Hastings

Book 1 in the Conquest Series

By

Griff Hosker

Hastings

Published by Griff Hosker 2023
Copyright ©Griff Hosker

A CIP catalogue record for this title is available from the British Library.

Contents

Real people used in the novel

Duke William, The Bastard, Duke of Normandy
Bishop Odo of Bayeux. His half-brother
Robert Malet Seigneur of de Caux
William Malet his son
Durand Malet his second son
Robert Guiscard de Hauteville – later Duke of Sicily
Robert, Count of Eu
Hugh of Gournay
Walter Giffard
Robert of Mortemer
William de Warenne
Count Enguerrand
Geoffrey Martel, Count of Anjou
Guy of Ponthieu
Waleran of Ponthieu
Taillefer – Knight, juggler and troubadour
Earl Godwin – the Earl of Wessex
Harold Godwinson – Earl of Essex and later King of England.
Tostig Godwinson – Earl of Northumberland
Gyrth Godwinson – Earl of East Anglia
Leofwine Godwinson – Earl and ruler of Kent and the land north of Lundenwic
Ealdgyth – daughter of the Earl of Mercia and the niece of William Malet. Also known as Edith
Edwin – son of the Earl of Mercia. Upon his father's death, the earl
Morcar - the second son of the Earl of Mercia and later Earl of Northumberland.

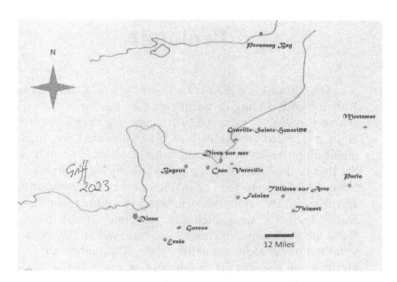

Part of Normandy and Maine in the 11ᵗʰ Century

Prologue

I am Richard fitz Malet and I was born a bastard to Lord Robert Malet. Living in Normandy that was not a mark of shame for Duke William of Normandy was also a bastard and yet he ruled the duchy. It meant that while I was the son, albeit illegitimate, of a Norman knight, I would not inherit the title or the lands. At least not while my stepbrothers lived. I had three of them: Sir William was the eldest, then Durand, and the youngest, who was just a little older than I was, Robert. He was named after our father. It also meant that I did not sleep in the hall. My home was in the mean dwelling of my mother and her father. My mother was Herleva and she was the daughter of an Englishman, Geoffrey. He had come to Normandy when Lady Ælfgifu had married my father. It was said that she was descended from King Cnut and her daughter, also called Ælfgifu had married Ælfgar, Earl of Mercia. I am still unsure if my father's marriage was politically motivated. Duke William wanted the English crown, and connections across the narrow stretch of water that separated England from Normandy were always useful. I confess that I only learned such things later in life. In my early years, I just tried to avoid smacks and punches from, it seemed, everyone who lived on the manor. I was called Richard by everyone except my grandfather and my best friend, Bruno, they called me Dick.

I saw little of my own father, Robert Malet, the Seigneur of de Caux, for once he had enjoyed his night with my mother and I had been born, I was forgotten. Forgotten is the wrong word. I was the son of the seigneur and had to be educated and when I was old enough, I was given to the priest of the manor and taught to read and write. Father Raymond often punished me for using the wrong word. I made fewer such mistakes but it still happened. I was not forgotten for I could still be trained to use a weapon and ride a horse. I was, therefore of some use. He died, in any case, when I was still a toddler and my stepbrother, William Malet became the new Seigneur of de Caux.

It was my mother and grandfather who brought me up. My grandfather was a mighty warrior and he used the double-handed axe favoured by the English housecarls. He had long ago ceased to be a bodyguard and his age meant that he no longer rode to war with the seigneur and the others. Instead, his duties were to train young warriors, he had trained my half-brother William, and to stand duties on the hall. I saw little of him except at night but then my mother died. My mother had never been well, so my grandfather said, since the day I was born. I had been, apparently, a particularly large baby and she had suffered. I often heard her waking in the night to drink some potion made by the women of the manor. Those early years saw me with my mother every waking and sleeping moment. She worked in the hall as a serving maid and I knew the kitchens as well as any. Once I could crawl, I was placed in a pen in the buttery where I could do no harm and when I was able to walk then I was allowed to help in the kitchen. I fetched vegetables from the vegetable chamber. The cook, Gunhild, liked me and acted as a sort of grandmother. She was even more gentle with me than my own mother and I adored her. I think she and my grandfather liked each other, for when my mother died and I was left in my grandfather's charge, Gunhild would visit more often. Sometimes she would stay for the whole night. I could not be certain for my grandfather had the only bed in the mean dwelling in which we lived and I had a paillasse in the room with the table and the two chairs. I shared the paillasse with Bruno and Hrolfr, my grandfather's two hounds. They were warm and I enjoyed a cosy little nest.

My life changed the day my mother died. I could no longer spend the days in the warmth of the hall's kitchen. That was made clear when Father Raymond had finished the funeral service and, as Gunhild returned to the kitchen, spoke to my grandfather and to me.

"The Seigneur has decided, Geoffrey, that the boy, Richard, in addition to his lessons with me, will also be trained to be a warrior. That will be your duty. I shall have him from prime to terces and you shall have him for the rest of the day."

"He is so young, Father." I glanced at my grandfather. He had already begun to teach me how to hold a wooden sword.

Father Raymond was not an insensitive man and he nodded, "Aye, but now that the seigneur has a wife and will one day have his own son, he wants Richard here to be as you were for his mother, a bodyguard. Growing up together and sharing the education and the training can only do them both good. When they go to war, and we both know that day will come, there will be a bond there that may save the life of the seigneur's sons, when they are born. Richard will be able to help me educate the children when they are born."

I was too young to realise then the implications of his words, but now I do. I was disposable and my purpose in life was to protect my step-nephews.

My grandfather was already upset at the death of his daughter and, being a widower, I was all that he had left. After the priest had given his news, he picked me up and held me close, "I shall have to be mother, father and grandfather for you, Richard." He held me tightly while he spoke to the priest, "And when does this begin? Can he be allowed a day to mourn his mother?" Even at my young age, I heard the bitterness in his voice.

The priest shook his head sadly, "You should know, Geoffrey, that you are tolerated here by the seigneur. Do not do or say anything which might jeopardise your position."

"I will take the boy with me and return to England."

"That can never happen. You could leave but the boy is now part of the seigneur's demesne."

"Then he is a thrall."

"No, but he serves the Malet family. Take him for the day but tomorrow make sure that he is brought to me. His education begins on the morrow. You may have your one day."

My grandfather took me back to our home and called the dogs. He took me for a walk in the woods. The dogs loved charging around the woods and stalking prey. They would come back to my grandfather's whistle. When we were alone, he spoke to me in English. I had to speak Norman in the kitchen, the hall and to all the others in the manor but my grandfather had always spoken to me in English. I think it gave him comfort. I found it easy to switch from one to the other.

"Grandfather, I do not mind learning with Father Raymond. Mother wanted me to be educated. She always corrected my words when I made mistakes."

"It is not the education I mind; it is that you will be tied to the seigneur's children. My life has been one of service to the Malet family and they do not treat people well. They are Norman and see we English as inferior."

I did not understand what he was saying then. I did later, but to me, life was all a game. I had played the game of kitchen and made that something I could enjoy. I would do the same with Father Raymond, and training to be a warrior seemed like something I would enjoy too.

My half-brother had no children yet but there were others who were ready. They were the sons of some of his knights and oathsworn. My grandfather worked with the sons of the household knights. All were still considered boys and while I was the youngest, I was as big as they were and my grandfather had already begun working with me from the time I could toddle. I knew how to use a slingshot and how to hold the wooden sword in two hands. It was all a game. The lessons with Father Raymond were harder but any frustration I had from the morning was dispelled in the afternoon when I was able to take out my anger as we sparred and worked with weapons. Those years were good ones. They changed when…no, Taillefer taught me to tell a tale better than that.

Chapter 1

Pays de Caux 1050

My grandfather was kept on for two reasons. The first was that he had been the bodyguard of Lord William's mother. She, however, had died not long after Lord Robert. He was also kept on because he was a good warrior and he was English although he had Danish blood in him. He was able to teach the men of Lord William's demesne how to fight against warriors armed with a Danish axe and who did not fight from horseback. The Saxons and Danes who lived in England preferred a shield wall. As I came to learn, the Normans had embraced the horse. Also descended from the warriors known as Vikings, the Normans now had an edge over their blood kin. When my grandfather was not training young warriors to use the sword, he was advising the knights and men at arms on the best way to defeat a man swinging a two handed Danish axe. Even though old, my grandfather could swing the axe with such ease that it was beautiful to watch. The knights respected my grandfather.

Thanks to my grandfather, I never felt myself a Norman. My grandfather felt that my mother had been used by Lord Robert and he did not like it. He was English and his daughter, my mother, whilst brought up in Normandy was English. It followed that he regarded me as English. He continued to speak to me in English whenever we were alone but he risked the wrath of Lord William if he spoke it in his presence. Father Raymond was French and he also taught me French and Latin. I was not a natural student and it took punishment for the knowledge to penetrate. But sink in it did, eventually. My punishing lessons with Father Raymond ensured that my Norman was perfect. As I approached my tenth year on this earth, Lord William had yet to have his sons and his daughter. It was when they were born that my life would change. By the time Lord William's sons, Robert, and Gilbert came along to be taught by the French priest, I had learned enough to be able to help him teach whilst still learning. I saw my future in those lessons. I was there to be used by the Malet family. The blood I had inherited must have made them feel that I owed the family some sort of loyalty.

When we worked with my grandfather, it was different. My grandfather never deferred to me or gave me an easy time but I felt an equal with the other young men training to be what Lord William called pueros. Pueros were not squires but were young men training to be warriors. Only a few men would be squires but every pueros would fight for Sir William in one shape or form. I got on well with the other four despite the fact that I was younger than they were. Baldwin, Odo, Guillaume and Bruno were like blood brothers to me and I felt more affinity with them than my half-brothers. Their fathers all served my half-brother. Three years earlier Lord William had been with Duke William when they had fought for the French king at the battle of Val-es-Dunes. He had done well but Bruno's father was killed and somehow that made Bruno and I even closer. We were both orphans. He was a similar height to me, and my grandfather often paired us together and fighting against someone of a similar build helped us both.

My grandfather was helped in his training schedule by Alain. He was a horseman from Brittany. I never discovered the real reason he had fled his homeland to serve with my father, Lord Robert, but he had and he had stayed. He had a wife and three daughters. It was he who taught us to ride. Those lessons began almost as soon as we began training when I was just four. I think at that age you endure falls easier. We all fell from the backs of the ponies we were given. He wanted us to be good horsemen and so we trained, at first, without saddles. We learned to grip with our legs. By the time I was seven and using the simple saddles, we were far more competent riders. The horses we then rode were little more than ponies but even Lord William and his knights rode small horses unless riding to battle. The riders' feet almost touched the ground.

Alain explained why riding a horse into battle was important. My grandfather listened and nodded so I knew that Alain was speaking the truth, "A horse can get a rider into battle quicker than a man on foot and get him out just as quickly."

Baldwin asked, "Is that not cowardly, master?"

"The aim of war is to win, Baldwin, by any means possible. Sometimes riders need to pull away and reform ready for another attack. Men on foot cannot do that."

My grandfather nodded, "A shield wall is fixed to the earth and may not, nay, dare not move. Holding a shield and an axe is tiring."

"Aye, we horsemen can ride away from the battle to fetch fresh weapons. We can even drink some ale or wine and then return to the attack. We have mobility and can move around the flank. A shield wall is a solid line of shields but lances and spears can find weaknesses. It is not time yet, but when I deem the time right, I will teach you how to hit a circle no bigger than this." He made an O with his forefinger and thumb. I later found he was exaggerating and the circle we were asked to hit was as wide as an O made by two hands, but we all tried to emulate the Breton who was the most skilful man I ever saw on the back of a horse at the manor.

Our training was divided into two sessions. My grandfather gave us sword, spear and shield skills while Alain taught us to ride and to lance. We also had to practise with our slingshots as well as bows each day while the two old warriors watched on. We gradually improved although we never used metal weapons. The lances and spears were fire-hardened shafts of wood and the swords were also heavy wooden lumps. For that reason, we wore no mail. The result was that we all had bruised and battered bodies at the end of each day. It made us harder and tougher. My grandfather knew war on foot and taught us how to use the shield both for offence and defence. He instilled in us the need to hurt our enemies even if that meant striking a blow to the knee or the leg. "A wound always slows a warrior down unless, of course, you are fighting a berserker and then you take off the head."

We were young and we were malleable. Alain found that Bruno and I, in particular, were natural riders. We soon learned to walk our horses backwards, to guide them with our knees and best of all, how to use a horse as a weapon. By standing in the stirrups and pulling back the head, I was able to make the horse rear when its natural reaction was to flail its hooves. I imagined the terror of a man on foot facing such deadly weapons.

Our work did not cease when the sun set. We then had to take food from Gunhild's kitchen to the hall and serve those there. It was as hard as the martial training had been and, with muscles aching and bruised already, it was taxing too. When we were not serving, we stood behind the gathered warriors and their wives and waited to be waved forward. The standing sapped energy from our legs but taught each of us patience. It was as I stood behind my half-brother that I learned of events beyond the little world of our hall and our manor. He and his brothers spoke of England and the duke's ambitions there. I learned that the English King, Edward, was a pious man and having been brought up in Caen at the court of Duke William favoured the Normans. King Edward was descended from the royal family that had ruled England before Cnut had won the crown in battle and, some said, treachery. When Cnut died, his heir, Edmund Aetheling, had fled and lived in Denmark. Duke William wanted, my half-brother said, the crown of England. It was as I heard these words that I realised my half-brother was held in high esteem by the ruler of Normandy for he was privy to such information.

When the food was eaten and the hall emptied, then would be the time when we would eat. Our food would be that which was left but Gunhild always kept some behind for the five of us and we ate well and filled out. It was after my mother died that all pretence went from my grandfather and Gunhild. She shared his bed each night and I slept, still, with the hounds. I learned to ignore the sounds from the bedchamber.

Duke William arrived for the christening of Robert, the first of my half-brother's sons. I did not know it but there was another motive. If I thought we were worked hard before, the visit of the duke increased it tenfold. Our training with weapons was forgotten as the hall was cleaned and repaired. A new warrior hall had to be built for the men who would accompany the duke. I thought it a waste for who would occupy them after the christening? It was not my place to say anything and we worked hard to make sure that the man who would be a king was comfortable. I knew how important it all was when I was given a new blue tunic and a pair of new leather shoes. My hair was trimmed by the castle barber and I was scrutinised by Gunhild to ensure that I would not let anyone down.

We waited by the gates to the castle as the column of mailed men approached. Duke William was still unmarried and he brought bachelors with him. I would come to know many of them but the first time I saw them I could not help but notice their martial manner. We were dressed in tunics but they wore hauberks that came down to their knees and their horses were at least four hands taller than the ones ridden by even my half-brother. Their mail and their helmets glinted and gleamed in the late afternoon light from the west. It was when the duke dismounted that I was slightly disappointed. He was a smaller man than he looked on his horse. Although only ten, I came up to his shoulder. He handed his helmet to a squire and then clasped my half-brother's hand. The smile told me that they were close. We had been told to line up and bow as they passed but we were totally ignored. The christening would be the next day but the feast would be that night and we were all inspected by not only Gunhild but also Lady Hesilia, my half-brother's wife. Our hands were examined and our nails were checked for dirt.

We then waited. The duke's squire, a youth of perhaps seventeen, and the other squires joined us. Roger, as I came to know, was a good man. He had ambitions but he was neither cruel nor vindictive.

"I will be the one to serve the duke but I know not this kitchen." His eyes landed on me, "You will stay close to me so that I can ask where are the things I need. You will have to serve your master and watch me. Do not get in my way." I shook my head and he smiled, "This will be a good lesson for you. Lord William is held in high regard by the duke and you will have to perform duties like me someday. Watch and learn, Richard."

He knew my name and that was a good lesson. I was now happy to serve this squire because he had used my name.

We stood behind the lords while the duke's half-brother, Odo, said grace. The hall was filled with candles and made the colours of the tapestries hanging from the walls seem to dance. I was Roger's shadow. He made it easy for me. When he served the duke, I brought the same to my half-brother. Lady Hesilia seemed to approve for she gave me a half-smile. Until that moment, I did not know if she even knew I existed.

It was as the food was finished and we hovered with jugs of wine that I first met Taillefer. He was not only a knight but also a juggler and minstrel. After the food was finished, he sang us the song of Roland. He had a wonderful voice but more than that he was a genuinely funny and talented man. Over the next ten years, I came to know him well but my judgement that first night never changed. I could see that Duke William was also fond of him as was my half-brother. When he had finished his song, I was desperate to speak to him but I knew that my place was behind my half-brother. I emulated Roger and kept my face forward although our eyes scanned our lords to see if they needed their beakers and goblets topped up. Baldwin and Bruno were charged with ensuring we had a good supply of wine. I copied Roger and once my jug was getting close to half-empty nodded to Bruno who fetched another and exchanged it.

I also listened.

"So William, how many men can you field?"

"You go to war, my lord?"

"King Henry of France needs our help in his war with Anjou. Count Geoffrey Martel seeks Maine and as it borders our land it might be useful if we were to show the Angevin that we will not cede our land easily." I saw my half-brother nod. "So, how many men?"

"I have my brother and the knights who served my father. I have six household knights and between them, my brother and my father also had six. There are twelve mounted men at arms as well as squires and pueros. As for my feudal commitments…"

The duke shook his head, "We need speed. I want every man to be mounted. Better that we leave the spearmen and archers to work their fields. It is our horsemen I wish to blood."

"Blood, my lord?"

Bishop Odo of Bayeux, the duke's half-brother, leaned over, "If England is not added to our lands, William Malet, we may need to take it from them. That is why they must be blooded."

I heard in the duke's voice his annoyance, "Brother, let us not get ahead of ourselves. I have yet to visit with King Edward. We need young men blooding. Roger here is now a pueros. I would have him knighted before too long." He nodded towards us, "And your young men, how many of them will come to war?"

My half-brother caught my eye, "If we are to bring these young cockerels then there would be twenty such pueros and squires."

I tried to keep a straight face as I realised that I would be going to war. I remembered when my grandfather had used the word pueros. He had told me it was young men who were warriors but had yet to be knighted. Some of them would take the route of squires while others would become like Baldwin's father, a man at arms. I was never sure if I was a page or a squire. The title was immaterial. If we went to war then our job would be to look after the horses and, when the knights and men at arms fought, ensure that they had replacement weapons. From my grandfather's words, there would be danger and no chance of glory. My friends and I had spoken of this and knew that it was worth the risk for by catching the eye of some noble we might be trained to be a knight. As my grandfather had said, there was little chance of that for me. When Robert, the half-brother closest to me in age, grew into a man, he would become a knight. His as-yet-unborn siblings would also become knights but I was the bastard and the best that I could hope for would be if I became a man at arms.

"Then bring your men to Falaise at the end of the month. This will not be a long campaign because I have to visit England in the autumn. Perhaps I might bring you."

As we later sat in the kitchen, our masters having retired, and ate the plentiful leftovers, we spoke of what the campaign might mean. Roger was the most senior and Bruno asked him, "Will you be given your spurs before we take the field?"

Roger shook his head, "No, for I would have to have trained another to take my place. The best that I can hope is that I do some deed that the duke notices and, at some time in the future, he gives me my spurs."

I was curious, "You have land?"

He nodded, "My father has a manor close to Ouistreham. He is old and will go to war no longer. He was a brother in arms of the duke's father, Robert."

Baldwin was keen to get on, "And when you are knighted, who will become a squire to the duke?"

Roger smiled, "You are too young for that yet. If I am knighted, it will not be for a year or two. You have much to learn, Baldwin son of Henri. Do not be impatient."

I was not included in the guests for the christening. The small church was packed with lords and their ladies. Instead, we practised in the yard. My grandfather became cross with us as our minds were not on the training but on the prospect of action. Eventually, after cuffing Guillaume on the back of the head, he told us to put down our wooden swords.

"Enough! I will tell you what is expected of you and then you can get back to real work. The Angevin would have you for breakfast if you went to war with your heads in the clouds. You will each be leading a horse with mail and weapons on it. Some of you may have two horses to lead, for another will have the tents that you will use."

"Do we have to take pans and cooking gear?"

For his interruption, Bruno was rewarded with a clip about the head. "The duke will take servants for such tasks but you will have to watch Sir William's horses and groom them. You will be the ones to saddle their horses and ensure that they are ready at a moment's notice. It is you who have to be certain that they do not throw a shoe at a critical time. Before you leave you will need to visit the farrier and have every horse shod. You will be responsible for using the whetstones to keep spears, lances, swords and axes sharp. You will fetch the food from the kitchens and wash and clean all the platters and goblets.

Baldwin's face fell. This sounded worse than the training we endured.

My grandfather saw his face and smiled, "You will be close to war, Baldwin, for you will have to ride close to your lords with their spare spears. When a spear is shattered then you will have to ride next to your lord and hand him his new one without being killed. If his horse is killed, you will have to take the spare." I opened my mouth and then closed it. My grandfather read my mind, "The pueros will have the first responsibility to do all that I have said but in the heat of the battle you must be ready to do your part." He patted his belt where a dagger lay in its scabbard, "Like me, you will each have a dagger. That will be your only weapon. The rules of chivalry are not set in stone. In theory, all of you should be safe from harm but in the heat of battle who knows? You may have to defend yourself."

Odo shook his head, "With a dagger?"

My grandfather laughed, "With your fists if you have to. The battlefield is not the place for faint hearts. Keep your eyes and ears open and, who knows, in two months' time I may still have five young men to train."

His words were not reassuring but they had the desired effect and we trained harder than we ever had. It was only after the departure of the duke and the visitors that I was able to really speak to my grandfather. He must have been waiting for just such an opportunity too for he initiated the conversation. "When you ride behind Sir William, do not be foolish. You owe him nothing except for the service any warrior owes the lord who feeds him. You are too young to risk your life for him. Let the others do that. Do not shirk your duty but be mindful that I want you to return here. I still have much to teach you." He smiled, "I would not say this in the practice ground but you are the best of the five. You may be the youngest but you have natural skills. Given time you will become a great warrior, but you need time. Hopefully, I will be given enough time to help you become the warrior that lies within you. Sir William will use you if he can. Take every insult and do not react. The likes of us can be executed without a moment of hesitation. Always remember that." He went to his chest and brought out a sheepskin. He untied it and there were four blades within. One was a short sword. It was not as long as Sir William's. It did not have a real tip and there was no fuller. There were also three shorter blades. He took one and handed it to me. It was a single-bladed dagger with a curved end. It was as long as my hand and half as much again. "This is a seax. It is a weapon used by the Saxons. It is not a stabbing weapon. It is a slashing weapon. I would have you keep it." I took it and removed it from its sheath. I had never seen a blade like it. He then took a second dagger. This was only as long as my hand. He took it from the scabbard and I saw that the blade was just the thickness of one of my fingers and a little finger. It was long and pointed with a needle-like tip. "This is something I had made for me when I was in England. I call it a bodkin blade for the tip is like the bodkin needle used by women. It is small but the end will pierce mail links. Take them and keep the bodkin hidden. They may be of some service to you."

That was the moment I knew I would be a warrior. I had been given killing weapons.

My half-brother rarely took an interest in me but at the end of that week, I was summoned to the hall where he and his squire, Eustace, waited for me. "Richard, you are to come with us on the campaign. Eustace here will use you as he sees fit. If you are to be anything more than useless baggage then listen to all that he says. The horse you will ride is more valuable than you are. The duke needs as many men who can ride as possible. Alain says you are a good rider and that is the reason you are coming. You are part of my mesne and I will not take anyone with me who looks like the sweepings after Caen market. You will wear boots and a well-made tunic. You shall wear a cloak. Do not harbour any illusions, Richard. You may have my father's blood in you but you are still a bastard and the result of too much wine and a moment of weakness. You will never amount to anything but I will use you while you still live and when you die, I will give your boots to another. I want this clearly understood before we leave. Do you understand?"

I was seething inside but I heeded my grandfather's words. I gave a bow and said, "Of course I understand, my lord. I am nothing."

He smiled, "Good. Take him away, Eustace, and try to do something with him."

After Eustace tossed me an old cloak, I was led to a room where women were sewing. I knew that at least two of them were illegitimate daughters of my father while others were the daughters of parents who had died. It was not charity that ensured they had a roof. They were thralls in all but name. I was asked to take off my tunic. I wore a pair of short breeks beneath else I would have been naked. I was keenly aware that all the women and girls were staring at me. I felt myself reddening. Eustace seemed unconcerned. He threw a tunic at me and said, "Put this on." I did so and it was clearly too big. He waved over a woman, "Make the adjustments to this garment and I want a second the same size as this."

"Yes, Master Eustace." The woman grabbed a handful of cloth and then took a bone needle from her sleeve. She pinned it and did the same with the other side. She grinned, "Now take it off."

I pulled it over my head feeling the cold air. I donned my old one as quickly as I could. I was then whisked off to the tanner, Bergil. He normally made leather jacks to be worn by those who wore no mail. While Sir William and even Eustace would have their boots and buskins made by a bootmaker, the tanner would cobble together simple ones for ordinary folk.

"Bergil, make the boy some boots. Whatever leather you have shall do."

"Yes, Master Eustace."

The squire turned back to me, "When the women have done, collect your tunics and present yourself in the main hall tomorrow morning dressed as though we are going on campaign."

My half-brother had set the tone and Eustace regarded me as something he might have stepped on in the hog bog. When he had gone Bergil smiled, "Sit on this bench, Richard." I hauled myself up and he used a piece of wood to measure my feet. He made marks on the stick. "I liked your mother. If his lordship had not had her then there were many who might have wed her." He shook his head, "I know that some maids are wed at twelve but it is not right. You are lucky to have your grandfather and Gunhild to watch over you." I realised then that the relationship was an open secret. He wandered over to a shelf and took down a pair of boots. "I made these for my son." He shook his head. "Better that someone uses them." His son had died the previous winter of the coughing sickness. It mainly took the old but Fótr had always been a sickly boy. He had been older than I was when God had taken him. The tanner smiled as he put them on me. "They may be a little big but I am sure some of the women who sew for his lordship will have needles to sew a pair of socce for you. When your feet grow you can discard the socce. Keep the leather waxed and oiled. It will keep out the damp, make them more comfortable and they will last longer."

"Thank you, Bergil,"

"There are many people here who liked your mother. You have more friends than you know."

That was proved when I returned to the women. Despite the demands made on their time, they had finished the two tunics and even sewn the gryphon symbol of the Malets on the breast of the tunic. I thanked them and hesitantly asked them about the socce. Matilde, who was the oldest of the women, smiled and said, "The work of moments. I will drop them at your grandfather's when we finish for the day."

Sir William thought he ran the manor but in truth, it was women like Matilde and men like Bergil who ensured it ran smoothly. Their rewards would be small but one thing that

21

could be said about the Malet family was that they kept their people safe, and in the parlous world in which we lived that was enough.

I was presentable enough when I met Eustace. My friends, it seemed, had also been selected. In the case of three of them, it was because their fathers were going to war but Bruno had been chosen, like me, because we were the best. The others had the same tunics but, somehow, mine seemed to fit a little better. He took us out to the stables where Alain awaited us. We had all ridden the ponies and horses that belonged to Sir William but we were now to be given our own and, at the same time, be introduced to the sumpters that would carry the mail. First, we collected our saddles and saddle blankets. These were not the war saddles used by the knights with the high wooden cantles to keep them in the saddle. They were very simple leather ones without wooden cantles that would not prevent us from sliding up and down the horse's spine. They were to protect the horse. The lessons in riding without a saddle would now come to our aid. We were given our own bridle and reins. Alain had taught us how to tie the reins to suit us. Until now we had never had our own and we could fasten them once and then leave them. Similarly, the stirrups would be adjusted once and then left. With our horse furniture, we left the stable and headed for the pen where the horses were tethered. If we thought we would choose our own horses we were in for a disappointment. Alain chose the horse that each of us would ride. These were not ponies but they were only a little bigger. He had obviously made his decision before we reached the pen for he just pointed and said our name and the name of the horse. We knew some of them for we had ridden them but mine was a new one. He was a chestnut-coloured horse with a white blaze and two white socks.

"Richard, Blaze."

I went to the horse and, having known what we were about, had a carrot in my hand. I slipped it to him as I stroked his mane and then slipped on the bridle and reins. I fitted the saddle and then checked all around him. He was a gelding. The knights and men at arms preferred a stallion.

22

They liked a horse that would fight in battle. I was happy with Blaze.

I saw Eustace grinning and wondered why. Alain said, "Untether your horses and mount."

I did so, carefully, for I did not want to be unceremoniously dumped from Blaze's back. All the other men who would be going to war were gathered. They already had their horses and it was clear that we would be engaged in some sort of activity related to the campaign. The knights, of course, were not there. The pueros, squires and men at arms were. Once we were mounted, the command to trot around the inside of the pen or gyrus was given. Alain had named it a gyrus for he said that the Romans had used such a term and he admired all things Roman. I dug my heels in and Blaze responded. "Canter." I urged Blaze on and found myself catching up with Odo and his mount. It was harder to control my new horse but I managed it. Then Eustace and four squires suddenly stood on the lower rung of the pen and they all shouted, "Catch." They threw a fire-hardened spear at each of us. Eustace threw mine and he threw it hard. My hand came up almost as though another was controlling it and, more by good luck than anything, I caught it. Bruno managed as well but the other three failed and their failure was greeted with hoots of derision. We had been initiated.

Eustace shouted, "You need to practise, between now and when we leave, throwing a spear for your knight to catch and catching one yourself. You may not have to throw one but oft times there will not be the luxury of handing one."

Alain said, "But before then you have lessons in loading panniers on the back of the sumpters and leading a train of them."

If I thought we had worked hard before then it was in those first days of training that I came to know the true meaning of the phrase. Often, when I retired, I did not bother to undress, I simply collapsed. We were not hitting each other with sticks any longer but we had to endure kicks from sumpters that objected to panniers. Even loading the panniers was not without danger for carelessness could result

in a sharpened spearhead raking an arm. Baldwin and
Guillaume discovered that. However, the night before we
were to leave for the muster at Falaise, I felt confident that I
had made the necessary mistakes already to prepare me for a
campaign where a mistake, of any kind, could be fatal.

Chapter 2

It was a glorious colourful column that left the castle at Graville-Sainte-Honorine. Not all the men were leaving but enough were for women to shed tears as fathers, husbands and brothers left for war. Even Gunhild wept. The night before we had departed, she had given me a leather satchel with dried venison in it and another pair of socce. I knew the venison would last for months and was a godsend to a boy whose stomach could never be filled. She also gave me a hat that she had knitted. It would keep my head warm during the day and at night. My grandfather gave me his campaign blanket. I knew, from my words with him, that I would be learning lessons in this campaign that could not be taught at the castle.

Sir William and his brother Sir Durand rode at the fore along with their younger brother, Robert. He acted as a sort of squire to the two of them although he was only a little older than we were. The other household knights were next, then the men at arms, squires and then the pueros. We, of course, were at the rear. Behind us rode two men at arms, Robert of Lisieux and Richard of Dreux. We would not need their protection until we crossed to Maine where the Angevin were threatening, but as I learned, Sir William was a careful commander who husbanded his men, even callow youths such as we. This was the first time I had come into contact with Sir Durand and I did not like him from the first. He also seemed to dislike me and took great delight in ordering me about before any of the other pueros. Having said that, the others did not like him. We were used to taking orders but there was something in the way he gave his orders that seemed to almost curse us.

The five of us had been allocated our horses but the sumpters we led were a different matter. That first day, as we headed for the muster point at Rouen, we learned about the character of the sumpters we led. When we stopped to water them in the mid-morning, we spoke about the problems we were having. It was clear that Odo had the most difficult one, appropriately named Donkey, and so Bruno took him. Bruno was the best of us with horses although I was not far behind him. We had decided that we would look after each other. When we were men grown then we would be at the forefront of any fight and we swore an oath to be brothers in arms. Bruno and I were destined to be closer than the others as we were both assigned to help Eustace protect my half-brother. The other three would help their fathers. It made Bruno and me, both fatherless, like brothers.

The muster was at Rouen Castle and we saw that we were just one conroi amongst many. There would be no rooms for us and we slept in the hayloft above the stables. I was used to sleeping with animals but some of the younger sons of lords who were forced to use the stable were unhappy. It was there that our comradeship came to our aid. Chlotar was the son of a knight from the Cotentin, Charles de Hauteville. He was almost a pueros and had been with the duke on his previous campaign. As such he thought to throw his weight about and he chose to pick on Odo. Odo was the smallest of us and must have seemed like an easy target.

"You, runt, I would sleep there. I am the son of a knight and you serve a man at arms. Move your blanket before I throw it in the hog bog."

Odo was a tough boy and he squared up to the much bigger and older youth, "I was here first and this shall be my bed."

We were busy making our own beds but we all stopped and turned. Three youths were behind Chlotar. The four spread out to surround Odo. "Then you shall not only have a blanket covered in pig shit you will also have a beating for your trouble."

Before they could do anything Bruno tapped Chlotar on the shoulder and said, quietly, "Not while we are here." It was Chlotar who swung the first fist but it was a wide arching swipe that was easily ducked. Bruno was strong and his punch to the bully's middle doubled him up. A second youth turned to face me but my left hand easily blocked the punch that came for my head and I hit him hard in the ribs. I heard something crack and he fell to his knees. Bruno had

26

smacked Chlotar with an uppercut and he lay on the ground. Baldwin and Guillaume had easily overcome the other two.

Bruno nodded to me, "Let us awaken poor Chlotar."

We picked him up and walked over to the water trough where we dumped him. The water woke him. As he tried to rise from the water, Bruno put his face close to his and said, "You take on one of us then you take on us all. Steer clear of us."

This was my first encounter with a bully but all my later experiences reinforced what I learned from that first one. Bullies back down and more than that, they are not brave in battle. The fight lasted but seconds and yet gave us not only confidence but also a certain standing amongst the other boys who would follow Duke William.

Of course, Eustace heard about it and he gathered the five of us the next day, "I hear there was a disturbance in the stables last night." We said nothing. He nodded, "Remember this, if you do choose to fight, then you win." We nodded.

We stayed just two nights in Rouen while the last of the knights and their mesne arrived. We crossed the Seine to head towards Falaise and then the disputed borderlands. It was not a huge army. There were, perhaps, four hundred knights and with men at arms, squires, pueros and we boys the number rose to a thousand. The duke had ten servants but as they were armed, I knew that they had another purpose. We rode in our familia but I saw that my half-brother rode with the duke. It was Sir Durand and Robert Malet who rode with us. He was also my half-brother but was much younger than Sir William. Sir William's position with the duke meant that Eustace rode with us. We used the opportunity to find out as much as we could while he was a captive audience. We knew that he would not use his fists to punish us as we were in full sight of the rest of the army.

Baldwin was the chatterbox and he asked the most questions, "We fight with the French, Master Eustace?"

"We do."

"But I thought they were our enemies. The duke has fought against them before. Why does he fight with them now?"

I knew part of this for I had overheard the conversation at the feast but I was interested to hear what Eustace made of it all. "Count Geoffrey Martel has taken over Maine. The last thing that the duke and the French king wants is for Anjou to encroach on our lands. It would suit both leaders if Maine had an independent duke as its ruler. We go to restore the balance." He smiled, "Then it may well be that we become enemies of France once more."

"And we will see a battle?"

Eustace shrugged, "Perhaps, Guillaume, but more likely we will take back some of the castles that the Angevin have taken."

I knew that disappointed the others but my grandfather had told me that the taking of a castle was never easy and not the work of knights. Had we brought foot soldiers then they might have been used.

"Does the duke not covet England?" The heads of Eustace and my friends turned. I realised that I had spoken aloud what I had thought in my head.

Eustace studied me, "Ah, now I remember, your grandfather is English. Someone told me that he speaks English to you." I nodded. "Remember where your loyalty lies, Richard fitz Malet. You are Norman."

"Then we will be fighting against England someday." Bruno was a clever youth and understood far more than many of the men at arms and pueros.

Eustace sighed, "Bruno, there is an English king who is a close friend of our duke. Those who oppose King Edward live abroad. You have more chance of becoming a warrior than we have of fighting in England." He laughed, "You have yet to even see a real fight and yet you want to invade England."

Bruno reddened, "It was just a rumour, we heard."

"That is the trouble with listening at table, you hear but part of the tale."

Odo asked, "And do we do this alone?"

Eustace shook his head, "You need to listen more when Father Raymond teaches you. The French army will be heading from Paris and we will meet up further down the road. Now enough questions. Watch your sumpters."

When we reached Argentan, we were joined by the much larger elements from France. I was not there when the two leaders met but I guessed that Duke William would be less happy than the King of France. Was the King of France using Normandy to help him win Maine? We were there for two days and we saw little of my half-brother. When he returned it was with news. I was present, as a server of wine when he spoke with his brother, Durand, and his senior knights. I was invisible as I listened to their deliberations.

"The duke is cautious. He does not wish to ride into battle without knowing what it is we face. We are to make a chevauchée into Maine. We seek information and we seek to bring smaller numbers of Angevin to battle."

"Brother, we should not shy away from fighting Anjou."

"Durand, you have yet to fight in a battle of any type. You were not with the duke when we put down the rebellion. We will be circumspect. We are a small conroi. There are but fifty of us. The other knights will be doing the same. All is well."

Sir Charles asked, "And what will the French be doing while we bleed?"

"They will be the bait that draws the Angevin to them. They will head more slowly down to Le Mans. That suits us for there will be plunder for us and while we might not have the glory of a battle, we will be richer for this foray."

Eustace and I cleared away the emptied goblets and jugs to take them to the kitchen in the house used by Sir William. My four companions awaited us for we would have to wash them, I asked him, "A chevauchée?"

"A raid to take animals, kill warriors and draw men away from the advance of the French king. In addition, it will give Duke William valuable knowledge. He will want the border castles if he can get them."

"And we five, what do we do?"

He stopped just before the kitchen door, "You will not have to fetch lances for this but you may be called upon to defend yourselves. Those fire-hardened spears may become useful."

We entered the kitchen and as we washed and dried the beakers and pots, I cast my mind back to a conversation with my grandfather. He had wanted me to wear a leather vest on top of my tunic. When I had mentioned it to Eustace, he had firmly told me that we had to wear my half-brother's livery and as we would not be fighting we would not need the protection.

That night, as we nestled in the hay, I told my companions what I had heard. They were, like me, excited about the prospect of action but also daunted by our lack of protection. We were on campaign and there was little we could do about it. I examined the fire-hardened spear. It could hurt, of course, but only against someone like me, one who had neither leather nor mail. I was glad that I had two better weapons I could use.

We left, before dawn, to head south and west towards the Mayenne River. This time we led a single sumpter each and it was just laden with water, some food and some spare spears. This was a raid and the knights wore their mail. We would, if we were successful, take animals, food and treasure from wherever we raided. Each knight held a spear and was cloaked. This time it was Baldwin's father who led us. He would be the scout. Sir William, who wore a jazerant, a tunic with his symbol upon it, over his mail, seemed to know what lay ahead of us. It was also clear that we had been given the task especially by the duke for he came to see us off and clasped Sir William's arm. Within four miles we would be in Maine and I saw that the knights and men at arms wore helmets and coifs. The squires also wore either leather caps or helmets. Eustace also wore a leather brigandine studded with metal. The squires and pueros all had short swords and Eustace even had a round shield. I noticed that the banner remained furled. Sir William would choose just the right moment to unfurl it.

By terces, we could hear the distant tolling from an abbey and we could see smoke rising from a settlement. We stopped and Baldwin's father returned. Sir William turned and waved and Robert of Lisieux and Richard of Dreux, our rearguard, left us. There was a conference ahead and another of the squires, Henri rode back. "We are to raid a small village, Pré-en-Pail, there is a manor house with a ditch. You five must follow and wait just ten paces from the village. If your masters shout for a spear then take them one. When they dismount, you must be on hand to take the reins of their horses."

Bruno nodded and said, "And the squires?"

Henri grinned, "We use spears and draw swords." He wheeled his horse and headed back to the fore.

I saw that the knights had couched their spears and spread out in a double line with the squires and the pueros guarding the flanks. Bruno turned, "Come, we must show willing this day and stay as close to our masters as we can."

That was easier said than done as the knights and men at arms all rode much bigger and better horses than we. It suddenly struck me that we had not brought spares with us. They were still in Argentan. What happened if a knight was unhorsed? The answer came to me in a flash, we would have to give up our horses. It explained why our horses had been chosen by Alain and why they were not the ponies we expected. Blaze was a good horse and Sir William would need a replacement he could ride.

We trotted down the road and then when Sir William first raised and then lowered his lance, the double line took off as though at the start of a hunt. Even though we were expecting it, there was still a delay in our moving. We had sumpters with us and they slowed us as they had to be dragged. The result was that we were further back than Henri had commanded. I saw ahead that while there was no wall around the village, there was a tower on the hall or manor house. A bell tolled from the church as our mounted men tore into the few roads that crossed the village. We heard the screams and shouts. Those who could, fled inside their homes to bar their doors. Those close to the manor house sought refuge there but the speed of the charge took many by surprise. Even above the shouts, we heard the crack of the two crossbows released from the top of the tower. I saw that the knights held their shields tightly to their bodies and with mail encasing them it would take a lucky hit to cause a wound. As the horsemen used their spears, so they slowed and we closed with them. By the time they reached the manor, we were close to them. I saw Sir William dismount and Eustace rode to take his horse's reins. He shouted, "Richard!" I rode as fast as I could dragging the sumpter and I leapt from my mount clutching his reins and the tether. "Tardy! You should have been closer. He handed me the reins of Zeus, Sir William's mount, and he dismounted and then handed me his reins.

I had four animals to control and while three were relatively calm the sumpter was not. I put the reins of three horses in my left hand and then took the sumpter's tether. I wrapped it around the cantle of Zeus. The sumpter pulled but when Zeus gave a kick the sumpter calmed. I was able to control them easier and see what was going on.

Eustace had his shield held over Sir William's head. Sir William's shield was hung over his back. He was using a war axe to hack into the door. His brother and his squire were racing to help although Sir Durand appeared to be slower than the other knights and he and his squire hung at the back of the knights and men at arms. I was not the only one, it seems, who had failed to read the mind of Sir William. I was able to view the whole thing dispassionately for, holding the horses, we were in no danger. No one would waste a bolt or an arrow on us when there were warriors trying to get in. I realised the mistake of not having either mounted archers or mounted crossbowmen. Until entry was gained, the men on the top of the tower could shower stones and bolts on the attackers. I saw one knight, Sir Drogo, had been hit in the leg by one and his squire was tending to him. Once Sir Charles came to help his lord, the door soon gave way and with a cheer our knights raced inside. The squires remained outside for, like we five, some had horses to hold. That would have been the time for the villagers in their homes to race and attack us but they did not. They must have outnumbered us and with our knights occupied, we were vulnerable. They stayed within.

We could hear the fighting and the screams from inside the manor. There would be a lord there and he would have retainers and household knights. It was only when I heard a bone-chilling scream come from the hall that I realised Sir William must have known this was an enemy of Duke William. Maine owed its allegiance to Normandy but there must have been a recent shift towards Anjou. The two crossbowmen were hurled from the top of the tower. The screams, followed by the cracks as their bodies hit the cobbles marked the end of resistance. I counted the knights as they emerged. I saw that Sir Durand and his squire had swords that were still sheathed although they carried treasure with them. Only Sir Drogo had endured a wound but, as I later found out, many of those who had fought had suffered bruises not to mention dented and damaged helmets, shields and mail.

Eustace came out, "Tether the horses. We have a hall and village to strip."

I could see nowhere handy and so I took the spear and jammed it between some of the stones in the wall that ran along the outside of the hall. I tied the horses to it.

Eustace pointed, "Search the rooms on the ground floor. Remember to look under the boards."

"What do I take?"

"Anything. We have found horses and we can carry back mail, weapons, treasure, all…"

I had to step over two bodies close to the wrecked door. Two squires were pulling the mail from the dead man at arms. The door to my left was open and I entered. A dead servant lay on the floor. His tunic was bloodied and torn. He had around his neck, however, a chain which I took and donned. He had to have been the steward. I saw that he had well-made boots and I took them from him. On his belt hung a fine dagger and scabbard. I took all three and hung them from my waist. Along with them, I took a bunch of keys. Leaving him I looked around the room. There was a fine table and chairs. If there was a compartment under the boards it would be under the table and would take more than me to shift it. On the table were four candlesticks. I took

them. The walls were hung with tapestries. I left those and
headed for the door in the rear corner. I knew it would likely
lead to either the kitchen or servants' quarters but it was
worth a try. There were four doors leading off a very narrow
corridor which confirmed these were rooms and passages
used by servants. The first door I tried yielded a good result.
It was the steward's room and when I looked beneath the
bed, I found a small box. It was heavy and when I took it out
I knew it would contain coins. It did. I put the candlesticks
and the boots on the bed. I would use the blanket there to
make a sack. I found a short sword which I took as well as a
head ring. It looked to me to be made of silver. I put that
with the other treasures. He had a good coistrel as well as a
fine cloth to be worn about the neck and I took those.
Wrapping up my bundle I went next door. It was a storeroom
and there was a barrel of wine and jugs. I took the heaviest
barrel and as I could carry no more, I left.

Once outside I found Sir William speaking with his
youngest brother. He turned, "Richard?" He frowned.

"I did as Eustace told me to." I undid the bundle and laid
it out.

The frown changed to a smile, "I can see that you are
honest. Take off the sword and the chain of office but you
may keep the dagger, belt, scabbard and cloth. If the boots fit
no one then you may have them too."

Eager to please I added, "We have not yet looked for
treasure beneath the boards."

"Fetch your fellows, the ones with the fists, and find it."

I had turned to call them before I realised the implications
of his words. Eustace had told him of our conflict. He had
not said he wouldn't but I would now be wary of what I said
to the squire. "Baldwin, Bruno, Odo, Guillaume; we have
work to do for his lordship." My words made them stop in
their tracks and head for me. Sir William's orders took
precedence over everyone.

As we ran, sharp-eyed Odo spotted my new weapons,
"Robbing the dead?"

I shrugged, "His lordship said that I could keep them."

He shook his head, "All I managed was three copper coins."

We reached the room and I pointed at the table, "Eustace seems to think that, beneath this floor, there may be a treasure. Let us move the table to the side and search."

The table was oak and large enough to seat at least twelve people. It took some shifting but we managed it and we looked at the floor. Odo was the smallest of us but he did have keen eyesight. He spotted the boards, towards the edge of where the table had stood and close to the fireplace that had less dust gathered in them. We knelt down and began to blow, in one direction, the dust and then we took out our blades. It stood to reason that any secret hiding place would need to be easily opened. We might try to rip up the floorboards and never find what we sought. It was Baldwin's blade that prised open the floorboard that was attached to four others. I used my seax to help the others lift the hatch. Beneath it was an empty space. The entrance was narrow. I looked over at the steward's body. He was smaller than I was.

"Odo, down the rabbit hole. Guillaume, fetch a light." If anyone thought it amiss that I was giving orders they never said a word and both obeyed me. Odo slipped in and had to crouch. Guillaume did not bring the brand that burned in the sconce but one of the candles I had discarded from the candlesticks. He passed it to Odo who peered into the dark.

"I see a box not far away. He started to crawl and I saw that he was heading towards the fireplace. That made sense as the stone would be solid beneath the fire and would help protect the box. We heard the sound as the box was dragged over the stones beneath the floor. His head popped up, "There is another one." He disappeared and Bruno and I hoisted the box out. It was heavy.

Bruno went to open it. I shook my head, "Let his lordship open it. He has the steward's keys. If we break the lock we may be punished. This is our first raid, let us do everything right." He nodded.

The second box was smaller but seemed heavier. It also took two of us to retrieve it. We carried them outside. I saw that wagons had been found and horses hitched to them. A couple of milk cows and a bull were being attached to the back of one. At the very least we would eat well. Fine furniture and food were being loaded even as we arrived. My decision not to try to open it was vindicated when I saw Sir William examine the two locks. He nodded his approval.

Eustace said, "Go and find more treasure."

I had grown bold, "Can we not see what we have found, my lord?"

My half-brother looked at me and nodded, "Aye, your honesty deserves that." He fitted the key to the large box which finally yielded to the pressure. Inside were parchments and papers. Had we found them they would have been discarded but Sir William handed them to Eustace. "Hold these." Beneath them lay coins, they were mainly silver but there were a few gold ones. The smaller box opened more easily and within it were gold coins and some emeralds and rubies. It was a princely ransom.

The knight stood, "There, you have seen all, now is the time to find loot for yourself."

We had obviously pleased him and we hurtled off to search the houses now vacated by the villagers who had been driven hence. All the important treasure had been taken but there were a couple of items we each salvaged. I found a purse with a silver coin and ten copper ones. I also found a short sword and scabbard beneath a man who had not even had time to draw it. And we found food. To young men who were never full that was almost as good as the handful of coins we had all taken.

Sir William's horn sounded not long after we heard the abbey bell sound sext. It was time to leave. Some of the pueros were driving the wagons, their horses tethered to the back. Our sumpters were also laden and we headed back to Argentan. The journey back would be slower as there were animals to be driven. Four pueros were assigned that task. It was as we rode back in an ebullient mood that we learned of the fight. The lord of the manor had been slain along with his sons and brothers. The women were not present. A survivor told us that they were visiting an aged mother in Le Mans. It

had saved them from ransom but as we had the treasure of
Pré-en-Pail it was hard to see where the money would have
come from.

It was after dark when we reached the main camp and Sir
William went directly to the duke to report our success. Sir
Drogo was taken to the healers. It was a lively atmosphere in
our camp and we asked Eustace where we would be raiding
the next day. He laughed, "You do not raid every day. What
of the horses? We will have two days in camp. Sir Drogo
needs the rest and Sir William will divide up the treasure.
You five will be put to work helping the squires to sort it."

We were disappointed as we all wished for the excitement
we had felt when we heard the clash of arms and the cries of
battle.

We had, of course, to be up early to help the duke's
servants serve up the food. That was after we had ensured
that the horses of our conroi had been fed and watered. They
were accorded more care than we were. We were the last to
eat although we were now wise enough to snaffle food when
we were in the kitchen. The cooks turned a blind eye. We
were learning. After food, the knights disappeared and
Eustace and the squires arrived. The coins were counted and
placed in piles. The largest two were for the Duke and Sir
William. While we sorted through the mail, the weapons and
the clothes, the squires delivered the coins. The dead knight
had fine mail, a good helmet and a Spanish sword. They
were placed to one side.

"Sir Durand's mail is not as good as this. Charles, give it
to your master and the helmet. Who knows you may benefit
too."

The others were sorted. Eustace took a good mail hauberk
for himself and a better helmet. The other squires and pueros
took the lesser hauberks, there were six of them, the swords
and the helmets. We, of course, were disappointed. When it
came to the clothes and boots, the better pieces were taken
and we were cast the leavings. It was better than nothing and
I was given a pair of breeks. I recognised them as having
belonged to the steward. The tunic had been badly cut but
there were just a couple of spots of blood on the breeks.

Fortune also favoured me. The boots were too small for any of the squires or pueros and Eustace tossed them to me. It was the best prize any of us received and my companions were envious. I tried them on. They were marginally too big but when I grew out of my present ones, they would be perfect and they were well made. We had enjoyed our first encounter and been rewarded. It was a taste of the future.

Chapter 3

We rode again two days later and it was a repeat of Pré-
en-Pail. Having done this before, we were able to ride much
closer to the knights and did not need to be chastened. We
also knew how to loot. I realised that was what we were
doing. We were being bandits and robbing the people to
weaken their resolve. There was no glory in it but then my
grandfather had often told me that the only glory from war
came from troubadours like Taillefer who made slaughter
sound glorious. We were all a little wiser too and knew to
take some items for ourselves. We had seen the dispersal of
treasure and knew that the treasure and good mail apart, no
one would miss the odd item. I found a dented helmet. It was
a plain pot one and still too big for me but I secreted it, when
we returned to our camp in Argentan, amongst my growing
pile of belongings. I also managed to increase my purse. The
dead warrior whose helmet I had taken had a purse with ten
silver coins and a handful of copper ones. No one saw me as
I slipped it inside my bundle. That night we were all even
more excited about this raid. When the gear was divided, our
prudence in looking out for ourselves was vindicated when
we were given nothing of real value. We also heard, the next
morning as we served food, that the duke had found some
fortresses he thought he could take.

The next day we would be riding towards Ambrières-les-
Vallées which lay to the west and was close to the Mayenne
River. We were now used to the procedure. We moved
purposefully down the road and when we spied, through the
trees ahead, the smoke spiralling in the sky and smelled the
woodsmoke, then we knew that we were close to the large
village.

The first we knew of the ambush was when Robert of
Lisieux, riding behind us, cried out and as I turned I saw the
bolt sticking from his arm. Richard of Dreux shouted,
"Ambush! Ambush!"

The men who appeared from the woods at the side of us
were not mailed but they were armed. I had no idea of

numbers but I knew we had to defend ourselves. The five of us were the easy targets and leading a sumpter and riding a horse those attacking would seek us out. I let go of the reins of the sumpter and couched the fire-hardened spear. The sword I had found was back at the camp and I cursed my lack of foresight. I had not wanted to lose it and yet, if I had it with me I could defend myself better.

As I turned Blaze, I heard the horn of Sir William as he sounded 'fall back'. That was easier said than done as there were men attacking Richard and a wounded Robert of Lisieux. They and their horses blocked our escape. The five of us were also in danger as a dozen men and boys leapt from cover with wood axes and billhooks attached to poles. I dug my heels in and Blaze leapt forward at the youth with the wood axe who screamed and ran at me. I had the spear couched and I had struck at targets in the gyrus but I had never struck flesh. As the tip of my spear entered the youth's shoulder, two things happened. I was jarred so much that I was nearly knocked from the saddle and the end broke as the youth dropped his axe and fell to the floor screaming in pain. I retained the broken shaft as another young man ran at me with a billhook tied to a piece of ash. This time he would have the advantage. I wheeled Blaze to join the exodus back down the road. The young man made the mistake of swinging wildly and too soon. At least the five of us had practised. The ambushers had not. I smacked the wooden spear against the side of the youth's unprotected head and he fell like a sack of grain. I was about to dig my heels in and go to the aid of Robert of Lisieux who, despite his wound, had managed to kill the man attacking him, when I heard Bruno's voice.

"Richard!" I turned and saw that Guillaume was bleeding and barely able to hold on to the reins and three youths were attacking him. Bruno was trying to defend him. The knights, men at arms, squires and pueros were flooding back down the road, led by my half-brother Sir Durand, and I felt like a fish trying to swim against the stream as I went to their aid. I was lucky that I had already used the spear as a sort of club for when I rode behind the man with the spear I was able to raise the broken spear and smash it down so hard upon his head that it shattered. I saw the bone beneath the scalp as he fell and Blaze barged a boy a little younger than me, to the ground. The clip on the head from Blaze he received told me that the boy had fought his first and his last battle. I hurled the now useless spear shaft away and grabbed Guillaume's reins.

I pulled and shouted, "Hang on to the saddle."

Alain had trained us well and Guillaume, whilst holding on to his wound with one hand, gripped his saddle with the other. His legs held him in place. Once more the three of us were the rearguard. Guillaume's father must have passed his wounded son without realising it. I saw the man with the crossbow aiming at Richard's back as he led Robert's mount down the road. I shouted, "Ware crossbow." Richard turned but there was little that he could do to avoid being struck. I wheeled Blaze and my horse's head struck the crossbowman in the back. The bolt skied into the air as the man was knocked to the ground.

I was aware, as we rejoined the road, that Guillaume was no longer holding on as tightly. I turned and saw Bruno ride up alongside him and use his arm to support him. We found the others a mile down the road. Pursuit had long ceased. I saw a handful of pueros with levelled spears as we turned the bend. We had no healers with us but the three wounded men were being tended to by their squires.

Sir William raised his helmet, "Are there any behind you?"

I shook my head, "We have Guillaume here and he is wounded but there are no others."

Even as I spoke and Sir William nodded, Bruno said, "No, Richard, he is not wounded. He is dead."

I turned and looked behind me. Guillaume's eyes were open but he was clearly dead. Eustace came over and bowed his head, "I am sorry and we will have dread news to impart when we return to our home for his father also lies dead back at Ambrières-les-Vallées."

41

Richard rode over and nodded to me, "And I owe you a life too. I would be sorely hurt if that bolt had struck me. You have your grandfather's blood in your veins."

Sir William's voice cut through the chatter, "We were ambushed and we have been hurt. We will remember this day but for now, we must return to our camp. The duke should know that our enemies are now prepared. Bring our dead and wounded with us. The dead shall be buried in hallowed ground. Richard, take charge of the rearguard."

"Aye, my lord." The man whose life I had saved rode over with the now bandaged Robert of Lisieux. He handed me the reins of his horse. "You have shown that you look after others. Watch my shield brother for me."

"Of course."

I looked at Robert. It was his right arm that was bandaged but his left hung at his side too. I saw that some of the links on his hauberk were damaged and bloody. He gave me a wan smile. "The bolt went into my left arm. It was then my shoulder was hit. I think the bone is broken. I shall not be going to war for a while. I will try not to fall from my mount."

I knew that he was in pain. Every footfall from his horse must have made the bones in his shoulder grate together. He did not cry out for he was a warrior but his face was etched in pain. I rode next to him in case he should start to fall and Bruno had placed his horse on the other side.

"I will need a pitcher of wine this night if I am to sleep."

"We will find you one, Robert."

The man at arms, Richard of Dreux came over to us, "You are a good lad, Richard, as are you, Bruno. I am sorry that Guillaume and his father died. Poor Marie will be all alone now."

I said, "His father died well?"

"Aye, he was at the fore and the first to fall."

Bruno said, "We have coins we have collected. He was our brother too and his mother shall have them."

"You need not worry about Marie, for three of us are bachelors. One shall take her as his Danish wife."

When we reached Argentan, the rider sent ahead to warn them of our arrival meant that there were healers waiting as well as food. Bishop Odo greeted Sir William and he and Sir Durand were whisked away. We carried Guillaume's body to the church where he was laid close to the altar. The other dead lay close to Ambrières-les-Vallées. In addition to Guillaume and his father, we had lost five pueros and three squires. Guillaume's father had been the only mailed man we had lost and that had been, so we were told, because an axeman had taken the legs of his horse and he had been butchered as he lay on the ground. We waited with Guillaume's body in the silence of the candlelit church.

"How was he hurt?"

Bruno had been the closest and he answered Baldwin, "He thrust his spear at a man and missed. The sword sliced through his tunic and cut open his stomach. Had we had the time to stop we might have stemmed the bleeding." He nodded to me, "If you had not come with your broken spear then I might have joined him. A fire-hardened spear is not the weapon to use. I want a sword."

"Then let us find them. The next time we raid we find swords. I have mine already." They all looked at me and I nodded, "When we searched the first village for treasure, I found it and secreted it. I care not if I am whipped for the taking of it, the next time we ride I wear the sword and, if I can get it, I will find a leather brigandine."

The others all nodded. We were small and a warrior's brigandine would dwarf us but it would protect us. A simple sword, such as the one that had done for Guillaume, would not have penetrated leather.

Odo said, "Aye, and a helmet."

I saw then that he had a cut across his forehead, "You were wounded?"

"No Richard, I rode into a branch."

For some reason that made us smile and while Guillaume was not forgotten we were a little easier. We dug the grave and the priest said the words. I took out the coppers from my purse and gave them to the priest. He took them but I did not begrudge the loss of coins. They were in memory of the first friend I had lost. He would not be the last. I hoped that when my time came one of my friends would do the same for me.

That night, before I slept, I said my prayers as usual. This time I added prayers for Guillaume. I tried to remember the last confession he had made. Would God allow him into heaven? I resolved to seek absolution before we next went to war. We were not warriors but that seemed to make no difference. My grandfather was right and I was at risk. This was not a game and I had to change or end up like Guillaume.

Eustace came to speak with the four of us after we had served the knights. "Sir William wished you to know that you acquitted yourselves well yesterday but you all lost our sumpters. You will have to take the animals we captured in our first raid. He is also aware that you are the least well-armed of his men. The next time we raid, you may keep any weapons that you find." He looked at me, "Some of you have made a start."

"How did you know?"

He shrugged, "You were seen and your belongings were searched."

I felt my hands clenching in anger but I just nodded. I had no privacy and this was a lesson to be learned.

The duke had learned enough about the area and when a rumour spread through the camp that the French had failed to bring Geoffrey Martel to battle then the mood changed and a depressed air descended, especially amongst our conroi. There had been other losses but ours had been the most serious. The wounded men began to heal and we made certain that the next time we faced the men of Maine we would be ready. I took the short sword out and examined it a little more. It was at least as good as the one I had taken from the steward. I then examined my other treasures. The steward had been a very small man. His boots fitted me and the sword, in my hand was not unwieldy. As I sharpened it, I thought about the man whose boots I would wear. He had clearly risen well in the ranks of his lord. The steward held the keys and the treasure. He had to have done that through his mind and, perhaps, his charm. I had seen the way that those gifted with a silver tongue could rise high in some men's eyes. Taillefer was a good example, although his silver tongue, it was said, was backed by his skill with swords. As I worked the whetstone down a blade that had clearly not been sharpened for some time, I thought of the lessons I could learn from the dead steward. I was a bastard and could expect no inheritance. I would have to earn my place in the household of my half-brother or leave it and seek a place with another. Sir William was clearly a confidante of Duke William. It was better to stay where I was and ensure that I was well thought of. The clenching of my fists would have to cease. I needed to become one who accepted whatever was thrown at me. Inside I might seethe but to the others, I had to appear unconcerned with injustice. My grandfather managed it and so would I.

The others were envious of my sword and since the ambush, I was allowed to wear it. Baldwin said, "You have the luck of the devil; you find a sword and instead of having to give it up you are allowed to keep it."

Bruno smiled, "Baldwin, your father took weapons when we raided. Why not ask him for one?" There was silence. We all knew that Baldwin's father, unlike Guillaume's, was not a pleasant man and did not seem to care for his son. Bruno and his father had been close but Baldwin's father used his son like a servant. My grandfather said it was a throwback to their ancestry. The Vikings from which the Normans were descended were not sentimental about their sons. When their sons were younger than us, they were sent to war and expected to survive. We, at least, were given training.

When we moved, it was not towards Le Mans but towards the south and west. We were too lowly to be told anything of course. We were just ordered to load the sumpters we had captured and be ready to move. Richard of Dreux and Robert of Lisieux showed the four of us more concern than any of the other men at arms, including Odo's father. We had shown courage and they admired that. It was they who told us, as we loaded tents and weapons onto the backs of the pack animals, that we were heading for the small castle of Gorron which lay just to the south of the

Mayenne River, the border with Normandy. It was a small place and the castle was not a large one but it was strategically important. It was Robert of Lisieux who used that word. Odo did not understand it and Robert patiently explained that if we held it then one route into Normandy was barred. It was rumoured that we would be returning to Pré-en-Pail to build a castle there. When we took Gorron and after we had built a castle then the duke would have a more secure border with Maine.

As Bruno and I rode together, as we inevitably did, we spoke of what this meant. Bruno was very clever. Being an orphan meant he had to live off his wits. Having a grandfather, I did not feel that I was an orphan. "If we are to build a castle then the duke has given up on retaking Maine, at least for the time."

"Why did we not join with the French, Bruno? We are not large enough to take on the army of Maine but if joined to the French, we could."

He chuckled, "My father, before he died, told me that the duke was the most cunning man that he knew. If we had called to arms every knight, man at arms, spearman, crossbowman and archer, then we would have had an army the size of the French. We brought an army to raid. The duke remembered the rebellion a couple of years since. The loyalty of some knights is in question. We shall be home ere long and whatever happens next, I will win a sword." His words made me look at him and he shrugged, "The pueros and squires who died mean that soon we shall be elevated. You are a little younger than me but the same size and we both dwarf Odo. If we campaign next year then we will be asked to fight and I want more than a fire-hardened spear."

His words were prophetic. When our army reached Pré-en-Pail, Sir Gilbert de Hauteville was left with his conroi to build a castle in the town. I watched the duke, along with Sir William, Bishop Odo and Sir Gilbert select the hill where a motte and bailey would be built. One of Sir Gilbert's knights would have his first command. He and just twenty men would garrison the castle. I learned this from Robert of Lisieux.

"It is something that Richard and I crave. At Graville-Sainte-Honorine we are the small fishes. If we were chosen to serve one of Sir William's knights and garrison a castle then we would command others. Who knows, spurs might come." He nodded to Eustace, "Yon squire will be given spurs before too long. He is lucky. His father is a knight. We are like you, Bruno, we have no one to champion our cause. We have to earn recognition through a feat of arms."

Richard nodded, "Aye, had we gone with Robert Guiscard de Hauteville to Italy then we might be knights already."

"That carrot is out of the ground. We did not and there is an end to it. We could go now but we would be picking up the leavings of the others and besides, the Hautevilles left because of the duke. Sir William is too close to the duke for us to be given a warm welcome."

Bruno had sharp ears, "But if Sir Gilbert is a Hauteville…"

Robert smiled, "He is from the branch that supported the duke. This is his reward. The knight he appoints will be given the fiefdom but he will still owe revenue and service to Sir Gilbert."

My grandfather was right. I was learning lessons here that I could not learn in the manor.

This time when we passed through villages and towns they were given ultimatums, swear loyalty to Duke William or lose their livestock and defences. As the land bordered Normandy, it was a brave knight who would oppose our army with half a dozen men at arms. Gorron was different because it had a castle and there was a garrison. Some men fled west from the town through which we passed and we knew that the garrison would increase. More, they would be improving the defences. Eustace did not seem at all put out by the prospect. He occasionally rode with us as we headed south and west and since our action seemed more approachable.

"I am not worried about attacking a castle with a ditch and wooden palisade." He patted the mail he now wore. "I have mail and a shield." He had a round shield. Sir William carried one of the newer kite-shaped shields that almost wrapped around his body and protected not only his left leg but also the side of his horse.

"And what of us, Eustace?"

He looked at me, "You now have a sword but I doubt that you would have to assault the walls. Once they are breached then that would be a different matter. Every one of you will be expected to attack once the outer wall is ours."

Bruno showed how sharp he was, "And, of course, the more that flood over the walls the less chance there is for the knights to die. We are there for the weight of numbers and like the pueros who died in the ambush, we are expected to be casualties of war."

I might have thought the same but the new Richard fitz Malet would not say anything. I would bite my tongue.

Eustace gave Bruno a cold stare, "Aye, and I was once as you were, Bruno. I was at Val-es-Dunes and there, with just a fire-hardened spear, I speared a warrior who would have slain Sir William and I was promoted to squire even though I was barely older than you. Look on such challenges as opportunities to catch the eye of the duke or Sir William. You four have already shown that you have what is needed to serve Sir William. Build on that."

As we neared Gorron I worked out why the duke had chosen it as a target. The river Colmont protected one side of the town and castle. It could be improved. Thirty miles to the west lay the island of Mont St. Michel. King Edward of England had given the abbey and the island to Duke William and it was now a bastion to the west. Gorron would add to its defences. Bruno was right. Duke William was just trying to strengthen his borders and had no intention of trying to take back Maine, not yet, at least.

The duke had the town surrounded quickly and we erected tents beyond the range of crossbows. The castle was not in the centre of the town but on a piece of slightly higher ground. We occupied the town. I learned from the men at arms that sometimes the buildings close to the walls would be demolished to enable war machines to get close and hurl stones. It was clear that we would not be doing that. This would be a simple and quick assault. The duke did not want a resentful populace. The castle and the garrison would suffer but not the people.

As part of the mesne of Sir William, we approached the gates with bared heads to discuss surrender. The presence of a bishop, the duke's half-brother, ensured that we were allowed to speak with the defenders. The bishop demanded the surrender promising all that did so safe conduct. They, of course, refused. The bishop then promised dire consequences for any opposition. I would have taken the terms but the lord who spoke seemed arrogantly confident that they would be able to hold out. Even I could see that was unlikely to be an outcome.

Our leaders held a council of war while we made hovels for us. The tents were for the knights and the men at arms although the duke and senior knights commandeered houses. We found wood and made lean-to shelters. One of the bishop's men, Eudo, came for us just as we were finishing. He was not a pueros for he was a man who was fully grown and had flecks of grey in his beard. He had a broad stocky build and on his arm was a bracer. The man was an archer. "You four come with me." He led us away from the main camp to the river. I saw that fifteen others, the same ages as we, awaited us there. "You are to be used not to hold horses for the horses will be penned but to use your slingshots. There are stones aplenty in the river and we need not use lead to cast them. Today you will gather them and tomorrow when the horn sounds you will find me. You will assault the men on the walls with your slings." With that, he turned and left us.

I found a stone and sat on it to take off my boots. I would not risk giving them a dousing. I rolled up my breeks too and waded into the river. It felt icy but I knew that I would soon become accustomed to it. We already had a bag on our belts containing our slings and some stones. I only had eight and knew that I would need many more. I took off my woollen hat and laid it on the bank and then began to search for stones. We were all looking for perfect stones. Round ones flew true. We soon exhausted the river close to us and we moved along it. The four of us stayed together. When I had filled my pouch I emptied it into my hat and we only stopped when we could fit no more in our pouches. We returned to my boots and sat while our feet dried.

We were all excited at the prospect of using our slings. Odo was the smallest of us but he was the most accurate with a sling and he positively bubbled, "For the first time I can try to hurt a man. Pigeons, squirrels and rabbits are all very well but if I slay a warrior I can take his sword."

Bruno shook his head, "Only if you are the first to reach his body."

I nodded and offered words of caution, "And remember, if we are to hit the men on the walls then we will be within crossbow and arrow range. We will have to avoid those missiles."

We all knew that while we might avoid an arrow, especially one that was loosed into the air, a crossbow bolt flew too quickly. We had to pray that they would not waste their bolts on boys. Odo seemed to have a natural eye and was also becoming a good archer. We had not brought bows as we were not strong enough to send them far enough. We had a better range with our slings.

We served our knights and then ate. We ate well at Gorron for we had taken food from the town. Their homes remained intact but their larders were raided. None of us ever left a morsel of food in our wooden bowls. My prayers that night were not only for the usual ones but also for myself. I did not want to suffer Guillaume's fate. I decided that, when I rose, I would confess. I wanted to go to heaven when I died and be reunited with my mother. I realised as I wrapped myself in my blanket that her face was now becoming indistinct in my mind. I was forgetting her.

Chapter 4

My death must have been on my mind for I woke early while it was still dark. I went to the river and made water. I knew that further sleep was impossible and so I headed for the fire where the night sentries were already loading the pot that had bubbled all night with fresh ingredients. I joined them and helped. I had learned that willing helpers were always popular.

When Bishop Odo came everyone stopped and bowed, "Carry on. I woke and decided to break my fast early."

The pueros in charge, Geoffrey of Tancerville, said, "It will be a few moments, my lord."

"I can wait. A man needs a full stomach if he is to fight."

I said, meekly, "Bishop, could I make a confession?"

He frowned and then said, "Ah, Richard fitz Malet, why do you need to confess? What have you done?"

I shrugged, "Nothing, my lord, but I go to war today and I lost a friend a few days ago. I would not risk the fiery furnaces of hell."

He nodded, "How long since your last confession, my son?"

"A week."

"And what sins have you committed since then?"

"I might have killed a man when we fought at Ambrières-les-Vallées."

"Nothing more?" I shook my head. "Then you have committed no sins for you were obeying your lawful lord's orders but say three Hail Marys just to be on the safe side."

He was a much slacker priest than Father Raymond who would have questioned me at length. When the food came the bishop did not leave us. One reason was that he refilled his bowl three times but the other was that he spoke with me. He had known my father and was interested in my background. He seemed particularly interested in my grandfather.

"He is an English housecarl?"

"He was, my lord, and he trains the men of Sir William."

51

He nodded, "Do you speak any English?"

I did not know what to say for my grandfather only spoke English to me when we were alone. I did not wish to betray him. The smile the bishop gave me persuaded me to tell the truth. I did not wish to commit the sin of telling a lie, "I can, my lord."

"Good." He had emptied his third bowl and taking a piece of bread he wiped the inside of it, "Take care today, fitz Malet. This squalid little hole is not the place to die." He turned and left.

The early breakfast meant I was ready before the others and I made my way to serve Sir William and the other knights. Dawn was only just breaking. Eustace was impressed with my early arrival, "You show potential, Richard. Today is your chance to shine. The duke's master archer, Eudo, will be watching not only his bowmen but also the slingers."

I had already worked that out but I nodded. As I served the food, I saw that Bishop Odo had come for more food although he took less than he normally did. I saw his eyes alight on me and he turned to speak to his half-brother. The duke looked at me and then nodded. I had been noticed but what would it mean?

The others joined me to help serve and received a scowl from Sir William for their pains. I felt guilty for I had not meant to show them in a bad light. However, anything that would let my half-brother look more favourably on me was a good thing.

The knights ate more quickly than normal and it meant we could head back to our hovels and prepare. The knights went to organise their men at arms and we gathered our stones and slingshots. I strapped on my sword feeling, for the first time, like a warrior. We ran to find Eudo and that was not easy as we did not know where the point of attack would be. Bruno reasoned that it would be the main gate for although they had raised the bridge, timbers had been found to make a crude crossing of the ditch. Once the gatehouse and the wall that faced us had been cleared of defenders then, as at Pré-en-Pail, the gate could be attacked by mailed

men. Bruno was proved right and we received an approving
nod from Eudo as we were the first of the slingers, except
those of the duke, to arrive. I saw that there were twenty
archers. Normally there would be more but the duke had
wanted mobility and the archers we had were the ones who
were mounted. He berated and clipped those who were tardy.

He pointed at the gates, "There is our target but I will
wait until all the slugabeds are here. Examine it well while
we wait."

I saw that he now had his metal studded leather jack and
he had two bags of arrows. Each one held twenty-four
arrows. On his head, he wore a pot helmet and, of course, he
had his bracer. His bow was not yet strung and that would be
the last thing he did before nocking an arrow. The other
archers also had leather jacks and one or two wore a helmet.
Some of them were putting their arrows in the ground. It
made for speedier reloading. I took out my sling and selected
the five best stones I had. I held those in my left hand and
the sling in my right. I then looked at the gatehouse. It was
two hundred paces from us and, I daresay, had they wished
then the crossbowmen could have annoyed us by sending
bolts at us but crossbows suffered wear and tear when used.
They would save them and their precious bolts for the actual
attack. The wooden gatehouse was twenty paces long
although the gates themselves were just eight paces or so
wide. There were two towers on the gatehouse and I saw two
archers in each one. I counted six crossbowmen on the
fighting platform. There looked to be two knights or men at
arms. The two sides of the gatehouse that faced us were also
lined with warriors, but the archers and crossbowmen were
spread out. I counted just twenty in total. The rest of the men
on the walls were villagers and there looked to be thirty or so
of them. We would easily outnumber them but they had the
advantage that they could hide behind the wooden palisade
while we would be in the open. The men who would cross
the ditch would risk lillia, traps in the bottom as well as an
ankle breaker. It was clear to me why the duke had chosen a
determined attack on the gate.

"Come on, get a move on!" I turned as Eudo shouted at the last of the slingers who arrived out of breath. He pointed to the gatehouse. "When I give the word, the slingers will advance to the edge of the ditch and send your stones at the men on the walls. The archers and I will cover you with arrows while you run to get into position. I will shout when you are to fall back."

One of the late slingers said, incredulously, "But they will send arrows at us!"

One of the archers laughed, "Then move out of the way!"

Eudo nodded, "Aye, you are young and nimble, you can judge the flights."

"What if they use crossbows?"

I turned to look at Bruno. Eudo smiled, "Then they will have made a mistake for as soon as a crossbowman rises he will be a dead man. Archers do not miss."

I did not say it but I was thinking that would be little consolation for a dead slinger.

"Make way there!"

A column of twenty knights and men at arms arrived. Half had no shields but carried the wooden beams. The other half had kite shields and they were held before and above as well as along the side. It did not completely protect the men with the beams but it would be enough. The rest of the knights and men at arms arrived and spread out in a triple line. As they did so, I heard an order from the walls and some of the defenders who were some distance from the gates were ordered to close with the gate. The battle lines were now drawn.

The bishop and his brother arrived. The bishop carried a mace. He bravely turned his back on the walls and began to intone a blessing. We all knelt. I felt doubly blessed. He had given me absolution and now blessed me again.

"Amen!" We all echoed it and, to me, it sounded more threatening than when we spoke it in church.

I did not recognise the knights who would take the beams but none were from de Caux. A horn sounded and with a cry of '*God and Duke William*', they moved towards the ditch. It was then I saw the enemy slingers. They rose and sent stones at the shields. The clattering sounded like a hailstorm but it had little effect. The arrows showered down and they added to the cacophony. One or two embedded themselves in shields but did no damage. The cracks of the crossbows were a more threatening sound and this time, when they struck the shields, they stuck. I heard the ping as some struck helmets but not a warrior fell.

Bruno chuckled, "Eudo is clever. He wastes not an arrow or a stone but watches for the position of the men on the wall." I glanced over and saw that Eudo was not watching the gate but the walls as were his men.

The beams were slid into position and then the column moved back in perfect step. I wondered if the defenders would sortie to remove the bridge. They did not and I saw why, Eudo and his archers had strung their bows and had an arrow ready to nock. It would be certain death for any that tried it.

Quietly, for we were close to him, Eudo said, "Now, slingers, is your time. You have all seen where the danger lies. Go forth now and make a name for yourselves."

I confess I felt my bowels make themselves known and fear gripped me as the four of us headed close to the ditch. Bruno said, "Weave and make us a harder target." We did and as the slingers on the fighting platform rose I put a stone into my sling. I saw one defender fall backwards with an arrow in his chest. The boy looked to be younger than I was. One of our slingers fell when a stone smacked into his head. I saw the edge of the ditch appear and, aiming at a slinger who had just risen, I hurled my stone. It flew straight and true but did not hit his head. However, smashing into his hand was as good a hit. I heard the scream as it struck. This was a duel. The crossbows did not waste a bolt but the archers sent hunting arrows at us. Eudo and our archers were like guardian angels. Their arrows found the mark more times than not. I did not stand still but moved from side to side. It made me less accurate but I was a harder target. One of the knights pointed over to us and I aimed at him. The ping as my stone hit his helmet echoed across the field and I heard men cheer behind me. I had not killed him but he ducked down.

I became the target. I was lucky and most of the stones missed me. One did strike me but it was on the leg and my boots and socce stopped it from being a serious wound. It did hurt and I looked for the boy who had sent it. I spied him and stood stock still to ensure I hit him. He died silently. Odo was having the greatest success. A boy who can bring down a pigeon in flight more times than he misses can easily hit a bigger target, a stationary archer or slinger. My arm was aching when I realised that there were fewer missiles coming our way and I was relieved when Eudo shouted, "Slingers fall back." We needed no urging but we did so while facing the missiles. As I moved back, I saw that eight slingers had paid the price and lay dead. Glancing to my left and right, I saw that none were my friends.

"Well done, boys. The duke will be pleased." The archer we passed spoke out of the side of his mouth.

The horn sounded and a wedge of mailed men headed for the bridge. The archers also moved forward and it was then that the crossbows rose. The archers were ready and every time a cumbersome weapon was raised an arrow, sometimes two, would hit them and they would fall from the fighting platform. I knew then that the duke had planned well. Our castle at Graville-Sainte-Honorine, only had three crossbowmen and six bowmen. Here, our archers outnumbered theirs.

Eudo pointed to the wall to the left of the gate, "You slingers, run along the side of the wall until you are close to the inner bailey. See if you can hit any on the inner platform and clear the walls. The duke will soon break through these gates and you boys can clamber over the walls if there is no one there."

We ran and heard the sound of axes on wood. Stones clattered against shields held over the knights' heads and there were cries as the defenders were struck by arrows. The inner bailey was oval and had an incline up to the mound and inner palisade. I saw men manning the inner wall and others who were on top of the donjon. It seemed to me that more than half the town had sought sanctuary in the walls. The river came too close to the point where the two walls joined and there were no defenders. We were a handful of boys and I think we were ignored. When we reached the wall, everyone just stared at the donjon which was tantalisingly close. Inevitably it was Bruno who came up with a plan, "We can climb those walls."

The three of us nodded agreement but one of the older slingers shook his head, "We were told to clear the walls. They are clear."

I remembered Eudo's words exactly, "He said when the walls were clear we were to climb. I am with you, Bruno."

The four of us ran. I stuffed my sling into my belt for I would need both hands free. Some of the other, braver boys followed us immediately. Half a dozen hung back. The ditch had stakes in it but with neither stone nor arrow falling on us we could pick our way through. The bank was steep and so I took out my seax and dug it in. It enabled me to pull myself up. The others watched and copied me. At the base of the palisade, the ground was flat. The walls were about three paces high and looked too difficult to scale. There were no defenders here for there were no warriors trying to ascend the walls. The only threat lay in half a dozen boys and what could they do?

Bruno turned his back to the wall and making a cup of his hands said, "Dick, you are strong. If I boost you then you might be able to climb."

I grinned, "I am game." I could not take a run but, holding my seax in my right hand, I was propelled into the air. I rammed the seax between two of the palings and it held. It meant I could use my left hand to reach up and as my feet scrabbled on the rough wood I clumsily climbed until my left hand reached the top. No one had seen me and, pulling my seax out, I clambered over. Baldwin came next and, having seen me, copied me. I was able to reach down and pull his arm. Odo came next but the two of us were needed to help him. Bruno called over another boy and he joined the three of us on the fighting platform. Cries from both the inner bailey and the gate told us that we had been seen.

Bruno leaned over and shouted, "Do as we did. The boys from de Caux will hold these defenders." They were brave words but as half a dozen villagers detached themselves from the other defenders and ran at us along the narrow fighting platform, I was none too sure. Bruno was our natural leader and he took the fore, "Let us close with them. We use our slings and then, when they are close we use Dick the swordsman." Suddenly I wondered at the wisdom of bringing the sword.

We ran and I slipped some stones into my right hand. Odo was not only fast but he was nimble and he hurled a stone while we were still loading our slings. His stone struck the shoulder of a villager. Three of them had crude wooden shields and the men stopped to allow them to make a barrier. More men were racing from the gate. The knights had yet to breach the gates and we were most certainly at risk.

We heard a cry from behind. Baldwin shouted, "An archer has hit one of the other slingers."

Bruno shouted over his shoulder, "Salvation lies with us. Run as though your lives depend on it."

I slung a stone and it hit a shield. Bruno, Baldwin and Odo were throwing and running. The speed made the stones less accurate but when Odo felled one and he dropped to the outer bailey it cheered us. The defenders were twenty paces from us and I stuffed my sling back into my belt and drew not only my sword but also my seax. The others dropped behind me. Had the defenders had a throwing spear or a bow then I would have been a dead man. As it was, I would in all likelihood die. The platform was wide enough for two men and I was the only one with a sword.

My three friends hurled their stones and then a voice from behind shouted, "Duck!" We did and six stones flew at the men advancing towards us. Two men dropped and, as I rose, I lunged with my sword. It came up beneath the shield of the man on my right and blood spurted from his leg. Bruno had drawn his own dagger and he lunged at the man to my left. The man was not expecting it and he reeled. It allowed me to slash at the wounded man's thigh and the razor-sharp seax tore through the flesh. The blood spurted and as it splashed into the face of the man Bruno was fighting so my friend rammed his dagger into the man's neck.

Baldwin shouted, "Push!" He had seen what I had not. We had more weight than they did and as we screamed and pushed so two men, one already wounded, fell from the fighting platform. I almost tumbled to the ground but I kept my feet and Baldwin killed his second man, the one I had wounded. Stones from behind struck the others and suddenly there were no defenders between us and the gate.

Bruno shouted, "Come on Sir Dick, lead your men to glory." He knelt to pick up a spear and a shield. Baldwin grabbed a sword and we moved down the platform.

I was leading and I could both see and hear the consternation from the gatehouse. The fox cubs were in the henhouse. I heard a horn and suddenly the gatehouse and walls were abandoned as men ran for the inner bailey and the donjon.

"Slings!"

The men who were fleeing would have to pass us and after sheathing my weapons I drew my sling and we began to batter and bruise the fleeing men. We might have hurt more had we been on the other side but the shields of those that had them were on their left. Even so, a dozen men fell before they reached the gates. Even worse for the men of Gorron was that the gates broke and Sir William and Bishop Odo led our knights to chase after them. Had they kept the gates barred it might have delayed the inevitable but they did not and tried to allow as many as they could to enter. It was Bishop Odo and my half-brother who were first through and once they had entered the gates then the castle was doomed. A wooden donjon could be fired. We had won and more importantly, we slingers had played our part. I noticed that the tardiest knight and squire were Sir Durand and Charles who seemed to take the longest time to cross the outer bailey.

I looked at the others and we all grinned. Bruno was quick thinking, "Before the others get there, let us descend and take our just desserts."

We hurtled down the ladders that were placed along the fighting platform. The others were busy stripping the four bodies on the fighting platform. Bruno reached the man he had killed and took the helmet and sword from him. I ran to one of those we had killed who had fled the gate. I took his helmet, his sword, his dagger and his purse. I was about to take his mail when a pueros stopped me, "That mail is mine. Keep the rest but the mail is mine."

I could have argued, indeed Bruno would have, but the mail was not the best and I was not big enough to wear. I stood and bowed, "Take my kill with my compliments." We were all fast and had stripped five men before the rest of the army, all older and bigger than we, arrived. We withdrew to the warrior hall. Its door was open and, before any other had realised that, we had searched it and found more weapons as well as leather jacks, wine and food. We sat on the table and ate and drank.

Bruno said, "Let us share what we have. Which of us four does not have a sword?" Odo lifted his hand. "Dick, you have two." I nodded and handed him the one I had taken from the first raid. The other was a better weapon and had a better scabbard. "Do we all have enough daggers?"

We all chorused, "Aye."

"How about helmets?"

I held up mine as did Baldwin and Bruno. Odo shook his head, "It is no matter for my head is too small. We have done well and God smiled on us. We all have coins."

"Aye, we do." Bruno patted me on the back, "And following Sir Dick brings rewards."

"We followed your orders, Bruno."

"But you were the one who faced them alone."

Just then the door opened and Eustace stood there with a bloody sword. He looked around and then, after wiping his sword on one of the beds, began to laugh and shake his head, "I sought you out for I heard what you had done and feared that you lay dying somewhere. I come here and find four

60

veterans eating and drinking as though they have not a care in the world."

I jumped from the table, "I am sorry, Eustace."

"Do not be, for when he hears of your brave deed Sir William will be more than proud. The whole army talks of the four slingers wearing the Malet livery that chased the defenders from the walls."

"There were other slingers..."

"But you led. This day has marked the four of you. You are now brothers in arms. As far as I am concerned, you are pueros who will become squires."

As we left the hall, tired but replete and laden with our loot, I felt as though I was walking on a cloud. We had lost Guillaume but it was almost as though his sacrifice had been to make us warriors. I would light a candle for him and pray for his soul.

Chapter 5

Graville-Sainte-Honorine 1050

We had done all that was necessary and after Duke
William had garrisoned Gorron and sent for ransom, our
conroi headed home. Eustace was now to be Sir Eustace of
Graville-Sainte-Honorine. He had led the chase to the gates
and followed Sir William into the breach. We were accorded
praise all the way home. Our two guardian angels, Richard
and Robert, were particularly impressed at the way we had
handled ourselves. Our only detractors were the slingers who
had not followed us and their animosity was understandable.
Not only did they have no treasure or loot, the rest of their
conroi mocked them as cowards. As we did not see them
again it mattered not. They could have followed us. Our only
casualty had been the boy, Raymond, struck in the back. We
all knew we had taken a risk but it had paid off. Even Robert
Malet, the younger brother, was envious and he spoke to us
as we headed home. We knew him, of course, for he trained
with us in the gyrus. He was given private lessons in the
castle so we did not see him when learning our letters.

"Are you four reckless or so desperate for glory that you
will do anything?"

Bruno was the reckless one and he showed it in his reply,
"My lord, we are not as lucky as you. One day you will be
given your spurs no matter what you do on the battlefield.
We do not have that luxury. Even Richard here, your half-
brother, has no guarantees. You will be given coins by your
brother. Your mail and weapons will be made by the
weaponsmith. We have to rob the dead to take helmets that
are too big and already dented and the handful of copper
coins that rub together in our purses."

The noble reddened and said, "You are an impudent
fellow."

Bruno shrugged, "You asked and I told you. As for being
impudent? Aye, I am. I became so when Guillaume and his
father died and the only ones who noted it were we four and

the other men at arms. Loyalty, it seems, is one way. We owe it to your family but it is not returned."

Robert Malet dug his heels in and returned to the fore.

I shook my head, "Was that well done, Bruno? He will speak with his brother and there may be retribution."

Bruno smiled, "I have enjoyed some success. If I am kept on, and I hope I am, then I will become more skilful. If not, then I have enough of a reputation to be taken on by another. Robert of Lisieux crossed half of Normandy to find a place here and I can do the same."

He was right in that we now had a reputation. Our names were known when, before the assault on Gorron, we were anonymous.

The retribution came but not in the way any of us expected. That night as we made our hovels Eustace sought us out. He had yet to be dubbed and given his spurs and so was still called Eustace. He sat with us and poured wine from a skin into our coistrels. He ruffled Bruno's hair, "What am I to do with you, Bruno the Belligerent."

We all knew to what he referred but the nickname made us all smile and Bruno shrugged, "I am what I am and I cannot change me."

Eustace nodded, "And yet Lord William would have me try." He looked at me, "I am sorry Richard but Bruno's gain is your loss."

That confused us all and Bruno said, "I want nothing if my friend loses out."

"Richard, you were to be my squire but when Master Robert reported Bruno's words it had an effect on Lord William. He realised that Guillaume was unmourned and that you, Bruno, are an orphan. You are to be my squire."

"And if I refuse?"

I put my hand on his arm, "Bruno, this is your chance. Grasp it with both hands. This is right for you are the natural leader. If I am meant to win spurs then that will happen and if not…"

Eustace smiled, "And that will happen, Richard. Your modesty does you great credit and was one of the reasons I asked for you. Your friend is right, Bruno, I am happy for you to be my squire but I intend to mould you into a man who can be knighted. You do not spurn what God throws in your path."

I saw that the clever Bruno had taken in the words and saw their wisdom. "How will my life change?"

"You will still train with these three and be educated as now but you will sleep in my bedchamber as my chamberlain. You will serve me and tend to my horses. When we go to war then it is you who will fetch my lance. I am not a poor knight for I have an income from my father and my own livery. You shall wear that. When we enter our castle, you leave the slingers and join the squires."

He nodded his agreement.

Baldwin said, "Surely we are more than slingers."

"Aye, you are but the name was given to you by those who knew you not. Even Duke William heard of the four slingers from de Caux. I can almost hear the song sung by Taillefer to commemorate it."

As we snuggled into our blankets Bruno spoke to me, for we shared a hovel, "I am sorry I took this from you, Dick."

"Eustace gave me a hint that I may yet be a squire. He said I was modest and that was an attractive quality and our notoriety helps me. I will continue to do as I have done. I have stuck a blade in a man and it did not turn my stomach. I had feared it would. I can be a warrior. I am modest but I know that I have skills. I will dedicate my life to becoming better."

I think Bruno had feared our friendship would be soured. My words told him that it would not.

Our arrival home was like a triumphal parade from the days of Rome. Sir Drogo had returned home when we had won at the siege and he had been our herald. We were cheered and from the looks we four received then our tale had been told. We were still the lowest of the low and so I could not see my grandfather or Gunhild until all my tasks had been completed. The sumpters had to be unpacked and while servants and thralls took away the loot, we had to store the panniers and the saddles as well as groom and tend to our horses. I now saw Blaze as a friend. We had lived together for a month and I had learned his ways as he had learned mine. I spoke to him as I did to Bruno, Odo and Baldwin.

Alain the horse master must have come in as I chattered to my mount and I heard him chuckle. I turned quickly and he held up a hand, "I was not mocking you, Richard. It is rare that such a bond is created so quickly. If a dog or a horse does not like a man then I am suspicious. Blaze likes you and that speaks well of you. We all heard of your gallant charge and now I see that you care for your horse as much as your brothers in arms. It is all good. You have seen to your animals, now go to your grandfather."

I knew that Alain and my grandfather shared more than the training of the young. They were friends. The short campaign had shown me the value of real friends.

Gunhild was in the kitchen of the Great Hall and my grandfather was with his hounds. His rheumy eyes filled as he held out his hands to greet me. I dropped the sack containing my war gear, "Dick, you are home and safe." We hugged and he said, in my ear, "By, but you have grown in a month."

I nodded and opened the bag, "And I have a bounty from the battlefield." I took out my treasures one by one telling him how I had acquired them. He listened patiently.

When I had finished, he took the sword, "Not a bad weapon but not one for a warrior. Still, you have growing to do." He nodded at the purse, "Keep your coins safe and when you have enough then see Aimeri the weaponsmith and have him make you a sword. It will not be cheap but will be money well spent."

"I thought to give the coins to you, grandfather."

He shook his head, "Your mother should have been married and had a dowry. I spent it not. Whatever coins I have, are for you. You are my only blood kin and my days on this earth are lessening."

"Do not say that, Grandfather."

He smiled, sadly, "A man does not live forever no matter how much he wills it. Had I not been brought from England then who knows, I may never have seen you born. I could have died in some battle with the Welsh or the

65

Northumbrians. No, Dick, fate sent me here and lengthened my life. I believe I have had a good life but I do not wish it to end. There are still things that I may teach you."

We had no more time to talk for Bruno came to fetch me. We had to serve at the table.

We had a whole month of change. Eustace was knighted and Bruno, while he did not leave us properly, spent less time with us and more with the squires. My grandfather had taught him all that he could and Bruno worked in the gyrus with the men at arms and other squires. We were still friends and always would be, that never changed, but we saw less of each other. When the duke arrived with his half-brother, as well as Taillefer and his house knights, I wondered if we would be going to war again. We were sparring in the gyrus but our attention was on the hall. When the duke and Sir William emerged along with Bishop Odo and Taillefer, I stopped sparring and looked at Baldwin as they came towards us "What means this?"

"I have no idea."

When they entered, we all bowed but when the duke spoke to my grandfather it took us all by surprise, "You are the one called Geoffrey? The English housecarl?"

"I am, my lord."

"I have a task for you. I travel to England to meet with King Edward and I need one who can speak English."

"You need a translator, my lord?"

"In a manner of speaking. I need a spy to hear what the English are saying when they think I do not hear them."

My grandfather shook his head, "Then I am not your man, my lord. I am a loyal member of Sir William's mesne but I will not betray the people of my birth."

I saw that it angered both the duke and Sir William. Sir Durand looked as though his head would burst he was so furious.

"I command you, Geoffrey." Sir William sounded almost petulant.

My grandfather smiled, "And if I went, then how would you know I reported truly?" He tapped his chest and then his head, "You command the man but the heart and the mind are my own, my lord."

I feared that this would end badly. Sir William had a temper on him. Fatherhood, he now had two sons, had aggravated his temper. It was Bishop Odo who was the peacemaker, "My lord, I have a solution." He waved me over, "You, Richard fitz Malet, can speak English can you not?"

"I can, my lord."

"Could you act as a spy?"

I looked at my grandfather whose face had sunk like one of Gunhild's egg puddings when it was pierced with a knife. I knew this was fate and my decision and answer would affect the rest of my life. I thought back to Bruno's decision to scale the walls and attack the men of Gorron. I had to seize the moment, for to spurn it was the wrong choice. "Aye, my lord."

The duke and Sir William did not look convinced but Taillefer put his arm around my shoulder, "This is even better for while an old English housecarl might be suspected, a Norman boy who pretends he cannot speak English would be a perfect spy."

The duke nodded, "You are right and if he were with Taillefer the jongleur then he would be even more anonymous." He looked at me, "You showed courage at Gorron, do this well and there shall be rewards for you. We ride in the morning."

Sir William was clearly unhappy with my grandfather and he glared at him. He turned to me and said, "Take the rest of the day off to prepare. I want you bathed and smelling sweetly. I will have Sir Eustace's squire bring you a clean tunic and new breeks." He turned to my grandfather and jabbed an angry finger at him, "You, have his hair cut, Robert of Lisieux can take the training this day." He leaned in close for the duke and his half-brother had gone, "I shall not forget this disloyalty."

Sir Durand waited until his brother had departed and then snarled, "And this is not over, old man. You are tolerated here no more and this day you embarrassed the family before the duke."

My grandfather showed no remorse and walked back to our hut with his head held high. "I am sorry if I have disappointed you, grandfather."

His hand gripped my shoulder and I felt some of the strength that had made him such a powerful housecarl, "I am not disappointed for you did the right thing. I am English so how could I spy on my own people? You have English blood in you but you are Norman. You only speak English to me and when I am gone the words will die in your head and you will speak only Norman. I am angry that you should be placed in this position. If you are discovered then your youth will not save you." He stopped and, holding me in two arms, looked directly into my face. "Play the part of one who is slow of wits. Listen and do not speak. If you are playing Taillefer's servant then none will expect you to say much in any case. Now come, we have to fill the bath."

The bath was an old horse trough. We used it to do washing and once or twice a year we would bathe in it. It leaked a little hence the fact that it could no longer function as a water trough. Once in the house, I took off my tunic and boots and began to carry pails of water from the well to the bath. The kitchen was not far away and Gunhild came out for some air. The kitchen was the hottest place in the castle and that was why it was far from the donjon. Fire in a wooden castle was dangerous. A short while later two of the thralls from the kitchen lumbered over with a steaming cauldron of water.

"Mistress Gunhild has finished with this water. She said it would make for a warmer bath."

Geoffrey smiled, "Tell her she is too kind and spoils my grandson but we are grateful."

The cauldron topped up the trough and I discarded my breeks and stepped in. The hot water made the chilly well water lukewarm. My grandfather handed me the soap that we made in the castle and I rubbed myself all over. I immersed my head under the water and held my breath. My grandfather rubbed my hair while I was under the water.

When I emerged I saw that all of the body lice and some of the nits floated, dead, on the water.

"Stay there and I will cut your hair as his lordship demanded."

My hair was unkempt and needed cutting. I wondered if he would cut it in the style of Sir William and the duke. The hair at the rear and the sides was shaved and the top was cut short. It made them look almost priestly. When he brought the bowl out, I saw that he was going to cut my hair the way the men at arms wore it. He put it on my head and it came to my ears. He took out his sharpest dagger and began to slice hanks of hair. When that was done, he lathered up soap and then shaved my head at the sides and the back. He also shaved my chin. It was not so much hair as down but I knew that I would soon need to shave. Sir William did not like beards and moustaches. My grandfather still wore his hair long but he had shaved since arriving to serve Sir William's mother. Finally, he took out the finest bone comb and rid my remaining hair of the last of the infestation. That done I emerged and with a towel wrapped around me we emptied the water. The fowl that pecked close by the hog bog raced over to feast on the former residents of my hair and body.

I saw Bruno wandering over. He had my tunic and breeks. We all went into the hut. Bruno grinned at my head. I said, "I know not why you are laughing, Sir Eustace will soon have you cut your hair like Sir William's. I am just sad that I will not be here to laugh at it and mock you."

"It is true then, you go to England with the duke."

I nodded, "As a spy. I go to listen to English words and report back to the duke."

"Then you are destined for great things, Dick."

"Or an early death."

"Grandfather! I heeded your words and I promise that I will stay silent. I will not speak any English. I can play the mummer."

Bruno sat on the chair as I dressed, "I envy you. You will travel to a foreign land."

Grandfather shook his head, "It is not that different from Normandy, Bruno. The food is similar to that which we eat here. They have deer and wild boar. They drink more mead and ale rather than wine but other than that…"

"Yet your warriors look different for they are all like you are they not?"

He shook his head, "I was a housecarl. They are the equivalent of a knight. We do not use horses as you Normans do but our long axes can take the legs from a horse and a dismounted knight is an easy prey."

We both looked at my grandfather, "You think that we will have to fight the English?"

He shrugged, "I know our duke and King Edward are like brothers but there are others, like the Godwin family who do not like the closeness between the duke and the king. There may come a time, Bruno, when you have to fight Englishmen, or Danes or Vikings. When you do, be wary for they have skills you know not how to counter."

The voice from outside demanded that Bruno returned to his duties. It allowed my grandfather and me to spend the rest of the day and evening talking. He told me all that he knew of England and then, while we ate the food that Gunhild had brought, the three of us spoke of my future. It was, of course, all fantasy but even my grandfather, sceptic though he was, knew that the visit to England with Duke William might well change my life.

When I retired, my dreams were filled with strange images conjured by my grandfather's words.

The next day we all woke early. Gunhild always had an early start but my grandfather and I wanted to spend as much time with one another as we could and the loss of a couple of hours of sleep seemed unimportant.

"You will not need your sword and I shall keep it here for you. You will not need your money and I will put it with mine. Come and help me shift the paillasse." The straw-filled bag was changed once a year and I had often turned it. When we had moved it, I saw that there was a bossless shield lying beneath. Grandfather shifted it and then lifted out a small chest from the hole in the ground. He opened it and I saw small bags within. "These are my treasures. Put yours there." I dropped it in and he lifted one of the bags and

70

withdrew a chain with a medallion on it. It looked like the one worn by the dead steward.

"What is that?"

He handed it to me and I looked at it, "A double-headed eagle, grandfather?"

"The symbol of Leofric, the Earl of Mercia and my master. I wore this when I commanded the housecarls and before I was bodyguard to Sir William's mother." He looked at me, "My wife was a daughter of Leofric. You are related to a noble English family." I handed it back to him and he put it back in the chest. When we had replaced everything, he sat on the paillasse. "I was an important man then. I came to Normandy with hopes of more honour and a fine house." He shook his head, "Your father did not like me and relegated me to being a trainer of men. It broke my wife's heart and she died because she missed England. Had your mother not been a bairn I might have returned to England. Now it is too late."

I pointed to the ground, "Take your treasure and mine, go to England and make a new start."

"The events of today make that impossible. I should have gone yesterday or the day before but if I go now then the duke and Sir William will suspect I go to warn the English and I will die before I can board a ship. No, Dick, I shall die in Normandy. When you are there and if you get to King Edward's new abbey then say a prayer for me. I pray each day in a Norman church but the edifice of King Edward might ensure that I go to heaven. Every day I wake up I am surprised because I am old and I ache. It is good that Gunhild has salves and creams else I should not be able to move at all."

"I will but your words are foolish. You will still be alive when I return and we shall laugh at your morbid thoughts."

"We shall see, we shall see."

Chapter 6

Had I not been riding at the side of Taillefer then my journey would have been sad as my grandfather's words weighed heavily upon me. Taillefer was a young knight and he was the most interesting as well as the funniest man I had ever met. He was keen for us to begin to play our parts as soon as we could. "It is important, Richard, that you never let down your guard. I am a troubadour and people like my songs because they seem true. That is because I believe them myself and I sing them passionately. We shall do the same with the roles we play. You are to be an orphan…"

"But I am an orphan."

He laughed. He was a very kind and patient man, "When you make up a lie it is always better to base it on the truth. You are an orphan and I discovered you on the side of the road. We do not know who your parents were for you were young," He nodded, "I like this story for it makes me out to be nobler than I am. I am training you to be a knight."

"I could have brought my sword!"

He shook his head, "Even Duke William will have to surrender his sword in the presence of King Edward. The sword is immaterial. I am explaining why you are so muscled and look like a warrior."

"My grandfather said I should not speak and listen as much as I can."

"And that is good advice. I like that," he nodded. "You are a sad youth, aye, that garners even more sympathy. The duke and I have spoken of this. When I sing then you can blend into the background and listen to the words of the nobles. You have a good memory?"

"I think so."

"No matter. Each night when we retire you will tell me all that you hear no matter how trivial. I have the most marvellous of memories."

"What is your real name, Taillefer?"

He suddenly looked at me, "What an extraordinary question. Why do think it is not my real name?"

I shrugged, "I think that you invented it. I think you have invented yourself."

"You are a clever one and when I get to know you better, I may tell you the truth but for now, Richard the Orphan, keep those ideas to yourself."

"Of course."

"And in return, I shall teach you how to use a sword as well as I and how to juggle."

"I do not wish to be a juggler. I will be a warrior."

"And juggling teaches dexterity. You know that I can juggle with three daggers or small swords?"

"That is impossible."

"You would think so but I can." He patted his saddlebag, "I have no land and there is no lord to give me a roof. I survive because lords like me to entertain them and they pay me well. The duke is my best client but there are others. I am paid here to distract the English while the duke talks in private with King Edward. When we return to Normandy, I shall seek another employer. I have a good life."

As we headed for Rouen and the ship we would take, he regaled me with tales of his adventures. It had all seemed to begin just four years earlier and I realised that Taillefer was a human onion. He had many layers but no matter how many you peeled you could never get to the heart of the man.

That was also my first experience of loading horses onto a ship. The Normans were descended from Norsemen who used their dragonships to raid England. They were long, low and sleek. With shallow sides, the horses jumped aboard from the quay. There were two ships to take us and I was able to watch the duke, Bishop Odo and his oathsworn board the first one. Taillefer and I were on the second with the servants. I was pleased with myself when we managed it. I was excited to be sailing but disappointed that the journey to the sea was so slow. We twisted and turned around every bend in the Seine and it took almost a day to reach the mouth of the estuary. There we waited for two days until the winds swung around and that was when I felt the real power of the sea. It took a whole day and night to sail across the channel. Even when we reached the river Thames, we had a long journey up the river to the king's palace at Thornley Island just outside Lundenwic and on the Temese.

The voyages were enlivened by Taillefer. I am older now and I think I understand what he was doing. He seemed to have adopted me and was trying to be as a father to me. He taught me things he thought my father should have taught me. I realised as the scales fell from my eyes that although my grandfather had done his best, he had come to the task as an old man and the lessons he had taught me, while good ones, did not help me as much as the ones from this exciting young Norman. The lessons were lessons in life. He taught me how to read people as easily as a priest reads a parchment. The other lessons were on the use of hands. The juggling apart he taught me how to use my hands to deceive someone. By moving one hand you distracted them. He also gave me sword skills. He was a truly great swordsman. He had three identical swords for he used them to juggle. He used them to practise and I juggled daggers instead. The river voyages were enlivened by our practice.

As we neared the quay where we would disembark, Taillefer gave me some warnings. "We are not in Normandy any longer. There will be men who will smile but their smiles hide daggers. The duke comes for political reasons but he and the king are friends. Keep your eyes open for those who do not seem to like that friendship. Only eat and drink when you have seen another eat or drink. Do not be the first to do so. Better to go hungry than be poisoned."

"That is possible?"

"These are people who throw the bones to win a crown. King Edmund Ironside died when sitting on a garderobe. Be on your guard."

We watched the duke and his entourage disembark and then we followed suit. Getting the horses off proved easier than getting them aboard. I think they had endured enough of the voyage too. We were not greeted by the king or any of his nobles, after all, they would have had no idea exactly when we were due to arrive but it was clear that we were expected. Ælfgar, an illegitimate son of the Earl of Mercia, and half a dozen mounted warriors met us to escort us through the city to the new palace and abbey that were the monuments to King Edward. I was at the rear with the servants of the duke and we followed the Mercians and Duke William as we rode the mile or so to the hall. Both the hall and the abbey were imposing but not as imposing as the ones in Rouen and Caen. I knew that Duke William would notice the differences. Having said that, they were still building the abbey as they were the hall.

I had never met a king before but the one I took to be the king turned out to be Earl Godwin of Wessex and the one who was the king looked like a priest. That there was warmth between the king and the duke was clear. They embraced and although we could not hear the words their heads were together and they spoke at length. If there was harmony there then there was animosity in the eyes of Earl Godwin and the ones who proved to be his sons, Harold, Tostig, Leofwine and Gyrth. I could have deduced that before Taillefer's lessons. I needed my newly acquired skills to read the others.

The English leaders, the duke and the bishop entered the abbey and we remained without. It gave me the chance to see the hall that was also under construction. I could see that it was habitable and, when completed, would be a fine stone hall but I was disappointed in it.

Taillefer called over one of the English housecarls. He spoke in Norman and the housecarl did his best to answer the questions. "The hall is new?" Taillefer kept his words simple.

"There was a hall close by that was built in the time of the Dane, Cnut. This was an island, Thornley Island, and the king used the water as a natural defence. It is close to the river and the king can travel between here and his palace at Grenewic easily."

Taillefer turned and pointed at the Roman walls. It was clear that repairs had been going on and we spied new mortar. "And the rest of Lundenwic?"

The housecarl shrugged, "Is not the place for visitors. King Edward chose this site for his abbey and hall as they are outside the wall. I think that in the fullness of time, he will turn his gaze to the city and make it fit to be his capital, but for now he builds the abbey where he will be buried."

I was desperate to ask questions but knew I had to play the part of the sad, silent orphan. Taillefer did it for me, "Yet the king looks young."

"He is and yet he has been cursed with no sons. Even a daughter might guarantee the succession."

Other housecarls had drawn closer to us and my English came to my aid. Two who were standing just a couple of feet from the one who was speaking smiled. One said, quietly but loud enough for me to hear, "And that suits the king's father-in-law, the Earl of Wessex."

The other said, "Hold your tongue."

The first man shrugged, "These cannot speak English."

"And we serve the earl's son. Show loyalty and hold your tongue."

Throughout the conversation, I stared at Taillefer and the man he was speaking with. My face was like a stone. I was not sure how valuable the information was but I stored it in my head.

When the royal and ducal parties emerged, we entered the hall. The king apologised for the construction but assured the duke that within, it would be warm and comfortable. It was still built in the style of the Danes who had ruled England for so many years. There were no bed chambers but the king had a bed on a raised dais with curtains around it. I guessed that the hall would be used for feasting and when it was cleared then mattresses were brought out. Along with the others who were not knights, I was taken to the kitchens. We would sleep in the storerooms. I chose the one closest to the kitchens. The residual heat from the fires would keep me warm. I found a corner where I could lay my blanket and cloak and then presented myself to the cook.

There were six of us who were Normans and I took my lead from the others. The cook spoke no Norman and a priest translated. We were each allocated to an English cook who would fill the platters that we carried. We would then take the platters and serve the table. The priest told us that he would act as a steward and direct us. When the platters were empty, we would return. I was comfortable with the work. It was what I had done for some years. However, some of those who were the squires of the duke's companions clearly thought the work beneath them and spoke their minds. The cooks could not understand the words but they did the tone. The priest coloured. I kept my silence. I dutifully took my platter and had it filled with river fish. The steam rose before me when I stepped from the heat of the kitchen to the cool of the corridor that led to the hall. It was only thirty paces long but the noise began to rise when I was halfway along. By the time I reached it, there was a cacophony. What surprised me was that there were less than thirty men seated at the table but the hall seemed to echo and reverberate with the words.

The arrival of the food made the two churchmen stand. Bishop Odo and the Abbot of St Peter's Abbey placed their hands together and silence descended. The prayer spoken by the Abbot was in Latin but my lessons with Father Raymond meant that I understood it. It was a longer grace than was normal and reflected the piety of King Edward. When they sat the noise rose once more.

King Edward had grown up in the Norman court and was more comfortable with Norman than either English or Danish. My ears might not be needed. As I placed the platter before Taillefer, he winked at me and that made me feel better. Going back with the empty platter, I turned sideways to allow those coming with fresh ones to pass. It was on the third visit that I realised some of the other Normans had only made the journey once. The cooks noticed and I was greeted with smiles. It was a beginning.

The last platters were to be left on the table. Cheese and hams were placed along the table. The priest asked us to stand behind our masters in case we were needed again. I was now starving but I stood patiently and watched. The duke, his half-brother and the king drank sparingly. The rest drank as though the barrels and jugs were about to run out. I looked at the English nobles and saw that they all sported facial hair and wore their hair long. Unlike Taillefer and the Norman knights, they also wore rings and gold about their necks. It was just an observation but Taillefer's lessons had been heeded.

King Edward turned and said, "We hear that you are a fine singer, Taillefer. Before we retire for the night we would hear a song."

Taillefer rose and I handed him his rote which was placed against the wall, "I will give you the Chanson de Roland." The king nodded his approval. Taillefer was clever. The song could not possibly insult the English before him as it was about a battle in the mountains between Franks and Moors. It was a tale of heroism, loyalty and courage. The words Taillefer sang were written by a friend of his, Turold. I knew that because it had come up on the voyage. However, the version sung by Taillefer was not exactly the same as Turold's. Taillefer liked to use certain words which he thought were more musical. The sound was more important to Taillefer than the accuracy. The song was greeted with applause. Part of that was the fact that many of the audience were so drunk that they would have cheered the reading of a list of ingredients for a pie. When he had finished Taillefer took a bow. The king rose and it was the signal for the end of the feast.

The priest waved us over along with the English servants and we were given the task of clearing the tables and then, when they were empty, moving them so that the sleeping mattresses could be fetched. The result was that we were not finished until the king was asleep and the cacophony of the feast was replaced by a different melody, snores, burps and farts. The priest waved us away, making the sign of the cross as he did so. "Now you may eat."

Back in the kitchen, the cook had cleared his preparation table. It was now cleaned and laden with the food that was left. Two of the cooks waved me over to sit on the bench between them. The ones who had been less than diligent were forced to sit at the end of the table with the least tasty morsels.

I helped myself to the leg and thigh of a fowl and some fine white bread, a rare treat. The man to my right filled my coistrel with ale and raised his to toast me. "Here's to women, beer and song, may none of them be flat."

I nodded and said, "Salut!"

The man on my other side asked, "Are you the servant of the troubadour, Taillefer?"

I feigned ignorance and one of those seated opposite asked in poor Norman, "Edgar asks if Taillefer is your master."

I nodded and answered in Norman, "He is."

Edgar continued in English, "He has a fine voice." I just gave the vacant smile of one who has not understood a word.

I was ignored. The man who could speak Norman was a trencherman and he filled his mouth so full that he could barely chew and kept washing the food down with the ale. What I learned that night was as valuable as gold. Earl Godwin and his sons were the most powerful men in the kingdom. The earl's daughter was the queen and the men along our table thought it inevitable that when King Edward died childless the earl would become king. The only man with a better claim was Edward the Exile now living in Hungary. He was dismissed as being no threat to Earl Godwin. As I helped the cooks to clear the table, I wondered what the purpose of our visit was.

As I headed to my store room one of the squires, Aimeri de Landvielle, took my arm, "Do not get too friendly with these savages. I know you are a simple country bumpkin and only here because your master can sing but do not get too close to them. You are a Norman. Remember that."

I played my part and nodded, "Yes, master. I am sorry. This is my first time serving in such an august company."

He laughed, "August? They must have driven the pigs hence to make us chambers!"

I slept better than I expected but not for long. The abbey bell tolled for prime and we were woken. The cooks were already preparing the food and we had to serve it. The process was shorter than the feast and we were finished and cleared by terces.

Taillefer greeted me. I saw that he had a sword in his belt and two across his back, "Ah, Richard, let us take a walk

through this city. I would look on the cathedral." He turned
to the duke, "Do you need me, my lord?"

"No, Taillefer, the time until the feast this night is your
own."

As soon as we were out of the hall, we headed for the
river and I told him all that I had learned. "You did well."

"The other squires managed to annoy the English in the
kitchen, my lord."

He nodded, "They have yet to learn that they have to fake
a smile."

"Why is the duke here, Taillefer?"

"Simple, he comes to win a kingdom. The king has no
heirs and Earl Godwin seems to take it as his natural right, as
Earl of Wessex, to inherit the crown. King Edward favours
the duke. Now keep your eyes open here in this city. There
are men who might seek to either rob us or do us harm."

"Then why take the risk, my lord?"

"We cannot let them think that we fear them." We headed
to the market, called the Chepe, and perused what they had
to sell. Taillefer taught me lessons that day too. "Never buy
something the first time. If we return tomorrow the price
may be lower and will certainly not be any higher."

We visited the cathedral of St Paul and, as I had promised
my grandfather, I said a prayer and paid a precious penny for
a candle. When we rose and headed for the daylight Taillefer
said, "I cannot understand why your grandfather remains in
Normandy. I am not English but I would like to spend my
last days in the land of my birth."

"He stays, I think, because of me and there is a woman,
Gunhild, they are comfortable together."

It was as we emerged from the dark of the church and
into the light that we were accosted by three Saxons. I saw
that they sported horsehair tied to their own hair. It was
white and was the symbol of Wessex. Earl Godwin's men.
They spoke to us in execrable Norman, laced with equally
bad French.

"Why do you Normans not stay in your rat holes in
France and leave England to those who have the right to be
here."

Taillefer stood balanced and looked relaxed. I knew he was ready to spring at a moment's notice. "England? Not long ago this was part of Denmark. I think that this land belongs to whoever wants it but rest assured, my friend, we want nothing from it."

He spoke slowly but, even so, it took some time for the words to penetrate. The leader who, like Taillefer, had more than one sword said, belligerently, clearly intending to initiate a fight, "Our land is not good enough for you? Is that it?"

Taillefer sighed, "If you wish to fight us, then do so quickly for your breath and your awful Norman make me wish our acquaintance to cease as quickly as possible."

He was ready with his quick hands and as the leader drew a sword, Taillefer had one drawn and drew another in the twinkling of an eye. The leader's two companions were slower than he was and, seeing two swords in Taillefer's hands, drew his second.

Taillefer said, "Richard" and as he flicked his right hand at one of the two slower men, confidently tossed the other sword to me. We had practised this on the ship and I easily caught it and blocked the leader's strike at Taillefer. I think that he could have danced away anyway but he nodded his thanks and drew his last blade. A crowd had gathered for we were in the open space before St Paul's. The three of them had their swords and I could see from their faces that they had expected three on one. I was a youth and they had dismissed me. We had not discussed this but I knew that all I had to do was protect Taillefer's back and he would control the rest. What he did that surprised even me was to begin to juggle the two swords. They looked mesmerised until the leader suddenly lunged with one sword at Taillefer's throat. Taillefer caught his two blades and making a cross trapped the Englishman's sword. He twisted his hands and the sword flew up to land, point down in the earth. There were squeals from the women who watched. The leader now had a sword in his left hand but he knew he was outclassed. He went to reach for his embedded blade and Taillefer stroked his sword across the back of the Saxon's right hand. The edge was razor sharp and cut through to the bones. They had endured enough and the three fled. Those watching clapped and cheered. Taillefer was a showman and gave a bow. He sheathed his swords and I handed him the one he had tossed to me. Drawing the Saxon's sword from the ground he handed it to me, "A present and a remembrance. You did well and I thank you for your blow."

"Which you did not need."

"Nonetheless it helped. They knew they had two opponents and that worried them. Let us return to the hall. This will interest the duke."

I examined the sword as we made our way back. It was a well-made sword and had good balance. I knew it was a good weapon and it highlighted Taillefer's skill. We did not get to see the duke and Bishop Odo until the middle of the afternoon. There was a small chapel close to the hall and the three of them retired there and I kept watch at the door. I caught the odd word but I knew that Taillefer would tell me anything that was of importance.

When they came out the duke handed me a couple of silver coins, "You have done well and your inclusion on this trip was well justified. Taillefer says that you handled yourself well this day. Good. Tonight do the same as last night for there is another feast but there will be more nobles at this one."

"When do we go home, Duke William?"

He smiled, "You yearn for home already?"

"I do, for there I can continue to learn to be a warrior."

Taillefer shook his head, "The lessons you learn here are even more valuable. I will try to keep up with your training."

That would have to wait for I had to change my tunic and wash up. The duke was mindful of the impression that we would give. Bishop Odo chastised the other squires. Some of them gave me baleful looks, realising who had informed on them. I did not care. When I returned to Normandy, I would rarely see them and Taillefer had given me confidence in my own abilities.

When I was sent up to the hall with the first platter even I was taken aback. I could not see how any more could have been accommodated in the hall for it was overflowing. More than that the king and the duke wore their finest fur-trimmed clothes. The king had on his crown. I was exhausted by the time we took the cheese and meats. It was the Bishop of Lundenwic who stood to demand silence and when there was, it was King Edward who rose to his feet. I felt the same as I had when we had prepared to scale the walls at Gorron. I truly believed that if Taillefer had drawn one of his swords he could have cut the air like a slice of cake.

I kept my eyes fixed on Earl Godwin. He and his sons were seated at the table that butted up to the king's and all of them were staring intently at King Edward. His voice was gentle and I saw men at the rear of the hall straining to hear his words.

"Friends, for I believe that this day all of you are my friends, as you know God has not blessed me with an heir." The queen's eyes were on her father, the earl, "I have come to the conclusion that he does not wish my line to continue. When I lived in exile I was welcomed by the family of my mother and by the Norman people. This day I repay that kindness as well as giving England that which it needs, a strong king." He turned to the Duke of Normandy. "This night I announce, before the most senior nobles in the land, that Duke William of Normandy is my heir and when I die then it is my will that he be crowned the King of England."

The only ones who banged the table, as the king sat, were the Normans and the clergy. They were the ones who approved. The rest did not and I saw the anger fill the face of the Earl of Wessex. I saw his eldest son, Harold, begin to rise but his father restrained him. Such an act would be an insult and, as I came to learn, Earl Godwin was a clever man.

The duke said nothing but he held the earl's gaze. Bishop Odo said, "Taillefer, a song."

"Of course." I handed my master his rote and as I gave it to him, saw lower down the earl's table, a man with a bandaged hand. It was the one who had tried to provoke Taillefer. If nothing else it proved that the earl had sent the men.

I wondered that night when I crawled exhausted into my blanket if we were to leave England and return to Normandy. We were not.

Chapter 7

We left Lundenwic but it was to visit one of the king's hunting lodges close to Wintan-Caestre. Blaze would have a chance to run. Although the visit had been planned, I believe that the king and the duke would have left in any case as there was a poisonous atmosphere in Lundenwic. It was the centre of Earl Godwin's power base and while he kept to himself, his sons were agitating and fermenting unrest. Duke William and his half-brother had not brought an army to England and the last thing that anyone wanted was for the Duke of Normandy to die in a riot. We rode for the capital of Wessex. Even then the king did not enter the burgh but went to a hunting lodge just outside the city. One of his many monasteries was close by and the hunting was good in the surrounding forests. The king did not hunt with us. We spent some days there and the pious king spent his time reading and praying. We hunted.

Duke William loved to hunt. It was in those days that I truly came to know Duke William of Normandy. Hunting boar and deer with a spear from the back of a horse was a combination of pleasure and practice for the duke. He could practise his skills with a spear and he enjoyed the chase and pursuit of animals that could hurt him. Bishop Odo and Taillefer were also skilled riders and huntsmen. I was there as a follower and a chaser. Along with the other squires and servants, our task was to start the herds moving towards our betters. Osric was King Edward's master of the hunt and he was loyal to the king. We were led to the places where the deer gathered. It was usual for deer to be hunted by nobles armed with bows but Duke William wanted to hone his skill with a lance. It was harder to make a kill and more dangerous. A stag could turn and gut both rider and mount with his wicked horns.

The first time we hunted deer, the beaters were spread out in a long line and we were driving them towards the nobles. It was easy and I enjoyed it. I was out in the open and unless the stag decided to turn on the herd's tormentors, we were safe. Osric had found a small herd and organised us into a line. His Norman was perfect for he was King Edward's man. I suspect that he had not led us to the largest herd but that would not bother Duke William. As we had left the lodge, Taillefer told me that the duke enjoyed the hunt as he saw it as practice for war. Osric nodded and began beating the small drum he had brought. Some of the other English beaters had wooden whistles. I knew how to whistle and joined the others in a cacophony of noise. The herd took off, led by a six-point stag. It was a young one. Osric had known where the herd would be and they ran up the shallow valley towards the nobles who were waiting with spears. We ran after them. Although our whoops, whistles and bangs were no longer needed, our pounding feet would keep the herd moving. I was a fast runner and I was the one closest to the herd as the duke and the nobles galloped at them. I stopped and waited behind a tree. The last thing I needed was to be trampled by either a horse or a maddened deer.

I peered around the bole of the elm tree and saw Duke William leaning from his saddle with his spear levelled. I was dispassionate enough to know that this was what it must be like for someone facing a charging line of Norman knights. The deer was a brave one and it went, head down, directly for the duke and his mount. Duke William was not the tallest of men, some said squat and that was surprising as his ancestor, Göngu-Hrólfr Rognvaldson, was said to have been a giant so tall that his feet touched the ground when riding anything other than the largest of mounts. The duke's size enabled him to jink his mount and yet keep his balance. He did not slow as he neared the beast's antlers. They were some distance from me but I was able to see that the duke easily controlled his mount with his knees and left hand and yet his right kept the spear steady. He pulled his arm back and then, suddenly shifting his left hand to move his horse to the side, thrust the spear deep into the animal's chest. It was a remarkable strike and he had to have leaned so far from his saddle that he would almost have tumbled to the ground. He rammed the spear so hard that it was jarred loose and the duke rose and leaned the other way as the dying stag's antlers sought to strike the duke.

Every knight with the king chose another target. Even Bishop Odo did not try to steal the glory by taking the stag. As the last of the squires reached us the hunt was over. The stag and six other deer lay dead. Duke William himself had dismounted to despatch any that had not been killed outright.

Taillefer had, naturally, killed his animal quickly. He waved me over and I ran to help him to gut it. He smiled, "This is an old girl. It is better to kill the old for it makes the herd stronger. The ones who survived this attack will seek a stronger stag. It is nature's way. Now, help me gut her and then fetch the horses." The sumpters and our mounts were at the place we had begun the hunt. Already Osric had lit a fire. Before the hunt, Taillefer had told me that the nobles would enjoy the roasted heart, liver and kidneys before we returned to the lodge. He had told me that in times past the heart was eaten raw as a sign of a young noble being blooded. All those who rode with Duke William had long since been blooded, not only in the hunt but in war. Roast heart was tasty. I cut some branches and threaded the bloody offal onto them ready to be cooked. That done I turned and ran back to the horses. When I passed the small stream, I stopped to wash my hands. The smell of blood could upset horses and the last thing I needed was to have to chase after a skittish horse. I had led two sumpters and I untethered them and rode Blaze back through the trees. By the time I reached the hunt, the air was filled with the smell of wood smoke. I heard the sound of Taillefer's melodious voice as he entertained the duke with a witty song about a huntsman and a maiden. It was bawdy and the duke and Bishop Odo were laughing as I neared them. It was not the sort of song for the court for it was both crude and rude. Taillefer could cater to every audience. It was how he came to be so rich. He knew how to make men laugh and ladies weep. Both brought him coins.

I tied up the horses and then returned to the deer. We had taken out the delicacies that would be eaten but the doe needed the rest removed. It was a messy job and I hung the entrails and bowels from the branch of a tree. It would not do for a noble to slip on them if they were discarded on the floor. The stag's testicles were being roasted for the duke and the bishop. Men believed that eating them made them more fertile. I wondered if that was King Edward's problem. My time with King Edward and Duke William made me ponder such things. I did not know it then but I do now, Taillefer took me into a different world. When I was in Graville-Sainte-Honorine, I was treated as little more than a servant. I was Taillefer's servant but he treated me differently. He seemed to think that he owed me a duty of care and needed to shape me into a warrior. My time in England made me a better warrior and, I believe, person.

Two days after the deer hunt, Duke William led us to hunt wild boar. Osric had found a small herd. While hunting deer was dangerous, hunting wild boar often resulted in fatalities. We would hunt them on horses. The squires would carry spare boar spears and ride close to their lords and masters. I had never hunted boar and I was afraid. I had seen, back in Normandy, a huntsman brought back to the castle. He had come too close to a boar and the boar's tusks had gutted him. It took him half a day to die and by the end he was begging for a warrior's death.

"You stay behind me. If I need a second spear then I will hold out my hand behind me." I nodded and he smiled, "I shall try to make do with one, eh?"

This time, when Osric led us, he was mounted and had his own boar spear. The boar spear had a bar just behind the head. Taillefer had told me that you did not want to bury the spear too deeply. Osric would not hunt but as he was leading he might be needed to come to the aid of the duke. The two of them, followed by Bishop Odo, would lead us. This time there would be no charging horses. We walked them. Osric knew where the wild boars were but even I could smell the stink of boar as the breeze brought their smell to us. Everyone could smell the small herd and I saw the knights grip their spears a little more tightly. The exception was Taillefer. He was a natural with every weapon. It was as though the weapon was part of him and moved of its own volition, obeying the thoughts of the troubadour. He was truly a remarkable man. Looking back now I can see that he became a sort of foster father to me. The time I spent with him made a bond that lasted until death.

Wild pigs have a keen sense of smell and good hearing. It makes up for their poor eyesight. They began to run as soon as we spied them. The wood in which we hunted had not only trees but shrubs and bushes. It afforded the animals good cover and they used it. Duke William rode after the largest boar. Bishop Odo would be there to help in case one strike was not enough. A wounded boar was a killer. My grandfather had taught me that. Some of the other animals did not follow the leader of the herd. They followed a young boar and it was that group of animals that Taillefer, Sir Roger and Sir Ambrose followed. I still did not know how Taillefer became as skilful as he was but he rode his horse with such ease and confidence that he easily outstripped the other two. I was lucky that Blaze knew Parsifal, Taillefer's horse, and he intuitively followed. It meant I was just two lengths behind Taillefer when he made his strike. It was still too far away but I would have needed to be riding Pegasus to have kept up. I was still close enough to see the spear rise and I watched with undisguised admiration as he found the perfect spot between the shoulders of the old sow. She was a big beast and had savage tusks but she tumbled over, clearly dead as I passed her. Taillefer reined in. Sir Roger and Sir Ambrose, followed by their squires, galloped off after the young boar and the others.

I dismounted. "I am sorry I could not keep up with you, my lord."

Taillefer dismounted and, shaking his head, pulled the spear from the still body of the sow, "I did not expect you to keep up with me." He used some leaves to clean the blood from the blade. "I took you as a squire to serve the duke. When this is over, I will return to my solitary life. I expect no man to risk his life for me. The chances I take are my decision. I earn coins from the nobles but I am beholden to no man. I like the duke and he likes me but I am my own man and I like that."

I took out the seax and between us, we rolled the sow over, "Why do you not marry, my lord? I know that you must be rich for I have seen the coins collected on this trip."

He nodded, "You are intuitive, Richard fitz Malet." He stood and went to fetch the ale skin. "I seek the perfect woman. Thus far I have not found her. When I do then I will court and marry her and, perhaps, settle down in a home." He drank from the skin and then wiped his mouth with the back of his hand, "In truth, I think my quest is a vain one. I seek a Helen but if a maid sleeps with me then she has lost her perfection." He put the stopper back in the ale skin and leaned down, "My nature is a complicated one." He laughed, "You are the one who has come the closest to knowing me. When this is over and you return home, I shall miss you."

I used the seax to saw through the tough hide of the sow, "I could come with you, my lord, and be your squire."

He said nothing and I paused in my sawing to look up. His face was sad, "I am torn, Richard, for I like you but I fear that my reckless nature will, one day, bring me my death. I would not have you close enough to suffer my fate. No, when this is over you shall go back to your grandfather and serve Sir William." He smiled, "That is a wicked-looking weapon." By changing the subject so dramatically I knew that he wished for no more personal questions.

I nodded, "It is a Saxon weapon, a seax and it has but one blade. It is perfect for this." I continued sawing and then the two of us pulled out the offal. It was as we did so that the other two knights and their squires walked their horses through the trees towards us. One of the knights, Sir Ambrose, was limping.

Taillefer stood, "No luck?"

Sir Roger shook his head, "I wouldn't say no luck, just bad luck. Ambrose's horse stumbled and my friend's leg smacked into a tree."

"You are lucky it is not broken and so I would say, Sir Roger, that you had good luck. In my view, luck is all a matter of perspective. We are lucky that you did not have our success for this old girl is too heavy for Richard and me to lift so all is well, eh?"

I met many people in my life but none had the optimistic view of Taillefer. The two knights smiled at his words and between us, we managed to first cut a long stave and then ram it through its mouth and out of its rear. The other squires led Parsifal and Blaze while Taillefer and I laboured beneath the weight of the sow. We headed towards the smell of woodsmoke.

When we reached it, we saw the bishop tending to Osric's leg. The duke smiled when he saw our sow. "Well done, Taillefer. We have two beasts to eat at the king's lodge." The boar, the leader of the herd, lay dead and I saw that the heart, liver and kidneys along with the testicles were already threaded on skewers.

"What happened to you, Osric?"

Taillefer spoke to all men as though they were equals. It was a rare gift. The duke appeared to be unconcerned that the king's huntsman was hurt. Osric smiled, "Old Lucifer there," he pointed to the dead boar, "did for me. When he was struck in the shoulder he turned and rammed his tusk into my leg." He shook his head, "My spear found his eye but I shall miss the old boy. I have led hunts to find him these last ten years."

Taillefer patted the hunter on the shoulder, "There is a young man to take his place. He escaped the attention of Sir Roger and Sir Ambrose. Perhaps he is Beelzebub, eh?"

The laughter in the forest was a mark of Taillefer's skill. He knew just the right thing to say and to do.

As Taillefer and I had been responsible for the sow, I was allowed to slice a piece from the heart. I had never eaten it before and the taste was so powerful that I knew some of the sow's power now lay within me. Having said that, I could not have eaten more than one slice.

We ate the sow two days later at a feast at the lodge. It was a smaller gathering than at Thornley and a more pleasant experience. The other squires had come to know me, and my diligence and natural modesty seemed to make them like me. I was learning from Taillefer. Even when we had been attacked in Lundenwic he had not lost his temper. He had told me that there was no point in losing your temper as such a man always made bad decisions. "It is better to act coldly and dispassionately than be a wild berserker."

There was plenty of meat left for us and I enjoyed, each time we returned to the kitchen, some of the crispy crackling. When the hair had burned from the pig on the spit, the skin, doused with salt, bubbled and changed into the most delicious part of the pig. The meat, slowly cooked, was delicious but I liked the crackling.

With no queen in residence, Queen Edith was with her father and brothers in Lundenwic, Taillefer had free rein to sing the bawdiest of songs. He also sang the songs that the duke liked: the song of Roland and of his illustrious ancestor, Göngu-Hrólfr Rognvaldson. Those were the times I enjoyed the best. Every eye and ear were on Taillefer and smiles were on their faces. I felt like a fraud in that I was here to discover the secrets of the English but all that I had managed to uncover was the obvious knowledge that Earl Godwin and his sons sought the throne and the crown.

It was when a rider galloped into the lodge two days after the sow feast that our lives changed, indeed, our future changed. The man was Flemish and came from Count Eustace. We were in the hall that day for it was a cold one and the duke and the king were playing chess. The man abased himself before the king, "King Edward, I am here at the request of Count Eustace of Boulogne. We tried to land at the burgh at Douvres so that we could ride here and meet with you as promised. The men of Douvres attacked us and men were killed."

Before the king could answer, the duke, who was a friend of Count Eustace, asked, "The count, he lives?"

"Aye, he managed to board our ship. As I had landed my horse already, he sent me to find you, Duke William, and the king."

King Edward's eyes narrowed, "When was this?"

"It has taken three days to reach you for I had to evade the men of Douvres. I first went to Lundenwic where I found out where you were."

Count Eustace was married to the king's sister and this act of defiance could not go unpunished. "We return to Lundenwic."

We rode far more quickly to reach Lundenwic than when we had ridden west. For once the vacillating King Edward acted with more strength than at any other time. I guessed that it was the presence of Duke William. They rode at the fore and Taillefer and I behind the household knights.

"What does this mean, my lord?"

We were riding hard but we were both good riders. Alain's lessons had paid off and I was now, thanks to Taillefer, as confident a rider as any. He turned in the saddle. "This is provocation from Earl Godwin. Douvres is his burgh and this action was either condoned or ordered by the earl. He does not want Duke William to be the king's heir. It will be interesting to see the reaction of the earl when he is bearded."

The king's housecarls were all at the hall at Thornley. We rode there and arrived late at night. The leading housecarl, Leofwine, had heard of the outrage. "King Edward, I have summoned the rest of your men from the burghs and castles close by. They will be here by tomorrow." It was clear that he, like most of us, thought that the king would ride to Douvres and punish the miscreants.

It was also clear that the king and Duke William had spoken of the matter on the ride east. The king shook his head, "Tomorrow we will visit Earl Godwin at his hall in Lundenwic. Does he have men there?"

"He and his sons just have their oathsworn, perhaps sixty men."

"Good."

I knew that Leofwine led twice that number and the duke had more than twenty knights and squires. Was this the start of a civil war?

Chapter 8

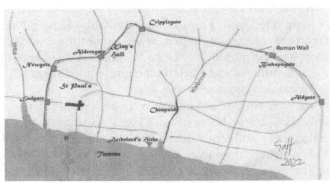

Lundenwic 1051

That night, as we prepared for bed, Taillefer spoke earnestly to me. I had never seen him so serious. "I know you have courage, Richard. Your actions at Gorron showed that but tomorrow you may need to have more than courage. You will need the reactions of a cat. Whatever happens, you stay to my left and behind me. Wear your new sword." He reached down and took a pot helmet from a bag. "I managed to get this from Leofwine. It was made some years ago for the son that King Edward never had. Here is an arming cap. Don them so I may see if it fits."

I slipped on the arming cap and the helmet fitted, but only just. I knew that if I tried to wear it six months from now it would be too small. "It does."

He looked relieved, "Good. Now you have no shield but that seax of yours looks strong enough to fend off a blade."

"I have other blades, my lord. I have the sword you gave me when we were attacked."

He shook his head, "The seax is long enough and strong enough. I pray that it will not come to violence but in my experience, if you do not prepare for danger then death soon follows."

We rose at lauds and none of us had enjoyed enough sleep. The breakfast was a spartan one but the bishop blessed us all. We left as the first rays of daylight appeared over the city walls to the east. We made for the Ludgate. Leofwine had ensured that the guards at that gate were loyal to the king and not to the earl. We entered and then headed for the earl's hall which lay close to the Aldersgate. The hall had been the king's hall until King Edward built the one close by the abbey. The earl had taken it and Taillefer had said it showed the man's ambition. The hall had a wall surrounding it and a guarded and barred gate.

The king wore mail. He did not look comfortable in it but he was flanked by Leofwine and Duke William. Both sat easily in their hauberks.

"Open in the name of the king."

A face appeared at the top of the gatehouse. Leofwine snapped, "Do you not see the king? This is the king's hall. Open it or suffer the consequences."

The gates were opened. I still wonder what might have happened had the men refused. Once inside we spread out. The housecarls and knights made a solid line and I was within ten feet of the duke and the king when the door to the hall opened. I knew there had to be a rear entrance when a couple of dozen men appeared from around the sides as the earl, his sons and his housecarls, all mailed but bareheaded emerged from the main door of the hall.

The earl gave a half-hearted bow and glared at Duke William as he said, "What means this unwarranted intrusion, King Edward? Why have we been awoken so rudely by a gang of armed foreigners?"

The king was calm as he spoke. He was emboldened by the wall of steel that surrounded him, "A king who demands entrance to his own hall is not intruding. Perhaps it is you who have intruded."

"I keep the king's peace and I use his hall to do so."

The king nodded, "Good, for it is keeping the king's peace that is the matter at hand. The men of Douvres have insulted my brother-in-law, Count Eustace of Boulogne, and blood has been spilt. I would have you ravage the town and hang those who committed the outrage."

I did as Taillefer had taught me and I watched the faces of those before me. I saw a glance between Harold Godwinson and his brother Gyrth. It was a look of triumph. The earl nodded as though he was going to agree but his words were of defiance, "Ravage my own burgh? Slay my own men? I think not, King Edward. If you wish to slay Englishmen then do so yourself or take your Norman bandits and have them do this."

The earl had misjudged the situation. I was able to think about it later on when the blood ran cooler. He thought that the king would back down. He had been known as a vacillating and insecure king. Many thought him to be a copy of his father, Æthelred the Unready. He was not but then again his father had not had the steely figure of Duke William next to him.

The king's voice was remarkably firm as he said, "Leofwine, arrest the earl and his sons."

The earl and retinue were armed and they were mailed but they had no helmets. Weapons were drawn and Harold and his brothers formed a wall before their father and lunged with their swords. The king was lucky that he had Leofwine and the duke flanking him or else he might have died there and then. Would the duke have been named king? The point was moot. Leofwine and Duke William stepped forward. The duke's sword beat down that of Harold but Tostig's found Leofwine's leg and Gyrth's, as the housecarl reeled, found his throat. The king's lieutenant died before the fight had even begun.

"Treachery!" I do not know if it was the bishop's call or that their leader had been murdered but the housecarls leapt forward to be revenged upon the killers. Perhaps realising that they had gone too far the brothers followed their father into the hall and the door was slammed shut. The earl's housecarls were not cowards. They had all taken an oath to protect the earl and his family to the death and they were prepared to do so.

I had no time to dwell on such matters for Taillefer and the duke were also targets. Taillefer had drawn his two swords. The housecarls who came at him, one with an axe and one with a long sword, had taken on more than they knew but I had drawn my sword and seax when Leofwine died and I was ready to defend Taillefer. My master blocked the swinging axe by making a crucifix of his swords. The second housecarl must have dismissed me for he lunged at Taillefer's middle with his sword. I was able to make a cross with my seax and sword. I forced the blade down and it scraped and scratched along the cobbles. The housecarl snarled, "Norman pup! You shall die."

What I did next surprised him. I brought up my two weapons and the tip of the seax tore a line along his bare cheek. At the same time, I stabbed at his side. It was a weak blow but it made him use his own sword to block it. Taillefer's right sword took the axeman in the middle and with contemptuous ease slashed his left hand across the throat of the swordsman.

The battle raged furiously with the housecarls determined to die well and Leofwine's men intent on vengeance.

"Behind me!"

I obeyed Taillefer and it was as I did so that I saw that not all the housecarls had thrown themselves into the fray. Three hung back and the scarred hand identified the leader. It was the man who had led the attack on Taillefer and while Taillefer was defending Duke William, they were making their surreptitious way through the battling warriors to Taillefer's right side. I disobeyed my orders. I had been told to stay to the left but if I did so then I could not use my sword effectively. I stepped to the right and was just in time to block scarred hand's lunge at Taillefer's side. Taillefer had quick reactions and his right-hand sword swept out to make the other two duck. I saw the look on scarred hand's face, he intended to kill me first. He raised his sword and brought it down towards my head. I did not know if my helmet would block the strike and, holding my sword above my head, dropped to my knee to halt the strike. The man wore a hauberk but by dropping I was able to ram my seax underneath it. The blow was blind but I must have torn into his thigh. The gush of warm blood came as a shock to both of us but in scarred hand's case it was the shock of death. I pulled out my hand, now bathed in blood. Scarred hand's companions had had enough.

"Let us leave, brother, and join the earl in Lincylene." They disengaged and disappeared behind the rest of the earl's men.

Another two housecarls had slain two of Leofwine's men and were advancing on Taillefer. Neither of us had any opportunity to prevent the two men from fleeing. I had killed a man with a blade and I had survived. I should have been terrified at the prospect of taking on a housecarl but Taillefer still lived. I swung my sword at the housecarl's side. The blow did nothing except to distract his attack and he turned to me, raising his axe above his head. Taillefer blocked the blow from the other housecarl and then brought his knee up to ram between the man's legs. As his head came forward Taillefer's two pommels smashed into the back of his skull. The axeman I had surprised kicked at me and as I tried to get out of the way I fell over a body behind me. Taillefer saved me and he slew the housecarl.

It was almost the last of the action. The most loyal of men had died and the vacillators, like scarred hand's companions, had chosen life and fled through the Aldersgate. Taillefer looked at me and saw that I had survived. He looked to his left and saw the king, duke and bishop still lived. He sheathed his swords and then held out a hand to help me up.

"I owe you a life, Richard. You surprised not only our enemies but me. I am glad you disobeyed my orders. You will become a great warrior. I know of only one other who was a callow youth like you and yet fought like a warrior."

"And who is that, my lord?"

He grinned, "Why, me of course."

It was a tantalizing glimpse into the life of Taillefer but he never expanded upon it.

The king shouted, "We need to mount men. The traitors will head for Wintan-Caestre."

My voice sounded remarkably strong as I shouted, "They will not, King Edward. They are heading for Lincylene."

The duke wheeled on me, "How do you know?"

"Two of those who fled, my lord, said that was where the earl was headed."

The king nodded, "There are allies in the north who would support him. This is war. This is rebellion." He looked at me, "You are Taillefer's squire are you not?"

"Yes, King Edward."

"I am grateful to you."

He turned and headed, surrounded by his surviving housecarls, back to his hall. The duke said, "This will delay our return." The count's man was still with us. "Find your master and have him return. His brother-in-law will have need of him."

"He will have returned to Boulogne."

The duke pointed south, "The river is there, hire or buy a ship and fetch him hither. At the very least we can punish the men of Douvres." He tossed him a small purse. "We will take over this hall and rid Lundenwic of the stench of treachery."

He and his half-brother left us as the Count of Boulogne's man hastened to obey the duke. Taillefer nodded at the men we had slain. "There are purses here and weapons. We shall share the bounty."

The other squires who had not been taken into the hall by their knights were also searching the bodies. Although tempted by the mail, I knew that it would be too big for me and I merely took it from the dead. Taillefer would make coin from selling it. I similarly placed the weapons to one side. I had enough and we could sell them. The purses I took. I reasoned that with enough coins in my purse when time allowed and I had grown, I would be able to have mail made for me by Aimeri the weaponsmith.

When Taillefer returned from inspecting the hall, he was impressed by my haul. "You took only from those we had slain?"

I nodded, "Of course."

"Good. Fetch our horses for the duke has said that we will use this hall until Count Eustace arrives."

"Are we going to war, Taillefer?"

He tapped the side of his nose, "Let us say that I may get the chance to draw my sword but like this little skirmish it will not be a battle commemorated in song."

"What? This was momentous."

"It might have been but the king will not wish the world to know that he almost lost his kingdom here in his capital. Had we delayed in coming then we would have met men mailed from head to toe. We took them by surprise but the king still lost warriors. The loss of Leofwine is a serious one." He whistled at Guy and Henri, Sir Roger and Sir Ambrose's squires. "Go with Richard and fetch your masters' horses. We stay here. Go carefully for we know not, yet, who is a friend and who is foe."

We did not go with drawn swords but we went whilst warily watching.

We reached the hall, now closely guarded by suspicious men. We were examined and then allowed to pass. We brought our horses and walked them back towards the city. The duke passed us as we neared Ludgate. There was a buzz in the city as word of the fracas spread. When we took the horses to the stables, we saw that the gate at the rear led directly to Aldersgate. The duke's servants were already preparing food and after we had tended to the horses, we explored our new home. The earl and his men had long gone. They had left in a hurry and we found things that we could use. There were clothes as well as coins. My purse was becoming increasingly heavy for Taillefer shared all that we found. He told me that he believed in fate and that if fate threw the bounty to the two of us then the two of us should share it. I now saw how he made his money. Each time he sang he was rewarded, in silver from knights and by gold from the duke and the bishop. I suspected that there would be more songs in the future.

Taillefer had found us a sleeping chamber to ourselves. The king's hall was well apportioned and the single chamber meant we would not be disturbed in the night by men with weaker bladders clambering noisily through a sleeping hall. As we unpacked our bags and hung our tunics to air them, I spoke to Taillefer.

"Does this delay our return home, my lord?"

"I am guessing so for the duke has sent for the count and that means he still has business over here."

"But I am no longer needed. The plot is known. My skill with English has been of some use but now it is redundant."

Taillefer smiled, "Your skill has yielded more results than you know. Had you not heard where the rebels were headed then time might have been wasted heading west. This way the king can gather his allies and prevent the earl from consolidating his hold on the north. Wessex might be Earl Godwin's but it is still loyal to King Edward. I fear, however, that we will be here for Christmas and beyond. Even if the duke no longer needs you as a speaker of English, you are a body with a blade and as such useful. We will use the time we are here to hone your skills still further but this morning has shown me that you have the natural reactions of a warrior."

Count Eustace arrived at the end of the week and the duke and Count Eustace, who had brought almost forty men, wasted no time in planning their vengeance on the men of Douvres. King Edward seemed to have forgotten the incident that had ignited this rebellion but the duke had not. The duke, count, bishop and senior knights, including Taillefer, gathered around a table to plan the revenge.

Count Eustace was an ambitious man. He had married the sister of King Edward and hoped for more than just the County of Boulogne. He had his eyes set on Flanders. To do that he needed allies and he and Duke William found benefits in working together.

"The burgh is well made and if we assault it then we will lose men, Duke William."

The duke nodded and picked at the meat on the platter before him, "How about a night assault?"

The count shook his head. "They keep a good watch and they are wary for they know we will want revenge."

Bishop Odo sighed, "Then it will have to be a bloody assault. We might lose men but the ones who survive will be better warriors for it."

Taillefer said, "There is another way." All their eyes swivelled to the troubadour. "We try a trick."

"A trick?"

"There is a tale of a war between the Greeks and the Trojans. To get inside Troy the clever Ulysses devised a plan to make the Trojans open their gates and allow them in."

The count took him literally, "You wish us to build a horse?"

Taillefer patiently shook his head, "Is there cover close to the burgh?"

The count nodded, "Aye, they built the burgh on the remains of the Roman fort. Close to it but outside the walls are the homes of the fishermen who use the harbour but they are below the walls and pose no threat."

"So long as we could hide our men there then my plan might work." He pointed to me, "We have one here who can speak English like an Englishman and we have clothes in this hall that belonged to Earl Godwin and his sons. If I dress as one of his sons and feign a wound then Richard can lead my horse and say we have been attacked by Normans and come to warn the burgh. When they open the gates then the two of us hold them open and the rest of you follow."

The idea, which sounded terrifying to me, seemed to meet with the approval of the others. Bishop Odo added a word of caution, "It has merit but is not without risks. I can understand your confidence, Taillefer, with your two swords you could hold off three or four men, but this pueros?"

"This morning, Bishop Odo, Richard saved my life and slew men. We fought not the town watch of Douvres but Earl Godwin's housecarls. I will dress my tunic with blood and gore. Their attention will be on that and if Richard here feigns a lack of control on his horse then they will not be able to close the gates." There was silence and Taillefer said, "At the very least it gives a night assault a better chance. With two of us inside they will need to overcome us and that means fewer men on the walls."

Everyone seemed convinced and they all looked to the duke. "The plan is a good one but why should the two of you risk your lives like this?"

"For gold, Duke William. When the men of Douvres are punished then Richard and I will be paid for our work." He smiled, "Regard it as another performance by Taillefer the troubadour."

The duke beamed. He liked Taillefer and showed it in word and deed, "Aye, Taillefer, you shall have gold for your service and I dare say there will be a song too."

"Perhaps."

"We leave before dawn and shall use the bridge. We shall leave the servants to guard our hall and when we cross the river, head due west as though we intend to head to Wintan-Caestre. If we ride hard we can be at Douvres by night and put your plan into operation before word of our departure reaches Douvres."

That night, as we retired early, I told Taillefer of my misgivings, "You have great confidence in me, my lord, but I have not. If I fail then all will be lost."

"If we fail, Richard, then you and I will be dead." He let the words sink in, "But I do not believe that we will fail. I have belief in the duke and the count. They want vengeance and the duke is keen to see how his knights fare not against housecarls but English warriors. If he is to hold on to the kingdom when King Edward dies then he will have to fight Englishmen. They will not simply give in. Duke William plans well. Play your part and we will return home even richer than when we left." He smiled, "You bring me luck and, if you wish, then I will make you my squire permanently."

Recent events had made me realise that I was not yet ready for such a task. I shook my head, "I will do this but I would return to Graville-Sainte-Honorine and my grandfather and friends. I have tasted fine food at the high table and enjoyed the heady conversation of kings, bishops and dukes but I am a simple fellow, Taillefer, and I would go back to my life."

Chapter 9

When we left, Taillefer and I were dressed in tunics with the white horse upon them, the sign of the Godwins, but we rode cloaked, cowled and hooded. Sir Ambrose and Sir Roger flanked and hid Taillefer and their squires me. Once we had clattered over the bridge we headed west and as soon as we were out of sight of any onlookers, for the sun had yet to rise, we turned east and headed for Douvres. This was the land ruled by Earl Godwin but the warriors had been summoned north. Civil war threatened and the two leaders, King Edward and Earl Godwin were marshalling their forces. The first act had come from the king who had sent his wife to a nunnery. It was, effectively, the end of their marriage. There would be no heir to threaten Duke William. Any hopes that Earl Godwin might have persuaded the king to rescind his proclamation had ended in the fight at the hall.

As we rode east, I went over the plan in my head. Taillefer was a master of words and he told me what to say. I just had to use the right words in English to do so. In that, I had been helped by my grandfather. He had not used the language of the court to speak to me but the words of the common man. My accent was of an Englishman. While my half-brother and the others at the manor had spoken Norman to me, my mother and grandfather had conversed in English. I could switch between the two without even thinking. Taillefer told me to put fear in my tone. "You must make them believe that you are terrified. I shall play my part and they will think I am close to death. My hands will hang down and I shall loll my head."

"But what if they do not open the gates?"

"You will tell them that I am Tostig Godwinson. They will admit the son of the earl."

As we crossed the Medway, I thought back to the conversation we had enjoyed in the King's Hall. I decided to make up my own name. I would say that I was Edmund. I knew that it was a popular name thanks to the last Saxon king who had opposed the Danes and almost defeated them.

I may not need to use it but Taillefer had taught me to pay attention to detail. I did not even see the mileposts that we passed. I was running through my words, my tone and my expression. Before we had left the hall, Taillefer had smeared animal blood on my face before, seemingly, almost soaking his tunic in blood. He had a small waterskin filled with fresh blood to splash as we neared the gates. He was a showman. As he had said, "It is like conjuring and juggling. You show them one hand but it is the other that does the magic. They will see the blood and not the men who might follow us."

We stopped on the way to water our horses and to eat but Taillefer and I were always hidden from view. We were the cloaked men surrounded by horses and warriors. We were the wooden horse.

It was dark when we arrived close to the manor of Coldred. We were now within touching distance of the burgh and our horses were weary. We walked the last couple of miles and did not take the road that led to the burgh but the one that passed through the village of Maxton. The fishermen were out at sea. The harbour was empty of fishing boats and we knew that the houses would pose no threat. We dismounted to rest the horses and prepare for the show. Taillefer and I would put on the cloaks we had found in the King's Hall. The white horse emblem was on the left side and, in the half-light of the lighted brands at the gates might be seen. The duke and the count moved their men as close as they could get to the wooden wall without being seen and then nodded. Taillefer and I did not speak. We had gone over the plan many times and knew what we had to do. Taillefer was confident that it would succeed but I was not. I was terrified of failure and letting down Duke William. My half-brother did not want the Malet name sullied by an ill-judged action from me.

We mounted and I took Parsifal's reins. I walked the horses back a few paces and then we slapped them to make them ride. I was leading Parsifal and Taillefer held two swords but they would be hidden from view. Men would see his hands hanging down and not the deadly weapons he carried. He was a great rider and would not fall off. As the horses picked up speed, so their hooves clattered on the stones. I shouted, "Alarm! Alarm! The Normans come and my master, Tostig Godwinson, is wounded." I kept shouting it as we rode up the twisting road that led to the gates. I heard men called to the walls. That would cause a distraction for the men on the walls would be looking at us, seeking our pursuers and moving along the walls so that the burgh was continuously defended. Behind us, the rest of our attacking party would be moving from shadow to shadow. Once the gates were open then they would run. I feared that our plan had failed for as I looked up, just thirty paces from the gate, I saw only faces on the wall and not the welcoming sight of the gates swinging open.

"In God's name, you must help us or Earl Godwin will lose a son." I used a pleading voice and looked up. I had adopted a pained expression for Taillefer said that making a story believable came with the tone and the face.

It must have worked for a voice commanded, "Open the gates but shut them as soon as the two men are within."

The gates yawned open. I knew that my part in this deception was vital and I prayed that Alain's lessons had been well learned and that Blaze would respond as I hoped he would. As we reached the gate, I let go of Parsifal's reins confident in the horse and his master. I needed two hands on my reins. After I passed beneath the gatehouse I stood and shouted, "Thank God!" I pulled back on the reins as I did so. The men to my left were trying to close the gate but as Blaze rose his flailing hooves made them recoil.

"Control your horse and move him."

The longer I could maintain the deception the more chance the plan had of success. "He is afeard, my lord, of your weapons. Give him space."

Duke William and the others were seen from the gatehouse. "Normans! This is a trick!"

The voice from above us was the signal for Taillefer to throw back his cloak and swing his swords at the two men on the other gate. Blaze and I already blocked one gate and I drew my sword and swung it at them to keep them at bay. The roar from the road told me that Count Eustace and Duke

William were racing up the slope just as fast as they could. Arrows and bolts flew from the walls but so long as our two horses stood in the gateway then there was no barrier. I think they saw me as the weak link for men ran at me and, one handed, I repeated the trick of making Blaze rear. This time an eager defender was struck on the head and fell but I was finding it hard to control Blaze and when the spear was thrust at me, I barely managed to flick it aside. A braver man than the rest suddenly launched himself from the gatehouse at me, like a human missile. I held my sword before me and it sliced into him but he knocked me from my saddle. I hit the ground hard. I saw first stars and then blackness. The blackness enveloped me and I found myself falling as though from a great height. I whirled and I flew and then there was nothing. I heard noises and feared that men were coming for me. I tried to move my arms but could not.

I was swimming in a sea of blood and my heart pounded in my head. I felt hands upon me and yet I saw nothing. I fell once more and I wondered if this was death. Would my mother be there to greet me?

"Lord Taillefer, he is coming round."

I heard the voices but my eyes did not want to open. They felt heavy.

"Richard, I thought you dead. God has answered my prayers. Open your eyes."

I forced myself to do so and was almost blinded by the light but, as my eyes adjusted, I saw that the light was just one candle. A priest held a beaker, "Drink this."

A hand lifted my head and I drank what tasted like nectar but the smell of herbs told me that it was some medicine.

The priest nodded, "I will see to the others, my lord."

Taillefer laid my head on the pillow and sat next to me, "You are a brave young cockerel, Richard fitz Malet. You need not have risked all. The duke was at the gate."

"I did not want to let anyone down."

Taillefer's normally laughing eyes clouded, "This is my fault. I am reckless and risk my life on a daily basis and you have tried to be like me. I am sorry, Richard."

I smiled, "What happened to me?"

"The man you skewered knocked you from Blaze and you hit the ground hard. You had a bloody coxcomb and the bone of your skull was broken. There was much blood. The priest who tended you knew not if you lived or died but you are made of sterner stuff. You have lain here for a day. They think you will heal with time but you will have to stay here."

"You will be leaving me?" Was I to be abandoned?

"Just briefly. Count Eustace and his men will stay here while we return to Lundenwic. The king has returned to Lundenwic and the duke needs to speak to him. I will return as soon as I can and then we can take ship and return home. The count and his men have had their vengeance and we can sail with him when the healers say you can travel." My eyes felt heavy and as they flickered shut, I saw a smile on Taillefer's face, "The sleeping potion works quickly." As darkness overtook me once more, I heard Taillefer's voice fading away, "Sleep is the best medicine, Richard. Dream your future."

And I did dream. I saw my grandfather and he was standing in a shield wall bravely exhorting the housecarls with him to fight. Then I saw that the men fighting him were Normans. The duke was raising his helmet. When I looked back, I saw that my grandfather had changed to become Earl Godwin and I was charging at him with couched lance and mailed from head to foot. I never reached him for I fell into the spiralling pit once more.

I woke and it was not candlelight that greeted me but daylight that streamed in from the wind hole. The shutters had been opened and a cold wind blew in. The priest who had tended me smiled and said, "Good, the sleep has done you good. Your heart does not race like a stallion but is measured. That is better. Sit up, for you need to eat. You have eaten nothing for two days or more."

He fed me like a baby and I ate the thick soup as though I had not eaten for a week. When I had finished, he took the bowl and then handed me a beaker. He smiled, "No potion this time, just ale." I drank greedily. When I had finished, he put down the beaker and put his arm under mine, "You need to make water." He led me to a pot in the corner.

"I cannot."

He shook his head, "This is not a matter of choice. Your bladder needs to be emptied or it will burst. Force it out."

I tried and nothing happened then suddenly it burst forth and I screamed at the pain. It came as though I was a horse.

The priest smiled, "The pain will soon cease and this is the start of your recovery. Tomorrow we shall take off the bandage from your head for the air will heal the wound. The day after you can walk about a little."

It was my first battle wound and I did not enjoy the recovery for I hated being idle. The next day, when we emerged into the open, the cold hit me even though I was cloaked. The priest, Abelard, walked with me but allowed me to walk alone. If I started to fall, I knew that he would arrest my descent for he was a kind man. As we stepped out from the citadel, I saw skulls atop the gatehouse. There were eight of them.

"Abelard, who are they?"

"They are the ones who were punished for attacking Count Eustace. They were the leaders and they were tried." He leaned into me, "They admitted, before they were hanged, that they were acting on the orders of Earl Godwin."

Taillefer had thought as much. Earl Godwin saw it as a provocative act and hoped that in the war that ensued, he would emerge victorious. For all that I knew he had succeeded. If the king had returned to Lundenwic then that suggested he had won.

My actions resulted in notoriety, fame even. The men from Boulogne who watched the walls greeted me warmly. They gave me a nickname, '*Horse Dancer*'. Abelard told me that both Taillefer and I had been hailed as heroes. Our action meant that only four men, apart from me, were wounded and the burgh taken quickly. After my first foray into the world, I was asked to dine with the count and his men in the burgh's Great Hall. Abelard came with me. I was embarrassed when the knights banged their beakers on the table and shouted my name. I was no Taillefer. If anyone deserved the applause it was Blaze.

I was not seated next to the count but I was close enough to hear his words and he was kind enough to speak to me, "Richard fitz Malet, I see a great warrior in you. You are young but you controlled your horse better than some of my knights. You are raw clay but I can see that from that clay will be created a knight like Taillefer."

"When will he return, my lord?"

"We are all keen to get home and it will be soon. The enemies of King Edward have miscalculated and the king has managed to create an alliance that inspires fear in Earl Godwin and his dwindling supporters. It will not be long."

In the end, it was a fortnight before the duke rode in with the bishop, his half-brother, and Taillefer. I had begun the practice of climbing, each day, the ladder to the fighting platform and walking circuits to build up my strength. Speaking to the sentries made it a pleasurable experience and when we saw the approaching metal snake, my spirits soared. I saw that behind the Norman knights marched housecarls. I almost ran down the ladder to greet Taillefer.

As the duke and Bishop Odo entered the burgh, they stopped to look down at me. The duke spoke, "Richard fitz Malet, the hero of Douvres. When we saw you last, you lay with blood coming from your head and we feared that you had died. I am pleased that you are not. I promised a reward and you shall have one. I have penned a missive for your half-brother. I have asked that you become one of the legal heirs to de Caux. There are others before you but it ensures that you will be trained as a knight and even if it is just a grange, you shall inherit land."

I knew that what he said was important and I was almost bereft of words. Taillefer had told me that in such a situation you gave a long bow and said, '*Thank you, my lord,*' to give you time to think.

"Thank you, my lord. I am just pleased that I could have been of service."

It was the right reply and the duke and the bishop beamed. "Better and better, Richard fitz Malet." They turned their horses and headed for the stables. Taillefer dismounted and walked over to me. He bodily picked me up to hug me,

"If you were my squire then I could not have a better one. The taking of Douvres deserves a song with you at its heart. It is a shame that this will remain a secret." He turned and walked Parsifal towards the stable.

"A secret?"

"Aye, the war that never was is over. The earl and his sons are banished from this land and have taken ship already. King Edward wishes all evidence of treachery and betrayal hidden. He wants peace to reign in this land. He has asked the duke and the count to return home for he is trying to heal wounds."

"Does the duke still inherit England on the king's death?"

"He does but he agrees with King Edward. There are some in the land who think that it was we who instigated this. By quitting the land we allow King Edward, who is a kindly man, to tend to his country's hurts. Hopefully, he will live long enough so that he can bring peace to England."

"And you, Taillefer, what of you? I know that my future is in Graville-Sainte-Honorine but is yours in Rouen or Caen?"

He shrugged, "For a while but I would travel the Empire. My fame has spread and I would reap the reward. The emperor can hear my songs and if the rewards heaped on me by King Edward are anything to go by, I will need a bigger chest for my gold."

Part of me was envious. I liked Taillefer and I wanted to share his adventures. I knew, however, that as much as we had got on, my presence would inhibit him. He was a free and reckless spirit and did not need to be tied down by a dullard such as me.

We left a week later from Douvres and sailed to Boulogne. It took just a couple of hours. Indeed the lighthouse at Douvres could be seen from Boulogne. We stayed for two nights in Boulogne and then headed for Rouen. As well as the reward of the parchment I now had a sumpter, given to me by the count to carry the weapons and treasure I had accumulated. A purse of silver from the duke had also made me wealthier than any, other than the duke's squires. At Rouen, I was feted and praised along with Taillefer.

Taillefer looked genuinely sad to see me leave alone for the ride home, "I know that our fates are entwined, Richard, and we shall fight alongside each other again. You are like the younger brother I never had." He laughed, "I was the younger brother." Once again, I was given a glimpse of his early life but that was all. The onion still remained intact.

It took just a day to reach Graville-Sainte-Honorine and I was excited to be heading back to speak to my grandfather, Bruno, Baldwin and Odo. I had much to tell them. I knew that I was changed. It was not just the scar on the back of my head or the laden sumpter. I knew that I had changed inside. When I had followed Bruno over the walls of Gorron, I had been that, just a follower. I now knew that the next time I would be alongside Bruno leading. Taillefer had made me a man.

I know not what I expected as I reached the boundaries of the manor but it was not the silence and downcast looks that I encountered. I knew some of those who tended the fields and when I waved and greeted some of them, they just looked at me and then averted their gaze. I stopped doing so after a mile. I could not think what I had done to cause such silence. Had I been away so long? When I neared the castle and the manor, I was full of trepidation. I rode to the gyrus for it was the afternoon and I knew that men would be practising and I would find my grandfather. I heard the clash of wood on wood and the commands but the voice was not my grandfather's. As I rounded the barn and saw the gyrus then I was seen. It was full but the long hair of my grandfather was missing. Everyone stopped and stared at me.

Alain tethered the horse he had been schooling and walked over to me. I had expected greetings and shouts from my three shield brothers but there was just silence. Alain came and held Blaze's reins, "Dismount, Richard."

"My grandfather?"

"Is at home. Leave your animals here and we will tend to them. Bruno and the others will bring your gear. You shall need them. I am sorry."

"He lives?"

He took my hand in his two and squeezed it, "Best that you go home, he will be anxious to… Just go, eh, Richard."

I ran for I was fearful. I knew of men who were my grandfather's age struck with an ailment that stopped them from moving. Had he been struck with just such an affliction? Gunhild was just coming from my home. I do not know if she was coming to see me or if it was luck but when she saw me, she burst into tears and held her arms open. I hugged her, "Why will no one tell me what is happening?"

She took my arm, "Come, but be ready for a shock."

I was ready for anything but when I entered the small dwelling we shared I saw a sight that even now makes me wake in the middle of the night shivering with shock. My grandfather had bloody scars where his eyes had been.

"Geoffrey, it is Dick. He has come home." She led me to him and put his hand in mine. "I will fetch some ale. Your grandfather will tell you the sorry tale."

I sat next to my grandfather and squeezed his one hand with my two. He said, "You are whole?"

I nodded and then cursed myself. I could barely speak when I said, "I am, Grandfather, and I thought I had much to tell you but I can see," I cursed myself again, "that what you have to say is of more import. Was it an accident?"

Even as I said the words, I knew that this was no accident. I knew he had been punished but I could think of no crime so heinous that it would have been warranted.

"You see that Bruno and Hrolfr are no longer here?" I looked up and saw that the familiar place they inhabited was empty. The mat on which they slept was no longer there.

"I can."

"Sir William and his brothers went hunting and they asked me to bring my hounds along with those of Sir Durand and Sir William. Bruno and Hrolfr were the best of hounds. It was they who found the scent of the stag and led us to it. Sir Durand had his spear ready but the deer came at Bruno and Hrolfr just reacted. He leapt on the stag and fastened his jaws around his neck. The stag was dead when Bruno joined in. Sir Durand was apoplectic with rage and he hacked off

Hrolfr's head. I went to hold his arm and he knocked me to the ground before slaying Bruno. I reacted and my hand went to my sword." He hung his head. "I loved those dogs. Along with Alain and you, they were my only companions."

I squeezed his hand for he was silent, "What happened next?"

"There was a trial. I laid hands on a knight. I think that Sir William was inclined to leniency for I did not actually draw my sword but it was half drawn and Sir Durand demanded blinding."

It was done and there was nothing that I could do about it but from that moment revenge burned in my heart. Sir Durand was my half-brother but that would matter not when the time was right. I thought back to the duke's visit and Sir Durand's words. This was a deliberate act on his part. Taillefer had taught me well and I could now play a part. I would be cold and dispassionate. I would plan and I would plot but it would all be inside my head. To the outside world I would be dutiful but inside would beat the heart of a killer.

He had no eyes but my silence spoke to my grandfather, "This is done, Dick, and cannot be undone. My life was almost over already but I will never see the girl that you wed nor the children that you sire and that saddens me. Swear that you will not take matters into your own hands."

Taillefer had taught me the power of words. Words could be used in many ways and I chose mine carefully. I would not make an oath that I was bound to break. "I swear, grandfather, that I will serve this family faithfully until I am dismissed. Is that good enough?"

"Not really but it will do." He squeezed my hand back, "Now give me your news."

It took some time for I needed to tell the tale to calm myself down. I had just finished and he had no time to respond for Bruno, Baldwin and Odo came with my treasures. Bruno held out his arm and I clasped it. He said quietly and earnestly, "If you want vengeance, Dick, then know that I am your shield brother and will go with you into the jaws of hell if you ask."

My grandfather became the old teacher once more and he barked, "None of that, Bruno son of Bergil. Dick has said that he will serve the family faithfully."

Bruno looked at me and I nodded.

There was warmth in my grandfather's voice as he said, "Now his tale is a good one. Is Baldwin there?"

"I am, Master Geoffrey."

"Then go to the kitchen and ask Gunhild for a jug of ale and beakers. I would hear your tale again, Dick."

The telling of the tale lightened the mood until Sir Eustace appeared at the door, "Richard, you have insulted Sir William. You have been back some time and not reported to him."

I stood and faced up to the knight, "So I am to be punished like my grandfather for an implied insult? Do I lose an ear? A nose?"

Sir Eustace's face became stern. "Do you know to whom you speak?"

"I do." I proffered the parchment. "I was rewarded by Duke William, Sir Eustace. I have friends like Bishop Odo and Count Eustace. I have been offered a place as Taillefer's squire so do not threaten me."

My grandfather growled, "Dick, your oath."

"Fear not, grandfather, my blades will stay sheathed but I will not be bullied nor threatened, by any."

I was suddenly aware that my three friends had stood behind me. Sir Eustace shook his head and then smiled, "I will take your harsh words, Richard fitz Malet, for I understand how you feel. When we speak to Sir William, choose both your words and your tone well. I forgive you for what you have done for me but no more. Understand?"

I feigned a fawning smile and bowed, "Of course, Sir Eustace. You mean like this?"

He turned and we followed. Bruno hissed in my ear, "You tread a dangerous path, Dick."

I nodded, "As we did when we scaled Gorron's walls."

He chuckled, "I can see that life is about to become interesting."

We entered the hall and the three brothers were seated around a table. Sir Durand glared at me while Sir William had an expectant look on his face. "Well?"

I used a small voice, "I am sorry if I have offended you, Sir William, but I needed to speak to my grandfather and when he asked me about the duke, I forgot time."

His face softened but Sir Durand still glowered and glared. "That is understandable. The rumour is that you acquitted yourself well and have upheld the family honour."

I turned to catch the eye of Sir Durand, "I always strive to serve my family as best I can." I took the parchment, "Duke William asked me to give you this when I first saw you." I handed it to him but kept my eye on Sir Durand.

Sir William read it and his face clouded over. He read it again and then handed it to Sir Durand, "You know I do not need to do this, Richard."

I nodded, "And if you do not, Sir William, then I will understand. If I am not to have that which the duke wishes then I will return to Rouen and let him know. I can then take up Taillefer's offer to be his squire."

Sir Durand hurled the parchment contemptuously to the ground, "This is intolerable! We are to give the bastard land and respect. It is the start of anarchy."

Sir William nodded to his squire who picked up the parchment and handed it back to him, "Durand, remember that Duke William is also a bastard and, besides, it seems that our half-brother has earned great honour." He held up his hand for Durand was about to speak, "Enough. I am the Seigneur and my commands will be obeyed. From this moment Richard fitz Malet shall be trained as a knight. We will find him a small grange so that he has an income."

"Thank you, my lord, but I would not cause division in the family."

Sir William shook his head and turned his eyes on his brother, "There will be no division. Is that clear?" The words were addressed to Durand who, after an uncomfortable silence, nodded. I was accepted, albeit reluctantly, into the family.

Chapter 10

My grandfather died just six months after my return from England. He simply gave up. The only things that kept him alive were our talks and the words of others who came to speak to him and tell him of my skills. Alain came each day and was with me the night my grandfather died. He entered after Father Raymond had heard my grandfather's confession and administered the last rites. The priest blessed us and left.

I held one hand and Gunhild, who had not left my grandfather's side the whole day, held the other. She wept but silently. My grandfather's hearing had not deteriorated and the slightest sound of a sniffle brought a reprimand. He wanted, he said, no tears for his passing. There would be but the three of us were determined that we would obey his wishes. He spoke to us intermittently. Having no eyes we could not tell if he was awake or asleep. Sometimes he would be totally silent and then suddenly he would speak. He spoke of his youth in England serving the Earl of Mercia. He smiled when he told us of battles where he and his fellow housecarls won the day against the Welsh and the Danes. Just as quickly he would change to talk of my mother and then his wife but in the last part of his life, those few short hours before God took him, he spoke largely about me and Gunhild. Towards the end, they were words about me. I did not know he was so proud of me. He spoke of my courage, fortitude and honour. I felt guilty for as soon as I was able, I intended to kill my half-brother, Durand. He begged me to have Aimeri make me a hauberk. It was as though he had recovered his sight.

"You are almost a man grown now and you need a hauberk."

I tried to laugh it off, "You cannot know my height, grandfather."

"I know, now, that your voice comes from above me and I feel the strength in your hands while mine are weak and feeble. War will come, Dick. Duke William has been promised the English throne and I know my people, they will not give up the crown without a fight."

"King Edward was hale when last I saw him."

"And I was hale when last my eyes saw you." He became silent and then said, "Gunhild, I would kiss you."

There were tears in her eyes, which she wiped away before bending to kiss him. She raised her head and could not stop the tears coursing down her cheeks. Too fearful of her words betraying her tears she mouthed, "I love you, Geoffrey," and made the sign of the cross.

He was silent again and then said, "I am tired, Dick, it is time. I shall sleep."

Nothing looked different but we all three knew that he had passed. Alain put his finger on my grandfather's neck and nodded. He made the sign of the cross, "Farewell, my friend, you were unjustly punished and God will welcome you to a heaven filled with your old comrades and he will punish the perpetrator of this foul act."

I leaned over and kissed him on the forehead, "And I will try to be half the warrior you were. You were as my father and I thank you for making me the man I am. I hope that you will be proud of me but a man must do what is right and I shall."

Both Gunhild and Alain turned to look at me. Alain said, "Geoffrey's soul is but a little way above our heads. Be careful, Dick. Durand is a wicked and a dangerous man. His elder brother will side with him over you. The duke's parchment will mean nothing."

I nodded, "I know that. The grange he has given me is a hog bog. There is neither a dwelling upon it nor animals within. He has made a token gesture. Do not fear. When Durand dies, I will ensure that none know it but I. I have no intention of being punished for something that is right and just. You have to trust my judgement."

Gunhild put her hand on mine, "Geoffrey said that you were the cleverest person that he knew. I trust you but I want to be there when you wed. I want to see Geoffrey's great-grandchildren and I want you to have a good life. Think about that."

The funeral took place in the village church and not the chapel on the manor. It was Father Peter who interred him and not Father Raymond. Sir Durand forbade him. My three companions defied the edict from Sir Durand that none were to attend the funeral as did Gunhild, Alain and the other servants from the kitchen. My grandfather was popular. I paid the stonemason in the village to make a stone. I had not spent any of either my loot or my reward. I husbanded it. As soon as my grandfather died then I began my new life. I was the last to leave the grave and I knelt and picked up a piece of the earth, "You will be buried here, grandfather, in a land that is not yours but know that wherever I travel you shall be with me. When you look down from heaven, for surely you will be there with my mother, I would have you proud of me and all that I do."

The first thing I did was to begin to build a house on my grange. My three friends and Alain helped me. As it was on de Caux land even Sir Durand could not stop us. We hewed the trees and dug the holes for the posts. Packed with rubble they were firm and, as the weeks passed following my grandfather's death, the house took shape as we added daub and wattle walls and then a roof. I knew what I wanted, a simple house with four rooms. I wanted a stable, for Blaze was now mine as was Mary, the sumpter. I was still a pueros serving Sir William but that was my only commitment to the family. I still trained every day but my lessons had stopped as soon as Sir William's sons began to attend. In truth, we had learned all that we could from the priest. It meant we had our mornings to either practise or build. The building was quickly made for we had stronger bodies and so we worked hard. After a month we had a roof and over the next weeks, we added plaster, wind holes and doors. The wind holes had shutters and the stable could accommodate four horses. I was planning for the future.

Sir Durand constantly criticised everything I said and did. It was as though I had been the one responsible. It took all my self-control not to challenge him to combat for although he was older than I was, I was the better warrior. Bruno was the only one who could give me a challenge. My time with

Taillefer had given me skills that they could not comprehend. I could switch sword hands mid-combat and fight just as easily with two weapons as one. Taillefer had begun the work and I had practised every day. I knew that if things continued as they were then Sir Durand and I would come to blows.

The duke's visit brought matters to a head. I was becoming increasingly angry with Durand although I did not show it and was looking for a chance to hurt him in some way. Although I was called a pueros I was a squire in all but name. I had good weapons and a good helmet. My grandfather's old hauberk fitted although it was not good enough for a real battle. The rings were too large. When Aimeri made mine, I would have the smallest holes he could fashion. It would treble the cost but be worth it. I had already spoken to the weaponsmith but as it was winter the earliest that I would need such an item would be summer. He said he would begin to make the links when time allowed.

The duke came with some nobles I had not met. Bishop Odo did not come but Robert, Count of Eu, Hugh of Gournay, Walter Giffard, and William de Warenne did. I was not aware of it then but the meeting was something of a council of war. The extra guests meant that the hall was bursting and the stables were full. I was lucky that I now had a roof and a stable. I still lived in my grandfather's home but that would soon change. I also had better clothes. They had been made by Gunhild and the ladies although I had paid for the cloth that we bought at Rouen market. My boots were well made and now that my hair was cut in the Norman style, I looked no different from the other squires. We waited at table. I was disappointed that Taillefer was not there. Sir Ambrose was and he told me that he had heard Taillefer was in Italy.

I was now used to serving at the table and although I did not have to do it every day, for sometimes I had other duties, the kitchen was a familiar place. Gunhild ran it efficiently and I was popular. I must have been the subject of conversation for when I returned with a full platter halfway through the meal, I saw beaming smiles when I was seen. I was embarrassed more than anything else but I smiled and endured it. Taillefer would have loved the attention but I did not, not least because Sir Durand glared and glowered at me the whole time.

While the food was being served, I heard news of England. It was one of the reasons for the visit of so many nobles. Earl Godwin had died but his four sons, Harold, Tostig, Gyrth and Leofwine, had returned and King Edward's Norman friends and counsellors were now ejected from the country. It did not matter that King Edward had named William as his heir for the land was ruled by the sons of Godwin. Tostig held the north, Leofwine the midlands, Gyrth the east and Harold the south and London. As the king was still hale and hearty it did not pose a problem, yet.

When we had finished serving the food, we took our places at the rear. I saw that some of the squires had managed to disappear, leaving just five of us to serve the table. Sir William did not have a troubadour and with no Taillefer, there was no entertainment after we had eaten. To my acute embarrassment, Duke William stood and pointed at me. He was red-faced and I had dined enough times with him to know that meant he had drunk well. When he spoke, I knew he was drunk for we had said that the taking of Douvres was to be a secret.

"I am no Taillefer but even I can tell the tale of Richard the Horse Dancer." Those like Sir Ambrose who knew the incident laughed and banged the table. The others looked interested, bemused but interested. The duke then told the story. He did not do it half as well as Taillefer who would have added dramatic pauses as well as quietly spoken sections but it met with the approval of the lords who banged the table.

As the duke sat down Sir Ambrose said, "And what of the battle of the king's hall?"

The duke nodded and drank some more wine, "You tell it, Sir Ambrose."

Sir Ambrose made a better effort than the duke and he made it seem like a bloody battle. He told it so well that there were shouts for more stories and, worst of all, every eye was fixed on me.

William de Warenne was barely twenty and looked to be the youngest knight in the hall. He said, "Sir William, why is your half-brother not yet a knight? It seems to me that he has shown enough to be so rewarded."

Sir William was uncomfortable while Sir Durand was just seeking an escape from the hall. Sir William gave a weak smile. "Richard is young and he would admit that he has plenty to learn. He is of an age with my young brother Robert and he has yet to win his spurs."

I saw Sir Eustace open his mouth to say something and then think better of it and drink instead.

The duke was not so drunk that he had not understood the conversation for he said, "Richard, what do you think? Are you ready for spurs? Say the word and I will dub you here and now."

It was an important moment in my life but I knew that I was not yet ready and that I did not want to put Sir William in a difficult position. I shook my head, "Duke William, I am humbled that you think me ready. Sir William is quite right and I have much yet to learn. Besides, there is no prospect of war. When there is a war, I will have the opportunity to show my skills where it counts, on the battlefield."

My words met with almost universal approval.

The duke wagged a finger, "Do not be too sure. King Henry of France conspires with Anjou and some Norman rebels. Within a year you may have your wish, Richard fitz Malet."

His words took the attention from me and the hall erupted in spirited conversations.

The next morning I rose early and went to practice with my three shield brothers. Baldwin and Bruno had also been serving and as we sparred discussed the events of the evening.

"If we go to war, Dick, will you be with the pueros or Sir William?"

I shrugged, "No one has said. I hope to be with you three and the pueros."

That pleased them. The lords were deep in conference when Sir Durand, Sir Eustace, Sir Ambrose and the lesser knights emerged. William de Warenne was not at the council of war and was with the half dozen knights and their squires.

"Richard fitz Malet, would you don mail and fetch a sword? I would have a bout with you. Sir Ambrose told me that you have learned tricks from Taillefer. The best place to see such tricks is when you are defending against them. If we are to go to war then I need all the practice I can get."

Sir Durand snorted and sounded like a disgruntled pig, "Tricks do not win either battles or war, my lord."

I held my tongue for Sir Durand's wars had been even briefer than mine. I smiled, "Of course, my lord, but my hauberk was handed down from my grandfather and is ill-fitting."

"No matter."

Bruno said, "And I shall be your squire and help to dress you." He escorted me to my grandfather's house.

We took out the padded undergarment. Gunhild had modified my grandfather's and it fitted me well. The hauberk hung like a sail in a flat calm. My arming cap was also well made and the helmet had a nasal. I strapped on my good sword and habit made me fasten my dagger. I had dug up my grandfather's treasure from his home. I reburied it at my grange and used grandfather's old shield, which had covered the chest, as my shield. I had Aimeri fit a boss. It was a round shield but they were better to use on foot in any case.

Bruno whispered in my ear as he fastened my baldric, "William de Warenne has a good reputation, Dick. Do not underestimate him."

"I have nothing to lose if I am defeated and I will give him a good bout."

We emerged and headed for the gyrus. Everyone had vacated the centre and William de Warenne waited with an expensive-looking hauberk, a fine helmet with reinforcing strips and a sword that looked like it came from Toledo. He had a round shield too but his was well-made and not a repaired Saxon one like mine.

We saluted each other and then began the dance that
always preceded a fight as men weighed up their opponent. I
had rarely fought with my shield but my sword felt like an
extension of my arm. We were well-matched in height and
when he swung his sword at me it was a safe attempt to test
my reflexes. I brought my shield up quickly and countered it
but the lack of padding on the shield and its age made my
arm shiver. I would need a much better shield in future. I
waited to make my first strike. I knew that I was fit and
prepared. I had not drunk much the previous night and the
longer the bout lasted the better chance I would have. He
took my caution for fear and advanced towards me using
both shield and sword offensively. I blocked each blow but
stepped back cautiously.

Sir Durand's mocking voice came from behind me, "All I
see is a frightened boy. Show some spirit, runt, and do not
embarrass the Malet name."

I remained cold and dispassionate. If anything his words
steeled me for I knew my strategy was the right one.
Taillefer had said to keep loose arms, quick feet and a cold
mind. William de Warenne came again and this time the
flurry of blows from shield and sword almost broke my
defence but I held and danced out of the way. What they did
do was to break the guige strap on the shield and it fell to the
ground.

William de Warenne looked disappointed, "Do you wish
another?"

I whipped out my seax, "No, my lord, I am comfortable
with this. Lay on."

This time when he lunged at me, I saw the sweat on his
brow and the blow, which I took on my seax was weaker
than the others. Without a shield I was more mobile and
holding his sword with my seax I pirouetted around and
smacked the flat of my sword against his back. There was a
huge cheer from those watching. William de Warenne lifted
his helmet and laughed, "One blow and you win."

I bowed, "A lucky one, my lord."

"I do not think so. Another turn or two?"

"As you wish."

We sparred for another ten minutes. He was tiring and looking for more tricks. I tried to make it last as long as I could but eventually, I saw that he was sweating too much and was weakening. I swung at his shield and when he raised it dropped to my knee and had my seax at his middle before he knew.

There was a huge cheer. "You were well trained and I can see what Sir Ambrose means. When we go to war, if Sir William would allow it, I would have you fight beneath my banner."

As the alternative meant taking orders from Sir Durand, I was happy to nod and say, "It would be an honour, my lord."

The fight did a number of things for me. It showed even my closest friends how much I had improved in the months away from them. In addition, I was accorded more respect by almost everyone, including Sir William who had witnessed the end of the fight. The exception was Sir Durand who seemed to think that I had somehow insulted him. I wished that it had been he who had fought me. It would have been so easy to slip a blade into his side and give my grandfather's soul, peace.

A week after the duke and his party had left us, I was summoned to meet with Sir William. Baldwin's father, Henri, was there. He had assumed the command of the men at arms now that Guillaume was dead. Although his younger brother Robert was there, Sir Durand was absent.

I stood and Sir William waved me to a seat, "When you returned with the letter I wondered at the duke's decision. I thought it was hasty and ill-judged. I was wrong. I spoke with those who witnessed all that you did and can find no fault in any of your actions. In fact, if anything you were too modest. You deserve the grange. I was remiss not to have done so before but there are three thralls you shall now have to work your fields. They can live in your grandfather's old house." I looked up when he said that and he shuffled uncomfortably on his chair. "I know that you are bitter about what happened to your grandfather and I wish that it had not been necessary." He leaned forward and put his hands on the table, "You are now of this family and we must support each other. You understand, do you not?"

I decided to be honest. I knew that I now had a place with William de Warenne if I chose it. He had made it clear before he left that the temporary attachment for the next campaign could be made permanent if I chose. I shook my head, "Even if that was an injustice? What Sir Durand did to my grandfather's hounds was wrong."

"They were dogs, Richard."

"And if they had been your hawks, my lord?" He said nothing. "To take away two of my grandfather's friends, albeit canine ones, was wrong and to blind him too was inexcusable. I can never eradicate that from my mind and my heart."

Robert was of an age with me and he asked, "Then why do you stay if the sight of my brother causes so much pain to you?"

"I confess that I thought to leave but I have those here on the manor who are close to me and Sir William is right, I am of Malet blood and this is my home. The duke made it so." I emphasised my last words for I knew that if the duke had not given me the parchment I would still be living in my grandfather's home.

Sir William nodded, "And I am the duke's man as well as his friend. Just promise me this, Richard fitz Malet, that you will not seek vengeance on our brother. It matters not if you like it or not, Durand is your brother too."

"I cannot in all conscience promise that for I think that Durand is a wilful man. I will say that unless provoked I will not cause him harm." I saw that Sir William was unhappy about that and I continued. "I have seen the way he looks at me, my lord, and I do not trust him. I will defend myself if I am attacked."

Silence filled the hall. Eventually, Sir William said, "I will speak with him."

"Then all is well."

Chapter 11

I have no idea what was said for after that meeting I rarely came into contact with Sir Durand. I was busy with my grange. The thralls had all been captured when Sir William had fought alongside the duke against rebels. They had belonged to one of those who opposed the duke. The three came originally from Denmark and had been ship's boys aboard a Danish longship. They had been captured ten years earlier and now spoke Norman and accepted their fate as slaves. Sir William had fitted them with a yoke. When they were brought to me by the steward, I took them to the blacksmith and had the yokes removed. It appalled Henry, the steward.

"What if they run? Sir William will be unhappy."

I nodded, "Then the thralls are still his lordship's?"

"No, they are a gift to you and go with the grange."

"Then they are mine and if they flee then I will have to work my land alone." I saw the blacksmith, Bacgsecg, smile. He had more Norse blood in him than most Normans and I think he liked the three Danes.

"It is on your head then."

He left us and I faced the three who rubbed their red chafed necks. I smiled, "I will ask Gunhild for some salve. You are to sleep in my old home. It is a good one and you will be comfortable. When I have done, fetch your gear from the thrall hall and when you are settled meet me at the grange."

The eldest of them, Carl, was also about my age and he looked at the other two before speaking, "Why did you take off the yokes, master? The steward is right, we might run."

I nodded and saw that the smith and his boy had stopped working to listen. "Aye, you might and where would you go? You would be in Normandy and the marks on your necks and the brands would mark you as slaves. Even if the three of you split up and Galmr and Erik went elsewhere your fate would be the same. You would be taken again and enslaved. The yokes would be back on and who knows what treatment you would receive. If you want to run then do so now. I am unused to owning any man and if you are not here, I will continue to work my grange myself. I am a warrior and until I marry and have children then the grange is somewhere to sleep. If you stay then it will be a farm."

They nodded at my words and Carl said, "Men say that you are a good warrior and a fair one. Your words confirm that. We will stay and you shall find us loyal and hard-working."

We had made a good start. I gave them my grandfather's old boots and clothes. He would not have wanted them to go to waste and I left the paillasse and bedding that was in the house. Bruno and I had made a new bed for my first house.

My life settled, over the next year, into a comfortable pattern and I confess that, my grandfather's death apart, life was comfortable. Gunhild and all the servants treated me almost as Gunhild's foster son. She was popular and by association so was I. I was now well-skilled and every day that I trained improved me. Even Bruno found it hard to keep pace with me. As I rarely even saw Sir Durand, I was spared the reminder of what he had done and the pain of my grandfather's death faded a little. I no longer had to visit the home I had shared with him as my thralls lived there and I was able to make peace with myself. I still woke at night wondering what might have happened had I not been in Lundenwic with the duke but at home. In the cold light of day, I realised that what had happened would have happened even if I had been there. The hounds would have done what they did and Sir Durand would have also followed the same path. It was in the darkness of night and the terror of my dreams that I was haunted.

My time was then divided between training with Bruno and the others and working with my thralls. They threw themselves into the work and when I got to know them discovered that one reason for their happiness was that Carl and Galmr had been Sir Durand's thralls and he had treated them badly. They worked tirelessly and once they knew my thoughts, worked largely unaided.

War was coming but it would not be at the instigation of the duke. He knew he needed time to build up his army following the divisive civil war that he had ended with his victory at Val-ès-Dunes. The prospect of taking over England meant he needed a much larger army than existed. We were preparing for a war that would be preparation for a greater conflict. The duke was doing all that he could to avoid a war for he was not yet ready. Taillefer was a clever man and when I had been with him he had explained such matters. The duke had not given cause to his enemies to make their alliance a belligerent one. He had not tried to regain his Maine land and so we prepared for war but in secret.

Odo asked, "How does the duke know that there will be a war?"

They all looked at me for my time riding with the duke meant that they thought I knew his mind. I did not but Sir William now spoke to me more frequently and he told me that there was an alliance made up of Henry of France, Count Geoffrey of Anjou, Count Renaud of Clermont and Count Guy of Ponthieu. Even if we mustered every knight and warrior in the land we would still be outnumbered. I gave the others the names of our enemies.

Odo shook his head, "We would be assailed on all sides. Only Brittany would come to our aid for they hate Anjou. Nor would we have the knights of Maine for that still belongs to Count Geoffrey Martel. How can we win?"

Again they all looked at me, "The duke has a clever mind and he will already be working out how best to do this. I will not be with you but I know that our training may well be the difference."

"You still intend to fight under de Warenne's banner?"

I nodded, "So long as Sir Durand is here, I will never be given my spurs. Robert has done less fighting and yet I know that this campaign might well see him dubbed. I do not begrudge him the honour but I might have a better chance serving a young noble such as William de Warenne." I smiled, "It will not change us, my friends, and we will all be involved in the war."

Bruno shook his head, "I would still be with you."

I suddenly realised that more than a year and a half had passed since I had returned home, a year since my grandfather's death. The measure of that time could be seen in the neat field of vegetables I had and the goat that was milked each day by Galmr. My thralls made cheese with its milk. I knew that I had grown. The clothes I had worn in England were now worn by my thralls. The boots I had first worn were also theirs. I had new boots, and clothes to accommodate my larger frame, and I was now used to my hair cut in the Norman style. To all intents and purposes, I was a young Norman and there was little difference between me and my half-brother, Robert. His clothes were finer and he had a better helmet and sword but other than that, had we sat at the same table, strangers would not have known which one was the bastard. Duke William had made that change with his parchment and command. I owed him and Taillefer everything. I knew that Sir William would never have given me the grange or the right to my name without it.

I was aware, however, of my limitations. Until I bought a bigger horse, and I knew that it would be me who bought it, there was no point in paying for a hauberk. Blaze could not carry me into battle. I would therefore be serving de Warenne as a pueros or squire. I would need a lance but I also needed a hide or leather vest to protect my upper body and I needed a shield. I could have made a shield myself, I knew how but I had enough coins left from my grandfather's chest to pay for a good one from Aimeri. I went to see him in the late winter for I wanted to prepare myself as much as I could so that when war came, I would be ready, I would be well prepared for whatever I needed to do.

"Aimeri, I would have a shield for this war."

He nodded, "A good one will not be cheap. Not to be offensive but you saw when you used your grandfather's that a weakness is soon exposed."

"And no offence taken." Once the duke had sent the parchment my position had changed. I was now officially part of the family and men spoke to me differently. "I know and I care not for the cost."

He looked relieved, "Then I would use a bronze and iron alloy for the boss and the rim. It is a durable material and affords protection. Of course, in war, such things are often damaged and you would have to have them repaired from time to time."

"Accepted."

"I can cover it with leather to protect the wood although we will varnish it and add protection." I nodded, "And the design?"

I did not want it to reflect the Malet family and so I came up with a unique design that would mark me on the battlefield. Taillefer had done so and I was still trying to be as much like him as I could. "Red and white chequerboard." One reason for my choice was that I knew that Gunhild had a bolt of white cloth and a smaller one of red. Red squares could be sewn onto the white. It would not cost me a fortune but I would look more like a knight and it would hide my hide vest.

"I will let you know when it is ready."

I gave him the coins before I left. Grandfather had always paid men who did work for him first. It was his way and was now mine. The tanner, Bergil, worked, not in the manor but in the village. Even there he was isolated as tanning was a smelly craft. I told him what I needed and he shook his head, "I can do it but it will cost. I could do it cheaply but you need hide that is well-cured and tanned. You need one that can take a blow from a sword."

"It matters not."

Nodding, he measured me and gave me a price. It was much less than I had expected and I paid him happily.

As I headed back to the manor and castle, I was smiling for I had all in place to send me to war as a warrior. My time in England had changed me. I had seen the benefit of a good gambeson to be worn beneath leather or mail as well as a well-made arming cap. I had both. The helmet was adequate and the sword taken from the housecarl was the equal of a knight's. If I was successful then the battlefield would become my marketplace where I could choose better weapons from those I slew. I laughed at myself and was glad that no one was watching. Where did my confidence come from? It had to be Taillefer but my grandfather had grounded me well. The thundering hooves brought me from my reverie and I turned to see Sir Durand and his squire, Charles, charging down the road as though going into battle. They made no attempt to move off line and I had to jump into the drainage ditch to avoid being trampled by their horses' hooves. They both laughed as they passed. My boots were soiled and my tunic was muddied. Neither was a disaster but the incident fuelled my anger.

I no longer ate, as I had done, in my home with food brought by Gunhild. I now ate in the warrior hall. I dined with the lesser men at arms, archers, crossbowmen and spearmen. Sir William had forty warriors he could lead into battle. Henri, as captain dined in the castle hall. In addition, there were eight knights who served him including his brother and Sir Drogo. It was interesting that Sir William chose Sir Drogo to be the carrier of his banner rather than his brother.

I cleaned myself up and changed into a clean tunic before I entered the hall. Gunhild was not only the cook but also a housekeeper and she made sure that I had a plentiful supply of clean breeks and tunics. It was in memory of my grandfather. When I reached the hall the other three were waiting for me. Our action at Gorron meant that they no longer had to wait at the table in the castle hall. We sat together with the other pueros.

Phillippe, one of the older pueros, obviously had something to tell us. He was waiting until I arrived not because of who I was but because he wanted the largest audience he could. "Now you are here, Richard, I can give you all my news." Bruno's eyes rolled for Phillippe was a gossip. What was important to him might not be to us. "I was in the stable tending to Sir Durand's horse, it was covered in mud. A rider had just arrived from the duke and he told Sir Drogo that the muster is at the end of next month. We go to war."

Bruno deflated the pompous Phillippe by saying, "And why did not Charles, Sir Durand's squire, groom the horse?"

We all knew why. Phillippe was desperate to ingratiate himself into Sir Durand's good favours.

Phillippe said, "That is not important. We go to war."

Baldwin knew that better than any and he shrugged as he broke off a piece of bread to dip into the tripe stew, "We all know that. My father has told me to keep my blade sharp."

Phillippe's voice became smaller, "I thought it worthy of note."

I smiled, "It is good that you told us, Phillippe. Thank you."

He smiled, "We all have the chance to do as you did at Gorron."

Bruno was a quick eater and he had finished his stew. He was mopping up the last of the juices and he said, "At Gorron, we outnumbered the defenders and they were merely villagers. We will be fighting greater numbers of men who will be warriors and they will seek to devour our land. I do not think that the war will be won in the same way as we defeated the Angevin. Tomorrow, I shall rise before dawn and practise with Horse Dancer. Perhaps there are tricks he can teach me to help me have songs sung about me."

They all jeered good-naturedly at me and I shook my head, "I told you, Taillefer composed no song about it."

"Aye, but we all heard Sir Ambrose tell it. Do not be so modest, Dick. Taillefer taught you his tricks. Teach us too."

I was still a student and anything I taught them would not be as good as that taught by Taillefer but it enlivened the training and Odo proved to have quick hands and took to the juggling quicker. I still had the most experience in life-threatening combat and, as we sparred, that showed. I was always a heartbeat quicker than the others. The place where we were even was on horseback. We would be riding with other horsemen and carrying a couched lance. Ours would be shorter versions that we could throw if so ordered but I knew that throwing a spear also threw away the ability to keep an enemy away. We rode at hoops and speared them. We stabbed at man-shaped sacks filled with straw. It helped to marry our eyes and our hands but it would not replicate the actual sensation of sliding a metal head into a soft body nor the jar as the spear hit a solid body. War would hone such skills and I knew that there were French youths doing as we did. I was under no illusions. Many of them would be better than we were.

The closer the time came to the muster the more we trained as a mesne. It was necessary but it brought us close to Sir Durand and my three companions suffered because they associated with me. I was not the only one who had to endure his unjustified criticism. The other three did too. Unlike me, they could not speak back. So long as I used his title then I could argue back. He did not like it and began, increasingly, to find fault with the smallest mistake. Sometimes he criticised when there was no fault.

A week before I was due to leave and ride to Eu and Lord William de Warenne, I was as prepared as I could be without a bigger horse to my name. I had had my shield for a few days and the leather jerkin or brigandine was also ready. We were having a last practice and I was keen to use my new shield and see how my brigandine fared. Sir William had ordered his knights to charge at the pueros. We were there to act the part of French and Angevin knights. None were using metal-headed spears but even a pole could hurt. Bruno was effective with a spear and when Sir Durand picked him out and charged at him, I knew that Bruno would win. Sir Durand had a couched lance but he did not have the control that was needed. He did not keep the shaft tucked tightly into his side and he did not use the cantle to keep it steady until the thrust.

Bruno still rankled after the criticism the previous day when Sir Durand had told him to wash his hands for he looked like a beggar and I knew, even though I could not see his face that he would seek vengeance. I was heading for Sir Drogo and Sir William, and Baldwin and Odo flanked me. Sir William was making a more measured charge and keeping the line. Sir Durand, as ever, was eager to show that he was better than we were. He was not. He was better mailed, mounted, armed and protected but he was not as good as Bruno. Sir Durand took the hunched body of Bruno to be a sign of weakness. It was not. He was preparing to spring into action. Sir Durand stood in his stirrups and pulled back a wavering weapon. His blow was wildly inaccurate and even had Bruno sat upright he would have missed. As it was, the spear haft struck fresh air while Bruno put all his effort into a strike at Sir Durand's middle. Not only did my half-brother lack skills with a spear, his shield skills were also lacking. The spear protected his left side and Bruno struck at his middle. It punched the air from the knight and threw him from the saddle. I smiled as he landed on his back.

We three rode at Sir William and Sir Drogo. We assailed the two of them and were getting the better until Sir Eustace led the rest of the knights to slam into us. I managed to knock the standard from Sir Drogo's arms but the spear that smacked into my head meant I was dead. Sir William's squire sounded the horn to end the practice and we all lifted our helmets from our heads and those who had them slipped their coifs back.

Sir Drogo was grinning, "An interesting situation, Richard. I lost the standard yet you would have lost your life thanks to Sir Eustace. Would you have done the same in a real battle?"

I shrugged, "My lord, these practices are necessary but they are a game, are they not? In a real battle then the heart will send blood to your head and body and who knows?"

I knew that I would be able to fight cold but if Sir Drogo had thought he was going to lose the standard then he might have reacted differently.

Sir Durand had been helped to his feet and his brother dismounted to confront him, "The standard would not have been under threat had you not been so reckless and left the line. Why did you not hold the line?"

"I am a knight, brother, and seek honour."

Sir Drogo snorted, "And where is the honour in being dumped upon your arse by a pueros?"

We all smiled but Bruno laughed out loud. Sir Durand shouted, "I want that boy whipped! I am insulted and my honour impugned."

"Charles, take my brother and have his hurts seen to. The fall has clearly knocked the sense from him." The squire led the horse and the knight away from the gyrus. "Sir William nodded, "You four did well but, Bruno, learn to do as Richard does and control yourself."

"Yes, my lord."

We were in high spirits for we had not lost and the dumping of Durand brought a smile to us all. He was not a popular man. We took our horses from the field and I went to my small grange. I took the saddle from Blaze and hung it from its hook.

Carl said, "I will walk him to cool him down, master, and then we will water and feed him."

"Good." They were good men and responded well to the kindness and respect that I showed them. I had already decided that when I returned from this campaign, I would free them and offer them the chance to be my servants and be paid. The idea of owning a man did not suit. I took off my leather jerkin and gambeson and donned a clean tunic. I washed my face and dried it. Then I headed, with my wooden platter in my hand and my cloth over my shoulder, to the warrior hall.

There was a lively atmosphere in the hall. I knew that Captain Henri found the castle hall much duller for his son had told us that. Since Gorron, the two had become much closer. Here was an easy atmosphere. Men at arms like Robert and Richard had seen what the younger men could do and we were treated with respect. When Bruno walked in, he was cheered.

Odo made a mock bow, "Here he is the dumper of Durand!"

We all laughed. We could say what we wished for there were no knights to tell us off. As we sat and ate, wiping our fingers on the cloths over our left shoulders, we spoke of the practice. "You did well to strike so cleanly, Bruno."

He shook his head, "Odo, any man could have done what I did. Sir Durand is a poor warrior. If he were not a knight then he would be relegated to holding the reins of the spare horses."

We all laughed because it was true.

Baldwin said, "Aye, and it is men like my father, Robert and Richard who might suffer trying to save him from enemies."

We all nodded our agreement and I added, "And Charles is little better. He is so desperate to impress his knight that he does all that his master says."

Bruno wiped his hands and then using his knife, swept the bones into the bowl in the centre of the table. The hounds would enjoy the bounty later. The thought made me sad as I remembered the two dogs who had been my bed companions. As he poured wine into his beaker he said, "I am not sure that I wish to be a squire. The duke will need horsemen who are mailed and well-mounted. I hope for purses in this campaign. I would be independent of men like Sir Durand."

"And do not forget knights' horses. The French are well-mounted. Take a knight's horse and you are halfway to becoming a sword for hire."

Robert had been listening and he shook his head, "A knight is hard to unhorse let alone slay. Set your sights lower, Bruno."

I smiled, "Robert, I bow to your experience but did not Bruno unhorse a knight today? And if this had been a real battle then his spear would have found Sir Durand's throat."

"Sir Durand is not a French knight, Richard."

"And yet there may well be French knights as poor as Sir Durand. Let us pray that we meet them!"

He shook his head and smiled. We were too ebullient to be downcast.

Sir Eustace appeared at the door of the warrior hall. This was an unusual event and we all fell silent. I wiped my hands on my cloth and watched. He came over to us and said, "Bruno, Richard, come with me. Sir William has sent me to speak to you."

It sounded ominous. I could not think of anything other than Sir Durand that would have sent Sir Eustace from his feast to speak to us. Once outside he said, "Bruno, Sir Durand has demanded that you be whipped." He saw Bruno begin to open his mouth and held up a hand, "For once listen

and then speak." We both respected Eustace for he had
treated us fairly when he had been a squire. We nodded.
"You will not be whipped but Sir William wishes no bad
feelings to disrupt the harmony of the conroi when we go to
war. Bruno, you are to join Sir William de Warenne next
week."

"Yes, my lord." He paused, "Am I no longer to be your
squire?"

He shook his head, "I am to have another and that
saddens me for I thought to make you a better warrior than
me." He shrugged, "Such things are decided by the stars.
You will leave on the morrow, before dawn. Richard, you
shall go with him. Sir William has a letter he will send to
you, Richard, when it is penned. It will ask Sir William de
Warenne to take Bruno for this campaign." I knew that
Bruno had mixed feelings about this. He and I knew each
other well. He would relish the chance to impress another
lord but he would not like Sir Durand to think he had won.

"When the campaign is over, Sir Eustace, what then?"
Bruno asked.

"You return here and continue your training." He smiled,
"You have more chance of loot this way, Bruno."

I shook my head, "This is not right, my lord, and you
know it. Bruno did nothing wrong."

He sighed, "It is the way of the world, Richard, and you
cannot change it. Do not see this as half empty but half full.
You get to go to war with your best friend and the mesne will
be more harmonious."

Bruno put his hand on my shoulder, "He is right, Dick,
and I know that it will be hard for me to keep a smirk from
my face each time I see Sir Durand." He gave a half bow to
Sir Eustace, "Tell Sir William, I accept his offer."

Shaking his head Sir Eustace said, wryly, "Very
magnanimous of you, I am sure. Sir William will sleep easier
in his bed knowing that."

Chapter 12

Eu 1054

We reached Eu just a few days after leaving Graville-Sainte-Honorine. Sir William de Warenne served Robert the Count of Eu and we arrived at his castle in the middle of the day. It lay on the coast, just south of Boulogne, and there was a camp outside the castle. I sought the standard and familia of Sir William. We dismounted and walked our horses through the camp. I was not wearing my chequerboard tunic nor my brigandine. They were on Mary's back along with my spear and spare sword. She also carried Bruno's war gear. He was lucky that the Seigneur had allowed him to keep the small horse he had used at Gorron. The young noble's standard was easy to spot and we made for it. William de Warenne was sparring with his squire, Geoffrey. When he became aware of us, he stopped and smiled, "You have come early. That bodes well, Richard fitz Malet, and you have brought a companion. Did I not see you at Graville-Sainte-Honorine?"

Bowing he said, "You did, my lord." He handed over the parchment I had given to him when we left Graville-Sainte-Honorine.

Sir William read it and after a brief smile nodded, "A new sword is always welcome, no matter what the circumstances. Welcome, Bruno son of Bergil."

I wondered what the Seigneur had written. I doubted that I would ever know. The nobles were like a secret society and always closed ranks. Even Eustace, who came from a noble family, was the same. It confirmed, in my mind, that Taillefer had humble origins and explained why he felt an affinity with me. I hoped he would take part in this campaign.

"Geoffrey, take them and show them where the horse lines are. Can you make hovels?"

I nodded, "Yes, my lord."

"Good. Geoffrey, have them make their hovels close to the squires."

"Yes, my lord." He glanced at Mary as he walked us to the horse lines. "I see you have a design upon your shield, Richard. Does your tunic match it?" I nodded, "Whose is it?"

I looked down and said, in a small, wee voice, "Mine, Master Geoffrey."

He laughed, "I would say that was both premature and pretentious had I not seen for myself your modesty."

I felt I owed him an explanation, "Taillefer told me that you need to be identified on a field by both friend and foe. Friends so that they can recognise you and foes so that they fear you. The red and white stand out and," I shrugged, "I had the material."

He laughed again, "Better and better. I wear Sir William's livery. What about you, Bruno?"

"I have no design upon my shield and I wear the tunic of Sir William. I know not if this shall be permanent."

He stopped, "You would wish to leave the Lord of de Caux?"

"In truth, I know not for I was not privy to the letter. I do know that I was sent hither by my lord. I shall take each day as it comes and hope to profit from this war."

"Wise words and a healthy attitude." The young lord and Bruno hit it off from their first meeting.

We continued to the horse lines and he helped us to tether the animals, unsaddle the horses and unpack the sumpter. As we headed for the place where we would sleep, he said, "The Count of Ponthieu and his fellows are gathered to the east of us. It is good that you came early, Richard, for we leave before the muster is complete. Count Robert is a clever man and would pre-empt any mischief caused by the French and their allies. The French king is mustering his men further south. We have to play fox and ducks. We need to marshal our smaller numbers so that we can defeat their greater numbers. If Count Robert can manage that, it will be a fine trick. Like you, Bruno, I hope for the chance of treasure and for glory. There are many lords we can impress."

The rest of the mesne were friendly too. We were new and a novelty. My name was known thanks to Sir Ambrose and his description of me as Horse Dancer. I had to retell the tale when we ate. Another thing I had learned from Taillefer was how to tell a tale. Gradually the tale became better as I learned to gauge the audience. Once again, that was Taillefer's teaching. Sir William attached the two of us to some pueros who were led by his brother, Sir Radulf. Sir Radulf was the elder brother of Sir William and the heir to the title of Seigneur. The two of them were just a few years older than I was. As he was still in the castle of the Warenne family, Arques-la-Bataille, just a couple of miles down the road, we left the main camp to join him. We did not travel alone. We went with the other thirty pueros that the Count of Eu had allocated to Sir Radulf.

We were lucky and knew it. Sir Radulf had been, until a couple of years earlier, a squire and he had been dubbed by the duke himself. He and Sir William de Warenne were cousins of the duke. Sir William would not lead many men, just three of the Warenne knights, and would serve with the Count of Eu. Sir Radulf and his men had been given the freedom of being the scouts for the army. Sir Radulf was keen to impress but he was, as I came to know, far from reckless. He was cautious. We spent the three days we were at the castle by the coast learning the calls from the horns and the signals from the standards. He was at pains to explain our role. There were only forty of us in total and so it was easy for him to gather us around him.

"You will be the first conroi that I command and while I will be the only knight and one of the few with mail, we will fight as though we are knights. We shall be the eyes of the count. Our task is to find the French and the men of Ponthieu. When we do, we let the count know and we keep them in sight. If we have the opportunity then I intend to bring them to battle. The word has come to me that the French are raiding and pillaging eastern Normandy. It is why we will be moving a week early. We will not be using our sumpters but we will ride armed and armoured. We carry what we need and anything else will be provided by the French."

I looked at the others. Three of the pueros had mail hauberks but only Sir Radulf had a war horse. We would need to take French horses as soon as we could.

We practised and when we did so, we were placed with other young warriors. Inevitably we became friendly with some, namely Ralph, Walter and Roger. We got on well and they became the replacements for those we had left in Graville-Sainte-Honorine.

When the rider came from Eu, it was to order us east, towards Mortemer. It was too far to travel in one day and we stayed the night at Blangy. It was there, as we camped in the outer bailey of the castle that we learned of the French attacks. They had launched an attack not with one army but two. One was led by King Henry and the other was led by Guy de Ponthieu. Duke William, we were told, was heading to the Seine to confront the King of France and his larger army. Our task was to stop the privations of the Count of Ponthieu. He had split his men into smaller groups and they were plundering Eastern Normandy. This was a chevauchée intended to draw an army to battle while making the raiders richer. Although we would go to battle mounted, we had foot soldiers and servants with us and we moved at a walking pace. Bruno and I had the smallest horses and so we often walked, much to the amusement of Sir Radulf and the others.

When we reached Blangy, we heard the full report of the raid. There were refugees in the castle who spoke of rape and pillage. It offended all of us. We might not be knights but that did not mean we could not be honourable. When we had raided Gorron there had been no such rape. We had looted but maids and the old were safe. We killed the warriors and that was all. Sir Radulf's squire, Roger, came to tell us that we would rise before dawn and he wanted us armed and ready to fight.

We retired early for we all knew that a tired warrior made mistakes. I groomed Blaze and fed him oats and I made sure he had plenty of water. That done I prepared my weapons, sharpening and honing each of them. Like Taillefer, I had more than one sword. The short one I kept on my saddle in case I needed it. That was sharpened too. I put a good edge on my spearhead and my daggers. Finally, I found a priest and confessed. A man could not commit many sins in his sleep. As I wrapped myself in my blanket, I prayed to God that he would watch over me and I asked my grandfather, now assuredly in heaven, to protect me also. It helped me to sleep.

We were on the road by lauds. We rode on cobbled surfaces and I wondered at that. The sound of our hooves clattered and cracked in the silence of the early morning. Sir Radulf knew what he was about. His captain of arms, Guy, was a veteran who was coming to the end of his time as a warrior. He knew what he was doing. As dawn broke and we watered our horses at a village as yet untouched, I found myself next to him, "Captain Guy, why did we ride on roads that would alert our enemies to our presence?"

He smiled, "I was told you had a clever mind, Richard fitz Malet. There should be no enemies this close to Blangy. They are further east and nearer to Mortemer. If there were any this close then they would only be scouts and we would be able to deal with them." He nodded towards my spear, "Keep that to hand and be ready to react quickly. Sir Radulf asked for this task and he asked to lead young warriors. You are all chosen men."

For some reason that made me feel more confident. Back at Graville-Sainte-Honorine, I had never been chosen. I wondered if I could have a better home somewhere else.

We found the French, or some of them at least, close to the manor of Conty. There was no castle and we surprised some knights and horsemen who had ridden in to pillage and loot. Although some were still mounted, most were on foot having dismounted to rob the houses and church. Sir Radulf gave the command although I suspect that it was Guy who initiated the order and we galloped with raised shields and couched lances into the village. We had taken them by surprise. Most had their shields upon their backs and their swords were sheathed. I was under no illusions. The French invaders would outnumber us and the more of them that we could kill the fewer would remain to fight us. I struck a light horseman in the back as he tried to flee to his horse. This was the first time I had struck someone with a long spear and it was harder to shake the body from the end than I expected. I had to slow Blaze and let the weapon trail behind me. The other pueros had the same problem and it was Guy, Sir Radulf and Roger who began to draw ahead of us. I determined to stay as close as I could and to learn from the experience.

I dug my heels into Blaze's side and reached the bulk of the raiders. They had reached their horses and were trying to mount them so that they could face us on more level terms. There were knights and mailed men would have an advantage over us. Only a handful of our men were mailed. The second man I speared turned to face me and having his shield before him made a harder target. I thrust the spear beneath his shield and it tore into his thigh. I doubted that it would be a mortal wound but the blood spurted and he fell. I pulled my spear back and saw a knight mount his horse. He was side on to me and his shield was still across his back. I stabbed with the spear and aimed for his side. He glanced to the side and seeing the spear used his mailed left hand to try to deflect the spear. He was only partially successful. My arm drove the spearhead into the hauberk covering his thigh and into his leg. He wheeled his horse away as I pulled my arm back. The spear that hit my shield came as a complete surprise to me and I cursed myself for failing to remember that there were other Frenchmen and they would try to get at me. I wheeled Blaze and standing in my stirrups hurled my spear at the pueros who had tried to hurt me. He was slow to raise his shield and my throw was a good one. I hit him between his neck and his arm. The blood that spouted told me that he was dead and I drew my sword. I would recover my spear later.

I dug my heels in and followed Guy who still had his lance and was hurtling after a knight and his squire. The squire also had a leather hauberk and a shield but his spear had gone. I was not so arrogant that I thought I could take on a knight and so I followed the squire. He glanced over his

shoulder and turned his horse's head slightly to block off
Guy's attack on the knight. I urged my game horse on and
when I reached his horse's rump, swung my sword overhand
to smash into his back. It did not hurt him much but he had
not seen my approach and he naturally jerked his reins to the
right and out of the path of Guy. I say that I had not hurt him
but his face was effused with anger when he turned and,
taking his reins in his left hand, he drew his sword. His
wheeling horse and my strike meant that we were side by
side. The advantage I had was that my shield was between us
and his was that he was older and therefore had more
experience. I had yet to fight in a battle from the back of a
horse. He drew and swung in one movement and my shield
suffered its first real blow from a sword. Aimeri had made it
well. Beneath the leather red and white chequerboard he had
embedded nail heads for both strength and to afford more
protection. He had also padded it slightly so that the blow,
when it came, made my arm shiver a little but did not harm
me.

   I saw ahead that Guy and the knight were duelling and we
had slowed too. I saw no others around us. The skirmish had
spread over a large area and there would be many such
battles going on. I concentrated on my own. He must have
thought that he had more advantage fighting sword to sword
for he savagely jerked his horse's reins around to bring us
side to side. He was facing back towards Conty. I brought
my shield over to lie horizontally over my cantle and lifted
my sword to counter his first strike. He had a good sword
and it was better than the one I had taken from the Saxon in
Lundenwic. Mine did not bend but his rang truer. I let him
take the next swing while I gauged his strengths and
weaknesses. His strength was just that; he was well-muscled
and my right arm knew it had been hit. If we continued to
trade such blows then he would win for his sword would
bend mine or he would wear me down. I had to end this
quickly or ignominiously retreat. I would not let Guy down.
I used the metal side of my shield as a weapon and swung it
horizontally at his side. He was not expecting it and I hurt
him when I hit his ribs. In that heartbeat, as he winced in

pain, I lunged with the tip at his shoulder. Luck smiled on me for I must have found a seam on his leather hauberk. He shouted in pain when the tip found flesh. It cannot have penetrated more than a fingernail but it shocked him. Taking advantage I stood in my saddle and brought my sword down on his shoulder. He was strong but his reactions were slow and although I did not cut the leather, the blow was so powerful that my sword broke the bone and, unable to hold the sword, he dropped the weapon.

"I yield, I yield."

"Well done, Richard." I looked up and saw that Guy had defeated the knight and taken his sword. "You did well." He nodded towards the fallen sword, "You had better pick up your sword. Along with the horse and the purse on yon squire's belt, today has been a profitable one."

The squire was glaring at me. The knight also looked unhappy. It was one thing to be defeated by a knight but a man at arms was quite another.

By the time we reached Conty most of the riders had returned. The French bodies were laid out and had been searched already. Another knight and squire had been taken and they sat disconsolately. Sir Radulf beamed when he saw us ride in. "You have done well, Guy, a knight and his squire."

"The squire was nothing to do with me, my lord. That was all the doing of Richard fitz Malet." The four captured men all looked at me when my name was spoken. I knew it was nothing to do with me but the Malet name was well known. My half-brother was closer to the duke than the duke's cousins, the Warenne family.

Sir Radulf was a generous man and he beamed, "Then you shall both have the ransom."

Guy bowed but I shook my head, "I shall have the sword, purse and horse, my lord, but I give the squire his freedom."

I had surprised all six men. The squire shook his head, "But you beat me fair and square. I barely laid a blow on you. Why?"

"You were my first combat and my blow hit your back. I will take other ransoms I hope but my act is one to put me in God's good books."

The squire took his purse and tossed it to me, "I shall remember your name and the red and white checks, Richard fitz Malet."

We had taken enough sumpters and poorer quality horses for our captives to be taken back to Sir Radulf's castle. The squire who was unhurt was sent with the ransom demands and the other captured animals were all sent with an escort of those who had been wounded. Two pueros had died and that was sad. That night, as the Count of Eu arrived with the rest of our men, we buried them in the small churchyard. Before he left, the wounded squire told me that his horse was called Louis. He was an improvement on Blaze for he was a couple of hands taller. Not yet a warhorse, he was an animal that would allow me to spare Blaze all the work.

Bruno, Ralph, Walter and Roger had all taken weapons and purses but not a horse. I was the envy of all of them. Bruno was happier than I had ever seen him at Graville-Sainte-Honorine. His father had died in the service of Sir William but Bruno had not been afforded any special treatment. He had nothing. I knew that but for Duke William, I would be in the same position. Sir Radulf made a point of speaking to us all and Bruno appreciated that. As we ate the food prepared by the grateful villagers, he spoke to me in confidence, "I like this mesne, Dick, you seem to have influence. Could you ask Sir Radulf if it could be permanent?"

I nodded, "Of course, but it means we will not serve together."

"And that is sad but I feel I have no future in Graville-Sainte-Honorine but amongst this company I do. There will be no Sir Durand."

I nodded. It had crossed my mind to do the same but I was tied to the Malet family and I did not want to risk falling foul of fate.

I had no chance to speak to Sir Radulf for there was a council of war. The French were close by and clearly spread out over a large area. When he returned, he told us that we would be seeking battle with the men of Ponthieu over the next few days. Count Robert intended to bring our men to bear in numbers and destroy the raiders piecemeal. The local men had told us that the French seemed to be operating in bands of four or five hundred. The count's plan could work. We were told that we had to travel light. The foot soldiers who had accompanied us would guard the baggage at Conty and in the event of a defeat we would have somewhere to which we could retreat. I had to choose my horse and I picked Blaze. This was not the time to get to know a new horse. Blaze was reliable and we knew each other. That was more important than size.

We stayed a little closer to the knights and men at arms this time, although Sir Radulf sent his best scouts ahead of us as we moved steadily eastwards. It became clear that the raid on Conty had been the furthest extent of the men of Ponthieu. We gleaned much from our prisoners who were happy to chat with each other, somehow thinking that we had suddenly gone deaf. It was clear that the French were further south and facing Duke William. The Count of Ponthieu must have thought he had free rein to raid. He was in for a shock.

It was an hour after the sun had reached its zenith when the scouts rode back. They reported to Sir Radulf who, in turn, reported to the count. We crowded around the scouts and begged for information. "The enemy is just five miles ahead at Mortemer. They have their warbands spread out across four or five miles for there are many rich farms close by."

"How many do we face?"

The scout laughed, "Enough to make us all rich men."

Sir Radulf was not away for long and he quickly gave his orders. "We have done being the eyes of the army. Now we become the teeth." He pointed to half of the men, the ones who had followed us from Eu, "You twenty men will be with the Count of Eu. "The rest of you," he pointed specifically at Bruno and me and then swept his arm around the others who were wearing his livery, "shall be with my brother. The Warenne family shall earn great honour this day."

I was happy about that. Sir William and his men, along with those of Hugh of Gournay and Walter Giffard also joined us. The loyal knights of eastern Normandy would be with the Count of Eu and they had a particular interest in those who had ravaged their lands.

The smoke in the sky, even as we set off, was a good indication that the enemy warriors were close and ravaging the land. We rode in columns as we headed east and we were the column on the extreme left. Sir William and his brother, Sir Radulf, led the knights to our right. Riding in a column of, in our case two men, and in Sir William's three, meant we could travel quickly and easily form a line when we needed to. We followed Guy. There were just ten paces between us and the mailed knights. I knew that our job was to stop any who would hinder the knights. We would be going after the smaller fishes and they would deal with the knights.

It was the Count of Eu and his men who made the first contact. There was a cheer from our right as the knights formed a line. Sir Radulf anticipated that we would be in action soon, especially when we saw women and children fleeing from ahead.

"Form line."

The knights would be riding knee to knee while we would have space between us. It meant our line was as long as the numerically superior knights ahead of us. We had to pick our way over obstacles but when they cleared, we saw the men of Ponthieu and the men of Mortemer. The land around was flat and farmed. We dressed our lines and then the horn sounded and we galloped towards the enemy horsemen. As at Conty, some of the men were dismounted and when they heard the horn and the sound of thundering hooves then they ran for their horses.

Guy waved his lance to the left where there were horse holders, "Pueros, there is your target." He wheeled his horse and our line veered to cut off the fleeing men on foot and capture the horses. Men who were surrounded and afoot were more inclined to surrender. Guy was the best mounted and as there was no need for a solid line, he spurred his horse and caught up with the first man. His technique was flawless.

He did not couch the spear but stabbed down at the neck of the man as he passed him. As the man fell and the horse continued, the spear naturally sprang free and he was ready for the next man.

I aimed Blaze at the back of a liveried man at arms. He only had a sword and it was still sheathed. He had, in his hand, a small chest. He put the value of coins above his own life. I had decided to emulate Guy and I held my spear to stab. The man was cunning and he threw himself to the ground as I neared him. It availed him little for I threw the spear into his back and drew my sword. Guy had almost reached the horse lines and I shouted, "Bruno, come with me and we will block their escape."

I had seen that the road headed north and while they could attempt to flee across the fields, the inviting road was a better prospect.

"Ay, Dick. We shall be as two Horatios at the bridge." I smiled. He had listened to Father Raymond's lessons.

We had to jump a small wall and my choice of Blaze as my mount was vindicated for we soared over it and landed on the road. We wheeled our horses and then stopped. The first two men had mounted their horses and were still looking over their shoulders at Guy and the other pueros. When they turned, they had a real shock. My shield was before me and Bruno still had his spear. They must have thought me the easier option and came at me. Bruno had an easy kill for the two men still had their shields over their backs. As Bruno's victim slipped from the saddle, the horse of the man coming for me veered towards his companion. I slashed my sword across his chest and he tumbled from his horse and over the wall.

We dug our heels in and headed down the road to the tethered horses. The fourteen or so men who had fled for them lay dead, dying or so incapacitated as to make them no threat. Guy shouted, "Jean, William, guard the horses and the prisoners. The rest, come with me. Our lords need us."

I saw in the distance a furious fight. On the one side were the Warenne brothers and their knights whilst on the other were the Count of Ponthieu and his brother, Waleran. It was

151

a classically confused fight. This was not an open battlefield. There were small dwellings, walls, trees and plenty of bodies. Survival would be not only a matter of skill but also luck. We each rode to the nearest man and, in my case, it was a mailed man at arms. His horse was at least five hands bigger than Blaze and I knew that I had my work cut out just to survive.

His spear had gone and he had a sword. The squire's sword I used was a better one than mine but I was not yet used to its weight. He rode at my sword side. My red and white chequerboard tunic might have confused him for it was unique on the battlefield but he stabbed his sword at the centre of it in an attempt to end the fight quickly. Even my quick hands could not bring the shield over quickly enough and his sword tore the tunic but was then stopped by the hide beneath. The tanner had done a good job. His eyes told me that he thought there was nothing beneath the tunic but a gambeson and flesh. As he pulled his arm back for a strike at my head, I used the flat of the blade to smash across his chest. His back rolled into the cantle and I stood in my stirrups to bring my sword down at his neck. As with the squire, while I did not break flesh, I broke a bone and his arm dropped. He was a wily old warrior and did not drop his sword but he used his left hand to make his bigger horse rear and I had to pull Blaze from the path of the flailing hooves. The man rode off and made good his escape.

I saw that Sir William de Warenne was engaged with Guy of Ponthieu. I saw his standard bearer behind him. I shouted, "Bruno!" and pointed my sword at the standard. He nodded and followed me. He, too, had lost his spear and with drawn swords, we two pueros rode at the knight holding the standard. If we could take the standard then the heart would go from our foes. He saw us coming and wheeled his horse to face us. His squire also saw us and he put his own mount next to his knight.

I rode at the squire who guarded his knight's left. We were shield to shield but the one he held had no boss and mine did. I punched at his shield with mine and as he reeled from the blow I stood in the saddle and brought my sword down at his helmet. He could not bring his shield up and I dented the helmet. This was a fight to the death and while he could not bring his shield up, I struck his helmet three times in rapid succession and he slipped from the saddle. As he did so, his horse rode away and I was able to get next to the standard. I let go of my shield and it was held by the guige strap. I grabbed the standard and pulled at it. The knight was engaged with Bruno and as he tried to hold on, so Bruno was able to deliver a mighty blow to the knight's arm. The mail hauberk prevented the blade from severing the flesh but Bruno was strong and the sword fell.

"Surrender, my lord, and you shall live. Do not and I will slit your throat." Such was the venom in Bruno's words that the knight nodded.

I lowered the standard just as Guy of Ponthieu shouted to Sir William, "I yield. I yield." It was the end of the battle for us. Waleran of Ponthieu lay dead, slain by Sir Radulf.

Sir William de Warenne lifted his helmet and lowered his ventail, "I am right glad that you two came to serve me. You have taken a standard and captured a knight. You are both worthy warriors."

Bruno sheathed his sword and nudged his horse a little closer to Sir William, "Then may I ask a boon, my lord?"

"Of course, anything you wish."

"I would join your mesne, my lord, and become part of your familia."

"Of course, and you, Richard?"

I was being given a chance to free myself from the shackles of the Malets and the tyranny of Sir Durand but I shook my head, "No, my lord, I still have a grange at Graville-Sainte-Honorine but I thank you for the offer."

He smiled, "As you wish but you may join me at any time. Graville-Sainte-Honorine's loss shall be my gain."

Chapter 13

The single battle of Mortemer ended the war. The destruction of his ally left King Henry of France with no alternative other than to ignominiously slink back to France. Duke William had not even had to draw a sword for the Count of Eu and the Warenne brothers had won the war for him. I had a second horse, sword and purse for my pains. The helmet was too badly damaged to be of use but I took it anyway. Aimeri could reuse the metal. Bruno did even better; Sir William generously allowed him to keep the ransom of the standard bearer. In hindsight that was not surprising for Sir William had captured a count and his ransom would be a mighty one. After returning what we could to the people of Mortemer, we began the long and slow ride home. We were all in high spirits. Bruno and Guy tried to persuade me to follow Bruno and serve Sir William de Warenne but I had made up my mind. For good or ill, I was a Malet and I would follow my path. We reached Arques-la-Bataille and feasted for some days. Duke William arrived on the second day and that feast was even better.

Bruno and I did not have to serve at the table, and Sir Radulf also insisted that we sit with the other knights. Here my star had risen. I found it ironic that the duke and other Normans held me in high esteem but at Graville-Sainte-Honorine I was seen as little more than a hired sword with a hog bog for a grange.

Sir William not only had the ransom but also the promise of land. Duke William did not specify which lands but he was a man of his word. Ponthieu was confiscated by the duke, and the other rebellious lords who had fought against us were exiled and their lands were taken. One, Roger fili Episcopi, was given Mortemer. Bruno and I thought that unfair as the knight had been with Duke William and had done nothing to merit the reward. I wondered what treat lay in store for Sir William.

I left Varenne, Sir William's home, a fortnight after the battle. It was a sad parting for I was losing my best friend and I knew not when I would see Bruno again. Leading Blaze and my second captured horse, Zeus, I rode Louis and the captured weapons hung from Zeus' panniers. Blaze deserved the rest.

My half-brothers had returned immediately after the cessation of hostilities. They had not fought and had no reward for their service. Every lord and his mesne owed the duke forty days a year of service. They had given that but had nothing to show for it. As I rode into the manor, the pueros who were practising stopped to watch me. Baldwin laughed, "I see you have landed on your feet again, Richard fitz Malet. You have the luck of the devil."

Odo shouted, "Where is Bruno? He was not hurt, was he?"

I dismounted and tied my horses to the rail. I shook my head and said, quietly, "He has joined the mesne of Sir William de Warenne."

Baldwin shook his head, "His lordship will not like that."

I shrugged, "There was nothing to tie Bruno here. He was ill-used was he not? This is Sir Durand's doing."

Odo nodded, "He made our lives a misery when on the campaign. His brother seems to let him do as he wishes."

Odo's words depressed me. I had spurned the opportunity to escape. "I shall stable my horses and then deliver the news to Sir William."

"I do not envy you that, Richard." Baldwin brightened, "And when we eat this night, you can tell us what it is like to fight in a real war and not sit across a river, staring at an enemy."

Carl and the others were pleased to see me and show that they had not been idle in my absence. I had not expected anything less. We took my horses to the stable and I made a sudden decision although it had been on my mind for some time.

"I am pleased with all that you have done for me and I would like to reward you."

Carl grinned, "You need not, master, for our lives are better here than they were."

"Nonetheless, I would give you freedom. I shall have papers drawn up so that you will no longer be thralls."

Rather than looking pleased, they all looked worried. Carl said, "Where will we go?"

I laughed, "Nowhere. You shall still stay here with me but I will pay you. The three of you shall have half of what is grown on the grange and I will pay you a stipend each year, I cannot say how much it shall be. That will depend upon my purse."

My words had pleased them and Carl, their spokesman, voiced their thanks, "For my part, master, just the freedom is enough and we will happily work for you." A sudden thought struck him, "As we are no longer slaves, does that mean we are allowed weapons?"

I had not thought of that, "I suppose so, but why do you need weapons?"

"A weapon, even just a dagger, shows others that we are free men and there may come a time when you wish to go to war with us. We are your men and we would if you would allow it, fight for you." He emphasised the word, you. He was right of course, and if I ever became a knight then I would need followers. That dream had seemed a long way off but the Battle of Mortemer had seen squires knighted. If I attracted the attention of Duke William then I might be dubbed. He had offered it once but I was not sure it was meant for I was still young, but the dream was a little closer now.

I first took my tunic to Gunhild and gave it to her for repair. I also gave her the silver cross I had taken from the dead squire. It pleased her. Then, suitably attired, I went to the Great Hall to present myself to Sir William. He was with his brothers along with Sir Phillippe and Sir Roger.

He smiled, "Ah, the wanderer returns." He looked beyond me, "And Bruno?"

There was no way I could make it any easier and so I was blunt, "Sir William was impressed by him. He captured the standard bearer of Count Guy and so Sir William offered Bruno a place in his familia." It was not exactly the truth but little could be gained by telling my half-brother that Bruno had requested the move.

He nodded, "Then I wish him well."

Sir Durand snorted. He sounded like a pig, "Good riddance. We have more bastards here than enough."

It was an insult aimed at me but before I could react Sir William snapped, "Brother, if you cannot be polite then leave us."

He stood, "Aye, for the air grows foul."

Sir William sighed and shook his head, "I apologise for Durand, sit, take wine and tell us all."

Sir Eustace nodded, "Aye, Richard, for all we did was to have a staring contest with King Henry and his knights."

With no glaring Sir Durand, it was a pleasant talk and Sir William proved he had been listening when he said, "So it was you that took the banner?"

"Aye, Sir William, but only when Bruno had disabled the knight."

"The next time we go to war then you shall ride at my side."

Robert shook his head, "King Henry was beaten, brother, there will be no more war."

"There you are wrong Robert, for Count Geoffrey Martel brought no troops, did he? King Henry was not beaten, the Count of Ponthieu was. As our ally is Eustace of Boulogne then our northern borders are safe but Maine is now Angevin and that is the way they will come next time. It will take them time to recover. By then you shall be a knight and you can emulate Richard here and do great deeds to grab the eye of the duke."

Robert smiled, as did I, but inside I was thinking that Robert and I were of an age but because he was legitimate and I was not, it was he who would be knighted as a right and I would have to earn it.

The first thing I needed to do was to school Zeus and Louis. Both had riders who were not Norman and had been schooled differently. I asked for Alain's help and my grandfather's old friend happily indulged me and within three months the horses were mine. He also helped me to make a better saddle. By that, I mean a wooden war saddle that would hold me in my seat. The wood before and behind me would be made for my body. The ones I had taken from the squires were made for them and I slid around. We made a new one and although tight it helped me, when I charged with a couched spear, to be able to take the force of the blow. I spent more time learning the techniques of the spear and the lance. I did not neglect my swordplay but I knew that my weakness lay with the spear and I wanted to be as good as Guy had been.

The year passed and I grew. Odo had not grown as much and he had decided that he would never be a man at arms. He had practised more than we had with a bow, and as there was no captain of archers in the manor he decided he would aim for that. He would still continue to train with us but he would also join the archers and strengthen his upper body. He knew it meant he would never be a knight but he had good skills with bow and sling. It was a natural progression. Of course, it meant another of my shield brothers would not train in the gyrus for as long as we did. He would join the archers at the butts for part of the day. We did not go to war but Sir William, knowing that we had a war ahead, made us practise our manoeuvres. I avoided Sir Durand in all these encounters and, for his part, he seemed unwilling to risk sparring with me. When I dined I now had two companions, Baldwin and Odo. With Odo missing during the day, it was just Baldwin and me who trained with the young pueros. When Bruno had been with us then he and I had been the leaders. Now that he was gone, the others naturally flanked me and took me as their leader. My horse was eager for war. Baldwin still rode the small horse that was the same size as Blaze. Whilst not war horses, Zeus and Louis were warrior's horses. I could spar on horseback with Sir Phillippe and only be at a slight disadvantage.

It was more than a year after the Battle of Mortemer that two things of moment happened. The first was that Robert, my half-brother, was knighted. The second was that Roger of Mortemer gave refuge to an enemy of Duke William. Count Ralph, nicknamed, the Great, was a Frenchman. That he was the father-in-law of Roger of Mortemer was not considered when the new Lord of Mortemer gave him refuge, and the castle and the lands were taken from him by the duke and given to William of Warenne. I wondered, not for the first time, if I had made the right decision in returning to Graville-Sainte-Honorine.

The knighting of Robert was the cause for great celebrations. Sir Durand took particular pleasure in it. As usual, he made snide and sneering comments directed at me. Since his dismissal from the table on my return from the battle, he had not made the mistake of voicing them before his elder brother. He chose to do so amongst the lackeys who fawned around him. The men who did so were the worst of warriors and were despised by men like Sir Phillipe, Sir Eustace, Sir Roger and my two companions. I endured the insults but I also stored them to fuel my need for vengeance.

I threw myself into my training and made sure that each day I sparred and jousted against both Baldwin and Petr who had shown himself to be a good pueros. Sometimes I even took two on at once, using, as Taillefer did, two swords. I rarely managed to win and that was no surprise for my two sparring partners knew every trick and blow that I used. It did not matter for it was good to train my reflexes. Sir Robert, whom I liked, was not too proud to ask for lessons from me. Sir Durand would never have done so but I did not mind training the young knight. It could only help me when it came to war.

Our routine was upset as the year came to a close for there was a visit from Earl Ælfgar of Mercia and his wife Ælgifu, the sister of Sir William. They brought with them their sons Edwin and Morcar, as well as their daughter, Ealdgyth, and half a dozen housecarls. I was invited to the feast to celebrate their arrival partly because I was a relative but, more importantly, because I spoke English and I would make the housecarls feel more comfortable. Consequently, I was seated at one of the lesser tables. I did not mind because the housecarls reminded me of my grandfather. They wore their hair the same way and all had the same facial hair as he had. They were good company.

My deeds at Douvres were known to them and when they spoke, with smiles on their faces, about the incident, I was emboldened and spoke more openly than I might have done. It emerged, as we spoke, that they had little time for Harold Godwinson. It was he who had persuaded King Edward to take East Anglia from Earl Ælfgar and give him the harder task of ruling Mercia which suffered constant raids from the Welsh.

Edmund was the captain of the housecarls and I warmed to him for he spoke openly to me, "Harold Godwinson seeks the crown. Between you and I, Richard fitz Malet, the king himself visited the earl before we left and I think that this sudden visit came as a result of that. King Edward is a saintly and kindly old man but he is like clay in the hands of the sons of Godwin. We were there when the crown was promised to Duke William but, back in England, it is as though there was no such promise made. I fear that if your duke wishes to rule England, he will have to bloody his hands to get it." He looked around conspiratorially, "You should know that the earl rose against not the king but Harold Godwinson two years since. We did not lose but neither did we win. Let us say that Earl Harold now knows that the men of Mercia are a force to be reckoned with."

"There is peace now?"

He nodded, "We came to an accord." He drank some of the cider, "Earl Ælfgar is a good warrior and knows how to lead men. Duke William, if he has to fight for the crown, will find him a worthy adversary."

I glanced up at the head table and saw that the earl and Sir William had their heads together. I guessed that the same message was being passed between them. I enjoyed that evening. It was not just the company of the housecarls but the obvious discomfort of Sir Durand. Edwin and Morcar were happily chatting to Robert who was a likeable young man while Durand just drank himself into a stupor and when his face fell into the apple sauce and pork, I could barely contain my mirth. Two squires had to take him hence and I saw the anger on Sir William's face. He had disgraced the family and that would never do.

The next day I was asked to accompany them as they went hunting in the woods. They were housecarls and did not ride. Honour demanded that we should walk. Once again Durand disgraced himself by refusing to come. He used the excuse of a bad stomach but everyone knew that it was because he did not want to hunt on foot.

I wore my leather brigandine and a leather cap that Carl had made for me. I carried two javelins as well as a boar spear and these days I rarely went anywhere without a sword hanging from my belt. I chose the shorter sword for convenience. I was assigned to the six housecarls and both Baldwin and Odo attached themselves to us. They carried the spare spears and Odo had his bow slung over his shoulder. Hunting on foot was always a challenge. We had the master of the hunt with us and his hounds and he carried a bow. Two other huntsmen came with us. They had bows too. There was a clear protocol, the three huntsmen as well as Odo, Baldwin and I would not interfere unless one of our betters was in danger.

Gilbert the huntsman knew the woods well and the dogs soon picked up a scent. The tracks we saw were of both deer and wild boar. The dogs would know the prey and Gilbert might be able to guess but for the rest of us, we were in the dark. The earl and Sir William walked close to the trail while the rest of us had to dodge between trees and shrubs and avoid tree roots. We walked in silence. The breeze came into our faces but animals seem to have better hearing than men. I knew the woods well and I led for even though we were not on the path, I knew the best routes through the trees. My grandfather and I had often walked them with the hounds. I could almost see where the hounds had stopped to sniff. I had only hunted boars once and that had been in England. Then I had followed Taillefer. Times had changed and now I led.

The boars, when we surprised them, burst from cover and the leader led his pack directly for the fastest way from the danger. That was the path where both the earl and Sir William stood along with Sir Robert. The housecarls were fearless and they raced to get to the side of their lord and master. I was younger and knew the woods and I was able to get ahead of them. As I ran, I readied the javelin. There was no way I could hope to make a kill but I prayed that I could distract the leader of the pack of boars sufficiently for either the earl or Sir Robert to make the kill. I was twenty paces when I threw the spear and it hit the rump of the boar. It did not penetrate very far for it fell out but the beast's head jerked to the side and it was then that Earl Ælfgar rammed his boar spear into the neck of the boar. In turning its head it had made it easier. Sir William and Sir Robert both acted promptly and they both speared the boar ensuring that it died quickly. The rest of the herd escaped.

Edmund put his mighty mitt around my shoulders, "Bravely done, my Norman friend. You put us old men to shame."

I shrugged, "I know these woods well."

As we headed back to the castle, the boar carried by the two huntsmen as well as Baldwin and Odo, Sir William waved me forward. "The earl would like to thank you."

Earl Ælfgar was no longer a young man. This close to him I could see that his hair was grey and thinning. He spoke in English and so I knew that I had been the subject of a discussion, "Thank you, Richard fitz Malet. I am slower than I used to be. I might have been able to strike without being gored but your timely throw meant I did not have to."

I saw the gratitude in Sir William's eyes. I was not sure how I would benefit from this action but it had done me no harm. My star was rising as Sir Durand's fell. Perhaps I would not need to kill the man to have my vengeance. He seemed to me to be a man who might well destroy himself without any help from me.

Our English guests stayed for a month and that gave me the chance to spar once more with housecarls. The six of them were quite happy to do so as they rarely got to practice with Normans. The three of us rode at them while they made a very small shield wall. It was hard to find a way through their defences. Their round shields were bigger than ours and they all wore a coif beneath their helmets as well as hauberks that reached to the ground. They, in turn, found it hard to strike a blow against horsemen. We all suffered bruises but each one was a good lesson learned. As we drank cider after the bout, we discussed the practice.

"When we fight the Welsh then we only have to fear their arrows, and our shields and mail mean that we housecarls are rarely hurt. The Welsh just run away when they have angered us enough to make us charge. Our normal enemies do not use horses. When the Danes and Norsemen come, they fight on foot and we have the measure of them. It is good that we are allies for if we fought, I do not know who would be the winner."

I nodded, "Either you or we would have to do something different. If we both fought the same way then the result would be a stalemate."

We were all warriors and it was easy to speak with one another. None of us became angered and we all learned something from the discussion. After they left us and returned to England, I was summoned to speak to Sir William.

"You did well during the visit of the English and I know you kept your eyes and ears open. I need to speak with Duke William but I do not wish to attract attention. I will take just you, Richard, Robert and, of course, Geoffrey, my squire."

"I will be honoured, my lord."

"You will wear my livery for this visit."

I was excited as I prepared Louis that night. I had never seen Caen and knew it to be a mighty citadel. It was where Duke William felt most comfortable. We took a ship and headed across the mighty Seine Estuary. We would not travel up the Orne but landed at the small fishing port of Ouistreham. It was easier than waiting for the tides. It was a short ride to the walled city with the recently built round donjon. Sir William was a close friend of the duke and we were admitted immediately. To my great delight, Taillefer was there. He greeted me like a long-lost son and I saw the amusement on the face of both the duke and my half-brother.

Duke William waved a hand, "No, Taillefer, do not mind me. Greet the pueros, after all this is your court."

Taillefer grinned, "I apologise, Duke William, but I have missed this boy."

"Then take him hence while I speak of more important matters with the Seigneur de Caux."

Once outside I said, "Where have you been, Taillefer?"

"Where have I not been? My songs are in demand and kings, dukes, princes, and even popes like to see my tricks with swords. You know better than any that it is all just practice."

"You met the pope?"

He lowered his voice for we were in the inner bailey and there were many people there, "A disappointing man. Perhaps I expected something different." He shrugged, "God did not appoint him, his friends did. Still, I met the man and Parsifal and I were blessed. That cannot hurt."

"And you are back for good?"

"Perhaps. I like the duke and he seems to like me. I feel at home here but if a duke or prince offers me work then I go. I am like the squirrel that stores up his nuts for winter. My winter will be when I am old and stiff with age. If I refuse a prince then who knows what will happen." He stopped and, putting his hands on my shoulders, faced me, "But you, tell me about you for you have grown. Why, it seems to me that you are ready for a hauberk."

I laughed and as he put his arm around my shoulder we walked from the castle into Caen and I told him all. He had not heard about my grandfather and there was no reason why he should have. When you consort with kings and princes then the matter of the blinding of an old man is of no consequence.

"I am sorry, Richard. I only met this Sir Durand briefly but I did not like him when I did." He stopped, "And you harbour vengeance in your heart."

"How…"

He gave a sad smile, "I too have been hurt and sought vengeance and you and I are very similar. Do not walk that path, Richard, allow the fates to punish him for they surely will. Men like Sir Durand are always punished. Take satisfaction in that he will be punished and he will suffer."

Taillefer was wise and although I did not answer him directly, his words sank in and had an effect. I told him about my bout with Sir William de Warenne, Bruno's falling out with Sir Durand and then my role in the battle of Mortemer.

He laughed and hugged me tighter, "It was you and Bruno! I heard how two pueros took a standard and I should have known it was you two. I am pleased."

I concluded by telling him of the visit of the earl and the hunt. He became serious, "Aye, and that explains Sir William's presence and coincidentally, mine. I have just returned from England. Harold Godwinson tightens his grip on the land. His unpleasant brother, Tostig, has been exiled and I believe that the man you met, Morcar, will be the next earl. King Edward does little these days but watch his new abbey and minster as it grows. He prays and lives like a hermit in his hall. He lets Harold do as he wishes. I came to tell the duke. I spoke with King Edward, for I was invited to sing at a feast. It was nothing like the one we attended. There were less than a dozen people there and none of them had power. I came with a message to the duke. King Edward still wishes the duke to be his heir."

I stopped and with a puzzled look on my face said, "But I was there when the duke was named heir. Why should King Edward have to confirm his words?"

He leaned in and spoke in my ear, "Because, my young friend, Harold is spreading the word that Duke William forced King Edward to name him. Harold and his powerful friends speak of King Edward's desire to have an English heir. As the king is alone so much who is there to gainsay those words? And there is something more. Edward Ætheling, Edmund Ironsides' son, has returned from Hungary. If he was placed on the throne then there would be an Englishman who had the right to be king on the English throne. Harold could manipulate him. My words had an effect and I suspect that the earl came to Normandy, not just to bring his wife to see her brother but to warn the duke of the danger."

We had reached the centre of Caen and the busy market, "Come, I shall use some of my wealth to buy food and drink.

It is a long time until the feast and I enjoy your company, Richard fitz Malet."

He told me of Italy and the treasures he had gained. He pointed to a new sword on his belt. One of them was a short sword with a curved end. "It is from a place called Thrace and whilst I cannot use it for juggling I like the way it looks." He took it out and handed it to me.

I was now a better judge of weapons and I balanced it in my hand, "It has a nice feel but it is much shorter than your other swords."

"When I saw your seax I admired it. Every weapon has a different purpose. Your seax, in the right conditions, would be a more useful weapon than my sword. So too with this. If we had to fight indoors where the ceilings are low, it would be of more use. With my fast hands, I could use it to great effect."

I saw then his mind at work. He was contemplating situations that might arise in the future and preparing for them.

I pointed to the beard and moustache he had grown, "And when did you grow those? A disguise?"

He laughed, "I think that although we have spent little time together, you know me as well as any man. Aye, and when I went to Italy, I used the mountains. There was snow and it was cold. It helped me in England too for my hair was longer and I looked less like a Norman. Do not fear, I will visit a barber before too long. Duke William likes men who are clean-shaven around him."

Chapter 14

Varaville 1057

When the French came again, they did so from a totally different direction and this time came with the Angevin as their allies. Ponthieu and the northern borders were now safer and while we were north of the Seine and protected, we also knew that the French were up to something as messages came from the borders to tell us of castles being fortified along the eastern border. We had stayed in Caen for a week and whilst I was not privy to the many conversations and councils that Sir William attended, Taillefer let me know what was going on. We had the bond that exists between shield brothers and those who have put their lives in one another's hands. It was Taillefer who told me of the meetings between King Henry and Count Geoffrey. I saw, as he spoke, of the dangerous world in which he lived. He was a spy. He feigned friendship with the French but he was always Duke William's man. It explained why he was so often absent from the Norman court. He was not just fattening his purse, he was filling Duke William's mind with information.

It came as no surprise when we were mustered and ordered to sail to Caen. The duke was mustering his army at Falaise. Sir William commandeered many ships. Baldwin wondered why we did not simply march to Falaise. I had learned much from my talks with Taillefer and I understood more of the geography of France. As we sat in the ship, gently heading south and west, I took out my seax to carve a map in the wood. "Here is Paris, here is Le Mans and here is Angers. The French king has learned not to divide his forces. They can meet here." I made a cross at Dreux. "From there they can strike north towards Rouen or towards Caen and Bayeux. By mustering at Falaise the duke ensures that he can counter either threat." I put the seax away and swept the shavings from the deck before a sailor could see me. "I do not think that they will head for Rouen as the Seine is a mighty barrier."

Baldwin laughed, "We have with us a mighty general, Petr. He has rubbed shoulders with counts and dukes and he knows what is in their minds."

I laughed with them because they were right. I was being a little pompous, "I am sorry, my friends. I have picked up a little knowledge and as they say, that can be a dangerous thing. We shall see what we shall see when we reach Falaise. What we all know is that we will be outnumbered once again and we will need all of the duke's cunning just to survive."

I had disembarked the most and when we docked, I helped the other two unload their mounts. I had taken Louis again for he was the better schooled of my two newly acquired horses. The saddle kept me firmly on his back and although it was unlikely that we, as light horsemen, would charge with couched lances, I knew that if I did so then I would keep my seat. It was not far to Falaise and we rode it in one day. We were in Normandy and the heartland of Duke William's domain. We rode without helmets. My arming cap had now been reinforced with a leather hood. It was not as effective as a mail coif but it would afford some protection to my neck and throat. Baldwin, Petr and Odo had also emulated me and each had a tunic that marked them. When we fought, we would recognise our friends and that was always a comfort.

Sir Eustace had been promoted to carry the standard of de Caux into battle. I knew from the Battle of Mortemer that it was not only a prestigious honour but also a position of peril. I did not envy him or his squire, Hugh. There were twenty of us who were light horsemen. When battle came it would be Robert, the man at arms who would lead us. I wondered how he would feel for he had, at Mortemer and Gorron, ridden at the side of Richard, his friend. I knew that I missed Bruno. I would be seeing him I knew but he would be riding with the men of de Warenne.

When the Seigneur of de Caux had followed the duke in the last campaign he had not drawn sword. It had been the men of Eu who had fought Guy of Ponthieu. I was known and as we rode into the huge camp beneath the impressive

donjon and tower of Falaise it was I who was greeted. I saw
Sir William smile and Sir Durand scowl.

Bruno spied us and shouted, "Dick, Odo, Baldwin!"

We turned and saw a warrior wearing a mail hauberk and
the livery of William de Warenne. I waved back, "When we
are settled, I will seek you out."

Baldwin said, "Perhaps you should have stayed with
Bruno, Richard. He looks to be a man at arms."

I smiled, "I have put my feet on a path that will lead me,"
I shrugged, "I know not where but to deviate from that path
strikes me as perilous. None of us knows the journey we take
until it is over. I am happy for Bruno and happy that I go to
war with the two of you."

It was August and with a cloudless sky, we did not bother
with hovels. When we had seen to our horses and made a
camp with our saddles, shields and spears, we headed
towards the men of Mortemer. Bruno was speaking with Sir
Radulf and Sir William de Warenne when we neared them
and we respectfully stopped and waited. When we were
spied, I was greeted like an old friend by the two knights.

Sir William grinned, "Now I know we shall win for we
have Horse Dancer and the taker of standards with us. It is
good to see you, Richard."

"And you, Sir Radulf and Lord Mortemer."

Sir William laughed, "I still cannot get used to the title.
Go with your friends, Bruno. You may have an hour and then
return. We have to plan our ride on the morrow."

"Yes, my lord."

He put his arm around my shoulder and led us towards a
tent. "You have a tent?"

He nodded, "I am a man at arms now, Dick. You should
have stayed with me."

"You have a horse that can carry you?" I patted his
stomach, "You have grown bigger since I last saw you,"

"Sir William is kind and the ransom I received enabled
me to buy a courser and the mail. Sir William himself
promoted me. If I can impress him, I may get my spurs."

Baldwin said, "You have luck, Bruno."

"We earn what we get. Dick had the chance of this but for some inexplicable reason chose to stay where Sir Durand gets away with whatever he will and faithful old retainers are blinded."

I did not like the direction the conversation was taking and I changed the subject, "So you ride as scouts?"

He nodded, "We have heard that the French and the Angevin are at Dreux. The duke wishes us to keep in contact with them. The rumour is that they intend to head for Caen or Bayeux."

Odo grinned at me, "Right again, Dick."

I nodded, "They go for the heart of the dukedom. If they take either then they split Normandy in twain and the duke will have lost."

Bruno put his arm around me again. He had grown and was now a handspan taller. As I had also grown, we dwarfed poor Odo, "With we four the alliance of the devil stands no chance. They have to cross the River Dives and that means we can stop them."

"You know, Bruno, that they will outnumber us and that it was Ponthieu we defeated and not King Henry?"

"I know but Sir William has been training us hard. He is a good leader and a skilled warrior. I am happy to follow him."

We left and headed back to our camp. I will not deny that I was envious but I did not resent Bruno his good fortune. He had seized his chance when it came.

I was disappointed when we passed Duke William that Taillefer was not with him. I had hoped that he would be but my last encounter had told me that he was the duke's eyes and ears. Wherever he was he would be in danger but he would be serving the duke.

Being on campaign and, as I was still a pueros, meant more work than back at the castle. Sir Durand, in particular, took great pleasure in ordering the three of us to do jobs that should have been carried out by his squire. The three of us endured the fetching and carrying. I saw that young Sir Robert took notice and he did not approve. It seemed to me that it was Durand who was the cuckoo in the nest and not me.

The news, when it reached us, was that the enemy army was headed west for the coast. It was not Bruno who brought the word but another of those with whom I had served, Walter. He too wore a short hauberk and his horse, whilst not a war horse, could cope with the weight. He reported to the duke and then, as he walked his horse back to the road to return to the Lord of Mortemer and the scouts, he spied me and stopped, "Well, Walter?"

"They are heading for the estuary of Dives. There they can cross and ravage the lands close to Bayeux and Caen."

"How many do we face?"

"Twice the number you see here. The duke will need a cunning plan." He mounted his horse, "I must return quickly for I would not miss the chance for action." As he swung his leg over the cantle he smiled, "Lord Mortemer has not allowed the new title to change him. He is still an eager young cockerel and we are lucky to serve him."

The duke was as decisive as ever and we broke camp that day and made three miles before we had to camp. Our mesne rode close to the duke. We would not be the scouts. When Sir William and his knights rode to battle, his banner would be close to the duke's. Bishop Odo also rode with us and he had a larger mesne and retinue than the last time I had ridden with him. I suppose that as Bishop of Bayeux, he had a vested interest in this invasion as one of the targets was his church. He led the knights of Bayeux. Ours was the smallest of the three mesne. I was flattered, and Sir Durand angered, by the attention I received. I think that the bishop regarded me as a good luck charm while knights like Sir Ambrose and Sir Roger knew my worth better than any.

The bishop waved me forward on our second day out of Falaise to speak with me. Sir Robert saw me move and he followed me. The bishop studied me, "I see you have still to buy a hauberk, Richard fitz Malet. It might save your life one day. You have the frame to carry one."

"I will buy one, my lord, when I think I am worthy to look like my grandfather. I am still learning."

"I can see that you do not suffer from the sin of pride, but your modesty may cause you hurt. At the very least you should wear a mailed coif." He nodded to Sir Robert, "See, young Sir Robert here wears one and the ventail adds even more protection."

"He is right, Richard. When we return home, we shall have Aimeri make you one. It is the least that the family can do for you."

I nodded, "I thank you, my lord. Will we fight, Bishop Odo?"

The bishop inclined his head, "Or will we watch as we did the last time King Henry came to plunder? My brother is clever and we all know that he is not afraid of any man. We will attack if he thinks we can win. We will try to stop the enemy from ravaging our lands as they did the last time. Does that mean there will be a battle? Who knows, but you pair will be ready, I can see that."

The conversation ended, we returned to our mesne. Sir Durand saw us together and snapped, "Robert, ride with your equals and not your inferiors."

Normally Sir Robert would have acquiesced but this time he said, "The air is cleaner with this brother. I will ride with him for he has proved himself more than enough in battle. I have yet to do so and I have not heard men boast of the prowess of Sir Durand Malet."

When some of the men at arms sniggered, Sir Durand and his squire spurred their horses to ride closer to Sir Eustace and the Seigneur. Sir Robert shook his head, "I shall pay for that but it was worth it just to get under his skin. I know not why he treats you as he does."

I had thought about it and had a theory, "It goes back to my grandfather. I think your brother knew he was in the wrong but his character means that he could not back down and apologise. He could not undo the blinding. The whole manor thought it wrong. I believe Sir William did too and Sir Durand thought it was me who was to blame. It is just the way he is."

"You are right. He was cruel to me when we were growing up." He shook his head, "When he turned his attention to you, I was grateful. I am sorry for that now. I should not have been happy that another endured what I did. Bruno did the right thing, he left."

Everyone I knew seemed to think I had made a mistake in not following Sir William de Warenne. Perhaps they were right. Bruno was with the vanguard and had more chance of action than we did, lumbering along with the ducal warriors.

When we caught up with the scouts, we were at the coast and the Franco-Angevin army was preparing to cross. The king and the duke were at the fore with their vanguard. The heavily armoured knights surrounded the two leaders and the sunlight glistened from gleaming hauberks. The whole column seemed to be like a giant metal snake. I knew that was an illusion and that there would be many such as we without mail but their heavy horsemen would outnumber us. Duke William, Bishop Odo, Sir William, the Count of Eu along with the Lord of Mortemer and his brother, Sir Radulf, were in a knot watching the enemy.

Suddenly, from behind us came a rider galloping hard. I was close enough to hear his words, "My lord, I am Sir Richard of Hérouville. I grew up not far from here." He pointed at the estuary, "They have begun to cross at the wrong time, my lord, the tide will turn and the crossing will be barred."

The duke whipped his head around to stare at the young knight, "You are certain?"

"I swear, my lord. Within half an hour the sea will stop any more men crossing."

"Then I am in your debt. My lords, return to your conroi. When I sound the horn, we attack those that remain on this side of the river. I want every lance to charge as one, knights, squires, pueros. Servants who can ride should join us. God has sent us hope and I will not spurn it."

It meant Odo, who was mounted, would have to fight on horseback. I had heard the words and I fitted my helmet and tightened the strap. I made sure that the shield was snugly secure and then I waited for Robert's command.

The seigneur said, "The ground closest to the river is too soft for mailed men. Use our light horsemen, Robert, to attack there. It will protect our left flank. For the rest, form a

line on me. Durand, guard the standard." I watched the
knights and men at arms spread from our position. Bruno
would be on the extreme right and we would be on the
extreme left. I would not get to fight alongside my shield
brother. My horse was bigger than Odo's and Odo was
almost in the river. Being small and riding a small horse had
advantages as my horse would sink in the sand closer to the
water. We were ready for the horn when we saw men
struggling to fight against the incoming tide. It very quickly
became clear that the crossing would have to cease.
Although half of the army remained on our side of the river,
it was the half with the fewer knights. The Franco-Angevins
who remained on our side knew what was coming but they
were tardy to form lines and Duke William seized the
moment. His horn sounded and we galloped forward. This
time the men led by my half-brother had the opportunity to
show what they could do and they spurred their horses. The
exception was Sir Durand and after fifty paces was a horse's
length behind his two brothers. The standard had no
protection from a knight on one side. Sir Eustace would have
to rely on Hugh, his squire. Soon Sir Robert would have to
close with Sir William to offer protection.

I had no time to wonder at the lack of effort for there
were Frenchmen before us who were kneeling to aim
crossbows at us. They were a screen only but their bolts
could kill. It would not matter if a man wore mail or not, the
narrow bolts could easily penetrate mail. I swung my shield
around and rued that I did not have a coif with a ventail. My
face felt exposed. The horns from the Franco-Angevin troops
told us that they were panicking. There was no order. The
real leaders were on the wrong side of the river. We had the
baggage train and the bulk of the army before us. Half of
them were on foot.

I saw the bolt that came at me, or at least I was aware of
it. I heard the crack and saw the blur. I ducked my head
behind my shield and prayed that the bolt would not strike
Louis. It was well aimed for it smacked into the boss of my
shield. It must have spiralled in the air. I peered over the top.
In those few moments since ducking behind my shield, I had

covered twenty paces and I pulled back my spear. The crossbowman was pulling on the string but Louis was a good horse and he was eager to get at the enemy. I rammed the lance into the chest of the crossbowman. He wore no protection. As Louis continued towards the French spearmen, I let the lance slip behind me as I had seen Guy do and the body slipped from it. The spearmen were belatedly trying to form a shield wall. They were hampered by the rising tide. Odo and those to my left were mounted and their horses made light of the water that barely reached their bellies. The men on my left would have a relatively easy time. With shields on their left, Odo and the others could choose where to strike their spears. A second rank was racing to put their shields behind the backs of the front rank but it was hit and miss. Some men stood alone and others had a man to their rear. I aimed Louis at a slight gap between two spearmen. Baldwin was almost boot to boot with me. The spearmen had the butts of their spears grounded to form a barrier. I had long arms and when I thrust my lance at the nearest man, I knew that my spearhead would reach him before his spear could get close to Louis. I smashed into his face and with no one behind him he fell. That allowed Baldwin to choose his target and his spear found the shoulder of the other spearman. As the head ripped flesh from the wound, the man fell and we were through their first line.

Robert was to my left and he yelled, "Destroy these spearmen. Leave the horsemen for the Seigneur."

It was the right order. If we did not destroy these men they could reform and threaten our knights. Baldwin and I reined in and turned to spear the backs of the men we had already passed. I saw Odo and the men from our left. They had left the river and were driving the survivors towards us. It was like fishing. The enemy had nowhere to go that was safe and fearing a spear in the back, front and side meant most men made poor decisions. As the last of them was slain Robert rode up. His spear was shattered and he held his sword.

"Well done, pueros. Form line and we will go to the aid of Sir William."

I saw that Sir William was fighting a furious battle of his own against a conroi of French knights. Sir Eustace bravely held the standard but they were beleaguered. Hugh was doing all that he could to protect his knight but I could not see Sir Durand. Had he fallen?

As in all such confused battles, we reached the fighting at different times. The Frenchmen ahead of us sensed our approach and began to turn to face us. It eased the pressure on Sir William and Sir Eustace. I lunged at the man at arms as he turned but his shield blocked my strike. He could not bring his spear around and so I used Louis as a weapon. I made him rear and his hooves struck the French shield. His horse shifted away from the blow but, even so, a hoof smashing into a shield will hurt and the crack I heard was the shield breaking. From the scream from behind the ventail, I guessed it had done the arm little good either. The horse needed little encouragement from its rider to flee towards the river. I let him go for the man at arms was no longer a threat. I pulled back my weapon and rammed it at the back of the man trying to wrest the standard from Sir Eustace. The head burst the mail links, tore the gambeson and then sank into the flesh of his shoulder. His spear fell and he, too, turned to spur his horse away. I saw the blood flowing down his back.

I swung Louis so that I was next to Sir Eustace and was guarding his left side, the side with the standard. He slashed with his sword across the face of the man at arms with whom he was fighting and as the man tumbled to the ground turned, "Richard! Sir William and I thank you."

I looked around for another enemy but our attack had driven the French from around the standard. There were four bodies on the ground.

"Our left flank is secure, my lord."

He nodded and shouted, "Sir William, our left is secure. What are our orders?"

My half-brother had lost his spear and he pointed his sword, "Men of de Caux, let us go to the aid of Duke William."

Two hundred paces from us I saw that the majority of the French knights had made for Duke William. His death would end the battle and give the Franco-Angevin alliance an unlikely victory. We dug our heels in and I saw that the battle was spread out over a large area. I had no idea of time but I was weary beyond words and guessed that at least two hours had passed. The tide would begin, soon, to recede. Would the rest of the Franco-Angevin army return to aid their comrades? We had to end the battle to the east of the river or risk defeat.

Hugh, Sir Eustace's squire, nudged his horse between us. He had no spear and his helmet was badly dented, "I thank you, Richard, for protecting my lord but it is my appointed task."

I nodded but added, "You are hurt."

"It is nothing and I am just a little dizzy that is all but if you would guard my left then the standard shall be safe."

We were in a loose line as we headed to the aid of the duke. Baldwin was on my left but I could not see Odo. Ahead I recognised the standard of William de Warenne and knew that Bruno would be close by. No one would be safe this day.

Our horses were tired and this would not be a charge. We would simply edge into the French and Angevin knights fighting with Sir Ambrose and the rest of the duke's familia. This time I would not be fighting a man at arms or a pueros but a knight. The advantage I held was my lance. Most lances were shattered and neither army had the luxury of replacements. This time they were knights of Anjou who turned to face us. My task was to help Hugh protect Sir Eustace and the standard. I would have to fix myself and stay there. I could not run. The four knights who saw the standard of the Seigneur saw a chance of glory and they rode, knee to knee towards us. It was not a charge, indeed it was barely a walk for their horses had carried mailed men for a couple of hours. They were lathered and weary.

I was, I think, ignored for, despite the red and white chequerboard, I still looked like a pueros as I wore no coif. Three of them came for Hugh and Sir Eustace while the fourth rode his horse to attack Sir William who was already engaged. The omission on the part of the Angevin knight proved to be his undoing. His shield was on his left and his sword was pointed at Hugh as I struck with my long weapon. It slid into the mail, gambeson and links as it had with the French man at arms but this time the Angevin knight clamped his arm on the shaft and it was torn from my grip by the movement of our horses. I had my sword in my hand before he hurled the lance to the ground. He wore a ventail and I could only see his eyes but they burned with hatred. As our swords clashed and sparked, I saw his eyes and he winced. The spearhead had penetrated deeply enough to cut muscle. He was bleeding from within his mail. I hefted my shield around to protect my body more and prepared for a slogging match. This would be a test of swords and strength. The Angevin knight had already shown me that he had strength. Did I have enough to defeat him?

I sensed rather than saw Baldwin as he edged his horse around the rear of the knight I was fighting. I put the image from my mind as I blocked another blow. I was using the flat of my sword to avoid blunting the edge. I knew that the inner steel of the sword added strength. When Hugh fell from his saddle, I knew why Baldwin had ridden around the rear of the knight I was fighting. He had seen what I had not. Hugh was in trouble. As the squire fell, I knew I had to go beyond a mere slogging match and end this. As he pulled back his sword for another strike, I saw that his movements were slowing and I stood in my stirrups. It allowed me to bring my shield before me and I swung down with my sword. His blow hit my shield and was so ineffectual that I knew he was hurting. My sword slid down the side of his helmet and bit through the mail links and his gambeson. I sawed the blade as I pulled it back and blood spurted. It was not the spurt of a cut but was a harbinger of death for it spouted and I saw the life leave his eyes.

Baldwin's attack had ended the threat to Sir Eustace and both Sir William and Sir Robert looked whole. The duke and the bishop had also been victorious.

Sir William said, "Well done." It was thanks to the twelve men who still remained. I saw Odo and Robert but others had died. I stood in my stirrups to look beyond the men before me and I saw that the baggage train was being looted. The rest of the enemy army had fled. I was about to sit down when I recognised Sir Durand and his squire. He had abandoned his position close to his brother and attacked the defenceless baggage train.

I sat as the duke pointed his sword at the river, "With me to the river. When the tide goes out again, we will drive the French and Angevin from our lands."

I dismounted and went to Hugh. He looked to have not a mark on him and yet he was dead. When I took his helmet from him, I saw why. It was filled with blood. I had been right and the dented helmet had been a sign that he was mortally wounded. "Sir Eustace, Hugh is dead."

He nodded, "We will give him all due honours when we return. For now, we have a war to win."

We walked our weary horses to the river where I could see the wet sand marking where the water had lain. We waited behind the duke and his men. I could see in the distance that the French and Angevin had thought better of another battle and were fleeing back to France and Maine. Their horses would be fresher and pursuit pointless. I knew, however, that the duke would seek to chase them if only to stop them from causing mischief. The lands through which they would pass belonged to him and his brother. We crossed as soon as it was safe to do so.

We only stopped when darkness came. Louis was almost a broken horse and I dismounted as soon as we stopped. We camped fifteen miles from the river and the villagers fed us. It was the next day when we returned to the battlefield. I sought the body of the knight I had slain. I found him but another had taken his mail, sword, purse and horse. The ones who had not followed the duke had benefitted from our efforts. I saw that Duke William was angry as he surveyed the pillaged field.

"All of you who followed me this day and won the victory deserve a reward and I will ensure that it comes to you. I will also punish all those who disobeyed me and perpetrated this outrage." He was glaring at the robbed corpses of the French and the looted baggage train.

We looked around to see who was missing and Sir Robert asked, innocently, "Where is our brother? Does he lie amongst the dead?"

As if in answer, Sir Durand and his squire rode towards us with a line of four laden sumpters. He had no idea that he was in trouble. He was smiling and his helmet hung from an unbroken spear, "Hail Duke William. I have found treasure from the King of France that I would share with you."

Sir William growled, "Durand, silence."

Sir Durand looked puzzled, "But we won and to the victor go the spoils."

The duke pointed an imperious finger at Sir Durand, "Sir Durand Malet of Graville-Sainte-Honorine, you will present yourself to my castle in Caen where you will be tried before a jury of your peers." He turned to Sir William, "Only the valiant efforts of the rest of your familia prevent me from exacting punishment here and now."

He wheeled his horse away and a shocked Sir Durand was left to face his brother, "I did nothing wrong!"

"You left my side and plundered the baggage train, that much is clear. Thanks to you a good squire is dead and but for Richard we might have lost Sir Eustace and the standard. The duke ordered us to chase the French king. You disobeyed him."

"I did not hear the order and so it does not count."

Sir Eustace shook his head, "I would not use that defence at your trial Sir Durand. You should have been with your brother. Do you see how few men remain? That is a testament to the duty of the dead."

Chapter 15

Sir William made a mistake. It was an understandable mistake for Sir William was an honourable man and the mistake was that he thought his brother was also honourable.

"We will bury our dead and then while Sir Eustace takes the rest of the mesne home, Robert and I will accompany you to Caen."

"But I did nothing wrong."

"Enough." We all dismounted and tethered our horses to broken spears. Odo went to find spades. The baggage train had been plundered but spades and picks were not considered loot. No one noticed that Sir Durand and Charles his squire had not dismounted. We should have noticed that they had not relinquished their hold on the tethered horses, laden with loot. He waited until all of us, Sir Robert included, were carrying the bodies of the fallen before he took off for the ford over the estuary. He was lucky and managed to get halfway across before anyone noticed and by then the tide was starting to turn. Richard and Robert were ordered to mount their horses and pursue the two but by the time they reached and untied their horses and rode back to the ford, it was too dangerous to cross.

Sir William waved me over, "Richard, you know the duke as well as any man. Ride to Caen and tell him that my brother has fled justice. He is now a fugitive. Tell the duke that whatever punishment he deems will be exacted. For my part, I shall disown and banish my brother from my lands." He shook his head, "I know not where the bad blood came from but I can see that his heart is bad. His demand for the blinding of your grandfather should have been warning enough."

"Yes, my lord, and I am sorry."

"You have nothing to be sorry for. You behaved as nobly as a knight in the battle and when you return to Graville-Sainte-Honorine we shall speak about your future. My brother's flight changes everything. I am just glad there is neither wife nor child. Go and be swift."

I had to wait for the turning of the tide. I rode hard and entered Caen just an hour behind the duke. I saw why Sir William had sent me for I was admitted directly as I was well known. The duke was in his hall when his steward told him of my arrival. He frowned, "I know that you have come from Sir William and your arrival so soon after me tells me that your news is urgent. Pray speak."

I did not know any soft way to say it and so I blurted out, "Sir Durand refused to attend Caen and he and his squire fled with their loot. I did not pass them and I am guessing he is seeking sanctuary with your enemies." The duke's eyes bored into me. "The Seigneur has disowned and banished him from the lands of de Caux."

He seemed satisfied and turned to his steward, "Make it known that Sir Durand Malet is banished from Normandy and returns on pain of death."

Bishop Odo shook his head, "Brother, a word of advice?" The duke nodded. "Such an edict tells our people that Sir Durand did not obey you. He is banished from his home. Let us leave it at that and if he is foolish enough to return then we can punish him then."

The duke pondered this and then nodded, "Tell Sir William that this stain on his family must be expunged by the Malets themselves."

I bowed, "I am sure that he will."

He smiled, "You must be exhausted. Stay for the night and dine with us. We have no Taillefer but you tell a good tale yourself and your words might rid me of my ill humour."

Just as Sir Durand's star not only fell but plummeted to earth so mine rose like a comet. I told my tales, they were well practised now and I amused the lords who were present. I saw what it was like to be Taillefer for even though I was a pale shadow of him and his skill, I was paid silver for my pains. I headed back to Graville-Sainte-Honorine with a full purse and a lighter heart. I did not have the spectre of Sir Durand. The manor and the castle would be a more pleasant place.

It was late in the evening when I reached the castle. As much as I wanted to go to my home and have a simple supper, I knew that I had to speak to Lord William. They had finished dining and his lordship and Lady Hesilia were about to retire when I entered. Sir William immediately asked for all but his wife and brother to leave. He nodded to Robert who poured me a goblet of wine. He waited until I had drunk a mouthful and then said, "Well?"

"The duke endorses your punishment, my lord, but he expects the family to punish your brother."

He looked relieved, "But that will be easier said than done. He will have fled to either France or Anjou."

Robert said, "Anjou."

"And how do you know, Robert?"

"He often spoke glowingly of Geoffrey Martel. He thought he had served Anjou better than the duke served Normandy. He thought that we should not have lost Maine."

Sir William shook his head, "And to think I did not know my brother." He looked at me, "And we shall seek him on the field of battle."

I could not hide the bitterness in my voice, "Then you had better look for him far from the front line. At Varaville he made no attempt to seek out the enemy. He was the reason that Hugh died. He was struck when your brother should have been guarding the standard."

"But you did your duty. I had a courser I was going to give my brother for he had expressed a wish to be married. The marriage will not be taking place and so the horse is my gift to you as weregeld."

Robert asked, "Weregeld?"

"Our ancestors, the Northmen knew what that was. It is payment for a debt of blood. It cannot recompense you for the loss of a grandfather but it will ease my conscience."

"Thank you, my lord."

As I headed back to my grange, I realised that I now had four horses. I could give Zeus to Baldwin and the smaller Blaze to Odo. I would still have Louis as a riding horse and my friends should benefit too. As I entered the grange, I realised that with my full purse from Caen, I could now afford to have a mail hauberk made. I was not yet a knight but I was getting closer to that goal.

I collected Geoffrey, for that was the name of the courser, from Alain the next day. Alain was delighted that the horse was going to me, "I named him Geoffrey in honour of your grandfather when I began to school him. When I discovered he was going to Sir Durand my heart sank but this is meant to be. Geoffrey is not just a good horse but a great one. He has heart and he has power but he is also gentle. Already he has sired four foals and all are healthy and strong."

Geoffrey was a grey with flecks of black on his hindquarters. We took to each other immediately and I rode him around the gyrus to cheers from the other pueros and men at arms. There were fewer of us now for some had fallen at Varaville but the battle and departure of Sir Durand had made us all closer. As I dismounted, I pointed to my stable, "And a gift for you, Baldwin, is Zeus and to you, Odo, Blaze."

"That is generous beyond words, Dick."

"Baldwin, we are shield brothers and my good fortune should be shared." They both nodded their gratitude. I beamed, "Does the day and the manor not seem brighter this day?"

We all laughed and Odo said, "Aye, for the shadow of Durand has been blown away. Perhaps Bruno might return."

I shook my head, "He has taken a different path. His shield brothers are different now and that is as it should be. When new pueros come it is we who will train them and they will become our shield brothers."

What the battle had not yielded was more weapons and so my three freemen had to use the old ones I had given them when I gave them their freedom. When I was not practising with the other pueros or working on the land then I gave them skills. If we ever went to war then they would serve with others in the levy, but I wanted them to have the best chance of survival and so I taught them all that I could. A week after my return I sought out Aimeri and put my purse on his workbench. I had removed a third of my fortune but the purse was still heavy.

"Aimeri, I would have a mail hauberk, coif and ventail."

He picked up the purse and after peering inside it, weighed it in his hand. "For this, you can have a good hauberk, not a great one such as a knight might use but then again, you are not yet a knight."

I smiled, "I just wish to be better protected. I have been lucky, thus far, but we know that cannot last and with a courser between my legs then knights will seek me out if only to take my horse from me."

"Good. You have your grandfather's wisdom and common sense."

The other change in my life, apart from the healthier atmosphere around the manor, was that I was asked by Sir William to take on the training of his two sons, Robert and Gilbert. Robert was almost eight and Gilbert six. They had been educated by Father Raymond but the seigneur had neglected their martial training. I had expected the instructors to be either Richard or Robert, the men at arms, but Sir William brought his sons to me as we practised in the gyrus.

His younger brother was with him. We all stopped and bowed, "It is time, Richard fitz Malet, for my sons to learn how to be warriors. We would have you begin the training."

"Me, my lord?"

He smiled, "Enough modesty, Richard. You have skills and everyone in the manor recognises them. Taillefer did a good job moulding you into a skilled warrior. More than that you are both gentle and kind. I would have my sons acquire your traits. My brother Robert will teach them how to be knights but it is you who will teach them skills with a sword." He turned to the boys who were each holding a small wooden sword. I wondered who had made them. "Boys, Richard is of our blood and you can trust him to do well by you. Heed his words and watch what he does."

"Yes, father," they dutifully chorused.

I waved Odo over, "Odo, you can help me." The two of us took them through how to stand and balance and how to move before they even raised their wooden swords. We had all learned those skills but Taillefer had elevated the skill so that it was almost like dancing. When we were satisfied, we taught them the basic blows and how to block them. For a week Odo and I were their opponents and then we let them spar with each other so that we could hone their skills. Surprisingly, it was the younger brother who proved to be the more natural swordsman as well as the most aggressive. I had expected it to be the other way around. From then on we curbed Gilbert's aggression a little and turned Robert's lack of it into an ability to block and deflect every blow that came his way. In that way, Robert learned to win when his younger brother tired. After two months their father and uncle came to watch them and were more than pleased with what they saw. Alain had begun to teach them to ride and this time it was Robert who was the more natural horseman.

Sir William led me away, "You have done well, Richard. My brother and I have given thought to your future. Would you be a squire and train to be a knight?"

I had often thought about this and I shook my head, "I like the life I lead amongst the pueros, my lord. I hope to be a knight one day but it will be because of some deed on the field of battle that will bring me my spurs."

"A good answer and one that is not unexpected. In that case, I would promote you to man at arms. Both Robert of Lisieux and Richard of Dreux commend you as does Captain Henri. It means you will be paid more but you will have duties at the castle." The men at arms stood watch on the walls when the mesne was not on campaign. It meant a weekly loss of sleep but I cared not for it was a step up.

"I am honoured, my lord."

Baldwin and Odo were both jealous and sad. We would no longer be riding to war together. I was surprised that neither of them had earned a promotion for we had lost men at arms in the battle of Varaville. Perhaps it was the gift of the horse and the making of my mail that had decided the seigneur.

The winter and the early spring passed quickly and I found little time to think of anything for when I was not training or teaching, I was standing guard. I learned to exist on less sleep than I thought possible.

It was February when my hauberk, coif and ventail were ready. Baldwin and Odo came with me to help me dress. I handed my leather brigandine to Baldwin. We had already agreed that he could have it. They first placed my coif over my arming cap. The ventail hung down. It felt heavy upon my head. Then they pulled the hauberk over my head, I do not know what I was expecting but it weighed more than I had thought it would. I tried to lift my arms and found them slow to respond. My grandfather's had fewer links and was lighter. This was a well-made hauberk.

Aimeri nodded, "Aye, Richard, it is hard. Wear this every day and become accustomed to it. Make it as a skin and over time you will grow used to it. Now don the helmet, baldric and sword." He showed me how to fasten the thongs on the ventail. Only my eyes were unprotected but I felt as though I was trapped in the mail.

Aimeri smiled at my obvious discomfort, "Aye, every warrior feels that way, Richard. You think you are bound by the hauberk. Well, you are but your skin is now mailed and you are like a dragon. There are weak spots, you, better than any, know where they are but you have more chance of surviving a battle thus dressed. Even if a bolt should pierce the links, it will be slowed and then stopped by your gambeson. A blade might tear the links but that is unlikely. So long as you care for it then all will be well."

Odo asked, "Care for it?"

"I have oiled it and there is the hessian sack that it is kept in. Rain is an enemy. After it has been wet then put sand in the sack along with the mail and shake it. When it is dry remove the sand and oil it once more. Do not worry, your tunic will also protect the mail but take my advice and your hauberk will last, perhaps, ten years."

I saw a shadow in his eyes and I said, "And if I outlive my hauberk then I will be lucky."

He nodded, "Men at arms have a shorter life than knights. A knight can be taken and ransomed but a man at arms is, more often than not, killed."

Baldwin nodded, "It is as my father said, Dick. You have been blessed and cursed with this promotion."

Just then his apprentice, Hrolfr, used the tongs to lift a horseshoe from the fire. He dropped it and Aimeri used his own tongs to pick it up. He plunged it into the water and then rounded on the unfortunate boy, "You clumsy lump! How many times do I have to tell you that a hot piece of metal, even though not afire can begin one?"

"Sorry, master."

"If you are going to drop it then do so in the water." He shook his head, "I use fire every day but it is an enemy as well as a friend. There is so much wood in here that if a fire started then much of my workshop would be ruined, not to mention my livelihood."

I felt sorry for Hrolfr as I had not known, until then, that a hot piece of metal, even a horseshoe, could be so dangerous.

I did as I was advised and apart from sleep, I wore the hauberk every day. I did not wear the coif and ventail when eating but other than that I had a second skin. Aimeri was right and a month after I was given it, I found it easier to bear and to wear. Geoffrey also bore my weight easily and I knew that Louis and Zeus would have struggled to carry me into battle. I would be able to ride Louis when mailed but not fight from his back. I liked that the hauberk was split so that it covered my thighs and afforded them protection. I had needed to make a new saddle already and the wearing of the mail confirmed it. I had one made for me as I now had an income.

One other effect of my promotion that was unexpected, was that the young women in the manor began to flirt with me. I know that as I was related to the Seigneur I was seen as a good prospect for one of the villagers' or farmers' daughters to marry but the mail and the courser seemed to act as pollen in a flower. When we rode through the manor, I saw their admiring glances. It was Baldwin and Odo who pointed out what soon became obvious.

We had ridden to the beach where we exercised our horses on the sand and in the sea. Alain assured us that it made for stronger horses and the animals seemed to like the sea. It made work for us as we had to groom the sand from them. As we were cleaning the worst of the sand from their coats Baldwin said, "Did you see, Odo, the admiring glances the new man at arms received from the young women when we passed through the village?"

Geoffrey needed much grooming and I was distracted, "What man at arms?"

"You, you goose!"

"I thought their smiles and waves were for you."

Baldwin laughed, "Whilst it is obvious that I am the better looking, Dick, you are the one with the fine horse, the mail and the Malet name. Should you wish to bed any of them then they are there ready and waiting to be plucked."

I stopped what I was doing, "My mother was plucked and then discarded. I will take no woman until she is my wife."

I had stunned them both, "But it is usual for a young man to spill his seed."

"Odo, do as you will, I will not. My mother died too young and that was because she was taken by my father. This conversation is at an end and we will not speak of it again."

From then on whenever we passed through villages and young women smiled and waved, I kept a steely and stoic look on my face. Baldwin told me that the girls thought I was a cold one. Some even began to whisper that I preferred men but at least I was spared their attentions. I had already made up my mind that I would not wed until either I had my spurs or I was a rich man like Taillefer. Then I would seek and court a young woman. I know the others thought it strange but a man cannot change his character.

We heard news from England, as we settled into our life in the garrison of Graville-Sainte-Honorine, that the Atheling, Edward, had mysteriously died in England. Foul play was suspected but there was no proof. The last heir to the throne was dead. As King Edward had named Duke William as his heir, it would be just a matter of time.

Chapter 16

Tillières-sur-Avre 1058

This time Duke William did not visit with us for a council of war, he sent Sir Ambrose to call upon Sir William and for us to muster for our forty days of service. We were going to war. My three men asked if they were to come. It was spring and I shook my head, "The grange needs work and with most of the men gone, Sir William will need his freemen to defend his land in case there is danger."

The three loved to be called freemen. It was highly unlikely that with Duke William's army in the field, anyone would be foolish enough to raid his lands but my answer gave the three of them purpose. We were to muster at Falaise. Since our victory, some of the allies of the French King and Count Geoffrey Martel had left the alliance to side with Duke William. The Bishop of Sees was the most important of them. Guy, Count of Ponthieu, had also sworn fealty to Duke William. We would not be using his men on this campaign but it was good to know we had them as reinforcements. Sir Ambrose told me that the duke intended to retake Tillières-sur-Avre and Thimert. Both had been lost to the French king and I think it was Duke William flexing his muscles. In England, Harold Godwinson was busy claiming victory over the Welsh and our duke wanted the English to know that Normans were more than capable of defeating not the wild Welsh but the formidable French.

Not all of the dead men at arms had been replaced and there were just nine of us who followed Sir William and the knights. I had thought to suggest to Sir William to make Baldwin a man at arms but it seemed presumptuous. As far as I was concerned, he was ready. After all, Bruno and I were men at arms and Zeus could easily carry him. He had no mail but I knew that he could wear his father's old hauberk. He led, instead, the pueros. At one time he would have been honoured but he saw me riding behind his father and he was, naturally, envious.

I learned all that I could from the others as I ate with them in the warrior hall. I learned that while Tillières was a strong castle, Thimert was a fortress. We would be besieging and that meant our warhorses would not be needed.

Robert of Lisieux had been at the siege of Brionne and understood such matters, "Duke William has, to my knowledge, prosecuted three sieges. He has not always reduced the walls and induced a surrender but he has always won. Sometimes it can take months."

Richard of Dreux had recently married and his wife was pregnant, "And I shall not see my son born."

Robert laughed, "How do you know it will be a boy?"

"I know these things. You are a bachelor and the ways of women are a mystery to you."

Robert shook his head and turned to me, "Married half a year and already he is an expert."

"So Robert, what is it that we will do at the siege if we are not to use our warhorses?"

"Oh, we shall ride. Each day men will ride the country to take what we can from the people and to ensure that no force comes to relieve the siege. When the archers and the men with the war machines have either reduced the walls or made a breach in the gate then we will be the ones who will take the castle."

"Archers? What can they do against stone walls?"

"Against walls? Nothing but there are wooden buildings and they often have thatched roofs. They can set fire to a building. With luck, the wind can spread the fire. If the fighting platform burns then the walls are weakened and they cannot defend themselves. Of course, the defenders will know when we use fire arrows for they will see the fires where the men ignite them and they can watch the flights of the arrows. Often, they will use water to douse the flames. It is like a game of cat and mouse. We try one trick and they try to counter it."

"Then why does Duke William want to retake the castle if it is so hard and may cost men?"

"Because they are barriers to an army trying to enter Normandy. When we take them and take them we will, then he will garrison them and improve the defences."

We left our home and rode with coifs around our necks and our helmets hanging from our cantles. We would be safe from any attack until well beyond Falaise. Our victory at Varaville had destroyed more than the baggage train and rearguard, it had broken their alliance and taken away the appetite for war. It was rumoured that both leaders were not well men. We learned the news at Falaise when we were reunited with the Lord of Mortemer, William de Warenne. This time we did get to see Bruno and I saw a real change in my oldest friend. He rode a fine warhorse which, so he told us, he had taken from a knight he had defeated at Varaville. He had also taken the knight's mail and sword. He had been lucky but I took comfort from the fact that my hauberk had been made for me. He was unsurprised by the cowardice of Sir Durand.

"I saw him, you know, towards the end of that battle. He and his squire were robbing the baggage train. As far as I am aware, the only men he and his squire slew were the unarmed drivers of the wagons. Good riddance."

I asked, "I wonder where he went?"

It was Robert who supplied an answer, "There are many rulers out there who would like the brother of a close friend of Duke William in their court. Durand may not be a warrior but he has knowledge and to the Count of Aquitaine or Anjou, that is worth more than having a sword. Never fear he will be punished for his misdeeds." Robert was a wise man.

I felt sorry for Odo and Baldwin. We did not look down on them and involved them in all our conversations but they were ordered around by every knight in the mesne. We were men at arms and looked after our own horses and equipment. The pueros were called upon to help the squires.

We took wagons laden with timber and rope to Tillières. The French knew we were coming and would, no doubt, try to dislodge us. We were confident. We had fought the French twice and both times Duke William had shown that he knew how to beat them.

I was a man at arms now and enjoyed a somewhat crowded tent. We erected our own while the knights sat and watched their squires put up theirs. The camp was protected by stakes. We had with us both archers and crossbowmen and they were put to use. Some of the border knights had also brought spearmen and slingers. We had workers enough. Captain Henri went to speak to Sir William to discover our duties. As he did, I surveyed the castle. It did not look particularly strong and still had a wooden donjon but the walls were made of stone topped with wood. Beyond the walls, I could see the buildings inside the curtain wall. There were plenty of them and most had a thatched roof. The wall bristled with men but I knew that less than half of them would be warriors. The problem would be to get over the ditch and breach the walls. The stone throwers were being assembled as was the ram. However, the defenders had raised the bridge which spanned the ditch and that would have to be filled. Such a task was not one for knights but mailed men at arms. I did not relish that thought.

When Captain Henri returned, he smiled, "The duke wants us to scout the land towards Thimert, tomorrow. He anticipates a swift reduction of this one and then we will try to take the more formidable one that is Thimert."

Rollo asked, "And we are allowed to raid?"

"We are."

It made us all smile. There would be profit in the ride and we would not have to labour at the siege lines. The duke was rewarding us for Varaville.

I sought out the pueros and found them labouring to embed stakes around our camp. Baldwin shook his head ruefully, "The sooner I become a man at arms the better. I shall need to do some great deed like Dick here and then I will not have bloodied hands from digging holes and sharpening stakes."

I pointed at the walls, "And here is the perfect opportunity for you to do so. This is much like Gorron and remember how well we all did there."

"Aye, perhaps, and we have more chance of scaling the walls than you, wearing mail." Odo rammed the stake into the hole he had just dug.

Baldwin swung the wooden hammer to drive the stake into the ground, "While you, Richard fitz Malet, will have to breach the walls." He nodded towards the walls. Behind them, we saw a tendril of smoke. "They will heat oil or water to give you a warm welcome. I do not envy you that."

Sir Eustace strolled over, "Enough talk and more labour. When you have finished the stakes, you need to fetch food and you, Richard fitz Malet, need to prepare for tomorrow's endeavours."

"Yes, Sir Eustace." As I headed back to our tent I reflected that Sir Eustace had also benefitted from Sir Durand's departure. He was now Sir William's second in command. Sir Robert was happy to defer to the knight whereas Sir Durand had refused to obey any request, however simple. Life was better without the spectre of the bad brother.

The horn for us to stand to came before prime. The duke was not taking any chances and did not wish a sortie to attack us while we slept. The night guards, Bruno and the men at arms of Mortemer, had hot food ready. I had stood a night watch and knew that boredom could be alleviated by cooking.

He grinned at me, "Once again, Dick, you have the luck. While we watch the walls and wait for the war machines to be built, you get to gad about the land making yourself rich."

I laughed, "As you are the man who took a knight's ransom, I do not think you need to be envious of whatever coins I can grasp."

He shrugged, "Perhaps you are right. I hope the duke begins to rain arrows on this castle sooner rather than later. I hate to be idle."

As I ate the fried ham on the slightly stale bread we had brought with us, I nodded, "We are to scout out Thimert and that bodes well for it means he thinks he can take this one quickly."

"Come, Richard, it will be daylight soon and I would be on the road and seeking coins."

"Aye, Captain."

I always rode just behind Robert of Lisieux and Richard of Dreux. With the captain at the fore that meant I was normally at the rear. The two men of arms whom I knew the best were always the rearguard. As they had shown on the road to Gorron, they were solid and dependable.

The roads in this part of eastern Normandy were narrow and twisting. Fields were lined with trees and hedgerows and the settlements were all small. Tillières and Thimert were the only castles and had the largest villages. We rode ready for trouble but not expecting it. As we left the camp, Captain Henri said, "We will ride to Thimert first and then raid on the way back."

Cantering down the road I said, "Robert, why do we not raid on the way there?"

"We would have to carry or lead whatever we took and there might be men waiting to ambush us on the way back. This way they will just be relieved that we have passed by and besides, our commission is to see the castle at Thimert. It was part of the duchy until King Henry took it. The duke would know of any improvements that they have made."

The people who lived in the area fled at the sound of our hooves. These were the borderlands and caution was always advisable. As we passed through them, we noted where there were houses that looked promising. Any that had defences of any kind, attractive though they might be we would avoid. Robert told me that we would take no risks. An animal we could kill and take back for food was treasure. Horses grazing in fields would also be worth taking. The fortress was less than twenty miles away and we reined in a mile from its walls. It was a formidable place. It had a ditch and a rampart topped with stone and a wooden palisade. The donjon must have been built on a natural rock outcrop and it stood proud of the walls. That was all we could see. The town also had a wall that lay just half a mile from us. Whilst not a substantial barrier it would slow down an attacker. While Captain Henri studied the walls, we watched for anyone taking undue interest in us. I saw that the gatehouse was new and was made of good stone. There were two towers and what looked to me like a small donjon.

It was Rollo who spied the column of riders leaving the castle heading for the town. There were sixteen of them and they were coming to shift us. I could see that at least half of them were pueros. I wondered why they had sent so few and when Captain Henri did not flee but said to fasten our ventails, I wondered what I was missing.

As I fastened it, I turned to Robert who anticipated my question, "They have not seen our full numbers and think we are pueros or light horsemen." He nodded at the four men at arms who had taken the opportunity to empty their bladders. "We will discourage them and then ride back at our leisure."

I fastened the ventail and slipped the mitts Aimeri had added over my hands. The palms were without protection but would help me to feel both the lance and the reins. I did not couch the weapon. None of the others had.

"Form two lines. Richard, behind me."

"Aye, Captain Henri."

He was both protecting me and also ensuring that the best of our men faced the enemy. With five in the front rank and just four in the second, we filled the road. We could see, from our vantage point, all the way to the walls but the road dipped just after the town and then rose to a slight rise fifty paces from us. The sixteen men disappeared and Captain Henri said, "We meet them at the charge. Follow me and keep together."

Rollo and Roger flanked me. Our boots touched. They had done this before and they waited until there was a horse's length between us and the others. We rode easily down the slight slope. It saved energy and helped us to stay together. On the slight slope on the other side, we dug in our heels. I had to rein in Geoffrey for the Seigneur had given me a good horse. With my helmet, arming cap and coif, all that I could hear was the jingle of our mail and the clop of our hooves. When Captain Henri and the others lowered their lances, we four did the same. I was expecting to see the enemy but I still had a shock when the four men rode over the brow of the rise. I saw their pennants first and Captain Henri shouted, "Charge!" for their spears and lances were yet to be lowered. Thinking about it later on, when the heat of battle was no longer on me, I realised that they had expected us to flee.

With five lowered lances against four men whose lances were still raised, there was only one outcome. The leader was a knight. I spied his spurs as he was tumbled from his saddle by Captain Henri. The five ploughed through and Rollo shouted, "Come with me to the right."

I wheeled Geoffrey and followed Rollo. Some of the pueros had moved off the road to avoid the spears and lances of our five men. Rollo had made the right decision and we both speared, in the side, two pueros whose shields were held on their left. They fell to the ground. I did not know it but another three had been felled and with more than half their number hurt or dead, they turned and fled.

"Take the horses if you can. We have no time to take mail and weapons." I saw that just three men looked to be dead. The others lay clutching wounds or were trying to crawl or ride to safety. I reached down and grabbed the reins of the pueros I had slain. This was war but I wished that I had only wounded him.

We headed back down the road with six horses. Captain Henri had managed to take the knight's horse. It was clearly not a war horse but was a good one, nonetheless. The horses meant that we could take more loot on the way back. We chose just four large farmhouses to raid. As we clattered into each of their yards, they fled. Nine mailed men were too many to fight. We dismounted and I fastened my lance to my new horse. I would not need it again. We burst into the house and took what we could. Rollo found a chest hidden beneath the floor while I found a good ham and a round of cheese. Robert had been outside and I heard a squeal as he killed a pig. It took three of us to put it across the back of the knight's horse. We emptied the other three houses that we had selected and with laden, weary horses, rode back into our camp. While Captain Henri went to report, we butchered the pig and made four large joints. We had enough fires to cook all four. We put the heart, liver and kidneys on skewers to cook for us. We would eat them while we waited for the four joints to cook. We had also liberated enough wine to ensure that we would all sleep soundly.

Both the Seigneur and the duke were pleased with our report. It confirmed that while the fortress was stronger than it had been, there was nothing to slow us when we reduced Tillières. We would not need to ride the next day.

As we ate, Baldwin and Odo joined us. We shared some of the pork with them. The cheese and the ham I would keep for when rations were in short supply. Odo, the fat dripping from his mouth, pointed, "The onagers are finished. They have tested them already and tomorrow they will try the range. The archers have been making the fire arrows."

"And what will the pueros be doing?"

Baldwin wiped his mouth with the arm of his tunic, "We are to guard the onager built by our men."

I nodded, "You know that means helping to load it and shift it back into position?"

Odo looked disappointed, "I thought we would be there to fight the enemy if they sortied."

"The duke has brought a mighty army. The last thing the enemy will do will be to attack in daylight. They would have to open their gates and they would be slaughtered. If the enemy attack it will be at night."

"What makes you so wise all of a sudden?"

I nodded at Richard and Robert, "When I ride with them, I ask questions and I listen."

When the stone throwers began to hurl their stones at the walls, I was disappointed. The first stone fell short and rolled into the ditch, to the jeers of the defenders. The engineers were clearly angered and their second ball sailed over the walls to crash either into the ground or we knew not where for there was no crash. Their third was more successful and managed to hit the timbers of the wall and there was a crack but that was all.

Robert of Lisieux turned to me and shook his head, "This will be a long day."

He was proved right. The rate at which they could send their stones was slower than I had expected and the effect was not as dramatic as any of us hoped. Sir Eustace came at noon to speak to both the engineers and the archers. A fire was lit and the archers prepared to send their fire arrows at the walls and the straw of the roofs. I anticipated more progress.

The archers lit the rags at the end of the arrows and released as quickly as they could. They were hurriedly sent and had mixed results. Some fell into the earth embankment and some hit stone. The ones that hit the wood were watched by the defenders and pails of water doused the flames before they could take effect. By the time the archers had exhausted their supply of arrows and the stone throwers had to be repaired, we had little to show for a day's assault.

Odo joked as we retired to our camp, "You could have saved the coin you spent on the hauberk for I cannot see you needing it."

I know not how the mind works. Perhaps Father Raymond does but Odo's words brought a memory of Aimeri's workshop and his berating of Hrolfr. I hurried to the tent of the Seigneur who was speaking with the duke, the bishop and the Lord of Mortemer, Sir William de Warenne. As much as I wanted to speak, I knew that I dare not interrupt them. I stepped nervously from foot to foot. Sir William de Warenne saw my dance and laughed, "Either Richard fitz Malet needs to make water or he has something important to say."

My half-brother waved me forward, "Come, Richard, speak."

"It is just I know a way that we can set fire to the walls and prevent the defenders from dousing the flames."

Bishop Odo smiled, "Unless this is some satanic magic, I would hear it."

"If we have a furnace such as smiths used then the arrowheads could be heated. The enemy would not know they were hot and when they strike hay or wood then they will burn. It will also allow the archers to aim a little better and to make more considered pulls."

I saw their faces as they took in my words. The duke said, "Fetch me Renaud, the master archer."

He was summoned and my half-brother said, "Whence came this idea, Richard?"

"I saw Aimeri our weaponsmith panic when a piece of hot metal struck the ground. If he was afraid then I knew hot metal and wood were a dangerous combination."

The grizzled and slightly lopsided archer came and knuckled his head, "My lord?"

"Tell him your idea, Richard."

I did so and I was even more nervous than the first time as I expected to be ridiculed by the archer who would see some flaw that I had not. He beamed when I had finished, "That would work, my lord, and we would not risk either burnt hand or wrecked bow. We will be saved the time of making the arrows."

The duke nodded, "Then build the furnace this night and have the men cook some meat upon it. Let the defenders think we feed the archers."

"Yes, my lord." Patting me on the back as he left, the archer ran to obey the orders.

"Once again, Richard fitz Malet, you have shown that the Malets are useful to their duke." He turned to the Seigneur, "Or some of them at least." Sir William said nothing but I could see that he was not happy about the stain on the family name.

I could not get away for some time as I was questioned about how I came up with the idea. By the time I reached the camp then all my shield brothers had heard that I had spoken to the duke. I explained my idea and they wanted all of the details.

The smell of cooking meat filled the camp as the archers obeyed their instructions. The smell must have drifted over to the town and I knew that they would be rationed. The smell of cooking meat was a powerful weapon.

The next day the stone throwers began to hurl their stones and the archers gathered in small groups. Renaud and his twenty best archers were first. They heated their arrows and then quickly went to their marks and began to loose. Odo stood to watch them. He had improved as an archer but was not yet considered good enough to join them full time. The defenders jeered them as the arrows struck the hay of the roof of a building we could see and slammed into the walls. The next twenty came and it was only when smoke began to rise from the wood walls and the roof burst into flames that they realised what was happening. By then it was too late as a relay of archers sent arrow after arrow into the town and the walls. The water the defenders used was too little and too late for the fire had taken a fierce hold. Once the burning thatch fell into the buildings then the daub and wattle ignited and we saw flames rising in the sky. The already weakened walls were soon breached by stones sent by the war machines. Their engineers had seen the success of the archers and it spurred them to greater endeavours.

As darkness fell, the town and the buildings in the bailey burned, fanned by a favourable wind. We were told to be ready for a dawn assault. By then, it was hoped, the flames would have died. It would be hot work but that was a minor consideration.

The men at arms and knights gathered along the edge of the ditch. Behind us were the pueros. Sir William would lead us and we were to attack one hundred paces from the gate. Bishop Odo and his men had the honour of attacking the gate. We waited in the dark behind a line of pueros. We could see no one on the walls but that was because, in many places, the fighting platform had collapsed, but we knew that there would be defenders. I gripped my shield. I would be fighting in mail and, for the first time, on foot. I was next to Rollo and Robert. I did not want to let either of them down.

The defenders had to have known that we were going to attack and would be waiting for us but the horn from the duke ended any doubt. We stepped forward. The pueros raced to the ditch and laid the ladders and wooden boards that they carried across them. Then they knelt in pairs to hold them while we crossed. I was lucky and it was a board that I crossed. I did not have to peer down to look for the rungs of a ladder in the dark. I held my shield above my head as I crossed and my caution was rewarded when a shower of arrows and stones descended on us. They had been sent almost blindly for there were gaps in the walls and only part of the fighting platform remained.

Once we had crossed, Captain Henri reformed us and with shields held before us and drawing swords, we headed for the tumble of stones that marked the breach. The knights of de Caux were heading for another breach and they would be followed by their squires. The pueros followed us. The huge sledgehammer that swung towards Captain Henri's head would have caught out many men for the wielder was hidden behind the wall and simply swung his hammer at head height. Captain Henri had his shield ready but, even so, the blow was so hard that he was driven back. Robert darted forward and swung his sword to hack into the middle of the blacksmith. Our swords did have a tip but they were, in essence, slashing weapons. With two edges they could tear through anything but mail and if we fought a mailed man then we used them like an iron bar. These were townsfolk and pueros. The men at arms and knights would be at the donjon. The men we fought were defending their town and their walls. The Norman occupants would have been evicted when the French took over and these had been given their houses. It explained their ferocious fight.

Robert's attack was followed up by Rollo and me racing to the right. It was not quite dawn and in the darkness of the shadow of the walls, we fought men who materialised from nowhere. You needed quick reactions, a good shield and mail that would hold. I had all three. The wood axe that came for my chest was blocked by the metal boss on my shield. The man had used the wood axe two handed and that left him open to a strike from my sword. It bit into his side and blood spurted. We had made an enclave within the walls and as the pueros came to back us, Captain Henri waved his sword to signal an advance.

We had open and clear ground once we had passed the ramparts and palisade. The defenders we had not slain were fleeing for the inner bailey and the donjon. The problem the defenders of Tillières had was that they were being attacked on all sides. As the sun peered over the east wall to illuminate the small outer bailey, I saw that Norman knights and men at arms were hacking down and slaying knots of men. They began to surrender and we advanced to the last defence, the wall around the donjon. The leader of the French garrison kept his gates closed and as the last defender in the outer bailey surrendered so Duke William ordered a halt. There was little point in risking bolts killing knights.

"Pueros, take the prisoners away and bind them." He waited until they had gone and then, with his oathsworn holding shields before them, called upon the garrison to surrender the castle. "I am Duke William and I call upon the garrison to surrender. Do so and those not of noble birth will be released and the nobles ransomed." There was silence from the walls. "You have until terce to make your mind up. That will give us enough time to build a small fire and heat up our arrows. Your wooden donjon will burn and you will die." He shrugged in an exaggerated fashion so that the defenders could see. "We will lose ransom but Tillières will be Norman once more."

Even before the archers had brought the firewood, kindling and arrows, the garrison surrendered. The attack on their outer wall was enough.

Chapter 17

Thimert 1058

We stayed at Tillières for a month. It was enough time to rebuild the defences we had destroyed and for a garrison to be installed. Duke William had another fortress back in his hands. We headed for Thimert and, as I knew, a much harder siege. We surrounded the walls and this time the stone throwers were put into operation far quicker than at Tillières. This, however, would be a harder nut to crack for the walls had more stone than at Tillières and the stone gatehouse was like a small donjon. The fire arrows would be wasted and so the duke began to batter the walls. We were also told that our service was almost over. The seigneur informed us that the duke had asked for sixty days rather than forty and he had agreed. Even so, we would not be able to reduce the walls in that time and Duke William had sent for other vassals, including the Bishop of Sees and the Count of Ponthieu. When they arrived, we would go home.

Until then, the knights and men at arms of de Caux, along with the pueros were given licence to raid eastwards. Tillières and Thimert, when we took it, would be the border with France and its ally Blois. Duke William wanted the will of the French and the men of Blois to be weakened.

This time it was my half-brother who led the chevauchée. Chartres was the most important town in the area and we clearly did not have enough men to attack it. The walls were stronger than Thimert. Instead, we raided the lands to the north and east of Chartres, the lands of the Beauce. Our task was two-fold. The men left to weaken Thimert's walls needed to be fed and we took from every farm, village and hamlet within twenty miles of Thimert. While the food we took went to the besiegers, the weapons, horses, and treasure went to us. Sir William was a wise man and he allowed us to keep what we took. It encouraged us to be thorough and by the end of the month, the lands between Thimert and Chartres had been pillaged of anything that was worthwhile taking. The farmers had fled either to France or to Chartres. The extra mouths would need feeding and our enemies would suffer.

When we saw the standards of Ponthieu and Sees in our camp, we knew that our service was over. Bruno had already left, for the Lord of Mortemer and had been relieved two weeks before us. With extra, heavily laden horses we began the journey back to our home.

There was a change in my life after Tillières. I had impressed everyone and especially my half-brother. The cold and distant man had warmed to me. I remembered growing up before my grandfather died when I had felt closer to my grandfather's dogs than my blood relatives. The departure of Sir Durand had changed all that and as we rode home, I was frequently summoned to ride with my two half-brothers.

"You know, Richard, attacking the walls of Tillières and seeing Thimert has made me realise that my castle is too small and insubstantial. I need stone walls and a castle that will guard the river. When we reach de Caux we will begin to look for a site. Robert and I would like you to come with us to find my new stronghold."

"Me, my lord? I am honoured but why?"

"Because you have shown that your Malet blood makes you one of us and the mind you have for war shows that you are a warrior. Everyone speaks well of you."

I was flattered, "I will be honoured, my lord."

"Perhaps the departure of Durand helped me to see more clearly what was before me."

Once back at Graville-Sainte-Honorine I threw myself into making my grange as productive as I could. I now had another four horses. While one was a horse I could use for war, the other three were valuable as animals for the plough and for my three men to ride when we needed them to. I also gave them the weapons I had taken. The purses I had taken enabled me to pay them more. They all seemed happy about that but Carl, in particular, was effusive in his thanks. When he came to ask my permission to wed, I was taken aback.

"Of course, but I did not know that you were courting."

"Master, you spend longer away from the grange than within it. We help the others in the manor and that brings us into contact with their families. Heloise likes me but as you are related to the seigneur, her father, Petr, thought I should ask permission."

"Of course, but where shall you live?"

He smiled, "Master, we know the grange better than any." He meant, of course, me but was too polite to say so. "We have found three plots of land that are not fertile enough to grow things. We thought to build a house each, with your permission, of course. Your grandfather's dwelling is too small and too far from the grange. This way the three of us could be closer to our work and have our own places. We would build them, my lord. There is timber enough for the frame and we each know how to make cob."

"Cob?"

"Straw and lime, mixed with earth are both fireproof and strong and all three are plentiful around here. We can build a home in six days and it will be ready for occupation in two weeks."

I laughed, "You seem to have it all in hand. Of course, you have my permission and I will give a dowry when you wed."

"You need not, master, for you are more than generous."

"I know that I need not, Carl. It is my choice."

And so I spent the next year building. At first, it was on my grange and then, when we had found the site, the castle that my half-brother would occupy. The seigneur would live in the new, larger castle and Sir Robert would have Graville-Sainte-Honorine. I would be his captain of men at arms. It was one of the best times of my life. The only better times had been either when I was with Taillefer or before the blinding of my grandfather. Not only did we build three very small dwellings for my men and Carl's wife, but also two extra rooms for the grange as well as a larger stable and a barn. When Heloise and Carl were married, I paid her to be my housekeeper and cook. I now had an income from Sir William and we produced more than we ate. Carl and Heloise sold it at Lillebonne market. I knew that the next time we raided I needed either animals or coin to buy animals. I wanted a sow so that we could rear our own pigs. Galmr had found some fowl that had fled their owners and we now had birds who could lay eggs. A pig and a milk cow would make all well. The wild apples that we grew gave us cider and the mash would feed the pigs too. Life was good and had changed dramatically since the departure of Sir Durand.

A month after we returned, we heard that Thimert had fallen and was garrisoned by Normans. Two months later Thimert itself was besieged by King Henry.

The hardest work I did was labouring on the new castle. Only the knights were exempt although Sir Eustace and Sir Robert did lend a hand through choice. Sir William had hired Guillaume of Rouen as the master mason. He and the seigneur devised the plan and Guillaume oversaw it. Sir William paid for extra labourers. Work was in short supply during winter and the men were glad of pay. They would earn coins digging foundations and infilling walls.

We had a crane erected and that, once the foundations were dug, speeded matters up. We worked on the donjon first. Sir William wanted a square one such as they had at Brionne. It was simpler to construct than a round one although not as effective defensively. As he had planned a strong curtain wall as well as a chemise wall to protect the base as well as a gatehouse similar to Thimert, it did not seem a problem. Once the huge stones for the foundations were laid then Guillaume had us make an inner wall. In many ways, the lifting into place of the huge blocks was relatively easy. Guillaume or one of his assistants would guide the block into place. The better blocks were for the outside. There they would be seen. The interior stone was of lesser quality as it would be plastered when finished. Once we had a pair of walls the height of a man, the hard work of packing the gap with infill began. We used wheelbarrows to carry the stones up a plank and tip them in. I think Sir Robert and Sir Eustace joined us as they saw the benefits of pushing the barrow. It hardened muscles and we were all stronger for it. Once we had the first floor built then it was a tricky task for the mason to fit the beams to the corbels. We were assigned the less technical job of building the chemise wall. The stones there needed not to be as fine as the donjon and they were not as heavy. More importantly, once it was built then the donjon would have protection for its vulnerable base.

I think it helped us to become closer as we toiled together. We worked no matter what the weather. Sir William ensured we were well fed and his huntsmen kept us well supplied with game. My three labourers joined us from November until March and they reaped the financial rewards of being paid and fed for their work. They also came to know others alongside whom they would be fighting should the whole of the manor be called upon to do so. Duke William often used the muster, called arrière-ban, and my three men were quite happy at the prospect.

By the time summer came, Heloise was with child and my three men were working my fields. The donjon was almost finished and Sir William released his men at arms so that we could begin training again. It was clear that Harold Godwinson would not let Duke William simply take over the kingdom and so Bishop Odo began to build ships. They took time and an invasion was not yet necessary but Duke William was a good planner. We had boys to train to become pueros and pueros to train to become men at arms. Both Odo and Baldwin came into the latter category although it became increasingly clear that Odo would be an archer. Captain Henri singled out Odo as being the one who would command the slingers and archers. Working on the castle had made my friend far stronger and he could now easily pull a bow. His natural eye made him perfect for the task and he was the best archer in the demesne. Some of the older men had died. It was not just war that caused the deaths of warriors. Old age and disease claimed men and Odo, whilst still young, had shown that he knew how to command. We returned to Graville-Sainte-Honorine and a more systematic training of young Robert and Gilbert Malet took place. We had trained them while building the castle but more often than not we were called upon to haul on ropes or to take wheelbarrows and shift stones.

It was while we were training that Bruno rode in. He was on his way to the new castle and the seigneur but took the opportunity to speak with us. He was delighted with the news about Odo and Baldwin. Indeed he was so busy congratulating them that he almost forgot his news. When I asked him what brought him hence, he slapped his forehead, "I am remiss. I am here to tell Sir William that the duke's enemies, King Henry and Count Geoffrey are both dead. Their lands are ruled by infants."

Odo frowned, "What does that mean?"

"It means, captain of slingers, that we have no threat coming from the north and the south. If Duke William can secure Brittany, then England becomes our next target."

"How do you know this, Bruno? I do not doubt your words but…"

"The Lord of Mortemer is closely related to the duke who often visits Mortemer. His men tell us."

"Brittany is both a hard country to take and has good horsemen. Some are the equal of our men."

"I know, Baldwin, but Duke William is cunning. We will only attack when the duke thinks he can win. Anyway, I had better deliver my news to Sir William. I will call in on the way back if I have gleaned any other information."

The news that there might be a war with either England or Brittany made us increase the time that we trained. When Baldwin and the other six pueros joined us as men at arms, we had much to do. Pueros, as I well knew, rode in looser formations. Baldwin and the others needed to train to ride boot to boot. His father had purchased him a better horse. It was not the equal of Geoffrey but, then again, he had been intended for a knight, Sir Durand. Baldwin had the money for mail but it was not as much as I had acquired. My grandfather was to thank for that. Even so, Baldwin had mail, a ventail, a coif and a helmet. The mail links on his hauberk were not as tight as mine but he could go to war. His mother made him a tunic to wear over the mail.

209

As I was now riding in the mesne of Sir Robert, like the other men at arms we wore his mark. He had a pennon on his lance and we each wore a strip of material on our tunics. When we went to war, we would follow him. Captain Henri and the other more senior men at arms would ride with the seigneur. Sir Robert had no knights as yet and just half a dozen men at arms. I was the most senior. It did not seem that long ago since I had been a pueros and given all the menial tasks. Now I was in command of five men at arms and half a dozen pueros. We were the younger ones but I quite liked that.

I was not privy to the finances of the manor, there was no reason why I should have been, but it seemed to me that Sir William had come into money for a castle was expensive to build and needed Duke William's permission. The Seigneur never baulked when the mason asked for more money. The stones that were used were the finest stone that could be bought. It was the same stone as had been used at Falaise. Expensive tapestries hung from the walls of the new hall. However, it was more than that. Crossbows were bought and men were trained to use them. He hired four full-time crossbowmen. He paid for thousands of arrows. He bought horses. He and Sir Robert now both had two good war horses. Baldwin was given Sir Robert's older one. He paid for more pueros and both Captain Henri and I were asked to find as many men at arms as we could. Helmets and coifs were commissioned and it was clear to me that we would be going to war and that the seigneur had acquired chests of gold. The manor did not produce much more. My grange had doubled its yield but we were the smallest grange in the manor and would be as a puddle compared to the lake of money de Caux had received.

Even though Heloise cooked for me, I still enjoyed, sometimes, the warrior hall. I liked Gunhild's food and the conversation with Baldwin, Odo, Robert, Richard and Rollo. Captain Henri now lived in the new castle and dined in the great hall with the seigneur. When the warrior hall was built then Robert, Richard and Rollo would leave us. I wanted to enjoy their company as long as I could. Inevitably we often

spoke of Sir Durand. He was like a spectre who haunted the
manor. We had all hated or disliked him to some degree and
that he was gone should have helped us to forget him but we
could not. Whenever his name came up, the one who did so
always looked at me first. I think that they believed they
were reopening a wound that had healed. It had never healed.
Taillefer had persuaded me against murder, for that had
crossed my mind, but now that he was a fugitive he was fair
game. I would not even need to murder him. I could
challenge him to a duel. I was confident that I could win.

It was Baldwin who brought up his name as we picked
over the last of the bread, cheese and apple pickles. "Has any
heard of Sir Durand or Charles since they fled?"

He was looking at me and the others all did so too. "Why
do you look at me? Why should I know?"

Odo gave a sad smile, "Because you still harbour a
grudge and wish him dead."

I nodded, you did not lie to shield brothers, "True, but all
I know is that he is beyond Normandy and therefore cannot
be touched."

Robert of Lisieux used some pieces of cheese to illustrate
his point as he spoke, "Here is Normandy and here is France.
Here is Anjou and here is Brittany." He pointed with his
knife, "When he fled, I thought he might have gone to
France. It would have been a short ride but none of those we
took at Tillières spoke of a Malet at King Henry's court and I
think that given our service in the battle, they would have
done." He ate the cheese that represented Normandy and
France. "That leaves Anjou and Brittany."

I said, "Brittany? When he fled the word was that he
would go to an enemy like Anjou or France."

"Count Conan is an enemy too, Richard, and the ride
there is shorter. From what I have heard the count is much
like Sir Durand. He is cunning and careful. Since the death
of Count Geoffrey, I have heard that Count Conan is eating
up Angevin land..." he popped another piece of cheese into
his mouth, "well, much as I am doing now. Would not Sir
Durand tie his horse to the Breton wagon? I am just saying

that if we do go to war with the Bretons then we may see Sir Durand again."

Rollo laughed, "You will need good eyes for he will be well to the rear."

We joined in the laughter but it set my mind to thoughts of vengeance. We might fight the Angevin for Maine but Sir Durand would stay away from such a fight. Brittany, on the other hand, was closer and smaller. The chances were that we would not come into contact with him if he had sought sanctuary in Rennes.

Chapter 18

Maine 1063

When war came it was not before time. I now led twelve men at arms and we had practised to the point of boredom and we were all ready to test our skills. Sir William's two sons, Robert and Gilbert, would also be coming. They would be going as squires although neither was really ready to be squires, as the sons of the seigneur they missed out on the training as pueros. They would be kept far from danger in the battle. The heirs to de Caux would not be risked.

The duke summoned us to Falaise and none knew for certain who we were to fight. The rumours abounded but I thought that Duke William would wish to retake Maine. The Angevin had been quiet since the death of Count Geoffrey. Others thought that Brittany would be our target as Count Conan had begun to take Angevin strongholds. My standing rose when we reached the camp for it was to be Maine that we would retake. Once more it was a mobile army. The archers and crossbowmen had been left at de Caux much to Odo's chagrin. He had been appointed commander of the garrison while we were away but I knew that he would rather have been with us.

We had tents with us, another sign of the seigneur's largesse. As we erected them Bruno came over. He was desperate to speak to us and I knew why, he was wearing spurs. I stole his thunder by elaborately bowing, "Sir Bruno, this is an honour beyond words."

He laughed and cuffed me gently about the head, "Dick, I knew I could count on you to bring me down to earth."

Baldwin said, "How did you win them, Bruno, for I would be a knight too?"

Bruno shrugged, "By just working as hard as I did at Graville-Sainte-Honorine. The difference is that the Lord of Mortemer, Sir William, knows how to reward men. The spurs were given to me at Christmas as well as a manor close to Mortemer. It is a small one but brings a healthy income."

"I am pleased for you. Do you know whence we ride?"

He nodded, "We have been here for a week and helped to set up the camp. The duke arrived a day later. Your old friend, Taillefer, is here too." He leaned forward, "And a Breton lord who leads Breton horsemen."

The presence of Taillefer was not news but a Breton lord was, "Who is he?"

"Alan ar Rouz, or in our language, Alan the Red. He has lands in Normandy and Count Conan and he fell out. It is Count Conan's loss for I have spoken to him and he knows how to war. Anyway, I have duties for I am Sir William's standard bearer and that means I have to stay close to him." He clasped my arm, "You know better than any, Dick, that the spurs change nothing between us. We will always be Bruno and Dick. I daresay we shall see each other in this campaign."

"Assuredly."

We had brought food and we cooked our own meals. As well as my men at arms I now commanded ten pueros. Captain Henri was now Sir Henri and he commanded the other twelve men at arms and twelve pueros. He had offered the position of squire to my friend and his son, Baldwin, but my friend showed great loyalty by staying with me. Now that he was a knight, the former captain spent more time with the seigneur and the other knights. We did not mind and the atmosphere around our camp was a happy one. We were at breakfast when Taillefer found me. I had not expected to see him when we arrived for his services would be in demand at the feast. I was honoured that he sought me out.

"You have grown, Dick, and now tower over me." He shook his head and put his hands on his hips as he surveyed me. "I take it that you have a new horse for Blaze would be crushed beneath the weight of you and your mail."

"Aye, and it was a gift from Sir William. And you? I thought we might have seen you at Tillières."

He tapped his nose, "Sometimes those who serve Duke William do so with their eyes, ears and our most deadly of weapons, our minds." He leaned in so that only I could hear, "I spent a long time in Anjou and Maine. This campaign will not take long for Maine is like an apple that lies on the ground and looks whole but when you lift it you can see the wormhole that has made the centre bad. When Herbert of Maine fled from Geoffrey Martel, he bequeathed Maine to the duke and since he died the duke has betrothed his son, Robert Curthose to Herbert's sister, Marguerite. We enter a land which is now ours by right although held by Count Fulk."

I smiled and nodded. It was good to be with Taillefer again and I was honoured by his intimacy.

He put his arm around my shoulder and led me away, "I have also been in Brittany. Count Conan knows I am Duke William's man and he used me as a conduit. He told me that Brittany does not wish to war against Normandy."

There was something in his voice and eyes that made me stop, "You do not believe him."

He laughed, "He is like the wolf that asks you to lie down with him promising that no harm will come to you. No, neither the duke nor I were fooled. We both know that he does not wish a war until he has devoured a little more of Anjou and has the income from those lands." I nodded and he turned me to face him. He was silent at first as his eyes bored into me and then he spoke, "I also saw an old adversary of yours, Sir Durand de Malet. He now lives at the Chateau de Dinan. He aspires to be the seneschal there." I nodded as I took in his words. "And you, Dick, are thoughts of vengeance now expunged from your heart?"

I could not and would not lie to him. I shook my head, "Vengeance is still alight in my heart. I will not fan the embers until war comes between us and Brittany. Your words give me hope that I might be placed a sword's length from him."

"Good. I would not have you jeopardise your position in the duke's eyes. He knows war with Brittany is coming but he wants it on his terms."

We rode from Falaise a week later. We left in six columns. The largest was that led by the duke and the smallest was ours. We had been allocated a land we had raided already: the eastern side of Maine. We headed for

Ernée. Whilst a town with a wall, we knew we had to get
beyond it before we raided. We were small enough as a
conroi to do so. Without archers and slingers, we could not
afford to try to assault the walls of a town. Villages and
hamlets without walls would fall to us. We had no wagons to
slow us. We would live off the men of Maine. We used a
different formation for this raid. We men at arms rode at the
fore, led by Sir Henri. Half of the pueros followed us and
then, after a gap of a hundred or so paces, the knights and
squires. The newer pueros would be behind the knights. The
formation was a compliment to me. I led young men at arms
and that meant we could take on stronger formations than
younger, less well armoured pueros.

We halted in the trees some thirty paces from the road
and two hundred from the walls of Ernée. I joined Sir Henri
and Robert at the fore. Our intention was to see if we could
circumnavigate the town without being seen. To our
amazement the gates were open and, even better, there was
no one there. I saw a merchant and boy leading two sumpters
enter the gates unchallenged.

Sir Henri smacked his thigh, "By God, we have them."
He turned and began to fasten his ventail, "Alan, ride back to
the Seigneur and tell him that the gates to Ernée are open and
we shall hold them for him."

"Aye, my lord," His squire wheeled his horse and took
off.

We all fastened our ventails.

"Richard, when you have the gates, assign the pueros to
guard them and we shall take the other gate."

"Aye, my lord." Even as he spurred his horse I said,
"Bertrand, you and the pueros hold the gates. Follow us
closely."

I led my men at arms towards the road. As with Sir Henri,
the grass muffled our hooves until we reached the packed
soil and stones of the road. Then they clattered. Still, no one
appeared either at the gates or on the gatehouse and Sir
Henri was fifty paces from the gates before a face appeared.
As soon as the man saw him, he gave a shout of alarm. The
call was repeated and we rode ever closer to the gates. Only

216

Sir Henri, Robert and Richard at the front had couched
lances. Holding ours aloft allowed us to be much closer to
the men before us. A bell from within began to toll. If
nothing else it told the farms and granges around the town
that there was danger. Two men tried in vain to close the
gates, but the horses of the three men at arms burst the gates
asunder and the men were thrown to the ground where they
were speared.

Sir Henri and his men formed a half circle until we
arrived. Sir Henri turned and nodded at me as we reined in.
He spurred his huge black warhorse and they took off
towards the southern gate. I couched my lance and the others
emulated me. I turned and saw that Bertrand had dismounted
four men to act as horse holders and the four riders had
ascended the gatehouse. The entrance was protected. I saw
Sir William and the rest of the conroi galloping up and I
shouted, "Men of Sir Robert, follow me."

Geoffrey responded immediately and I led my men at
arms along the small street that passed between the walls of
the town and the mean houses there. I knew there had to be
another gate on this side. It takes either a brave man or a fool
to step out, unarmed and try to stop a mailed horseman on a
warhorse and the men who lived along that row of houses
were neither. I saw, in the distance, two mailed men trying to
mount recently saddled horses and I lowered my lance. A
cantle was handy in battle for it held you securely in your
seat but trying to get your leg over it whilst encumbered by a
mail hauberk and without the aid of a mounting step was
almost impossible. I rammed the head of my lance into his
back while he was still trying to mount. I think he must have
died instantly for the head went through his mail and into his
horse. The terrified beast took off through the open east gate
and as the man's foot was still in his stirrup it dragged his
body and my spear through the gate. I drew one of my
swords. I now emulated Taillefer and wore a pair of crossed
swords in scabbards across my back. It meant I could not
carry my shield there but that was no hardship and I drew my
favourite sword. The other man had mounted and I swept my

sword in a blind swing before him. He reeled and, as he did so, Baldwin speared him in the side.

"Petr, close the gates."

"But, Master Richard, the horse." He pointed at the horse that had fled.

"It is going nowhere and Sir William will have my back flayed if any escape through this gate." He nodded and obeyed me. "Baldwin, take four men and hold this gate. The rest of you, with me." Without waiting to see who obeyed me, I galloped towards the west gate on the other side of the town. I saw the open gates of a stable. There were still horses within. This time, as we passed the centre of the town there were men making a half-hearted attempt at defence but as we approached from the east and Sir William from the north they found themselves assaulted on two sides. I slashed my sword at a man with a shield and a spear. I knocked him to the ground and then heard the crunch as Stephen, mounted behind me, crushed his body with his horse's hooves. I did not stop to waste blows killing men who could do nothing to stop us but headed for the west gate. The stable had been at the eastern side of the town but three men were fleeing on foot and they managed to get on the road. I galloped after them, "Hold, or you will die!" They did not stop and Geoffrey soon overtook the man at the rear. I swung my sword but used the flat of it to smack into the back of the man's head. He tumbled forward and after wheeling Geoffrey before them, making the other two stop, I levelled my sword at them and said, "Yield or die."

They were unarmed and both nodded, "Spare us our lives, we beg of you."

"Pick up your friend." I saw the expressions on their faces. "He is not dead."

By the time we reached the west gate of Ernée, the town was ours. I do not think above an hour had passed since we had ridden through. I lowered my ventail and hung my helmet from my cantle. I was sweating. A mail hauberk and helmet will do that to a man. I dismounted and walked Geoffrey to the square where Sir William was already issuing orders. He looked at me, "Well?"

"None escaped, my lord, and we lost no one."

He beamed, "Better and better. The pueros can stand watch this night and we will eat well."

I went back to the east gate. "Petr, now you can fetch the horse and the body of the rider that fled."

We ate well in the town and we profited. Duke William was imposing his will on Maine and his orders to Sir William had been quite clear. We were to punish whoever we defeated. Had any village or hamlet willingly welcomed us then it might have been different but Maine did not wish to return to the Norman fold. They had not liked the rule of Anjou either and wished for their independence. I was just a man at arms but I understood that viewpoint.

I now had another horse as well as the dead man's mail, sword and purse. I kept the horse but, as I did not need the mail, gave it to Petr. I knew he had coveted the mail when the horse ran off. I could have kept it and sold it on but I wanted to lead men who were mailed. Baldwin kept the mail from the warrior he had killed as well as his horse. That first encounter, I could not call it a battle, made us stronger for there were battles to be fought that would test us further.

I was summoned to meet with my two half-brothers. They had taken over the largest hall in Ernée. The richest man in the town had lived there and he willingly paid his own ransom. Charles d' Ernée had been given the manor by Geoffrey Martel and he was no warrior. He was a merchant and landowner who profited from peace. He cared not who ruled so long as he was left alone. Sir William recognised that and we profited from the encounter.

The knights were all there and I was the only one without a title. It did not worry me.

"We will head north-west tomorrow towards Dinan and the border. Lord Mortemer and his conroi are to the east of us and they will head south and east." He held up his hand and splayed out the fingers. "We are Duke William's hand and our fingers will grasp the treasure of Maine so that we can hold the land more tightly this time."

Sir Henri said, "We were lucky to take Ernée, my lord. Dinan is not only a stronghold, it is Breton."

219

Sir William nodded, "And we will only ride as far as the border of Brittany. When we reach the border then we sweep south and then east. We cast out a net and take as much as we can of this land. The duke is clever, Henri. By keeping columns striking into the heart of Maine, he prevents those who oppose us from rallying."

Sir Robert had changed since Sir Durand had fled and he was more assertive these days, "We do not change what we did here. It worked." He smiled at me, "The men at arms are the eyes of this conroi and we the knights are the fists. We are a good combination."

Sir William nodded, "And now let us enjoy some wine."

As we were drinking the wine, I confided in my two half-brothers. I was not sure if they knew that Sir Durand was less than sixty miles from us but I thought they ought to know. My news came as a surprise to them.

"Thank you, Richard, for this piece of news. We can do little about the man who has sullied our name for as yet we are not at war with Brittany." He toasted me, "You did well today, Richard fitz Malet. Sir Henri speaks well of you and Sir Eustace, too, is fulsome in his praise."

"They are too kind, my lord. I am still learning to be a warrior but I enjoy leading my handful of men."

"You are a natural leader." He held out his goblet and his son, acting as a squire, refilled it. "I fear that we will be away from Le Caux for more than the forty days we owe the duke."

Sir Robert held his goblet up and it was refilled, "So long as we profit then it matters not, brother. This is what we train for. Since Mortemer, we have practised more than we have battled. This will put steel into our men. We shall need it."

Gilbert, Sir William's second son, was helping his older brother and he asked, "Why shall we need it, Uncle Robert?"

Sir Robert had been drinking and he slurred his words a little. He waved his goblet towards the north, "Maine is a morsel that was Norman. Brittany is a rocky nut but England, ah, there is a rich plum waiting to be plucked. Duke William was promised the crown and he expects to have it but Harold Godwinson, so we have heard, has ambitions of his own. The duke is training his men to take not a rebellious county but a whole country and a rich one at that." His hand encompassed the room, "The halls in England will make us all rich men."

I had enjoyed enough of the heady wine and I left to return to the house we had commandeered. I guessed, from the contents, that it had belonged to the two mailed men we had slain for there was no sign of a woman's hand. There had been no spurs on the men's feet and so I assumed that they were like us, men at arms. We found some fine clothes in the chests and we took those too. The horses we had taken would be used as pack animals.

In the next ten days, we took villages, farms and hamlets as we worked our way around the border of Maine. When we reached Laval, we found our first real obstacle. There was a well-made wooden castle and a town wall. The castle and defensive wall were built on a rocky promontory overlooking the river. There was a bridge and I knew from my time with Taillefer, when we had spoken of such things, that the town was important because it was on the main road from Paris to Rennes, the capital of Brittany, and was close to Le Mans.

I thought that my half-brother would pass the walls and head east to join up with William de Warenne and ultimately, the duke. However, he approached the barred gates. He took his brother, his sons and me. We rode bareheaded and left our shields with the others. It was a sign that we wished to speak and taking his two sons who had no mail was surety for our good behaviour and intentions.

When we reached the wooden gatehouse, he slipped his coif from his head, "I am Sir William Malet, Lord of de Caux. I would speak with Lord Guy of Laval. I am here in good faith and bring my sons and my brothers as surety for a peaceful truce." He waved a hand to the trees that masked the rest of our men. "My conroi wait yonder. I would speak peace and not war."

I was unsure if any had heard him. To be truthful I was still bemused at being identified as his brother. This was the first time he had ever done so and it touched me. When the

221

gates swung open, I was startled. A youngish man stood there, also bareheaded and with open palms.

"I am Guy of Laval and I do not like shouted conversations from the tops of my walls. I know your name, Sir William, and that you are a man of honour. Dismount and we will talk here in my gatehouse."

He was being cautious. He would not allow us into his castle proper in case our intentions were martial. We might be spies. We dismounted and led our horses across the wooden bridge into the gatehouse. Despite the fact that it was made of wood, it was substantial and had double doors. If one set was breached then there was another to hold an enemy. The delay in our greeting was now explained as a table and two chairs were fetched. Sir William and Sir Guy would face each other and talk.

Sir Guy began, "I appreciate the offer to talk, Sir William, but the presence of your knights and your warriors suggests that your intentions are more belligerent than your words. Speak plainly I beg of you. I appreciate honesty. If you intend to conquer us then let me know. We shall let you depart in peace."

Sir William nodded, "I have also heard of you, Guy of Laval. This town would not be here but for you. I can see that the wood of this castle is fresh and only a fool would try to take it. I am here with an offer."

There was silence.

"Go on."

"Duke William of Normandy was bequeathed Maine by Count Herbert. The duke's son, Robert, is betrothed to Lady Marguerite. Duke William would have Laval as a bastion against his enemies. We do not wish to fight you. The duke would have you join him as the rightful ruler of Maine."

"I would keep my castle and my lands?"

"And, although I have yet to speak to him, I am sure that the duke would give you greater powers over this part of Maine."

It did not take the young lord long to decide. It was only a handclasp but as the Bishop of Laval was there too, it was binding. We took no treasure from Laval but we were fed and our horses enjoyed the rest. When we left to head for Le Mans, I learned that war was not always the way to win a land. Words could be just as effective. I had learned much about my half-brother.

If I thought we would simply head home after our bloodless victory then I was wrong. We had less raiding to do as Sir Guy and his men accompanied us and the lands within twenty miles of Laval surrendered without a fight. Indeed, when we joined up with Duke William and the rest of the army at Le Mans, there was a great celebration at the new ally. However, the people of Maine had chosen Walter, Count of Mantes and the husband of Herbert's aunt, Biota. He and the other nobles of Maine had gathered in Le Mans and we had to besiege the city. It took two months to starve the city into submission. We did not have to assault the walls but it was a hard two months. Sieges are dull beyond words. When the rains came, they made the land one of mud. When the winds came, they were lazy ones that did not go around a man but through him. Food was scarce and belts were tightened but when the city finally surrendered then Robert Curthose had his own domain. He and Marguerite were married in the cathedral and Duke William led his army home. He would leave his son as master of Maine. We made our weary way back to Graville-Sainte-Honorine.

Chapter 19

Graville-Sainte-Honorine 1064

The people who settled this land and became Normans had been Vikings. Some of them, like Gunhild, were still closer in nature to the Northmen than men like Sir William. When I had been young, Gunhild had spoken of three sisters who wove spells to trap men. I saw evidence of their work when an Englishman rode alone into the castle. He was looking for Sir William for he had not heard of the new castle. I knew he was English from his hair and his moustache. I saw him arrive and enter the castle and then I was sent for. It was clear why, Sir Robert spoke a little English but not well enough.

"Ah, Richard, this is Edgar and he is Earl Harold's man. That is all I have gleaned. I would have him speak to you for I need to fully understand his presence."

I nodded, "I am Richard fitz Malet and I speak English well."

His eyes narrowed and then he nodded, "I remember when the duke came to Thornley and spoke to the king. You were Taillefer's servant then." I nodded and he looked relieved. "The earl and a party of us were fishing off the coast north of here when a storm came up and we were shipwrecked. Guy of Ponthieu took us prisoner and chose to hold us for ransom. I escaped and I came south to seek Duke William. I do not know this land and became lost. My Norman is poor and when I asked for Lord William I was directed here."

There were many questions I wished to ask this Englishman not least why an English earl would choose to fish off the French coast. I turned to Sir Robert and told him all. He knew the importance of such events. "Tell him that he shall stay here as our guest. I will send to my brother and the duke. Assure him that he is not a prisoner and can leave whenever he chooses."

I did so and he looked relieved, "My journey here was perilous, Richard fitz Malet, and I feared for my life. This is not England."

The Seigneur arrived within an hour and he was pleased with what both Robert and I had done. We dined in the Great Hall and I became the questioner for Sir William. He spoke English quite well, having married an English woman but he was clever. By using me to ask the questions he could study Edgar and his reactions.

When the interrogation had finished, he nodded, "The Count of Ponthieu has behaved badly, Edgar, and for that, I apologise." I translated and the seigneur continued, "Nobles have a duty to those whom the sea throws up but Guy of Ponthieu is not Norman. The duke will remedy all."

The Englishman looked relieved. He was led to his bedchamber leaving the three of us to debate the matter. Sir William had spotted the same flaw in the story as I had. "This earl was fishing alright but not for fish. He was seeking information. Bishop Odo's fleet is being built and it would not surprise me that this earl wished to see for himself the danger it represented. God has delivered us the main threat to the duke. I will be interested to see how the duke deals with it."

When Bishop Odo and his oathsworn rode into the castle the next day we had our answer. Once more I was used as a translator. The duke had ordered his brother to secure the release of Earl Harold. There was a chest of gold with the bishop to recompense the count for the loss of ransom. As we rode north, the bishop confided in me that if Guy of Ponthieu was in any way belligerent then he would lose both his lands and his freedom. When he had sworn fealty to the duke, he had made a binding commitment. I accompanied the bishop as a translator but when we met Earl Harold, we found it unnecessary. His Norman was equal to my English. I was kept close by, however, as the bishop wanted me as a listener.

Guy of Ponthieu had to accept the bishop's offer, as having lost his lands once, after the Battle of Mortemer, he could not afford to upset the duke. The chest of gold was far less than what he would have received in ransom. Earl Harold was far from happy. Whilst he was no longer a prisoner of the count, he was now going to be taken by the man who would have the crown of England. I saw him and Edgar with their heads together as the bishop and the count discussed the release. Edgar turned and pointed to me. I saw a frown cross his face. There was no real reason why he should remember me although Edgar had. I suspect it was my association with the bishop that worried him.

Although I was of little importance to anyone, my knowledge of English meant I rode at the fore. As we headed south, I rode just behind the English earl and the Norman bishop. I could not help but hear their words, "Tell me, Bishop Odo, are you taking us to a port so that we may return home?"

Shaking his head the bishop said, "That would be ungracious. We are taking you to Caen for the duke would entertain you and get to know you better. After all, you are one of the leading nobles of England and when the duke inherits the crown, he will need to know which of his nobles should help him control the land."

"So I am still a prisoner?"

"Of course not, but as you discovered during your unfortunate voyage, the seas are dangerous at this time of year. We Normans know the sea and respect it. When the weather is benign then, I dare say, my brother will provide a ship to take you home."

The earl had no choice but to accept the bishop's offer. The words guest and prisoner were interchangeable in this context. I stayed with them all the way to Caen. I was there when, a few miles from his city, the duke greeted Earl Harold like a long-lost cousin. I was also present at the feast to celebrate the safe arrival of the most powerful man in England. Taillefer was, unsurprisingly, there and that made me happy. I was a minor fish at this great feast and I sat with the other minnows. I was able to hear what the knights of Caen thought of the incident. I listened as they spoke.

"This ensures that the duke will be given the throne of England. We can hold the earl until King Edward dies and then there is no opposition to us."

"We could sail now. King Edward would welcome us with open arms and we would win a country without drawing a sword."

The rest of them echoed the words of the two most vocal knights. I was not sure for I knew the English. I did not think that Earl Harold would go along with the duke. No matter what they said publicly, I knew, from the words of those with Earl Harold, that he still wished the crown of England for himself. The squires of the knights served them and as they were privy to the squires who served the top table they dropped little nuggets of news. One was of particular interest to me.

"I just heard, my lord, that Duke William has offered the burgh of Douvres to Earl Harold. It is a powerful position."

"Did the Englishman accept?"

Shamefaced the squire said, "I did not hear, my lord."

Sir Gille snapped, "Then next time bring me the whole tale or none at all. You have whetted my appetite and still left me hungry."

I knew how important the port and burgh of Douvres was. Perhaps the duke would win over the Earl of Wessex and it might suit them both. If Harold ruled England for the duke then Duke William could continue to take lands from Anjou and France while having a safe and secure England to fund him.

Taillefer sought me out before I retired to the warrior hall, "So, Dick, you are still at the heart of these matters."

I shrugged, "Just happenstance."

"Perhaps. Things, however, are coming to a head. The duke has let all his vassals know that he wishes none to threaten his lands should he be absent."

"Why?"

"Because if he is to have the crown of England, he will need to leave Normandy. His son controls Maine and Eustace of Boulogne the north. His only fear is Brittany."

I nodded, "Then we go to war again."

"Probably. You do not mind, do you? I hear you made coin in Maine and are now a rich man."

"I am but the English are my grandfather's people. I would not have them subjugated."

"Then you should be happy about fighting them for the Godwinson brothers would subjugate England. You heard that the people of Northumberland sent Tostig Godwinson from their land?" I nodded, "He is the worst of them but the other three are little better. Trust me, Dick, the English would be better off ruled by the duke than Harold Godwinson."

He was Taillefer and I believed him. Besides, it was good to be at his side again and we spent each day improving my skills until the message came from Brittany.

Duke Conan decided to defy Duke William. He refused to give his surety for good behaviour. That it was a mistake was clear to us all. The Bretons were good horsemen and had enjoyed success against the weaker Angevin but Duke William had honed his army to make it a formidable weapon. We prepared to go to war once and this time, as we would inevitably have to fight a formal battle, we took not only archers and slingers but also retainers. Erik and Galmr would come to war while Carl, Heloise and his son would stay at the grange. My two retainers would guard the baggage and, if it was necessary, join the other half-trained retainers to be brought into battle if things were going badly. Odo was delighted to be going to war and he showed his desire by walking with his slingers and archers. He had a horse and he could have ridden but he wanted the thirty men and boys he led to know that he was one of them. This time I led fourteen men at arms and fifteen pueros. Our success in Maine had resulted in more money for horses and weapons. Sir William's retinue had also grown. The men of de Caux would number nearer two hundred when we fought the Bretons.

We had a seventy-mile march to the muster at Avranches and at the first camp, I asked Odo if he regretted his decision to walk. He shook his head, "I regard this as a sort of penance. Each step I take will make me even more determined to be the best that I can be, I was fated not to be a man at arms but God gave me a good eye and a strong arm. I can use a bow, sling or crossbow. The march will make my legs stronger and besides," he grinned, "the men I lead know the best jokes. Your men at arms are dullards in comparison."

Baldwin and I laughed. Odo was making the best of what he had. I admired that trait.

More men joined us once we passed Caen and the road was a long metal snake heading through Normandy. When we reached the muster, we saw Breton standards. We had been joined by Breton rebels. As well as Alan the Red and his rebels, Rivallon I of Dol the Lord of Comburg brought a substantial retinue. I admired Duke William for his attention to detail. He was pretending to be supporting the Breton rebels when I knew he wanted Brittany as a vassal. To aid him he had been to Rome where he had been given a papal banner by Pope Alexander. It gave legitimacy to his endeavours. We spent a week at Avranches while we awaited the arrival of more soldiers. Duke William was taking no chances.

Duke William arrived and I had another surprise. Earl Harold and his companions were with the duke. They were mounted and they were armed. What did this portend? I saw Taillefer with them and knew that I would discover all, eventually. The morning after their arrival, we set off and headed to the coast. I saw half a dozen of Bishop Odo's new ships and realised that we would have watchdogs on our flank. We headed for Mont St Michel, the island and abbey given to Duke William by King Edward. The duke was teaching the earl about the Normans. Was he trying to seal his support? The crossing by Mont St Michel was always fraught with danger. There was sinking sand and a tide that could race in and trap a man. I was pleased when we reached the far side and were able to make a camp.

As I had hoped, Taillefer sought me out. He had much to tell me and, as was his practice, he did so away from prying ears. He trusted me to keep his secrets but that was all. "Well, Dick, I have much to tell you. Earl Harold has sworn an oath on holy relics that he will support the duke's claim to the English crown when King Edward dies. That will not be long in coming for the old king is ill and hangs on to life just so that he can see his abbey completed and consecrated."

"Will the earl keep his oath?"

"It was a binding one and such oaths have a way of punishing oath breakers. I am hopeful for today, when we crossed by Mont St Michel, two of the duke's warriors were trapped by the sands and it was the earl himself who rescued them. He put his life in danger when he did not need to. Perhaps you will come with me to England when the duke is crowned. I am invited already and I would need a squire. You could play the part."

"I would be honoured." I had already begun to think that I might ask Taillefer if I could be his squire. As much as I liked leading my men, life with Taillefer would be far more exciting and adventurous.

I did not see him for a couple of days as we left the coast to head south and west. When we reached Saint Broladre and camped, he came to speak with me, "We have found them, Dick. The Bretons are waiting for us at Dol de Bretagne. The duke shall have his battle."

He need not have told me for Sir William was summoned to a council of war by the duke but I was touched that one so great as Taillefer would stoop to confide in one like me.

My half-brother returned with the news that we were to be part of the right wing of the army and would be under the command of the duke's half-brother Bishop Odo. The duke would be in the centre and the Breton rebels would be on the left. Marching to war was one thing but a battle was something entirely different. We sharpened weapons, oiled our mail and checked every strap on our shields. It was as we did so that I noticed that many knights serving Bishop Odo now used a kite-shaped shield. I could see how that would benefit a rider but thought that it would encumber a man on foot. I decided that I would have one made but still trust to my round one until I had the merit of the shield proved to me.

We were roused while it was still dark and formed up on the ground north of the Breton stronghold. We were all in a state of high excitement. The duke's battle plan was a simple one. Our archers and slingers, along with the crossbowmen, would advance before us and they would initiate the battle. The aim was to kill Breton horses and make them charge us. Our missile men would flee back and we would counter charge. As we waited for dawn, Geoffrey stamped the ground and flicked his head up and down. He was, like his rider, ready for war. When the sun rose from the east, the land before us had no horsemen. The gates of Dol de Bretagne were open and Count Conan had fled. That day began a chase. This was not a measured march, our horsemen galloped through the town to catch up with the fleeing Bretons.

We all knew where they were heading; Dinan. It was stronger than Dol de Bretagne and if the count could hide behind its walls, he could be supplied by sea and we would bleed our men away taking its walls. They had a head start but our night guards assured us that they had not heard noises in the night and that meant the Bretons had fled while we had arrayed for battle. It was Sir William de Warenne, Lord Mortemer, who led the chase and it was he who finally caught up with the Bretons. They had reached the outskirts of Dinan but the mad chase had ensured that the bulk of the Breton army was outside the walls of the fortress. Only a fool tried to enter a stronghold with men stuck on the road. The count formed his men up to fight. Duke William would have his battle but it would be fought beneath Dinan's walls. The Bretons could use the garrison of the fortress to aid their horsemen.

Odo was with the rest of the slingers and archers. They would still be on the road and the duke's original plan would need to be modified. Our horsemen faced up in our three battles. The Bretons had one large battle line. Our horses were tired already and I knew that we could not charge our enemy. Their horses were tired too. We would fight from the backs of horses for that was our way but it would be at the walk.

I had some new men at arms who had fought alongside us as pueros but had never been in the fore. As we waited for every horseman to be marshalled into line, I rode along my line of men and pointed at the horsemen who faced us, "Forget where Count Conan is. All we worry about are those horsemen before us. Look for their banners. They are our target. Once we have slain them and driven them from the field then we can seek enemies whose ransom will make us all rich men." I was telling them what they wanted to hear. "Our task is to take out their men at arms and light horsemen first. Make no mistake, Breton horsemen are good. If you underestimate them then you will die. We keep together and listen to the horn of Sir Robert. God will be with us this day." Bishop Odo blessed our army. I felt that with him leading us we were guaranteed the support of the Almighty.

As we waited for the horn to sound the attack, I saw that the walls bristled with men. They would not be armoured but there would be crossbows, bows and slings. The sooner we could engage with their horsemen the better chance we had of survival. The rain of arrows would be brief. The wait for the horn was longer than I had anticipated and our horses recovered better than I had expected. The rest, while we waited, gave our horses the chance to recover but they would only have one charge to make. We would have a three-hundred-pace race to the Bretons. If they allowed us to hit them while they stood then we would win. In all likelihood, they would countercharge and that would shorten the distance between us.

As we waited, to the right of Sir Robert, Sir William and the other knights, I gave one last command, "We keep boot to boot and when we thrust we shout. Let us make these Bretons fill their breeks when the men of de Caux come to make war." It was the right thing to say for they all cheered.

The horn sounded and we moved forward. A horse does not go from stop to charge in an instant. It is a measured move and I had to rein Geoffrey back so that he did not get ahead of my men. Sir William and the knights were slightly ahead of us and it meant we would be slightly echeloned when we struck. I would judge the moment to lower my lance. I had chosen a lance rather than a spear as I wanted the extra length. It was not much longer than a spear but those inches could prove the difference between life and death if I could strike my enemy before he hit me.

I had worked out that we were aiming at men led by a knight with a red banner. It looked to be a silver gryphon on the banner. The men we would be fighting wore red tunics. The closer we came the easier it was to identify the man who would try to kill me. Arrows and bolts flew from the walls but they did little harm. One bolt clanked off my helmet but with my ventail up, it would take a very lucky hit indeed to strike my eyes. I had done this before but I feared for some of those we had only recently trained. The ride was exciting and it was too easy to get carried away in the moment. You had to judge your strike perfectly so that you hit before your enemy. You had to be prepared to take a hit, preferably on your shield and you needed to react to a second attacker taking advantage of your distraction. I knew that Baldwin and Petr could do that and they flanked me, but the others? It was too late to do anything about that for we were so close that lives would be measured in heartbeats and not hoofbeats.

I saw that the Breton man at arms I faced had a vest made of overlapping metal discs. In theory, it was stronger than my mail. We would see. He had no nasal on his helmet and his spear was the standard length. Pulling back my arm I aimed for the centre of his metal vest. If I could not penetrate it then I could, at the very least, make him reel and that would make his spear miss me. I had my shield covering my middle and both hands. I punched at the perfect time. Geoffrey's head had just dipped and the Breton's horse had reacted to the lunging lance. The head slid over the horse's mane. I was aware of his spear coming at me but I forced myself to ignore it and counted on my lance's longer length. The head hit the mail discs and to my surprise slid between two of them. Had it been mail it might have slowed the strike. The rider's speed, allied to my punch drove the head into his body. His spear fell from his hands but his cantle held him in place. The lance was torn from my hand as it had penetrated so far that the head was sticking out of his back. My crossed swords behind me now helped me to rearm myself so quickly that the light horseman in the second rank had no time to adjust his strike. My shield blocked and turned the spear allowing me to slash my sword at head height. The warrior was no veteran and his eyes were on his spear and my shield. He never saw the blade that hacked into his forehead.

I reined in Geoffrey for before me was a wall of spearmen and only a fool would risk a sword against footmen armed with long spears. All along the battle was a cacophony of noise. It was like a thousand weaponsmiths all beating metal at the same time. Added to that were the screams and shouts of men trying to intimidate an enemy or men screaming out their curses as they died. You only ever saw the battle that was close to you and I saw that the gryphon on the red background was down. Our closest enemy was defeated.

Sir William reined in and shouted, "Those with spears and lances take the fore. The rest follow."

I was the only one of my men at arms to have lost my lance and I slipped behind Petr and Baldwin to join the pueros. The line of men at arms and knights walked up to the line of spearmen. Our lances were longer and as the men wielding them were all mounted had the advantage that they could strike down. The Bretons had a choice, they either lifted their shields, limiting their vision or risked a spear. I saw one veteran lift his shield but he was able to spear Stephen's horse in the throat. The dying animal fell forward and Stephen was thrown from the saddle to land in the middle of the spearmen. Even as they butchered him, his falling horse crashed onto the veteran who had speared him and Baldwin and Petr took advantage and rode their horses over the carcass of the horse and the corpse of the Breton. I followed. Their spears struck again and again for the cohesion of the shield wall was gone. My sword was able to slash at the heads of the spearmen who were attacked on all sides. They broke and it was when they did so that we saw the Bretons had left the gates open. I assume it was to allow them to reinforce. Had it just been the spearmen who fled, then the Bretons might have held us a little longer but Count Conan and his oathsworn also fled to save their lives. It was the end of the battle outside the city and the start of the battle within.

We were lucky for we simply followed the fleeing foot soldiers and were able to enter the town. Sir William shouted, "Make for the chateau!"

I knew the reason for that command. It was nothing to do with the treasures that would be there, it was to take Sir Durand. The last we had heard he had taken refuge in the castle. Would he still be there? As we galloped through the gate, we slashed and hacked with our swords. We had to clear a path for the bishop's men and it mattered not if we merely scared them away, so long as they did not block the gate then our victory would be complete.

The main gate and the road that passed through it headed directly to the gates of the castle. They were open. Count Conan's flight had been the signal for the castle's garrison to join him. I wondered briefly if Sir Durand would have joined that flight but I believed I knew my half-brother. He would seek to leave a rich man. I led my five remaining men at arms through the gaping gates. There were men still fleeing but, as they were laden with treasure they could not defend themselves. Most simply dropped what they were carrying and ran from us. I pointed to Leo and Fótr, "You two guard the gates until Sir William arrives."

We dismounted and I tied Geoffrey to a spear that I rammed into the packed earth. I hung my shield from my cantle. "We search for Sir Durand."

"Surely he will have fled."

"Perhaps, Petr, but I think he would try to profit from this. Go carefully. He and Charles are snakes."

I headed for the Great Hall while Baldwin and Petr took the stairs that led to the chambers beneath it. The doors to the hall were wide open and I saw that it had already been looted by the servants. Their treasure lay in the inner bailey.

I heard a cry and ran back to follow its sound. Below me I heard the clash of steel on steel. Someone was fighting my two companions. Baldwin could handle himself but Petr was another matter. I cursed myself for allowing the young man at arms to put his life at risk. I drew my second sword. The stairway I descended was narrow but I had two blades to block any who tried to ascend. I saw a light at the bottom and when I reached the last stair, I saw that the light emanated from a low chamber. Petr lay on the ground and was bleeding. Baldwin was trying to fight both Charles and Sir Durand. Even as I raced to get to his side, Charles stabbed my friend in the thigh. The two had not seen me for their backs were to me but Baldwin's eyes glanced at me and that warned Charles who spun around, slashing his dagger at me. I did not hesitate but hacked down with my left hand. The blade was razor sharp and it cut through the bone of his left hand, half severing it. He screamed in pain and lunged at me with his sword. I blocked the blow. We were so close that I could not use the edge of my blade and the ceiling prevented my usual strike. Instead, I punched him in the face with the hilt of my sword and he fell in a heap. I was just in time to see Sir Durand swing his sword to hack into the side of Baldwin. I barely blocked it with my sword, but block it I did and Baldwin rolled away, trying to stem the bleeding thigh. Had the sword connected well, then my friend would be dead for the blade would have severed his leg.

"So, the bastard comes for me. You will die and with you my father's mistake."

"You are the one who has dishonoured your family." He swung his dagger at my face but I easily blocked it with the sword in my left hand. I swung my right at his thigh and he barely managed to stop it. I saw fear in his eyes. He did not want to die and was not a good enough swordsman to stop it. "You are disowned. Your name has been stricken from the family records. It will be as though you were never born."

Baldwin suddenly shouted, "Dick!"

Charles had half risen and was lurching towards me with his dagger in his right hand. I swung the sword in my left hand and almost took his head from his shoulders. Sir Durand thought he saw his chance and lunged at my middle. Taillefer had taught me to use quick hands and I brought my sword around to block it. Baldwin had either passed out or died already and I had to end this.

"When you find rats, you rid yourself of them. Die."

My left hand darted and I gave him something he did not deserve, a quick death. The sword came out of the back of his neck. I heard noises behind me and pulling out the sword, I whirled. It was Sir Robert.

"He is dead?"

"He is dead." I sheathed my swords and knelt by Baldwin. His blood was puddling. I ripped Durand's tunic and using the cloth tied it above the wound to stem the bleeding. I shouted to Sir Robert's squire, "Quickly, take him to a healer while I see to Petr."

"I will help." Sir Robert grabbed Baldwin's shoulders and the two of them manhandled my wounded friend.

Petr was not dead, for when I cradled his head his eyes opened. They widened, "Sir Durand!"

"He is dead. Where are you hurt?"

He pointed to his middle, "I was stabbed in the side and when I fell, I banged my head."

I was relieved, "Then you will live. Come, you are too heavy for me to carry. Lean on me and we will find the daylight."

It took some time but when we emerged, my men cheered. Baldwin was awake and a healer was tending to him. Sir William came over and while Petr was tended to, he clasped my arm, "You have rid our family of the dishonour Durand brought us. You shall have his spurs and be knighted."

I shook my head, "I will have his spurs but I do not want to be knighted for killing a rat. I am young and there are deeds yet for me to perform. I am content." He nodded but he did not understand. I am not sure I did but Taillefer had offered me the chance to be his squire and that, to me, was more important than a knighthood, at the moment, anyway.

The campaign was over and Count Conan had been punished. He sent word that he would be Duke William's vassal but as he did not do so in person there was not much doubt that it was a lie. My two men at arms needed to recover and I stayed with them in Dinan while they healed. My two half-brothers returned home. After they had gone, I was invited to a feast in the chateau. Earl Harold was there as well as Taillefer and as most of the nobles had departed, I was seated next to Taillefer.

Earl Harold and Duke William got on well. Along with Bishop Odo, there was much laughter and toasting of each other. I had not been in their part of the battle but Taillefer, who had, told me that they all fought well.

"It seems, Dick, that my hopes for glory fighting against housecarls have been dashed. The earl has promised the duke, once more, that he will support his claim for the crown. As the king is close to death, it may well be that I shall travel to England next year to see Duke William crowned. Will you come with me? I enjoy your company."

"Of course."

"Did I hear that your brother offered to make you a knight and you declined his offer?"

"I did not want to be rewarded for killing Durand."

He lowered his voice, "Those words might have fooled your brother but not me. The real reason, come, out with it."

I sighed, "If I was a knight then you might not wish to take me with you."

He laughed, "You goose. It would make no difference to me. When it is offered again then grasp it with both hands."

Baldwin and Petr were ready to travel by the end of that week. We had taken horses from the Bretons as well as treasure and mail. The three of us were laden as we headed north. It would not be a swift journey for Baldwin, especially, was still a little weak. It mattered not for we had all shared a subterranean struggle. When we had fought in the darkness beneath the Great Hall of Dinan, it had been as though we were fighting the devil himself. We three were closer because of that.

Chapter 20

Normandy 1066

Word reached us in the middle of January that King Edward had died and Earl Harold had been immediately crowned as King of England. Sir William, as one of Duke William's closest advisers, was summoned to Caen and when he returned he told us the news. I ate with the brothers at the new castle for this was momentous news.

"The duke is angry beyond words for a sacred oath was sworn."

Sir Robert said, "Then God will surely punish him for it."

The seigneur's sons, Robert and Gilbert, were dining with us and I saw them taking it all in.

"The duke has sent an emissary to England to discover the truth of the matter. After all, we only have a report from a sea captain. He may have misunderstood."

I said, quietly, "There is no mistake, my lord. Harold has always wanted the crown and it seems to me that he would do anything to get it. I could not break an oath but then I do not seek a crown."

Sir William nodded, "I forgot that you went to Lundenwic with the duke. I thought that when he fought so hard at Dinan that he had changed."

"He fought so hard at Dinan to win his freedom. He had to get home as quickly as he could for he knew how ill the king was."

"There is sense in what you say."

"So what happens now, brother? Do we wait for word from Caen or prepare for war?"

"We will be sailing to England, of that there is no doubt. If this is a mistake then the duke would go there to claim his crown but if Harold has stolen it then we will take an army. The Lord of Mortemer, the Count of Eu and myself have all been asked to go if it is a coronation."

I remembered the shipwreck of Earl Harold, "Will the duke sail in winter?"

"No, he will not. When summer comes we shall know one way or the other and we will sail when the weather is kind and the winds benign. So, Robert, to answer your question, we shall be going to England and it is my belief that it will be to make war."

"And that means taking all of our men, even those who fight on foot."

"It does, Richard. They did not get to fight in the Breton war but this time they will. The duke can muster two thousand horses but he and his brother plan on taking ten thousand men."

Sir Robert's mouth opened and closed like a fish and he shook his head, "There are not enough ships in the world to take such a large army."

"There will be by summer. Bishop Odo told me that he has six hundred ships already and by summer there will be almost eight hundred. Our ten ships will be but part of that fleet."

This was not an undertaking lightly taken. The seas between Normandy and England were not wide but they were dangerous. I had experience of taking horses on a ship and it was not easy.

Galmr and Erik would be furnished with captured helmets, shields and swords. I had a new shield made for me. It was a kite shaped one. I wanted both my leg and Geoffrey protected as much as possible. Baldwin and the rest of my men emulated me. I wondered if Baldwin would cope for his wound troubled him still. So long as he was mounted then he might survive but unhorsed he would quickly fall. I tried to persuade him to stay at home but he was adamant.

"My father is now a knight and leads Sir William's men at arms. How would it look if his son skulked at home? I have half a year to make my leg strong and I shall."

The training, even in the cold late winter and early spring, became more important than ever. Stephen's death had been the reason we had broken the shield wall. When we fought the English, the shield wall would be made up of men like my grandfather and would be a worthier opponent than the Breton spearmen.

The duke and his brother were busy with their own plans which became public when he came to hold a council at the new castle. It was a measure of the closeness of the duke to the Malet family. Durand's death had brought honour back to us. I was in the hall, not as a guest but as a guard. Count Eustace was there along with William de Warenne, William fitz Osbern, Robert, Count of Mortain, Alan the Red, Walter Giffard and many more men I had fought alongside. Conspicuously absent was Taillefer.

I stood behind the duke along with Baldwin, Richard and Robert. The duke stood to speak.

"My friends, we are gathered here because an oath was broken. It was not broken by any of us but by a Saxon, Harold Godwinson. When I heard that he had betrayed me, I sent a challenge. I offered to fight him for the crown or, if it was a mistake, to allow him to be my governor. I even offered him my sister as a wife. He did not even do me the courtesy of a reply."

All of this was news to us and while we men at arms were stoically silent, many of the nobles expressed their anger vocally.

"I knew what the answer was when he discarded Edith Swan-Neck and married the sister of Morcar and Edwin. He has bound his family to the Mercians." He shook his head, "There too is a betrayal."

I had met her and saw that Harold was a political animal. He was making an alliance with the Mercians. I might be fighting the housecarls I had come to know in the hunt.

"I have been to Rome and Pope Alexander has blessed the papal banner once more and given me this," he held up a ring. "This contains one of St Peter's hairs. We have the support of the pope. The emperor has also given us his support. The only threat comes from Count Conan but as he is busy devouring pieces of Anjou, we can leave him until we have the crown of England on my head."

Men cheered and banged the table.

He held up his hands for silence, "We will not rush into this. We have many ships but we need more. I want the fleet assembling after Midsummer Day, at Dives sur Mer. I will let you know where the army is to be mustered nearer the time. Every man in this hall must be ready to bring every warrior that he can. We will land on the south coast of England."

The council was then given the chance to make suggestions and to ask questions. I had many but I was merely a man at arms. Sir Robert was only there because he was Sir William's brother and, like me, he remained silent. One question I would have asked was why did the duke let it be known where he would land. Harold would know and if he disputed our landing then the war would end on the beaches. If I had been Duke William, I would have kept the landing site secret until we sailed.

When Sir Eustace burst into the hall our hands went to our weapons. He dropped to his knees, "My lord, Duke William, I beg you to come outside and see something wondrous. A sign from God."

The duke looked at Sir William who nodded, "Sir Eustace is a sensible fellow, my lord. I trust him."

We left the hall and Sir Eustace pointed to the sky. Everyone in the castle was staring into the heavens. There we saw a comet as it arched across the sky. Everyone made the sign of the cross and we all looked at Bishop Odo. He dropped to his knees and we all copied him. In the silence we heard his words, quite clearly, "Lord, we thank you for this sign. It tells the world that England will become Duke William's."

Any doubters were silenced by the celestial sign. When the lords left for their manors and the duke for Caen the next day, there was such a confident mood that many wanted to sail straight away.

I still wondered where Taillefer had been. Such a council needed him. He called in at Graville-Saint-Honorine on his way to Caen. He spoke to Sir Robert first and then asked to see me. As usual, we walked and talked outside.

He did not waste time on pleasantries but came to the heart of the matter immediately, "It looks like you will be coming with me to war, if you still wish to."

"Of course I do. When you were not at the council of war, I feared you would not be accompanying the duke."

He laughed, "I will always be at the duke's side. I swore an oath and unlike the earl, I do not break my oath. I was on the service of the duke. I shall say no more. I have spoken to Sir Robert first, for you are his man. He is sorry that you will not be fighting alongside the rest of his mesne but understands the needs of the duke outweigh his and Sir William."

"The duke?"

"Indirectly the duke. He wishes me to be a distraction to the English. When the earl was his guest, he was most interested in my skills. I need you to be my eyes and ears. I feel safer when you are close by."

"It will be many months until we sail."

"Perhaps, but know that I have sown seeds that will bear fruit. Earl Harold is not the only one who can wear a smiling mask of friendship." I could see that he wanted to tell me something. He looked as though he could burst. He beamed and put his mouth close to my ear. "One of the places I have been was England. It was a rough voyage but Parsifal and I survived. I sang songs for King Harold and his new bride and I became drunk."

I laughed, "You are never drunk."

"But I can act drunk and in my drunken stupor I confided to the king that Duke William planned to land on the south coast."

"But he does! Now he will be prepared."

"He is prepared but he knows not when. The duke wants his army to gather and to wait for an army that will land when the duke chooses. I spent time with Tostig, his brother, for he is in Flanders. He plans on raiding the south coast too so my words while true, will merely have one brother fight another so that when we arrive it will be a weaker army. Duke William is clever." He smiled at me, "You are right in that it will be some months before an invasion and Tostig will begin King Harold's war first. We have ships to build and to man. Now, I shall visit with Sir William and when I return, you should be ready to leave here for what might be a year or more. Say your goodbyes."

"But I will return?"

"You will and you shall have tales to tell your unborn children that will make their eyes widen in wonder."

He mounted Parsifal and galloped off. Baldwin and Odo came over and I told them what was happening. They were disappointed. "So, it will just be the two of us who fight together." Odo shook his head, "We lost Guillaume, Bruno left and now you."

"I will be with you at the invasion."

Baldwin shook his head, "You will be with Taillefer, the duke and the bishop."

"I will return here."

Odo was a wise warrior, "It may be, Dick, that many of us do not return for we will be buried in England, others may not return because we have won and been given English land. This invasion will change everything." He clasped my arm, "In case we do not see each other again, it has been an honour."

I clasped Baldwin who nodded, "And I thank you for saving my life. I would have died in that cellar were it not for you."

They left to return to the gyrus. Carl and Heloise took the news better than I thought. They had their own family now. Erik and Galmr were as upset as Odo and Baldwin. "You will be going to war and I shall see you. Until then, the three of you watch my land."

I had just saddled Geoffrey when Sir Robert arrived. "You have been honoured, Richard. You will see this war closer than any other man. I envy you the chance to be with Duke William. Your war begins this day."

"But I will return, Sir Robert."

"Perhaps."

My parting from Gunhild was a tearful one. I had forgotten her age and she knew not how much time she had left on earth. "You were your grandfather's life, Dick, and while he would be happy to see you risen so high, he would not want you to make war on his people."

"I do not think that Harold Godwinson would be his people. My grandfather was an honourable man and King Edward did promise the crown to the duke. I heard the words myself."

"Then fight with honour and be not cruel."

"You know that I will do as my grandfather would have done."

"Then all is well."

We left for Caen immediately. I did not ride mailed. I used Louis as a sumpter and he carried my war gear. I had taken all my clothes, for when war came I would need them.

Caen was a hive of activity. We were admitted to the Great Hall upon arrival. There were clerks with quills and ink. The duke was striding around and barking out commands. I watched intrigued while Taillefer enjoyed some wine.

"What is the duke doing?"

"When you have eight hundred ships, which by summer we shall, then you need crews to man them. He is sending orders to every Norman fishing port for the lords there to supply sailors. Then we have two thousand horses, they will need grazing and supplementary cereal. It is being ordered. Ten thousand men will require to be fed and he is ordering the building of granaries close to the camps where they will be mustered and assembled. Duke William has read well and will leave nothing to chance."

"Where is the fleet?"

"They are being gathered in the bay at Dives sur Mer."

I nodded my understanding for it was a sheltered anchorage and I now had an explanation of the shipwreck. Earl Harold had been spying on the fleet. He had a fleet of his own and had he discovered where Duke William's fleet was then he could have destroyed it while it was without crews. It was the easiest way to prevent an invasion.

"Come, the duke will be busy for some time. Let me take you to the weaponsmiths."

We had one weaponsmith at our manor, Sir William had two. We could hear the banging of hammers on metal long before we reached the workshop and when we did you could not hear anything. There had to be twenty weaponsmiths and their apprentices. With cloths wrapped around their ears to stop them from losing their hearing and hide aprons to prevent them from being burnt, it was like being in another world. I hope never to go to hell but the heat and noise of the workshop seemed to me like hell on earth. Taillefer tugged on my arm and led me from the cauldron of noise and fire to a large warehouse, recently erected, that seemed almost silent by comparison. We could still hear the noise but it was slightly muted and Taillefer was able to talk.

He waved an arm and I saw a vast array of helmets, swords, lances and maces. There were also a few mail hauberks. "The duke is investing much of the treasure he took from the Bretons and the men of Maine to fund this invasion. England is a rich country and when we conquer it then Duke William may well be the richest ruler." He tapped my chest, "And you will be rich too."

I shrugged, "I have money enough already, Taillefer. What would I do with it?"

He laughed, "Spend it, of course. You are an enigma, Richard fitz Malet."

Over the next months, I saw a different side to Taillefer. He spent long hours each day with the duke and his brother poring over maps. He studied documents which told of the tides and the prevailing winds. Taillefer was there to add his own observations to the maps and the documents. When he had travelled England, he had been observing. Since our first visit, he had spent many months in the kingdom. King Edward had welcomed him. Perhaps there had been collusion between the duke and the king. Had they anticipated this turn of events? I was used as a servant. I fetched food and drink or went to the library to bring as yet unused documents. In that way I learned more about the invasion than anyone who was not the duke, bishop or Taillefer. I learned that we were to land at a bay called Pevensey. It had a lagoon and the ships we used could land men there easily and, more importantly, could be defended. I discovered that the granary and camp were being built at Saint-Valery-sur-Somme from where it was but a sixty mile voyage to Pevensey. The duke had also prepared his defences. There was a wooden castle being built close to Dives sur Mer. It would be carried in pieces across to Pevensey so that we would have a castle within days of landing. The preparations were astounding. Mercenaries were hired. Duke William was clever. They were hired with the promise of rewards when we won. It was clever as it meant he would not have to pay those who died.

It was not all acting as a servant. Taillefer had been told by the duke that he could initiate the battle, wherever and whenever that came. We practised every day. Sometimes it was on foot but more often than not it was while mounted. Geoffrey was the same size as Parsifal and I now had both more strength and skills. I could not beat Taillefer but I could give him a better work out. Occasionally, the bishop and the duke would join us. The duke was not a tall man but he was powerfully built. He was also an excellent rider and one of his boasts was that he had never been unhorsed. Those were good times as our blades rang together in the inner bailey of Caen Castle.

I served when they ate but less wine was consumed than normal. It was as if the duke and his nobles were preparing for war while they ate. I had come to know the kitchen staff well and I did not miss out. One of the younger cooks had taken a shine to me. I did not return her affections but I knew how to play a part so that she saved treats for me. I did not think I was deceiving the woman. Had she asked me outright then I would have told her that there was no chance of a liaison.

It was in May that a messenger arrived from Count Eustace. Tostig and his Norsemen had raided the Isle of Wight and Sandwic. Although they had been driven off by the English fleet, the fyrd had been summoned. King Harold waited on the south coast for our invasion. His fleet even sailed close to Dives sur Mer to observe our growing fleet. Everything pointed towards an imminent invasion. I found myself smiling when the news was told. I knew that August or even September were the earliest that our army and fleet would be ready to sail. Fields lay untended as the English army waited to repel us on the beaches.

Chapter 21

Saint-Valery-sur-Somme August 1066

I now saw for myself the results of the ink written by the clerks. When we reached the village, I was greeted by the sight of a patch of grazing, all two hundred acres of it, ready for our horses. There were horse lines already embedded in the ground. In the distance I saw the granaries, built off the ground to prevent rats from feasting. Then there was the land reserved for tents. Bread ovens had been built and cess pits dug in preparation for the army that would board the armada. Duke William was ensuring that the army he took would be well fed with horses fattened on grass and an army without disease. We now awaited the army which had already begun to arrive. The Bretons had the furthest to travel while the men of Flanders were already here. The fleet was still at Dives sur Mer. The duke and his senior leaders were housed in the village. Even Taillefer had been assigned a tent which I, as his servant, shared. Our horses tethered, we walked amongst the other warriors. We knew some of Count Eustace's men from the incident at Douvres. It was good to talk to men you knew. Once you fought with a man, you were bonded for life or until a sword or spear took you.

Sometimes we walked around the bay and sea front. It was more than big enough to cope with the eight hundred ships that would ferry us to England. Until the rest of the army arrived it was quite pleasant to walk, almost alone, and stare across the sea to England.

"This will be the greatest adventure of my life, Dick." Taillefer smiled, "I will make a confession to you. When I took you to England it changed my life. I saw and did things there that might have been impossible without you. When we came to England my English was poor. You helped to teach me the language of your grandfather. You are my good luck charm and when we cross to fight, I want you there with me. I wish you to know that whatever happens after the battle, which I am convinced God will give to us, you shall be able

to wear the spurs given to you. The duke has promised that
you shall be knighted."

"But I like being your servant."

"You are more than a servant and besides, you will still
ride with me. You shall be Sir Richard, Taillefer's Olivier.
When we defeat the Godwinson clan, there will still be a
land to win and with you at my side, we shall lead men to
take it."

He made it sound so exciting. I was honoured that he
thought of me as Olivier, Roland's best friend. I would be the
subject of songs. As much as I missed my friends, Bruno,
Baldwin and Odo, they could never compare to the
adventure I was now enjoying. We spent the days either in
conference with the duke or practising. I groomed my horses
every day as well as Parsifal. They enjoyed the grazing and
the peace. They fattened up but I knew that eventually the
grazing would run out. We could not stay here indefinitely.

August came to an end and the weather changed slightly.
The duke had not yet sent for all his fleet but some ships had
arrived and he used them to discourage the fishing ships and
English warships that tried to spy on our camp. We heard, at
the start of September, that Tostig had joined with the
legendary Harald Hadrada, the famous Varangian, and they
had invaded Northumbria, using the Humber to sail close to
Jorvik. When, at the end of that first week of September, we
heard that King Harold had disbanded his army to allow his
men to harvest the fields, the duke sent for the fleet.

The small seaport and the fields around it were now
crowded with ten thousand men. The fact that not all were
Normans made for some fractious moments. The Bretons
and Flemish rubbed the edges of one another but the
personality of Duke William ensured that peace prevailed. It
was good to see Bruno again. He was still Sir William's
standard bearer. He could not believe that I had turned down
the knighthood.

"Dick, you and I are both good warriors but we cannot
count on a knighthood. I grasped mine with both hands. You
should have done the same."

I smiled and told him what Taillefer had said. "I think, Bruno, that my grandfather, while he might not be happy that we invade his homeland, would be overjoyed if that was where I was knighted. This is meant to be, and then Taillefer and I can ride this land and make it Norman. We are lucky to be part of this."

"Aye, you are right. You know this land and I do not. What is it like?"

"Like Normandy but the country is richer. That is why the Danes and the Norse raided it so often. The English had a king who paid the Danes a fortune each year to keep them from raiding." I leaned in, "I have been privy to many conversations and I can tell you that the duke intends to give lands and manors to every knight who survives. You will have your own manor."

"There is the rub, though, Dick, we have to survive and I have heard that the housecarls are hard to beat. You should know that for your grandfather was a housecarl."

He was right, "We are just lucky that their housecarls are their best and while they are the strongest part of their army, they are also the smallest in number."

"But the people of England will fight us. Even a farmer with a billhook can bring down a horse and rider. Our mail is good protection but once on the ground we are helpless. We are like crabs on their backs and easy prey."

"Serving with Taillefer has given me an insight into Duke William and his military mind. He will not sacrifice his army needlessly. We shall use cunning to defeat them."

If we thought we would sail quickly then the wind thought otherwise and we had to wait. While we waited for the winds and tides to be right, we heard that Tostig and Harald Hadrada had defeated Edwin and Morcar. The Norse now ruled the north of England and when a couple of days later we heard that King Harold had taken his army to dispute with them, then we prayed for the winds to change. They did not. In desperation, the duke ordered the relics from the church to be paraded around the bay. That night the whole army prayed that the march had been successful and when we woke, we found it had. The winds had changed and we could board the mighty fleet.

It took all day to bring the horses to the bay and it was in the middle of the afternoon and at high tide when we boarded. Duke William was aboard the Mora, a brand new ship and the gift of his wife. He was boarded first and he sailed out to the bay where he awaited us. As ships were loaded, they joined him. He had organised well and each ship's captain knew his allocated place. He wanted no collisions and, as the sun set and as the last ship left the shore, he hung a huge lantern from his stern and he led us out to sea and into the night. Every ship hung a lantern from its stern and as darkness enveloped us, we heard the duke's horn sounding. It was an eerie experience. Sailing at night was terrifying and the horn sounded like some stricken sea creature. It took many hours to cross the sixty miles but the wind was steady and pushed the laden vessels north. We were lucky that the seas were calm. On the way from Dives sur Mer a storm had blown up and some ships had been dashed on the rocks. The horn faded and we could no longer see the stern light of the Mora. We had to trust that God still smiled on the duke and his endeavours. As the sun came up behind us, we spied his ship, the sail furled, waiting for us, just off the coast of England. Behind us, the eight hundred ships seemed to make a bridge that reached to the horizon and beyond. How could any face us?

We reefed our sails to edge into the lagoon and bay at Pevensey. There was no horde of farmers with weapons to dispute our landing but it took time to navigate the narrow entrance. We were two ships behind the duke's. As we ground onto the mud, Taillefer and I leapt to the shallows. The archers who had travelled on our ship, all ten of them, joined us with nocked arrows. The duke had been the first to splash into the water and with the archers scampering ahead of us, we headed to the land. It was as we stepped from the water that Duke William tripped and landed face down on the shore.

Bishop Odo made the sign of the cross and we all wondered if this was an omen. Taillefer laughed and said,

"Why Duke William, you have England in your hands. It is a good omen."

The duke nodded his gratitude and took Taillefer's proffered hand, "Thank you, my friend." He pointed to the ruined Roman fort of Anderida and said to the bishop, "Brother, have a palisade join those walls. Until we have the castle erected, this shall be our defence. Now get some horses unloaded. Taillefer, take some men and find us a way through these marshes. They protect us well but I would find a better place for the castle."

"Aye, my lord. Come, Dick."

"Count Eustace, do not land the horses yet but have the foot secure this. Taillefer, I will come with you."

There were more than twenty knights that rode with the duke and we were forced to travel west in order to reach the track around the marshy lagoon. As we rode, I saw that less than a tenth of our ships had even entered the lagoon. The rest were still well out to sea. We only learned the names of the places through which we passed later. When we found the tiny village and port of Haestingas even I could see that it was a better place to have landed. One side, the west, was protected by another marshy lagoon, Bulverhythe, while the other, the east, had the marshy valleys of the two rivers, Brede and Rother. The houses were on a rocky outcrop that was the perfect place for a castle.

The duke's face was exultant when he turned, "Richard fitz Malet, you are well mounted, return to my brother. I want the fleet brought and landed here. The men who are landed already can follow our route. You can be their guide."

"Yes, my lord."

"Do not get lost!"

"No, my lord."

I was exhausted by the time I reached the bishop. He had already done as ordered and there was a palisade erected. He listened to my words and then shouted, "Hold the landings. Sir Aimeri, you and your conroi will stay here and guard this camp. The rest will follow Richard fitz Malet. I will follow when I have given my orders to the fleet." He added quietly, "He has found a good place?"

"It is well defended by nature and better than this one."

"Good. Do not begin your march until I am mounted."

I rode to a higher piece of ground and dismounted while I waited. The archers, crossbowmen and spearmen who had landed formed up. I saw Odo amongst them. He rushed towards me, his face alight, "I hoped I would see you. I kept looking for you at Saint Valery but you were always with the high and the mighty."

"Well today, old friend, we will march together. We have many miles to go but it will be to a better place than this marsh."

The ships would reach Haestingas before we did and that meant the duke could begin to erect his castle. The bishop and his household knights joined me and we were the only mounted men. We led a column of men six hundred strong. They were the ones who had disembarked.

It was late in the afternoon when we wearily walked into the fortified camp. The castle had yet to be built but the duke had ditches already dug and there was food cooking.

The next day while the foot soldiers erected the castle, the two thousand mounted men went on a giant chevauchée. The duke wanted to ravage the land formerly ruled by Earl Godwin. We rode for twenty miles around Haestingas taking animals, food and burning houses. He wanted to make the English come to fight us. From one captured thegn, we learned that King Harold had fought a battle in the north of the land and defeated the Vikings. He was heading back south. Duke William would have his battle.

The news of the battle was confirmed when Robert, one of his English kinsmen, rode in to offer support. "Cousin, King Harold is coming south. He is in Lundenwic and gathering an army already. I advise you to stay behind your ditches and walls."

"You do not know me, cousin, for that is not my way. King Edward willed this kingdom to me and an oath breaker stole it. We will watch for King Harold and even though he brings every man in England to fight us, we will do battle with him. We have God on our side and he will give us our victory."

We ravaged the land for the first two weeks in October and patrols of Breton horsemen were kept as outriders. It was they who told the duke that the English were coming and heading for a strong feature called Caldbec Hill. It was just eight miles from our castle. When men on the walls reported the English fleet were out to sea then we knew that Harold sought to trap us here. He would fight us on land while his fleet prevented our escape. Our ships were transports and his were warships. We were trapped.

If King Harold thought he had the beating of Duke William, he was in for a shock. The foragers were called in and the army stood to arms. Priests circulated hearing confessions. We were about to fight and while we believed that God had given us the right none of us wanted to die without absolution.

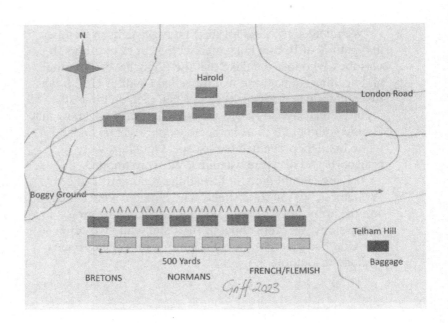

Chapter 22

The Battle of Hastings October 1066

Alan the Red's Breton scouts had kept us well apprised of the English movements. Men still raided but other than that we had kept close to the walls of the castle. The duke had us roused before dawn and we marched with our mail upon our horses to the hill called Hecheland. The enormous forest of Andresweald lay to the north of the English camp. We knew its position from the noise we heard coming from their camp. It was clear to us, for the Bretons had scouted well, that the English were camped on the main road to London. King Harold was preventing us from reaching his city.

Our huge column stopped and we donned our mail hauberks. There was an excited air, especially amongst the knights closest to the duke. While we had camped and waited, I had been with Taillefer and heard them discuss the battle as though it had already been fought. They knew that while Harold had defeated the Norsemen, he had lost men and they had been forced to march north and then south. Even I knew that was not good preparation for battle. However, I also knew that the men we faced were men like my grandfather. These were hard men who were used to marching rather than riding and, most importantly of all, they were defending their homes from invaders.

Once we had donned mail and men had helped each other to fasten ventails and don helmets, we mounted. The exception was Taillefer. He did not wear his helmet and his coif hung about his shoulders. He had reminded the duke of his promise to allow him to begin the battle. As we headed towards the Santlache, the Sandy Stream, Taillefer went over his plans for I was part of them.

"The English need to be disheartened before the battle starts and I am the man for that. I shall dance Parsifal, sing the Song of Roland and juggle my daggers and swords. I shall intimidate the English with my lance and when I summon you, I want you to ride to join me." We had taught

Geoffrey a few steps and we hoped that a dancing Geoffrey would distract the English enough to think that every Norman horse and rider was as skilled. "You will take out your daggers and juggle them too. Then we bow and ride back to our men. Hopefully, the English will leave their ridge."

It sounded simple and we knew from the scouts that the ridge occupied by the English was well chosen. It was narrow and had flanks protected by steep ground and rocks. The ground before it was steep. The duke and Bishop Odo both knew that our best chance of victory lay in the English leaving the safety of the ridge and attacking us. Harold had shown, in Brittany, that he was a brave and impulsive man. The saving of the two men from the sands at Mont St. Michel had shown that. The duke hoped he would be as impulsive here on his ridge.

It was the Bretons led by Alan the Red who reached our position first. They would form the left flank. Along with him were mercenaries from Anjou, Poitou and Maine. The duke and we Normans were in the centre and Count Eustace led the Flemish and French knights on the right. We marched in line of battle which meant that the archers were the closest to the enemy, then the largest contingent, the spearmen on foot, and finally, the horsemen. When we reached the position that the duke had chosen, we would simply turn to the right and our battle lines would be drawn. We marched in silence. It was not to keep us hidden, we could see English light horsemen, just a handful, watching us. It was to help us prepare for a bloody battle. In the distance we could hear mailed men moving; their mail and weapons jingling as they did so. They too were marching into position. They would know better than anybody where they were to fight for this was their land and King Harold had ruled it for many years. They would know every fold and every rock.

When we stopped, not long after the second hour of daylight, we saw the spears of the English as they rose over the ridge, marching to their positions. The men before us gave way so that the duke, the bishop, the standard bearers along with Taillefer and I could view the enemy.

The papal standard was held by Turstin son of Rollo. He would not be fighting in the fore but King Harold needed to see the standard for it was visible justification for our war and showed that we had the approval of the pope. It was Vital, one of the bishop's oathsworn, who pointed his spear at the ridge, "See, my lord, Harold and his banner."

The English king had placed his banner at the highest place on the ridge and he had an unobstructed view over the massive shield wall below him. I recognised housecarls in the front rank. I knew them by their dress and their size. They had their shields and spears before them. That meant, as my grandfather had told me, that their long axes would be hanging from their back. They would not need them for the first phase of the battle.

The duke said, "Brother, remember that I would have you and your oathsworn guard Turstin and the papal banner. Your swords and spears must keep that safe. While it flies it is a rallying point for us and a taunt to the enemy. When the time is right, your men shall be the reserve that seals our victory."

"Aye, brother, I am not happy for I would rather swing my sword at the enemy. I will stay with the boys, servants and priests on Telham Hill. We will keep up a prayer while you fight."

The priests were moving along our line offering absolution to our men. When the fighting began they and the boys and servants would fetch the wounded and heal them. As I surveyed the hill, I knew that this day would be a bloody one.

The duke turned to us, "You still wish to begin this battle, Taillefer?"

"Of course, my lord. Are we ready?"

The duke shaded his eyes to look at the sun, "I will sound the horn for the attack at the third hour of daylight."

"Then now is the time. Come, Dick, it is time for our show. Unfasten your ventail and hang your helmet from the cantle." I did so as we closed to within a hundred paces of the English. Our archers were a further one hundred and fifty paces further back. "Remember, I am the show and the entertainer. I will shout for you when it is time for your entrance. Until then, watch."

Taillefer was a master showman. He was a great knight but he was a greater showman.

He smiled, "This is what I was born to do, Dick. I shall sing the song of this day when I am too old to ride to war. Men will talk of Taillefer's taunting of the English."

"You take care, my lord."

He laughed, "I fear not these clods who lumber about the battlefield like grazing cows."

With his lance in his hand, he spurred Parsifal and rode to within forty paces of the English housecarls. Parsifal stepped proudly as he had been trained to do. I could see the English faces, for they wore no ventails, and they looked more bemused than anything. What could one man do? He rammed his spear into the ground and began to prance Parsifal in a parallel line to the spears. He shouted, as he took out his swords, "I am Taillefer and the greatest of knights. I come here to show you English that you cannot win this day." He spoke in Norman and so only a few of the English could understand. His voice carried to Harold for I saw him turn to the men around him and then point at Taillefer. The two had got on well in Brittany. Taillefer then began to sing the song of Roland. He sang it better that day than I have ever heard it sung. The melodious words and rhythm made the fact that they were in French immaterial and the English seemed to enjoy them. He juggled the whole time and never once dropped a sword. When he finished, he sheathed his swords and bowed. I saw a few housecarls bang their shields. I know not if it was in approval or in anger.

Taillefer rode back to pick up his spear. I wondered if now was my time but he shook his head as he caught my eye. He pulled the spear and rode at the housecarls. They presented a wall of spears thinking he was attacking and, at the last moment, he whirled Parsifal and came back towards me. He was laughing as though this was a huge joke. He rode back and this time the spears did not rise. They thought he was making them look foolish. This time however, he jabbed his lance into the face of a housecarl and when he pulled it back the man tumbled down the slope. Taillefer gave a great roar but it was his last for the housecarls ran at him. Even as he drew a sword, three spears impaled him and he was dragged from Parsifal's back. I was his man and I should have done something. I did nothing as he was butchered before my eyes.

It was only when a spearman ran from the lines to grab at Parsifal's reins that I reacted. Taillefer was dead but they would not take his horse. I spurred Geoffrey and couched my lance. Despite the shouts of warning from the housecarls, the man did not seem to hear them, intent as he was on taking his prize. It was an easy kill for he wore just a leather hauberk and my, as yet unused, spearhead slid through it and into his body. I transferred my lance to my shield arm and grabbed Parsifal's reins. He knew me and came with me. I descended the slope to cheers from our men. The spearmen banged their shields with their spears. Perhaps their Norseman heritage made them approve the act of a berserker, for that was what Taillefer had been. He had thought himself immortal. He had once taught me a word, hubris. I now knew what it meant.

I rode up to the duke. His face was a mask. "He died well. Take his horse to the boys and then join your brother. Today the three Malet brothers will fight as one."

My heart was in my boots as I rode to the hill. The man I admired most in the world was dead. My future had been butchered along with him on Caldbec Hill.

As I approached the men and boys close to the top of Telham Hill, I recognised two of them who came to greet me. It was Erik and Galmr. They had no mail and so were not needed to fight with the spearmen. Instead they had been assigned to guard the camp. I was pleased. "That was mightily done, master."

I nodded, "Watch Parsifal for me. Give him water and let him graze. He has lost a master and I have lost a friend. We will both need to grieve but now is not the time."

I headed back to the line of knights and men at arms standing behind the spearmen. Even as I did so, I heard the horn and the archers and spearmen began to climb towards the English. If nothing else Taillefer's sacrifice had told the duke that the English had few, if any archers. The English began to bang their shields and to shout, "Oli-crosse" others chanted, "Ut, ut, ut". It was a deafening and confusing noise intended to intimidate the archers and spearmen.

Sir William turned to me, "I am sorry about Taillefer's death, Richard, but I am happy that you fight with Robert and me. This was meant to be."

"And I will try to uphold the family honour."

Robert pointed at the unrecovered corpse of the man I had killed, "You have already done that, Richard. Ride at my side."

"I will, my lord."

The archers halted just less than a hundred paces from the English line. I saw Odo leading our archers. I knew that each archer had a bag containing twenty four arrows. They drew back and then began to send arrow after arrow into the shield wall. The metal heads smacked into shields and mail. Some English were hit, we could hear their cries, but not enough. They kept up their chants as the air was filled with arrows. The front ranks of housecarls and spearmen appeared to be intact and I could only hope that our archers were doing some damage. The archers the English possessed had some success and some men fell. As their arrow bags were emptied so the archers filtered back down the slope and through the spearmen to refill arrow bags. There were bodies left on the slope but I saw Odo who cheerfully waved as he passed us. Odo was the only archer with a mail hauberk. A gift from Baldwin and me after the battle of Dinan, this was the first time he had worn it to war.

We then watched the spearmen march up the hill. There were bodies to negotiate and if I had led the English, I would have made a last moment charge to drive them down the hill for the spearmen did not have locked shields. The front ranks of spearmen had hauberks but the rest had a greater variety of leather and metal studded brigandines. The arrows that came from behind the front line were now augmented by stones, huge lumps of wood and even maces. Some of those on the hill had fashioned stones with a rope attached and they flew into the air to crash down on the advancing men. By the time they reached the shield wall some had fallen already and there were gaps that the English exploited.

Robert turned to me, "This is not going as I had expected, Richard, I expected an English army weakened by a long march."

I pointed my weapon at the front ranks. "They are housecarls, my lord. They have the advantage of a slope and their front three ranks' spears can all reach our men. Wait until they draw their Danish axes. The battle is going as I expected and it will be both long and bloody."

He nodded, "And had your grandfather not come to Normandy with our grandsire then you might well be standing there."

The thought had occurred to me. My Norman birth was an accident in more ways than one.

Sir Ambrose rode down to us and spoke to Sir William, standing just ten paces from us, "My lord, when the horn sounds you are to advance your men with the rest of the line. The duke wishes the men on foot to be supported."

"Of course." He turned, "Today the men of de Caux will earn great honour and for those who follow Duke William, there will be land and treasure. We need to drive these men from the ridge."

Everyone cheered as though this was a foregone conclusion. Taillefer had thought so too and his butchered body now lay trampled at the top of the hill. It took some time for riders to deliver the duke's message. I saw wounded men making their way down the slope. It was not a flight but it showed that the English were having the better of the battle. It would not take long for the trickle of wounded men to become a rout of the rest.

Baldwin had nudged his horse next to mine and said, "Your ventail."

I realised that I had not fastened it following Taillefer's last command to me. I nodded and fastened it. We were all anonymous except for the design on our shields. Some men, the duke included, had no design. My chequerboard one and Sir Robert's were the only ones except for Sir William's in our mesne. I knew that it would draw attention to me. I was now Taillefer's man and I had slain an Englishman. They would seek me out. I rested my lance against Geoffrey and checked the guige strap holding the shield to my body and the smaller strap through which my armed passed. That done I held the reins and said, "Today, Geoffrey, you have your sternest test."

Baldwin nodded, made the sign of the cross and said, "Amen."

I picked up my lance and placed its butt on my foot. We waited.

The horn sounded and Sir William waved his lance forward. I wondered, as we began to move towards the streams and boggy ground, if those using a spear, a similar weapon to a lance but shorter would regret it. I had seen, when I had passed through their ranks, that some of the Bretons did not have either a spear or a lance but a clutch of javelins. Would they prove more useful? This was a day when a warrior used the weapons he trusted and in which he had the most confidence. Our lines became a little disordered as we picked our way through the boggy ground and crossed Santlache but Sir William slowed on the other side so that we could form ranks once more. We spurred our horses but it was not a charge. The ground was too steep and our spearmen were before us. King Harold had chosen well. As we drew closer, I saw how tightly packed the English were. The place they had chosen determined that. All that I could see was a wall of metal protected by wooden shields and sharp spears. How could we break it without the speed of a charging horse and the natural fear of a man facing such beasts?

"Make way for the horsemen!" The spearmen, grateful of the support, moved to the side to allow us to get closer. It made their ranks more solid and we, like my tunic, were a chequerboard. From the backs of our horses we could thrust further than they could but the English were arrayed in three ranks and spears were jabbed at us. I was lucky in that the spear that came for me struck my mail hauberk and not Geoffrey. I pulled back and jabbed at the housecarl who had tried to wound me. He brought his shield up and deflected the head but it scored a line along his cheek. Sir Robert took advantage of the distraction and thrust his lance into the housecarl's left shoulder. I stood in my stirrups, knowing that the man's shield arm would not be as strong and I jabbed down. I was right and the shield could not stop the blow which enlarged the hole in the byrnie made by Sir Robert and my triangular head ripped a large hole in the warrior. He was a brave man and a tough one but as Geoffrey snapped at him, Sir Robert's lance entered his head and he died.

We were not having it all our own way. It was Sir Eustace that was the first to die. Two housecarls had lost their spears and had swung the shields around their backs. They swung their Danish axes and one took the head of Sir Eustace's mount in one blow and as the horse tumbled, a second hacked through the chest of a falling Sir Eustace. Sir Eustace's squire foolishly tried to save his already dying master and he was speared while his horse had a leg hacked by the third axe. Sir Drogo grabbed the standard.

It was almost a stalemate where we were after that. Knights were reluctant to approach the Danish axes and the housecarls dared not leave their ridge. I kept a tight rein on Geoffrey and when a spear came at his head jerked it out of the way and then I thrust with my lance. The English learned that the warrior with the red chequerboard shield knew his business. I wounded three housecarls and suffered just a line scored in Geoffrey's flank. It was the spearmen who were suffering the most. We could move our horses back but those in the front rank, engaged in a bloody duel of their own could not. They killed their enemies and then they died.

The crisis when it came was two-fold. The Bretons had suffered more than we had and they began to edge back. At the same time, a cry went up that Duke William had fallen. It was hard to tell as he had neither a design on his shield or a distinctive horse. The men around him began to fall back to the Santlache. It was not a flight but the whole of our line began to move away from the housecarls. The dismounted men did not wait but they fled. I could not blame them as they had fought for longer than we had and endured more casualties.

"Walk your horses!" Sir William's commanding voice steadied us. It was the right decision. The housecarls would not leave their ridge and if we retreated then they would hold the field. The English had reinforcements who were on their way from Stamford Bridge. We had none.

The duke shouted, "Your duke lives still!" He lowered his ventail and pushed his helmet back to reveal his face but it was almost too late.

Even when Count Eustace shouted, "Your duke lives," men still began to fall back more quickly. A huge body of Englishmen, led by thegns, thought the battle was over and pursued the Bretons. It was Bishop Odo and his oathsworn who, with the papal banner, charged down Telham Hill. He would be swamped by the English but there was a chance that he might hold them.

Sir William shouted, "Let us rid the field of these English!" and lowering his lance charged obliquely to the Englishmen. Sir William de Warenne saw what the men of de Caux were doing and he led Bruno and his knights. Geoffrey had the chance to open his legs and he hurtled to close with an isolated Duke William. We caught the English in the open and our lances ran red with their blood. These were not housecarls. This was the fyrd led by a couple of reckless thegns. With Bishop Odo before and two conrois behind, they stood no chance. When we had finished and the survivors had fled, the Santlache became red with their blood. We called it the bloody lake after that, Senlac.

The duke ordered the recall of the rest of our men. Only Count Eustace's men had not been forced back and they descended in good order, facing the English. The English cheered as though they had enjoyed a victory. The duke consulted with his brother and his other senior leaders while we fed and watered our horses. Geoffrey's wound, which had seemed so innocuous now seemed dangerous. I walked him to the baggage on Telham Hill.

"Erik, I will ride Parsifal. Clean Geoffrey's wound with vinegar. You will have to hold his head tightly for he will not like it but the wound cannot become worse. Seal it with honey and give him this when you apply the vinegar." I handed him an apple I had taken on our raids.

Galmr looked at my surcoat which was now redder than it had been. "Master, are you hurt?"

I shook my head, "This is the blood of Englishmen. They died well and I was lucky."

"Then stay lucky, my lord, for we know that we will not find another master such as you in a hurry."

Their concern was touching. I mounted Parsifal. If he was missing his former master, I could not tell. However, he seemed eager to go to war once more.

I saw the English on the top of the hill as they shifted their own wounded and rearranged their lines. The battle was far from over. I rode Parsifal back to our line. Sir William was returning from a conversation with the duke.

"The English are proving a little stronger than we expected but their rash attack has given the duke an idea. We are to tempt the English into pursuit. He will not ask the Bretons to fall back as that might make them quit the field completely, although he has told Alan the Red that no ships will take any man back to Normandy unless he so orders. We are to fight for an hour and then Lord Mortemer and we will turn as though fleeing. Upon my command, we whirl and cut them down as they chase us. We then return to the fray. After a suitable passage of time Count Eustace will do the same on our right. In this way we will thin their numbers."

It was a plan but the English on the ridge looked to me to be almost as thick as ever. As we advanced up the hill, however, I saw that while the front rank was still mailed, the ones behind were not. Perhaps we had killed more than I had thought. Parsifal was the most eager of the horses to get to battle. He had not charged as yet and, perhaps, he had vengeance on his mine. I had to rein him in as we picked our way up the slope. The closer to the crest we came the more obstacles lay before us. This time there was no shower of arrows, stones and maces. An occasional arrow descended and one or two roped stones were hurled but that was all. I still had my original lance but every horseman had taken the opportunity to rearm and it was a wall of spears, lances and javelins that would prick, poke and stab at the men on the ridge. Many of the housecarls had lost their spears and their shields were around their backs. That meant they would swing their two handed axes. Many knights were riding their second horses or were fighting on foot.

Parsifal was a skilled horse and while he was still fresh I tried a trick that Taillefer had taught me. When I neared the axe-wielding housecarl I had chosen as my opponent, I stood in my stirrups to stab down at him. He had room and stepped back. His movement allowed me to jerk back on Parsifal's reins and make him flail in the air. The trick of Taillefer was that he had trained Parsifal to walk forward. When I released the reins, his mighty hooves crashed down to crush the helmet and skull of the axe man. More, it allowed me to stab at the unarmoured man behind him. I pulled out my lance and stabbed a second.

I heard an English voice shout, "Kill that Norman with the mad horse."

I calmly walked Parsifal backwards. The men who ran to obey the order and slay the horseman who had become slightly isolated were easy prey. My shield guarded my left and my hand darted like an adder's tongue. When I backed Parsifal between Sir Robert and Baldwin, all those who had raced for glory lay dead and we were now on the flatter ground at the top of the hill.

We now duelled with men who sought to kill our horses while we sought flesh and not mail. A cry from our right distracted everyone as the duke's horse was slain. It made us reel a little for the English thought he was dead. A second horse was fetched and he remounted. We had lost the ground we had gained. Perhaps the horse was not as good a mount as his first one, for a few moments after he had resumed fighting it, too, was slain. This time the two Sir Williams took the initiative and shouted, simultaneously, "Back!"

We knew what we were doing and wheeled our mounts to ride back down the hill. Those fighting on foot simply joined the other dismounted men to the left and right. There were just eighty of us who fled. We did not gallop but let our mounts use the slope. When Sir William Malet saw the bloody stream ahead of us and the hundreds of English who had followed us were spread out behind us, he ordered us to turn. These were not the housecarls and thegns. These were the farmers, the blacksmiths, the tanners and yeomen. They had helmets, spears and swords but no mail. Few even wore leather. They would stand no chance against us.

I urged Parsifal forward although, in truth, he needed little encouragement from me. An English voice shouted, "Back!" For most of them, it was too late. The ones at the back had a chance of survival but the ones at the fore had none. They would have been better to face us but they were terrified and we had their backs as targets. It was too easy. I chose my target and stabbed while selecting the next man to die. By the time we resumed our position, I had slain eight men. More importantly, we had pushed back the men on the ridge and were, once more, fighting on flatter ground.

I could see King Harold quite clearly. His standard was behind the main line and there was an unbroken phalanx of housecarls before him. Our trick had caused confusion and chaos in the English lines and one of Sir William de Warenne's knights, Robert fitz Erneis, saw his chance for glory. He and his squire galloped through the disordered fyrd, slashing their swords as they went. The squire was cut down before they even neared the standard but Sir Robert lasted long enough to cleave the helmet of a housecarl before being hacked to pieces along with his horse.

Perhaps that stirred the English for a fyrdman, wearing a leather apron and wielding a long axe, ducked beneath the sword of Duke William and brought it down to strike his helmet. I heard the ring and saw the dent but the duke retained his saddle and the axeman was speared by the duke's bodyguard.

We were all tiring but neither side was willing to concede. When Count Eustace made his feigned retreat, the men who chased him did so on weary legs. As with our attack, the result was a culling of the poorly armoured. Another result was that the two wings, the Bretons and the Flemish, had turned the edges of the English line. It was no longer a straight edge. It bowed and arched. My lance was finally broken as we edged forward to fight against what was the strongest part of the line, the men before King Harold and his bodyguard. It had served me well and the English badly. The fyrdman who hacked off its end gave a roar of triumph and raced at me to kill me and my horse. Taillefer had taught me well and my sword was out of the scabbard across my back and hacking down even as he lunged at me with his sword. My sword sliced through the helmet as though it was parchment. It was poorly made. His skull was dented and blood spurted. His sword tip touched the mail on my leg but did no harm.

The top of the hill was now a confused scene. We no longer had our solid lines. I could still see Baldwin and Sir Robert but there were dismounted Normans between us. Our horses were like islands in a sea of swords. It afforded us a good view and I could see that the two English flanks were tightly drawn in. The English standard still flew and the housecarls were as determined as ever behind their shields and axes. I heard the arrows from behind us and saw their steep flight into the air. Our archers had replenished their arrow bags and were sending them over the two lines to fall in the centre of the English line. This time the arrows had a devastating effect. Those who had them held shields over their heads but many of the fyrd had none and it was they who died first. However, the housecarls also suffered. They were tired. Wearing mail and holding a shield aloft were wearying. Some fell.

My half-brother shouted, "Now is our time, de Caux. One last charge and we can take this hill."

Even Parsifal was tiring but I owed it to his master to obey. I dug my heels in. The housecarl to my right did not see my sword come down and hack across his neck. I did not see the axe that came at my left. If I had still borne my round shield, I would have died for the axe would have taken off my leg. As it was, my shield took the blow and held true. As he raised his axe to hit me again, I leaned over and stabbed him in the face with my sword. Even in his dying, he tried to fight and his hand grabbed my blade. He held on even though his fingers were cut to the bone and he fell backwards. I drew a second sword and, as I did so, saw the standard fall. It rose again but I knew that the standard bearer had fallen. It was hard to see if Harold was still alive for the housecarls looked identical and all were smeared and besmirched with blood and gore.

The breakthrough when it came was dramatic. Duke William, flanked by Sir Ambrose and Sir Vital, galloped for the king. Other knights whom I did not know flanked him. I spied Bruno amongst them and I urged Parsifal through the maelstrom of bodies, hacking and slashing my sword as I went. This was a fresh blade and was sharp. Although some of those I slew were housecarls most were the fyrd. The arrows had ceased but I saw their effect and I recognised King Harold. He must have made the mistake of looking up, for an arrow was sticking from his skull. His fingers were clasped around it. If the English had worn a ventail he might not have been struck. It was Bruno who reached the standard bearer. Bruno slashed down and the brave English warrior, already pierced by arrows, fell. Another housecarl ran at Bruno with his spear. Bruno had his back to him for he was reaching for the standard. My sword came as a complete surprise to the man and the razor sharp blade took his head. As Bruno held it aloft, a cheer went up and many of the English, their king dead, his bodyguards slain and the standard taken, fled north.

The housecarls did not and they rushed to surround the body of their king. They were oathsworn and would keep their oath unto death. I would not risk Parsifal and I dismounted. Odo ran up to me, a bow and empty war bag in his hand. He had a short sword but it would avail him little against a housecarl. "Odo, hold Parsifal. I still have men to hew."

"Aye. We have done our part." Bruno and the others dismounted. We picked our way across the bodies and we heard the housecarls keening. They would not die easily. They were weary and their axes were nocked. Even blunted they could still kill. A blow could smash a skull protected by a helmet and I was glad that I had a long shield. The axe blow had damaged it a little but it would still protect my left side and so long as I had a sword in my hand then I had confidence that I would win. I looked into the resigned eyes of the housecarl who faced me. His helmet was dented and he had been wounded by an arrow, the stump of which still protruded from his byrnie. He nodded at me as I advanced. Even if he was mortally wounded, he would still try to kill me and take me with him. I waited for the swing of his two handed Danish axe. It was calculated. He had to strike first for he was so tired he might only have one blow left in him. As he swung, I stepped back. The axe head almost shaved me. I moved forward and swung my sword backhand across his throat. It gave him a warrior's death. The blood from his slashed throat sprayed me. And so we advanced. We slew them and they were so tired that few of our men were hurt. The circle grew smaller until the last man died.

Sir William shouted, "Mount, there are men to chase."

Even as I remounted Parsifal, I saw a knight, Sir Ralf of Exmes, dismount and hack the dead king in the leg. I still know not why he did it but it was witnessed by Duke William, who roared, "To mutilate a dead enemy is not to be tolerated. Sir Ralf, you are no longer a knight. Quit this field and take yourself from my sight." He then turned and shouted, "We have English to hunt. We have won this battle but not the war. We chase them until our horses can move no more."

We obeyed.

Epilogue

By the time we returned, it was so dark that we could see little. I had hoped to bury Taillefer. There was no moon but still Duke William searched for King Harold's body. The duke had a great sense of honour. He sent for Bruno and me as he had heard we had taken the standard. We went to the place where the standard bearer had been slain but the corpses were so badly hacked that we could not tell who was who. The duke sent for Edith Swan-Neck, the king's first wife who was at Watch Oak, close by. It was she who identified his body by marks on his skin that only a wife would know. The duke ordered my half-brother, Sir William Malet, to fetch the body and guard it. I helped to carry the body to our camp. My two half-brothers stood vigil over the body that night and Duke William's knights guarded the battlefield.

I returned, with Baldwin and Odo and, in the darkness, searched for Taillefer's body. When we found him, his body was almost unrecognisable. It was the two scabbards that marked him. We carried him back and laid him next to King Harold. It seemed right.

The next morning a rider came from King Harold's mother, Gytha. She offered the king's weight in gold if the body would be returned to her. The duke refused saying that the English would have one grave and our men another.

He spied me and called me over, "Young Richard fitz Malet, you have done great service here in England and I remember a promise made by my dear friend Taillefer. Take a knee." I knelt and, taking out his sword, he dubbed me on the shoulders, "Rise, Sir Richard fitz Malet. You are Taillefer's heir and along with his horse you shall have his treasure which is in Caen." He turned and shouted to the other men, "I shall send, this day, for more men. The battle is over but not the war." Everyone cheered. We had stood guard all night and the duke continued, "When the war is over and this land is at peace, you and your brothers shall all be rewarded with English manors, but for the moment we guard what we have taken and we honour our dead."

I rose and my half-brothers, Bruno, Baldwin and Odo all came to congratulate me. I smiled and accepted them but I would rather be what I was and Taillefer alive than be a knight. The world would be an emptier place without the unique enigma that was Taillefer. I had a large shadow to fill.

The End

Glossary

Chevauchée – A medieval raid normally led by knights
Coistrel – A wooden or leather drinking cup that could be carried on a belt.
Donjon - keep, keep was not used until the 14th century
Douvres – Dover
Hog bog - a place close to a farm where pigs and fowl could be kept
Jazerant - a padded light coat worn over a mail hauberk
Lincylene - Lincoln
Pueros – young warriors not yet ready to be a knight
Socce – socks also light shoes worn by actors/mummers
Ventail – a detachable mail mask

Canonical Hours

Matins (nighttime)
Lauds (early morning)
Prime (first hour of daylight)
Terce (third hour)
Sext (noon)
Nones (ninth hour)
Vespers (sunset evening)
Compline (end of the day)

Historical Background

A Danish wife was one where a couple married by common consent without a religious ceremony. It was a common practice at the time. It enabled lords to have more than one wife and for those lower down the social scale to be married.

The notion of fire arrows heated in a forge comes from the siege of Brionne in 1092 when Robert Duke of Normandy used the idea. I suspect he would have heard it from his father Duke William. Apologies for allowing my hero to take the credit.

Taillefer is a wonderful character for a novelist. Before the battle he dazzled all like Haley's Comet flashing across the sky. His only recorded reference was that he asked the duke if he could start the battle. The duke allowed it. Taillefer rode his horse before the English army, showing off riding tricks. Then he juggled with swords, sang a song and challenged any of the English who cared to try to fight him. One housecarl did so and was promptly slain by the skilful Norman. Growing cocky he then rode too close to the companions of the dead housecarl and he was surrounded and he and his horse were butchered. I thoroughly enjoyed making up a back story for him.

The various battles I describe are, in the main, historical ones: Mortemer, Varaville, and Dinan, but I have added others. The details of the battles are my fiction. I always aim to tell a good story but the historical figures I describe all played their parts. I weave my webs around real people but make up characters to bring them to life. The use of a forge to heat arrows comes from an actual battle at which the duke's son fought.

I made up Sir Durand but his brothers were real. I needed a villain and Sir Durand filled the bill.

The incident where Earl Harold was shipwrecked is well known. The only explanation I could come up with was a spying expedition. He did rescue two men from the sands of Mont St Michel and was clearly a brave man. His supporters said he never swore an oath but it is hard to see Duke William letting him return to England without one.

The numbers of ships and men, as well as the landings are all documented but history is written by the winners.

The incidents in the battle all largely happened the way I described them. Duke William had three horses killed. He was mistakenly assumed to have died and it was Count Eustace who shouted, 'Your duke lives.' The flight of the Bretons gave the duke the idea of feigned flight and it was that, allied to the use of archers that won the battle.

The series is called Conquest and the next books will be the story of how the Normans took Saxon England and changed it forever. It will end before the Anarchy series starts.

Companions of Duke William:

1) Robert de Beaumont, later 1st Earl of Leicester
(2) Eustace, Count of Boulogne, a.k.a. Eustace II
(3) William, Count of Évreux
(4) Geoffrey, Count of Mortagne and Lord of Nogent, later Count of Perche
(5) William fitz Osbern, later 1st Earl of Hereford
(6) Aimeri, Viscount of Thouars a.k.a. Aimery IV
(7) Walter Giffard, Lord of Longueville
(8) Hugh de Montfort, Lord of Montfort-sur-Risle
(9) Ralph de Tosny, Lord of Conches a.k.a. Raoul II
(10) Hugh de Grandmesnil
(11) William de Warenne, later 1st Earl of Surrey
(12) William Malet, Lord of Graville
(13) Odo, Bishop of Bayeux, later Earl of Kent
(14) Turstin fitz Rolf a.k.a. Turstin fitz Rou and Turstin le Blanc
(15) Engenulf de Laigle

These are the names of the knights we know who followed Duke William to England. There were others as these were the only fifteen whose names were recorded, I have made the others up.

Books used in the research

- The Norman Achievement - Richard Cassady
- Norman Knight – Gravett and Hook
- Hastings 1066 - Gravett
- The Norman Conquest of the North – Kappelle
- Norman Stone Castles (2) Gravett and Hook
- A short History of the Norman Conquest of England- Edward Augustus Freeman

Griff Hosker February 2023

Other books by Griff Hosker

If you enjoyed reading this book, then why not read another one by the author?

Ancient History

The Sword of Cartimandua Series
(Germania and Britannia 50 A.D. – 128 A.D.)
Ulpius Felix- Roman Warrior (prequel)
The Sword of Cartimandua
The Horse Warriors
Invasion Caledonia
Roman Retreat
Revolt of the Red Witch
Druid's Gold
Trajan's Hunters
The Last Frontier
Hero of Rome
Roman Hawk
Roman Treachery
Roman Wall
Roman Courage

The Wolf Warrior series
(Britain in the late 6th Century)
Saxon Dawn
Saxon Revenge
Saxon England
Saxon Blood
Saxon Slayer
Saxon Slaughter
Saxon Bane
Saxon Fall: Rise of the Warlord

Saxon Throne
Saxon Sword

Medieval History

The Dragon Heart Series
Viking Slave *
Viking Warrior *
Viking Jarl *
Viking Kingdom *
Viking Wolf *
Viking War
Viking Sword
Viking Wrath
Viking Raid
Viking Legend
Viking Vengeance
Viking Dragon
Viking Treasure
Viking Enemy
Viking Witch
Viking Blood
Viking Weregeld
Viking Storm
Viking Warband
Viking Shadow
Viking Legacy
Viking Clan
Viking Bravery

The Norman Genesis Series
Hrolf the Viking *
Horseman *
The Battle for a Home *
Revenge of the Franks *
The Land of the Northmen

Hastings

Ragnvald Hrolfsson
Brothers in Blood
Lord of Rouen
Drekar in the Seine
Duke of Normandy
The Duke and the King

Danelaw
(England and Denmark in the 11th Century)
Dragon Sword *
Oathsword *
Bloodsword *
Danish Sword
The Sword of Cnut

New World Series
Blood on the Blade *
Across the Seas *
The Savage Wilderness *
The Bear and the Wolf *
Erik The Navigator *
Erik's Clan *
The Last Viking

The Vengeance Trail *

The Conquest Series
(Normandy and England 1050-1100)
Hastings
Conquest

The Aelfraed Series
(Britain and Byzantium 1050 A.D. - 1085 A.D.)
Housecarl *
Outlaw *
Varangian *

281

The Reconquista Chronicles
Castilian Knight *
El Campeador *
The Lord of Valencia *

The Anarchy Series England
1120-1180
English Knight *
Knight of the Empress *
Northern Knight *
Baron of the North *
Earl *
King Henry's Champion *
The King is Dead *
Warlord of the North
Enemy at the Gate
The Fallen Crown
Warlord's War
Kingmaker
Henry II
Crusader
The Welsh Marches
Irish War
Poisonous Plots
The Princes' Revolt
Earl Marshal
The Perfect Knight

Border Knight
1182-1300
Sword for Hire *
Return of the Knight *
Baron's War *
Magna Carta *
Welsh Wars *

Henry III *
The Bloody Border *
Baron's Crusade
Sentinel of the North
War in the West
Debt of Honour
The Blood of the Warlord
The Fettered King
de Montfort's Crown

Sir John Hawkwood Series
France and Italy 1339- 1387
Crécy: The Age of the Archer *
Man At Arms *
The White Company *
Leader of Men *
Tuscan Warlord *
Condottiere

Lord Edward's Archer
Lord Edward's Archer *
King in Waiting *
An Archer's Crusade *
Targets of Treachery *
The Great Cause *
Wallace's War *
The Hunt

Struggle for a Crown
1360- 1485
Blood on the Crown *
To Murder a King *
The Throne *
King Henry IV *
The Road to Agincourt *
St Crispin's Day *

The Battle for France *
The Last Knight *
Queen's Knight *
The Knight's Tale

Tales from the Sword I
(Short stories from the Medieval period)

Tudor Warrior series
England and Scotland in the late 15th and early 16th
century
Tudor Warrior *
Tudor Spy *
Flodden*

Conquistador
England and America in the 16th Century
Conquistador *
The English Adventurer *

English Mercenary
The 30 Years War and the English Civil War
Horse and Pistol

Modern History

The Napoleonic Horseman Series
Chasseur à Cheval
Napoleon's Guard
British Light Dragoon
Soldier Spy
1808: The Road to Coruña
Talavera
The Lines of Torres Vedras
Bloody Badajoz
The Road to France

Waterloo

The Lucky Jack American Civil War series
Rebel Raiders
Confederate Rangers
The Road to Gettysburg

Soldier of the Queen series
Soldier of the Queen*
Redcoat's Rifle*
Omdurman

The British Ace Series
1914
1915 Fokker Scourge
1916 Angels over the Somme
1917 Eagles Fall
1918 We will remember them
From Arctic Snow to Desert Sand
Wings over Persia

Combined Operations series
1940-1945
Commando *
Raider *
Behind Enemy Lines
Dieppe
Toehold in Europe
Sword Beach
Breakout
The Battle for Antwerp
King Tiger
Beyond the Rhine
Korea
Korean Winter

Tales from the Sword II
(Short stories from the Modern period)

Books marked thus *, are also available in the audio format.
For more information on all of the books then please visit the author's website at www.griffhosker.com where there is a link to contact him or visit his Facebook page: GriffHosker at Sword Books or follow him on Twitter: @HoskerGriff or Sword (@swordbooksltd)
If you wish to be on the mailing list then contact the author through his website.

Printed in Great Britain
by Amazon

37345537R00159